I0825375

Arrows Align

K.S.RISON

Copyright © 2025 by K. S. Rison

All rights reserved.

No part of this book may be reproduced in any form or by any electronic or mechanical means, including information storage and retrieval systems, without written permission from the author, except for the use of brief quotations in a book review.

ISBN: 979-8-9931443-1-3 (Hardcover)

Edited by: Samantha | Radiant Editorial

Cover design by: Bianca Bordianu | Moonpress

Title page design by: Covers By Aura

Graphics by: Sunni Rae Art

Formatted by: Shelly | The Fiction Editor

A dedication...that's all I'm allowed to give you here.
The rest...you'll feel it between the lines.
Highlight with care, my little reader.

~Cullen Eros

AUTHOR'S NOTE

Before you dive into the world of dangerously attractive immortals, a gentle warning: this story contains mature language along with adult and intimate scenes that may not be suitable for all readers.

I hope you feel in control here. If you ever need a break, the story will still be waiting—perhaps with a smirking god or two.

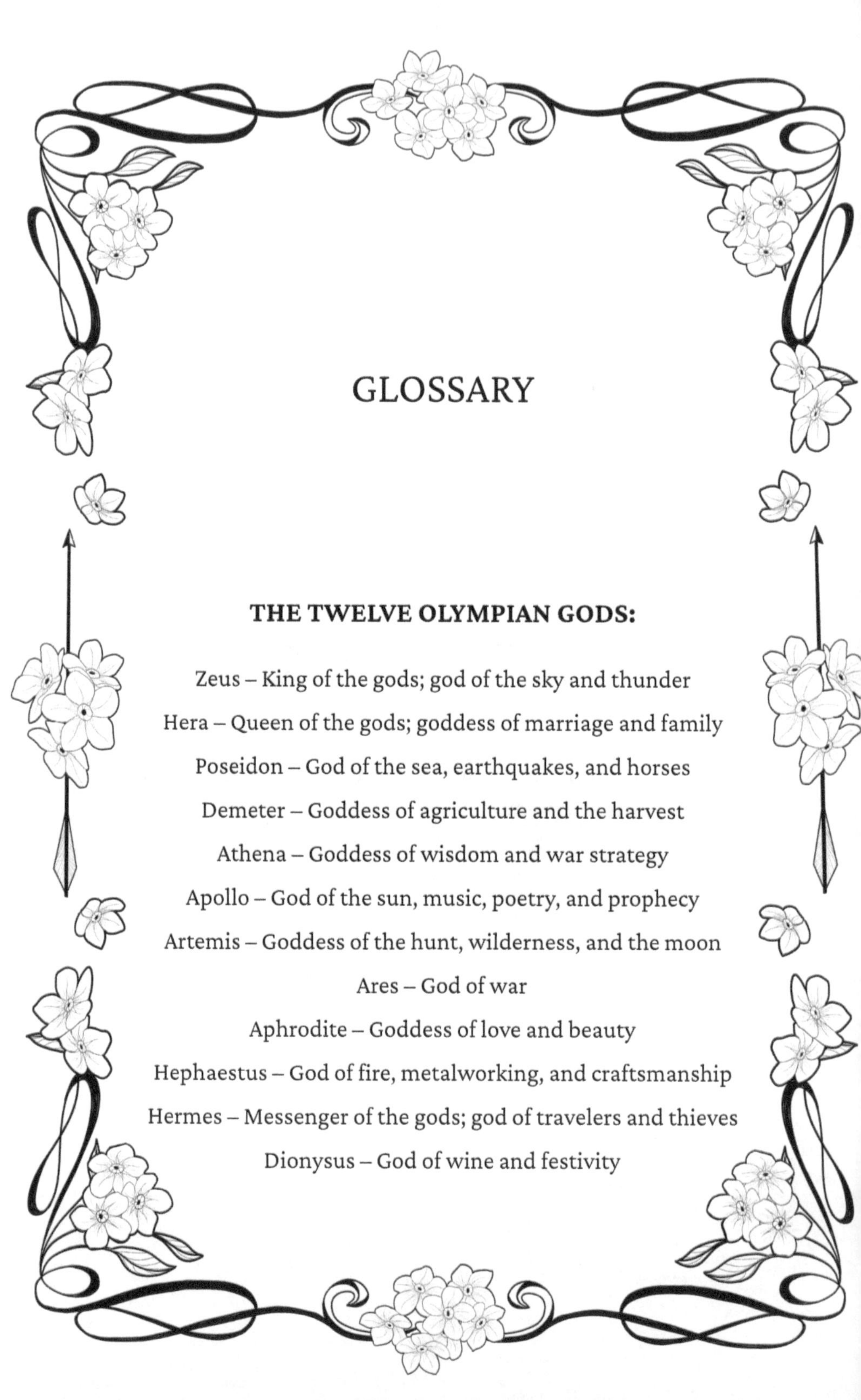

GLOSSARY

THE TWELVE OLYMPIAN GODS:

Zeus – King of the gods; god of the sky and thunder

Hera – Queen of the gods; goddess of marriage and family

Poseidon – God of the sea, earthquakes, and horses

Demeter – Goddess of agriculture and the harvest

Athena – Goddess of wisdom and war strategy

Apollo – God of the sun, music, poetry, and prophecy

Artemis – Goddess of the hunt, wilderness, and the moon

Ares – God of war

Aphrodite – Goddess of love and beauty

Hephaestus – God of fire, metalworking, and craftsmanship

Hermes – Messenger of the gods; god of travelers and thieves

Dionysus – God of wine and festivity

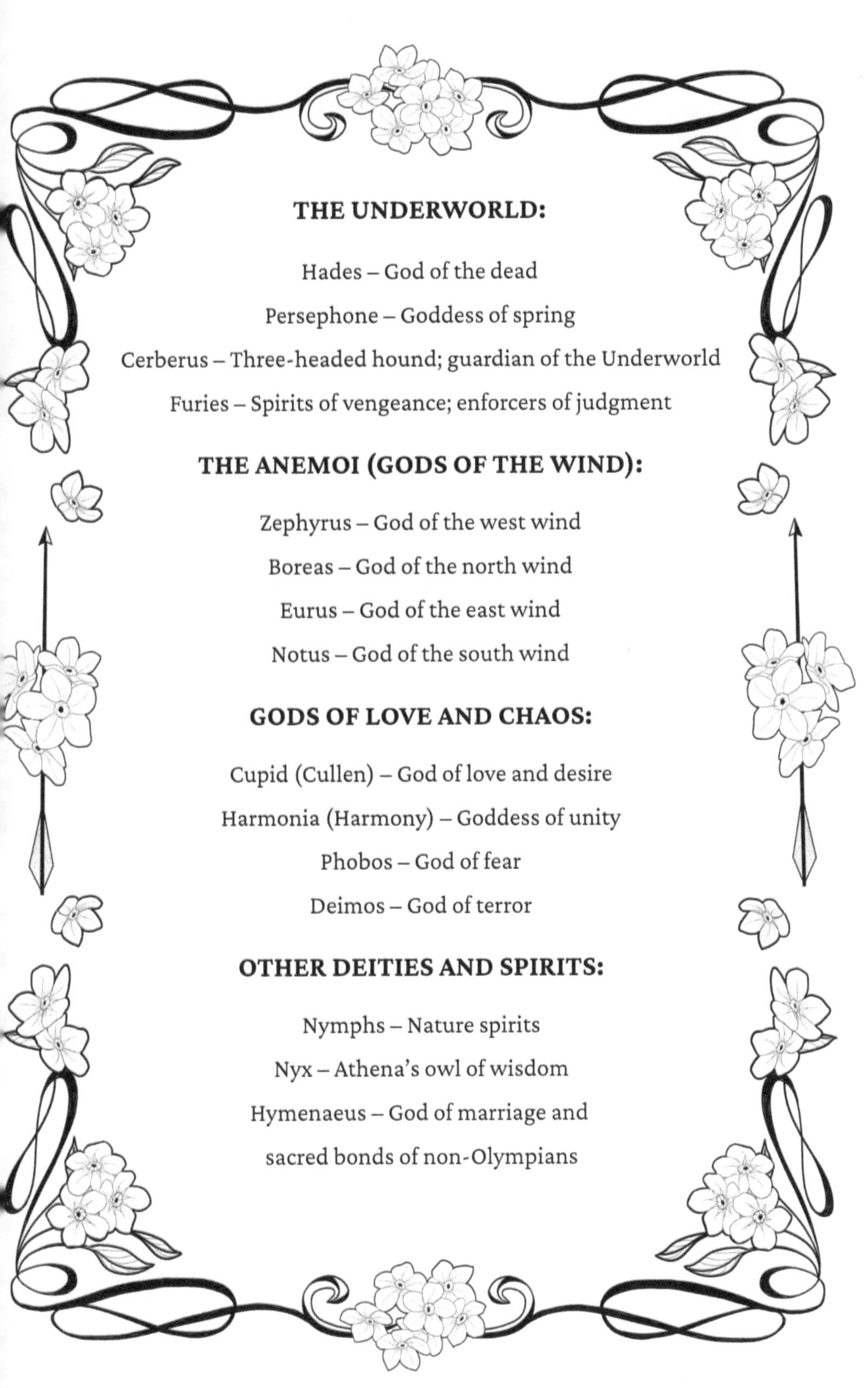

THE UNDERWORLD:

Hades – God of the dead

Persephone – Goddess of spring

Cerberus – Three-headed hound; guardian of the Underworld

Furies – Spirits of vengeance; enforcers of judgment

THE ANEMOI (GODS OF THE WIND):

Zephyrus – God of the west wind

Boreas – God of the north wind

Eurus – God of the east wind

Notus – God of the south wind

GODS OF LOVE AND CHAOS:

Cupid (Cullen) – God of love and desire

Harmonia (Harmony) – Goddess of unity

Phobos – God of fear

Deimos – God of terror

OTHER DEITIES AND SPIRITS:

Nymphs – Nature spirits

Nyx – Athena's owl of wisdom

Hymenaeus – God of marriage and
sacred bonds of non-Olympians

PROLOGUE
THE FATES

Spun.

Measured.

Severed.

These are the threads of existence, woven from the cloth of the abyss.

Thus began all that is.

Thus began the Titans.

We know this. We always know.

For we are all of these things at once—past, present, and future—and all are one.

Our eye has seen the Titans draw breath, seen how their raw power forged mountains, seas, air, sun, and stars.

How they spawned gods, goddesses, and mortals in their image.

But their creation was never sacred to them.

They saw existence as a fleeting canvas, beautiful only in its unraveling.

Volcanoes erupted, swallowing mountains.

Drought drank the oceans dry.

The sun went dark. Stars fell like ash.

At the center of it all was Cronus.

The First King.

But even power frays beneath the shears.

Even Titans fall.

From their tyranny rose the Olympians—twelve gods and goddesses, born of rebellion.

At their head stood Zeus, the last son of Cronus. The Storm King.

He did not rise to inherit a world of ashes.

He rose to conquer it—to shape it into something worthy of the gods.

Lightning cracked the sky wide.

Thunder rolled across the earth.

The very core of the world rasped beneath war.

Ten years.

The Titanomachy.

Ten long turns of the sun.

That was the price of rebellion.

Hephaestus, smith of flame and fury, forged the end: a torch no wind could smother, no ocean drown, no time erase—a fire unyielding.

And with it, Zeus struck.

Each blow frayed the Titans' strength—thread by thread—until their nature cracked.

But the fire did not destroy.

It stole.

It bound what it took. The essence of the Titans splintered, their power siphoned and reforged—giving rise to the Olympian Command, an unbreakable force woven into the order of the world.

The Olympians, forged in rebellion, now ruled with absolute authority.

Their voices could bend the will of mortals, silence lesser gods, as if the threads of fate pulled all beneath them to obey.

They stripped the Titans bare—hollowed them of pride and power—and cast them into Tartarus, the deepest pit in the Underworld. There, divine chains held them fast, binding their fury to the very walls that mocked their fall.

Just beyond their reach burned the torch—their stolen power—a taunting light they could see, could feel, but never touch.

The war ended. The Olympians rose. And from the wound left in the sky, a single tear fell.

A gift.

Nectar—the golden breath of immortality. The Olympians claimed it was a gift of season and ceremony, offered at the solstice's peak.

But the cosmos offers only half-truths.

The thread continues its weave.

Ages have passed since the last war of gods and Titans.

Time has buried the truth, leaving mortals certain that legends were only that—and nothing more.

They walk beside divinity, blind.

Unaware of the very strings being pulled.

But Fate remembers.

And Fate sees.

The thread shall stop when the fire of old returns—not in the hands of a god, but in the blood of one forged from a lineage long forgotten.

And when the lost rise once more, the bond that binds the gods shall shatter.

Behold the trinity of the threads: *Love. Strength. Death.*

Yes.

She will bring the gods to their knees.

And in her hands, at last, our death will come.

CHAPTER ONE
SKYE

S*hit, shit, shit*—where was it?

If I didn't find this damn shoe—

Meow.

"Marnie, sweetie, you're under my foot," I muttered, sidestepping the fluffball as I dug through another box, one shoe on, one shoe off.

The orange tabby wove around my ankles, her striped tail brushing my leg. I shuffled to avoid her, but she darted right in front of me—and my foot caught.

I stumbled, arms flailing—

And crashed straight into a towering stack of boxes.

They toppled.

I hit the floor with a solid *thud*, cardboard and packing paper exploding around me like confetti.

Flat on my back, I stared up at the ceiling for a beat, feeling like my organs needed a second to readjust. Groaning, I let my head roll to the side—and there it was.

Peeking out from the edge of a toppled box, as if it had been there all along.

I blinked, then laughed.

"Well, look at that...my shoe. Thank you, Marnie," I sing-songed.

I pushed myself up and dusted off my dress.

Marnie wound herself around my legs, purring like she'd orchestrated the whole thing.

"Alright, alright, you hungry little demon," I said, bending to scratch behind her ears. She meowed dramatically, as if I hadn't fed her in days.

Sighing, I set the box back in place and began gathering the things that had spilled out.

Damn it...not my new tarot cards.

They lay scattered across the floor, their gilded edges glinting in the light like fallen stars.

I crouched and picked up the nearest one.

The card's edge was smooth beneath my thumb as I flipped it over and read the title: *The Fool.*

A figure stood at the edge of a cliff, a small bag slung over one shoulder, flowers in the other hand, a dog dancing at their heels.

Above them, the sky was bright.

Below, jagged cliffs waited.

Danger? Possibly.

A small smile tugged at my lips. "Of course," I whispered.

The Fool—a fresh start, a new adventure, and usually...questionable life decisions.

Questionable life decisions.

Yeah. That sounded about right.

While Marnie devoured her dinner, I leaned against the windowsill, staring out at the narrow slice of the city visible from my studio apartment.

The place was hauntingly beautiful. People had even tried to buy it for the view alone—but I wasn't selling. I loved the hills of lights flickering like every night was Christmas. I loved how the black, exposed ceiling beams kept the space so dark at night it felt like its own safe little world.

Even with boxes left to unpack, I'd managed a few personal touches—a thrift-store painting of a little white cottage hidden in the woods, a small orange cat peeking out the window, reminding me of Marnie.

Then there were my books—my portal away from a world of debt and adult responsibilities—scattered across shelves and side tables. I'd read most of them more times than I could count, and some I even treated like journals, scribbling my thoughts in the margins until the lines between my life and the story blurred.

Still, it didn't feel like *mine.*

Maybe it never would.

Maybe a part of me would always want it to stay hers.

I kept her furniture. I even left her clothes in the drawers, exactly as she had. I couldn't bring myself to take them out. And now, I suppose her collection of tarot cards belongs to me, too. She gave me my first deck when I was old enough to understand what they meant—seventy-eight cards split into two groups: the Major and Minor Arcana. Each represents different milestones in life, and depending on how they're laid out—the patterns, the positions—they can reveal the past, the present, and the potential paths ahead.

I moved to the bookshelf where she kept them, tracing my fingers along the deck she'd given me, now sitting beside hers as if, in some way, we were still connected. Dusty blue, the faded gray lettering almost worn away—it wouldn't be worth much to anyone else, but to me, it was priceless.

It had been over a month since my aunt Lydia died.

I didn't think it was possible to dehydrate so quickly from crying so much.

Lydia and I always joked we were the family's resident black sheep—in a family full of entitled privilege. My parents were as emotionally available as a brick wall, hiding their disappointment behind tight smiles and practiced pleasantries.

They always complimented my looks, as if that were some kind of achievement—like my appearance was a ticket to a life they could be proud of, so long as it ended with me married off to some trust-fund husband they'd picked out like artwork.

Beyond that? Nothing.

No interest in my dreams, my opinions, anything that made me...*me.*

To be fair, I wasn't always sure what exactly those dreams even were.

My two older sisters were the perfect darlings of the family: obedient, refined, neatly slotted into the lives our parents had carved out for them. They never missed a chance to remind me how I was a disappointment, always with the same warning—*better use that pretty face while you've still got it.*

But Lydia had been different.

She never had children, never settled down, never conformed to anyone's expectations. She lived exactly how she wanted. At her funeral, friends and former lovers filled the room, telling stories of her life.

She had truly lived, and more than anyone else, she had seen me. Not just the pretty face my family paraded around, but the whole messy, daydreaming person underneath. She encouraged my wild ideas when everyone else tried to silence them.

Her sudden heart attack might as well have taken me with it.

My tarot cards, my substitute for actual companions, showed no warning. No insight, no comfort. Just silence when I needed answers the most.

To everyone's surprise—especially my family's—Lydia had left me her shop and the apartment above it in her will.

To Skye, be the magic you seek.

Simply put, my family—old money and older values—did not approve.

Taking over her shop was the final nail in a coffin I'd hammered shut myself.

They cut me off financially without hesitation, as if money had ever been my lifeline to happiness.

Mystic Soulstice was.

Is.

It wasn't just some abandoned corner store.

Mystic Soulstice was a little oasis in a busy—and sometimes harsh—city.

It offered everything from herbal remedies like hand-blended teas and tonics to infused lotions, incense, tarot decks, and crystals. Lydia loved connecting with her customers, so she offered all kinds of readings: tarot, palmistry, even aura readings when she felt a strong pull toward someone.

I used to count down the days to summer just to escape here. As a kid, I'd spend long, golden afternoons running up and down the stacks, watching the crystals catch the sunlight—like pixie dust had just fallen across them.

Lydia would guide my small hands, teaching me the uses of different herbs, how to feel the pulse of a crystal, lay out the tarot, and read the lines of a palm.

I remember tracing them once, thinking they looked like the veins of a leaf—and wondering if maybe we're all connected. Just part of the same pattern, repeating itself in skin and stone and root.

Lydia didn't possess *real* magic—

But there was always something otherworldly about her.

Just like the shop itself.

She used to pause mid-lesson, her wise eyes crinkling at the corners as she smiled and said, "Magic isn't always in the cards, my love. It's in the way we listen. Most of the time, that's all someone needs—a heart can mend when it's truly heard."

My phone buzzed, pulling me out of the memory.

Arrows Align.

The logo lit up my screen, followed by a message:

Liam
Still on for tonight?

I dropped onto the worn-but-loved couch, legs swinging over one arm and hanging off the side. I sighed—loud enough for Marnie to flick her tail in judgment.

Arrows Align had blown up overnight thanks to its mysterious Oracle AI—some matchmaking algorithm that promised to find your *perfect, real* connection.

Naturally, like everyone with Wi-Fi and poor impulse control, I downloaded it "just to see."

Now I was staring at a message from someone named Liam, wondering what in the divine hell I was doing.

I set my phone aside and closed my eyes.

Did I actually want to go through with this?

Apparently, yes—because the next second I was picking it back up. Liam's profile photo showed a guy with dark hair, green eyes, and rectangular glasses. His bio was a whopping two lines: *Works in finance. Loves to travel.* Riveting stuff.

Still...Lydia wouldn't have wanted me sulking in her apartment, wallowing in cat hair and grief. Plus, thanks to Marnie's earlier chaos, I'd found my other black heel and lost my last excuse.

I slipped it on and shoved aside the mountain of clothes covering the mirror.

The heels gave me a little boost—literally. Helpful when you're five feet tall and "vertically challenged," as my sisters so lovingly said.

At twenty-two, I had what people politely called *curves*, though most of my clothes just called it tight.

The blue dress hugged me like a corset, and I had to consciously think about breathing. But it brought out the blue in my round eyes, so I let it slide.

I'd twisted my brown hair up and off my neck, hoping the effort made me look like someone who actually wanted to be out in public.

Freckles dusted my nose and cheeks, soft and scattered. I used to hate them as a kid—tried to bury them under layers of makeup, hoping they'd disappear. But over time I grew into them. They reminded me of constellations—tiny stars across my skin—like I was made from them.

"This should be fun," I told my reflection, trying really hard to believe it.

When I opened the door, I had to admit—I was impressed. Dim lighting, exposed brick, and bookshelves that looked like they'd been stolen from a book lover's fever dream. The shelves stretched to the ceiling, packed with everything from leather-bound classics to aggressively loved paperbacks. String lights twinkled overhead, leading to a cozy bar area that opened into a maze of mismatched booths and wicker chairs.

I spotted Liam sliding off a barstool like he'd been waiting just for me. So...okay, I'd give him this—he looked like his profile picture, which in the world of online dating was basically a miracle. Bonus points for meeting me in a place where the books outnumbered the people.

"Wow, Skye," he said as I walked up. His eyes did a quick scan—respectful, but still definitely a scan. "You look amazing."

A blush crept up my cheeks, completely betraying me. "Thanks," I replied, mentally debating whether we should hug, shake hands, or... what?

I went with a friendly pat on the shoulder. Because apparently awkward was who I was now.

He grinned, either unbothered or politely pretending not to notice. "Books and booze. Can't go wrong, right?"

I chuckled, easing into it. "Yeah. Honestly, pretty dangerous combo."

He leaned in slightly, the corner of his mouth quirking up. "Maybe we can find some trouble later."

Liam waved down the bartender, and we placed our orders—whiskey neat for me, some kind of craft beer for him. When the drinks arrived, I took a slow sip, letting the burn of the whiskey settle into my chest, chasing away a tension I hadn't even realized I was carrying.

After a while, we wandered through the shelves, drinks in hand. My fingers skimmed the spines of weathered paperbacks and cracked hardcovers, deliberately passing over some of the spicier titles—I wasn't ready to admit my obsession with those just yet. Then a safer genre caught my eye. I pulled the book free and angled the cover toward him—just as he stepped a little too close behind me.

"What about this one?" I asked, holding up a fantasy novel with dragons coiled around a glowing sword.

He leaned in, his shoulder brushing mine. "Not bad," he purred, a slow smile tugging at the corner of his mouth. "But you strike me as someone who likes things a little...*darker*."

His voice was playful, but I felt an edge beneath it—

"Oh, look, a booth just opened up," he said, already moving, quick and eager to claim it before anyone else could.

I followed, slower, eyes still roaming the shelves even as I trailed after him. He slid into the booth and patted the space beside him—not across from him. I paused for a second, then sat down. The booth was narrow. His shoulder pressed against mine. I shifted, trying to make space, but there wasn't any.

"So tell me—" I started, trying to steer the conversation back to safer ground.

Then I felt it.

His hand on my knee.

My words stalled in my throat.

"You were saying?" he asked, voice dipping lower, fingers brushing just a little higher, like he was testing me.

My heart slammed against my ribs. The string lights above us flickered gently, casting golden shadows over his face—but I didn't need full lighting to catch the look in his eyes.

He knew exactly what he was doing.

His hand inched up, fingertips ghosting along the hem of my dress.

I froze.

No. Something...something didn't feel right.

"Liam," I said, my voice a warning. But he took it as encouragement.

"You're even prettier in person," he murmured, leaning closer, his breath brushing my cheek. "I was hoping you'd wear something like this."

I snapped back, every nerve in my body flaring. I jerked my legs away from him and scrambled out of the booth so fast the table shook, glasses clinking against one another. A couple nearby looked over.

"I...just need to—" I waved vaguely toward the bathrooms, not even bothering to finish the excuse.

I walked—fast. Not running, but close. My heels clicked sharply against the floor with every step.

I didn't look back.

The bathroom had a small vanity tucked in the corner. Thank god. I sank onto the bench, resting my head in my hands before lifting it to catch my reflection in the mirror.

Get a grip. I shook my head, trying to clear away the lingering unease that maybe I was overreacting.

I pushed myself to stand and made for the door, nearly colliding with someone as I swung it open.

"Shit, sorry," I blurted, stumbling back a step.

The woman didn't flinch.

She wore blood-red sunglasses.

Sunglasses...at night?

They wrapped around her face like something out of a futuristic runway show—oversized and angular, with wide tinted sides that blocked out her peripheral vision completely.

Her black hair moved swiftly, like dark snakes slipping out of a garden. She didn't look at me, just stepped forward until we were shoulder to shoulder...then paused.

"He put something in your drink," she said, her words sharp—like a fang just before it meets skin.

Before I could react—before I could even process—she was gone.

I stood there, blinking at the space where she'd vanished.

Okay...then.

I made my way back to the table, trying to look casual. This time, I slid into the seat across from Liam—I needed the space. Then I adjusted my expression into something neutral.

He didn't seem bothered. Just greeted me with a calm smile, casually sliding my drink back in front of me before taking a sip from his own.

I hesitated.

The woman's warning echoed in my head.

I looked down at the glass. The liquid swayed gently, disturbed by the push. Then...then I saw it—tiny bubbles rising from the bottom in slow, spiraling trails, like something was brewing beneath the surface.

My fingers hovered near the rim, but I didn't touch it. My eyes stayed fixed on the drink, gut twisting tighter with every second.

"Did you..." I forced my voice to stay even, though the sharp edge rose underneath. "Did you put something in this?"

Liam blinked, his mask slipping for just a fraction of a second. "What? No. God, why would you even—"

"Drink it," I said, cutting him off.

His smile faltered. "What?"

"Drink. It." I didn't look away. I didn't blink.

He stared at me.

One second. Two.

Then something in his expression shifted—twisted.

He moved to adjust his glasses, like the gesture might hide the crack forming behind his eyes.

"You're just a fucking tease," he spat, shoving back from the booth so fast my drink sloshed over the side, amber liquid dripping down the edge of the table and pooling on the floor in slow, poisonous spirals.

I watched him stalk toward the exit, every step echoing in my ears. Only when the door slammed behind him did I let out a breath.

My hands were trembling.

How could I be so—no. Fuck that.

Grinding my teeth, I yanked out my phone and stared at the Arrows Align app, its icon practically mocking me. Without hesitation, I pressed down on it, frustration boiling over as the screen flickered and the app began to wobble. It asked me to rate it with stars.

Ha.

My thumbs hit the phone harder, wishing I could give it zero. One tap—and it was gone. If only deleting the rest of the night were that easy.

I set the phone down—but it buzzed again. Cautiously, I moved to pick it up. If...if it was fucking Liam—

But it wasn't. Instead, a message lit up the screen:

> **Arrows Align**
> We are sorry for your negative review. A representative will contact you shortly to discuss your experience with Arrows Align.

What the actual fuck?

Why couldn't life just be simple?

I stared blankly at the screen, the adrenaline of my night finally ebbing. My tarot card flashed through my mind.

Of course.

I was *The Fool.*

CHAPTER TWO
SKYE

The doorknob jiggled, nearly coming off in my hand.

I really need to fix that.

I turned the key and pushed the door open. The bells and chimes above me moved softly, like a familiar voice saying, *You're home.*

It felt strange, standing in the doorway, opening Mystic Soulstice for the first time without Lydia.

I drew in a slow, deep breath. Her incense still lingered in the air—woven into the walls, tucked into every corner of the store.

I smiled. It felt like she was still here—like she might burst out of the back room any second, waving a stick of burning sage and insisting she'd had a dream about stars falling from the sky, so obviously the whole place needed cleansing.

Stepping inside, I let my fingers brush across the polished wood counter as I walked. I'd been cleaning, rearranging, and restocking for days, trying to breathe life back into the place.

Somehow, I'd managed to keep all the spider plants alive. But they kept having babies, creeping out of their pots and trailing across the shelves like leafy little invaders. At least they were cat-safe, so Marnie could stretch out on the windowsill cushions and bat at the shifting light from the chimes above the door.

Lydia had left me just enough money to give the shop a fresh start—

but not nearly enough to keep it afloat long-term. Every night, I ran the numbers down to the last penny.

Keeping this place alive would take a miracle.

Or some kind of divine intervention.

But today? I was choosing denial. I was opening the doors, putting on some music, because...this was fine. Not even the low-grade hangover from last night's disaster of a date would stop me.

The morning passed quietly. A few customers trickled in—Lydia's regulars, familiar faces I recognized from the funeral. Some smiled. A few hugged me. Hearing them say they'd still shop here, even without Lydia, was comforting in a bittersweet way. It meant something, seeing how loyal they'd been to her.

"Thank you again," I said, leaning back from a warm hug.

"Of course, dear. Let us know if you need anything," one of the sweet older women replied as the pair walked out the door with me following behind.

I waved as they left. But as I turned to close the door, something through the window caught my eye.

A young woman—practically bouncing as she walked—strode past, talking animatedly to herself. Or, more accurately, to the phone clipped to a selfie stick in her hand. She looked like a tourist: stylish, bright-eyed, and entirely out of place in heels on uneven cobblestones.

She passed the shop.

Then stopped.

Then—impressively—she walked backward in those heels until she stood right before the door.

Oh. She was coming in.

The bells above the door clanged so hard they sounded like they might fall off from the force of her entrance.

Marnie let out a low growl, clearly not thrilled about being disturbed from her perch on the windowsill.

I instinctively turned away, pretending to rearrange a display of incense-infused lotions, already bracing myself for whatever was about to come through that door.

Her voice hit me like a high-pitched canary before I even saw her.

"Oh my god, you guys! I just had to stop because look at this! This little shop is soooo cute. And it's, like, totally empty. Shame, right? I mean, let's save it, shall we?"

She had her selfie stick raised, phone angled perfectly at her face as she launched into full influencer mode. Her expressions were wildly exaggerated, all big eyes and pouty lips, as she gestured dramatically around the shop. On the screen, her reflection looked practically airbrushed: flawless skin, expertly blended makeup, and a sparkle filter that cast twinkling lights around her head.

Why did she look so familiar?

Her name hovered at the edge of my memory, just out of reach.

Before I could say anything, she turned her phone toward me like a weapon. "Owner, right?"

"I—"

"You guys! Isn't she just the cutest?" she interrupted, cutting me off with a shrill kind of enthusiasm.

I winced inwardly at the backhanded compliment but forced a smile. "Welcome to Mystic Soulstice," I said, keeping my tone polite.

Not that she heard me. Or cared to.

"So I just had to come in because look how adorable it is!" she squealed, spinning slowly for her phone. "You guys know how much I love small businesses, and this one is, like, totally worth saving!"

Totally worth saving.

She said it in a sing-song voice, like a jingle from a commercial.

Totally worth saving...

Aha.

It clicked—SmallShopSavior—the influencer.

I slowly rubbed my temple in a small circle, swallowing the cringe at the idea of my shop being framed as some kind of charity case.

Lifting my head, I noticed she had suddenly gone still. Her eyes were fixed on something behind me.

I turned to follow her gaze—straight to my sign advertising different readings.

"Oh, wow!" she said, flashing an overly friendly smile. "Is it cool if I do a live video of a tarot reading? My followers love this kind of thing, and it'd be, like, great for your business."

She tilted her head, still recording, waiting for my answer. I hesitated.

The word *no* sat right on the tip of my tongue, but the way her phone hovered—

I nodded.

"Sure," I answered, forcing a little enthusiasm into my voice. "I can give you a reading."

She beamed at me, and I couldn't shake the feeling that I'd just made a deal with the devil—a French-manicured one, which somehow made it even more terrifying. Before leading her to the back, I flipped the small wooden sign on the counter: *Be right back—reading in progress.*

The reading room was small and quaint, with velvet chairs and curtains and a low table set for readings. She followed me in, still livestreaming, narrating every step like a reality show.

"I'm about to get a tarot reading from the most adorable little witch I've ever met—she even has a cat!" she told her followers, voice syrupy sweet.

My stomach twisted at the word *witch*, but I swallowed it down. This was business. This was exposure.

She finally set her phone on the table, propping it at just the right angle so her followers could watch every moment unfold. Then, with a dramatic sigh, she settled into the chair across from me, smoothing her perfectly styled hair over one shoulder.

There was a beat of silence—just long enough for me to start shuffling the tarot deck, the worn edges sliding over my fingertips like silk.

Then she leaned forward, resting her elbows on the table, tilting her head just so for the phone.

"So..." she began, drawing out the word with theatrical weight, "should I get back together with my ex-boyfriend?"

Her voice dropped into a half-mocking, half-serious tone—but her eyes didn't quite match either. I kept shuffling the cards as she rambled on to her viewers, but her question hung heavy in the space between us.

Focus.

It felt like Lydia's hands were guiding mine, her presence lingering in the room like a soft echo.

Listen to what isn't said.

That was her rule. Lydia always said the key to a good reading wasn't in the words people spoke but in what they left out.

So I listened.

The influencer wanted to talk about a guy. But it wasn't really about him. I heard it in the way her breath caught on the word *boyfriend*. This wasn't about him—it was about whether she was enough on her own.

I laid the cards out carefully, one by one.

The first card: *Two of Swords.*

I took a steadying breath, looked up at her, and began. "The *Two of Swords* tells me you're standing at a crossroads. But it's not just about him. This relationship has you questioning yourself—deciding what you truly want versus what you think you should want."

Her fingers tightened around her phone, and her smile twitched—just a flicker. I flipped the next card: *The Tower.*

"This represents upheaval—sudden change. If you go back to him, it won't be the same as it was before. What you felt then is still there now. Getting back together might bring more confusion than happiness."

She stared down at the card, her cheerful mask slipping further. Her brows drew together as I flipped the last card.

Ace of Cups.

I tapped it gently. "This one is about emotional renewal—a fresh start—whether a new love or learning to love yourself. The real question isn't whether you should go back to him. It's whether you're ready for something that fills your cup...instead of draining it."

She looked up, surprise flickering across her face. And something else—vulnerability, maybe. "You really think I shouldn't go back to him?" she asked, her voice much quieter now, genuinely asking.

"I think you should trust yourself enough not to settle for something that doesn't feel right," I said gently. "There's something better out there for you—but you won't find it if you keep holding on to what's already broken."

Her gaze shifted from the cards back to me. "That was...amazing. I wasn't expecting that."

I shrugged, offering a small smile. "People usually don't."

She hesitated, then glanced at her phone, talking to her listeners. "Honestly, I didn't think it would be this...real."

She looked at me and continued, "I thought it'd be something more like Arrows Align."

I paused, the hesitation obvious.

Her eyes lit up, catching it. She leaned in slightly, a sly smile—her mask creeping once more across her face. "Oh? Not a fan? Do tell..."

I could see exactly where this was heading. Her phone, still angled toward me, just enough to catch whatever sound bite she thought she could get. I forced a polite smile, refusing to bite—

I started to pack up, hoping she'd take the hint that the reading was over. "I mean...it's just an app," I said lightly, brushing the table's edge. "Algorithms and data."

She didn't move.

"If you could tell the founder how to fix it," she asked, all innocent tilt and mocked curiosity, "what would you really say?"

I gave her a tight smile and shifted my chair back, trying to keep things polite. But she leaned forward, elbows on the table, relentless.

"Come on," she said, voice dipping into something softer, coaxing. "It tells people who to love. And if you don't match—or you don't like who it matches you with—suddenly you're broken. Alone."

I froze. That hit too close. Too damn close.

"It's pretending to be fate. I mean, someone like you—" she pressed on, eyes sinking into me. "You must see how messed up it is."

I inhaled sharply, blood humming under my skin. My mind flashed to Liam's hand on me. The spiked drink. The way the app had promised something...real.

Instead, it had handed me that piece of shit.

"I just think people would love to hear what you have to say," she added.

She looked at her phone, notifications beaming one after another. "You have a lot of people interested."

And there it was. Not curiosity. Not kindness. A hook baited and waiting for me to bite.

I looked at her phone. Still recording.

I carefully placed the cards down, safe from my anger, pressing my palms flat against the table. Then I leaned in, my gaze locked on the phone.

"I would tell them to burn it to the fucking ground."

She lit up like a flare, eyes gleaming as she whipped the phone back to her face. "Yes! Don't walk—run to this shop. She's serving *actual* magic!"

I leaned back, throat dry. Her phone was still recording, and I had the creeping sense that I would regret every word.

The moment she clicked it off, my muscles relaxed—like someone had been gripping me by the neck through the lens and finally let go.

“By the way, you can call me Bianca,” she said, her smile all teeth and no warmth. “SmallShopSavior is just for the followers.”

Bianca. Even the way she said her name carried a practiced condescension.

She stood, bracing herself with one hand on the back of the chair.

“Look, I can bring you customers—a lot of them. I'll send them your way, and in exchange, you give me a cut of whatever you make off them. It's a win-win.” Her eyes gleamed with a twisted hunger, like she could already taste it—her conquest.

She wasn't here to save anything.

She was here to *devour*.

I didn't want to be part of this—part of the lie. This wasn't what Lydia had built this shop for. She had filled it with love, intention, and something real.

But Lydia wasn't here anymore, and sentiment didn't cover rent.

I swallowed hard and forced the word out. “Alright.”

The grin that spread across her face was all sharp edges. “Perfect.”

She pulled out her phone, thumbs tapping fast. “Oh, you have AirDrop open, so I'll go ahead and send the contract. You should be getting it now.”

A pause. Then, with a too-sweet smile: “Content usage, reels, live mentions, tag tracking, commission breakdown...all the fun stuff.”

My phone buzzed.

I didn't move to open it.

Her voice kept going. But the words were slipping beneath the surface—muffled and warped, like I was hearing them through water. Like I was already too deep to breathe.

THE NEXT DAY, Mystic Soulstice was unrecognizable.

The door barely had a chance to close before another group pushed through.

Influencers—phones raised high—flooded the space like it was a photo op, not a shop. They posed beside the shelves, draped themselves over displays, and snapped selfies in front of the sign with fake-candid expressions, tossing up finger hearts and tilted peace signs like they were somehow bringing peace with them.

Some picked up crystals, holding them between fingers like props instead of sacred tools. One girl waved a bundle of sage like it was a magic wand, giggling as she declared she was "banishing demons."

Another nearly knocked over an entire tray of oils trying to get the perfect shot with "aesthetic lighting."

A lot was an understatement.

I'd even had to keep Marnie in the apartment upstairs. After the first day, people kept trying to pick her up or take selfies with her like she was part of the experience. One girl actually asked if she could borrow Marnie for a reel.

No.

Fuck...no.

I stood behind the counter, frozen in place, watching the frenzy unfold. It felt surreal—this swarm of people clamoring for appointments, talking about my "magic" like it was a trending novelty. A line snaked toward the back, customers buzzing about the live reading they'd seen online.

"Skye the Psychic" was trending. So was Arrows Align—paired with a clip of me muttering, *"Burn it to the fucking ground."*

I exhaled sharply, my fingers tightening around the edge of the counter. This wasn't what I wanted. It didn't feel like this place was Lydia's anymore.

And yet, the appointments kept rolling in.

CHAPTER THREE

SKYE

It had only been a few days since I agreed to Bianca's arrangement, but it already felt like I'd lost years of my life.

I was surviving off the shop's energy teas—and at this point, I was my own biggest customer.

One more hour until closing. One more appointment.

I laid my head on the counter, not caring if the wandering customers saw me.

I was tired.

The kind of tired even my soul could feel.

I closed my eyes and tried to steady my breathing, silently begging the next person not to ask if the lotions were *hex-free.*

My gaze drifted to the photo of Lydia and me, now propped safely on the counter after too many people had knocked it off the wall. Her arm was slung around my shoulder, caught mid-laugh as she tried to steal a bite of my chocolate ice cream—sneaky thief, that one.

Her hair—brown like mine—was pulled back in a loose braid, a few silver strands catching the light. She never dyed them. Said they were tinsel. *Even Christmas trees need a little sparkle,* she'd say with a wink.

She was the purest person I'd ever known. She never lied. Rarely got angry—except once, when someone barged into the shop shouting about sin and damnation, trying to shame the customers.

Lydia didn't raise her voice. She simply set down her book, walked over, and stared the man down with a steady, unshakable calm.

"This space is for peace," she said. "You'll take your fear elsewhere."

Her voice was soft, but it left no room for argument.

He left.

What would she think now? Was any of this worth it...in her eyes?

An image of Lydia surfaced in my mind.

Her eyes weren't angry—just disappointed.

Which somehow hurt more.

I squeezed my eyes shut, trying to will it away.

The bell above the door chimed—again.

Ugh.

I winced and peeled my now slightly sticky cheek from the countertop.

Then I looked up, and my breath caught.

A man had stepped inside. Man didn't do it justice. He was a walking romance fantasy.

Fantasy in a suit.

Navy suit, to be exact. It clung to his shoulders and lean, annoyingly perfect frame like even the fabric was trying to straddle him. His blond hair was slicked back with effortless precision, not a strand out of place, as if even they bowed to him.

My eyes locked on him—and refused to let go.

He looked completely out of place in my cozy, chaotic shop, like a wolf stepping into a den of rabbits. His eyes barely skimmed the shelves, uninterested. But the rest of the room? All the rabbits noticed him, practically lining up to be taken.

Customers froze mid-step, mid-sentence, openly staring.

And I was no better.

He moved through the sunset-lit haze like he knew precisely how goddamn magnetic he was—and didn't mind using it.

My mouth was dry. My body frozen. Maybe it was the lack of sleep, but I could've sworn he was walking in slow motion toward me—

"Welcome," I managed, my voice surprisingly steady despite the sudden flutter in my stomach. "Can I help you with something?" I added quickly, shuffling some papers to pretend I hadn't just been staring—and fantasizing about him taking me right here...on this counter.

He smiled—small, polite—and closed the distance until only the counter separated us.

"I've heard you offer quite famous readings."

His voice was smooth. I found myself nodding before my brain could catch up.

"Yes..." I said, hearing the pitch of my voice rise.

He moved to my sign advertising different readings. He tapped it with his knuckles. "Read me. Palm reading, perhaps? Please."

That *please* didn't sound like a request.

Behind him, a young woman shuffled forward with her belongings.

My last appointment of the day.

I hesitated. "I'm actually in the middle of an appointment right now. If you could—"

He didn't let me finish.

Instead, he turned to the young woman, who looked like she was hanging on his every move. A subtle, almost sinister smile played at his lips as he made a sweeping gesture toward her.

"Perhaps you'd consider rescheduling," he said smoothly, placing a hand over his heart like an actor mid-monologue. "I have a rather urgent matter that requires immediate attention. I'd be most grateful."

The young woman blinked, caught off guard. Then her expression melted into a dreamy haze, a slow, lovestruck smile spreading across her face.

"Oh, of course! I can come back another time."

I lifted my hand slightly, instinctively reaching over the counter. "Wait, no—"

But before I could do anything else, the man stepped forward—smooth, confident—cutting me off with practiced ease. He reached for the woman's hands, gently taking them in his before lifting them to his lips.

"Thank you, beautiful," he murmured, flashing a smile that turned her a shade of red I didn't even know existed.

My client practically floated out the door, casting him one last love-struck glance before slipping away.

All the while, his eyes never left mine.

"What a kind woman," he said with a smile that didn't reach his eyes.

"That wasn't necessary," I muttered, folding my arms.

I gave him a slow once-over. Guys like him didn't come here for readings—they came for attention, or to buy the building.

I narrowed my eyes. I wasn't about to be bought off by a charming smile and vague sense of urgency. "It'll be double my usual rate," I said flatly, testing him.

He didn't even blink. Just smiled—slow, amused, and annoyingly attractive. "Done," he replied, like it was pocket change.

Of course.

Damn it—I should've said triple.

I stepped out from behind the counter with an exaggerated eye roll, making no effort to hide it. "I'll need a moment to prepare," I said, brushing past him. "You can follow."

"I was hoping I would," he murmured, tossing in an infuriatingly effective wink for my own personal torture.

I paused for half a second. Smooth talker. Probably worked on half the city.

I shook my head and kept walking.

The hallway had never felt this long. Each step echoed off the walls, but all I could focus on was him—his presence behind me like gravity, like his eyes were unapologetically peeling away every layer of clothing I had on.

God help me.

I wanted to turn around, catch that look, and let it burn straight through me.

I stepped aside and swept the velvet curtain open with a practiced flick, though my fingers betrayed me with a slight tremble. He moved past me—close, far too close. There was plenty of space, but he chose to brush against me, the heat of his body a whisper against my skin. His scent wrapped around me—smoke and salt—like a beach bonfire after midnight.

His footsteps fell slow and sure on the wooden floor, nearly lost beneath the soft, ambient music drifting from hidden speakers—usually calming. Not now.

I gestured toward the small, round table at the center of the room. "Have a seat," I instructed, my voice thinner than I liked.

He lowered himself into the chair with effortless elegance, his eyes never leaving mine.

I sank into the seat across from him, trying not to squirm under his stare—or imagine what it would feel like if he touched me again.

"Name?" I asked, keeping my irritated tone casual.

He raised an eyebrow, a smirk playing at the corner of his mouth. "Shouldn't you be able to know that if you're psychic?"

I forced a smile. I was used to this kind of questioning—people showing up just to catch me slipping, to prove I was a fraud. Practically routine by now.

"I—"

"Cullen," he cut in smoothly, still wearing that amused expression. He clearly enjoyed getting under my skin.

"Palm reading, right? Then please—give me your hand, *Cullen...*" I said, letting his name linger on my lips like a challenge. I hated how much I enjoyed saying it—how easily it slid off my tongue.

I placed my hand palm-up on the table, fingers spread, eyes lifting to his with impatience.

He let out a low, amused chuckle and slowly laid his hand in mine, his touch unhurried, deliberate. The moment our skin connected, a jolt of something electric rippled up my arm. His hand was warm and strong. I wondered how many people he'd touched with these hands—what he'd done to them with those fingers.

My fingers curled around his instinctively—possessively.

I blinked, catching myself before I could lean in closer.

Get it together.

Something about him felt...off. And I knew enough to trust what I didn't trust.

"Do you have a specific question?" I asked, forcing my voice into something professional. "Love? Success? Or let me guess..."

I looked up through my lashes, letting the pause stretch just long enough to be suggestive.

"Problems in bed?" I purred, tugging lightly at my bottom lip with my teeth.

I held his gaze, daring him to respond to my quip. His eyes were golden—like the last light of a sunset. I'd never seen eyes like that before. He smiled slowly, almost proudly, and his grip on my hand tightened as he leaned in—too fast, a blur.

In an instant, I felt—

I gasped, my entire body locking in place. There was no pain—just a shock, sudden and searing, a ripple of energy that spread through me like wildfire. My chest clenched, and for a moment, I couldn't breathe.

"I—" I tried to speak, but the words caught in my throat.

I couldn't look away from him. It was like he held me there, pinned under his gaze, and I was powerless to resist.

The room began to swirl, the edges of my vision blurring, leaving only him. Everything else dissolved into a suffocating blackness—an abyss where light and hope were strangers.

I wanted to scream, but no sound came out. My body was no longer mine.

Then a sound emerged from within the dark—a distant echo of my voice, distorted and strange, like hearing myself on an old recording.

Love.

Strength.

Death.

The words were familiar—questions I often asked during readings—yet now they were twisted, corrupted. They repeated like a haunting chant, circling me, closing in until I could no longer tell where one ended and the next began.

Flashes of light erupted in the void, revealing fragmented, terrifying visions—nightmarish scenes bleeding into one another in a chaotic blur. Faces appeared, grotesque and melting, their features warping like wax under flame.

Then, just as suddenly, it all vanished—swallowed by an even heavier silence. But this silence wasn't empty. It pulsed with dark, living energy that made my skin crawl.

A voice emerged from it. *His* voice.

"I hope you do, little reader...*burn it to the fucking ground,*" he whispered.

The words echoed in my mind, louder and louder, until they roared inside me. Then a final image burst before my eyes—a fire, roaring and hungry, licking at my skin and dragging me into its core.

I JOLTED AWAKE, gasping for air, my body drenched in cold sweat. My heart thundered in my chest, pounding in my ears. For a moment, the darkness around me felt just as suffocating as the void I'd escaped. I couldn't tell where I was—

My room?

I blinked, disoriented, then fumbled for the lamp on my nightstand. Warm light spilled across the room, revealing my bed—and the fact that I was still wearing my clothes from earlier.

I looked down, pressing trembling fingers to my chest: no wounds, no marks—nothing out of place. But the panic wouldn't fade. My hands shook as I gripped the sheets, trying to ground myself.

How did I get here?

I scanned the room. Nothing.

Meow.

"Fucking hell—" I nearly fell out of bed.

Marnie was curled up beside me, purring softly. I scooped her up, cradling her against my chest. "You scared the shit out of me," I muttered.

But the question lingered, clawing at the edges of my mind.

What happened?

Where...who was...Cullen?

CHAPTER FOUR

CULLEN

I hated the city.

The noise.

The lie.

From up here, behind the floor-to-ceiling glass of my office, they all looked the same—tiny, frantic lives scrambling under the illusion of free will.

But their choices were never their own.

Mortals didn't see it.

That we were still here.

That the gods had never left.

They called us myths. Legends. Heroes.

Something to worship, mock, or tattoo on their ribs as if it meant they were part of something greater.

Let them.

Let them believe we were nothing more than stories.

Their lives burned out so quickly it was barely worth the breath to correct them.

I shifted in my chair, black leather biting into my back, and glanced around the office. Plastered on every surface of the white-as-bone walls, the glass door, even the custom-etched tumblers, was the Arrows Align logo: oversized red font, a golden arrowhead spearing through it like something being stabbed.

My mother's sense of humor, I was sure.

Everything in this building had been her design, down to the grout lines in the tile—measured precisely so they wouldn't snag her heels.

This tower was her temple now. Her obsession.

Meanwhile, I was stationed here, the golden boy fronting her matchmaking empire.

When all I wanted was to be home.

My real home.

Above it all.

A palace hidden in the clouds—secluded, untouched, mine. The only place that had ever felt like peace. Not that I got to stay long. My mother treated it like a borrowed privilege—granted me leave like a parole officer, always careful to include a time limit. A clear reminder: I didn't own my freedom. She did.

At least there was the bar.

I reached for the bottle tucked in the corner cabinet—one of the few indulgences I'd allowed in this sterile mausoleum. A splash of amber.

The only warmth in this place.

A mortal concoction. But it burned enough.

I used to care.

About the mortals. About their desires, their fragile hopes.

They had once called me Cupid—the one who inspired affection, the god who gave mortals the confidence to speak their truths, to chase what they wanted.

But centuries had a way of grinding that out of you.

Immortality had its own...vexations.

The monotony.

The stillness between centuries felt like rot.

I had been bored.

Deeply, bitterly bored.

Until—*very* recently.

Mystic Soulstice.

And the girl inside it.

Skye.

I loved the sound of my new game.

The way she tried—and failed—to hide her irritation when I interrupted her day? Amusing.

It had been centuries since someone's reaction made me actually curious. Intrigued.

I smirked at the memory, my jaw tightening as her face flashed behind my eyes—focused, sincere, utterly unaware of what was about to hit her.

She had actually wanted to give me a real reading. Thought she could see something in me.

I exhaled a quiet breath, nearly a laugh.

I should've taken her to bed first—felt her beneath me, burned that heat into my skin—before I cursed her with the arrow.

My fingers curled into a loose fist.

But no...

She had said it was urgent.

Urgent.

When the Olympian Command said move, you moved. I wouldn't have been allowed to wait long.

When Skye reached for my hand, I caught the flicker of hesitation in her eyes. She masked it quickly, flipping the tone, using my name.

The way she said it—drawn out, like it was meant to sting—

It only made me wonder how else I could make her say it.

The moment her fingers touched mine, it was like I was myself again.

Like my own thoughts belonged to me for the first time in days.

I actually questioned why I was there and why I was doing any of this.

But the second she let go...

The full force of the Command snapped back like a whip—stronger this time, as if it sensed my hesitation and meant to crush it.

My body moved on instinct. The arrow was already in my hand, already flying.

It sank straight into her heart.

She gasped, her eyes widening—not from pain but from shock.

The arrow didn't break her. It rewired her.

Something deep shifted inside her, like a locked door being blown open.

She froze. Her gaze locked with mine. Her lips parted like she was about to ask something.

But it was too late.

Her pupils dilated. I knew the spiral had begun.

Her world was already slipping into the darkness I'd lit from within.

Burn it to the fucking ground, I told her.

I wished I could burn with it.

This kind of task wasn't new to me.

Not by a long shot.

My mother—one of the twelve Olympians—wields Commands the way mortals drew breath.

Whenever her pride took a hit, whenever someone dared to steal a sliver of attention from her, she sent me. Her golden boy. Her executioner. Her favorite son.

I'd lost count of how many times I'd been the arrow in her hand.

They were always the same. Beautiful, sure, in their own ways. But fragile. Temporary. None of them lasted long once touched by the curse. Most collapsed into madness within hours, staring blankly at nothing while their minds unraveled. The stronger ones might last a day or two... but even they withered, unable to withstand the weight of it.

But Skye...

She felt entirely different.

Even after she collapsed—her body limp, unconscious in the chair—I could still sense it.

She hadn't broken.

Not yet.

And gods help me...I was curious.

I exhaled slowly and raised one hand.

The air grew thick with a sudden stillness, the temperature dipping just enough to raise the hairs on my skin. A chime of distant bells rang out as a breeze stirred the shop's hanging crystals.

Then the wind deepened. It curled around itself, forming a column of swirling air that shimmered with power. From within that current, he emerged.

Zephyrus.

Or—Zeph, as I called him.

He stepped out of the wind like it had manifested him.

His skin shimmered with a pale, silvery glow, like twilight caught on flesh. Long silver hair flowed as though it obeyed some invisible breeze that never touched the rest of the room. Robes seemed woven from the current itself, fluttering and drifting with no weight, seams, or start or end.

His gaze settled on me, calm and waiting.

I met his eyes without flinching.

He already knew what this was.

Knew how I felt about these *errands.*

But...here we were.

Again.

"Get her out of here," I ordered, flicking my fingers through the air.

Zeph didn't speak. He never needed to. His form dissolved into a silent current of wind that curled around Skye, lifting her effortlessly from the chair. Her body floated weightlessly, as though gravity had momentarily forgotten her.

I watched her, my gaze fixed on her face—now slack in unconsciousness, the tension gone.

There was a moment when I really looked at her.

Even like this, she radiated something...something real.

In that moment, I understood exactly why my mother was jealous.

The thought of it made me smirk wider.

I leaned back in my chair, twisting the band around my wrist. With a flick, the bracelet responded, summoning the arrow back into my palm.

I ran my fingers over its shaft—sleek and metallic. It shimmered with a faint pulse, like it had a heartbeat of its own. But the tip...

That was the true artistry.

Razor-sharp. Gleaming like liquid silver. Designed to cut through body and thought.

To break mortals and even gods from the inside out.

Usually, I didn't hold onto them after a curse. But this one?

Something about this one...

I pressed the arrow lightly to my forehead and exhaled.

It's over. It's done.

A knock pulled me out of the spiral.

"Come in," I said, voice flat, already twisting the bracelet again. The arrow disarmed in a flash of light, vanishing back into its place at my wrist.

The door creaked open, and Vanessa, my mother's secretary, walked in. She was beautiful, undeniably so, with perfectly styled hair, a fitted pencil skirt, and a blouse that left just enough to the imagination. She knew how to play the part, and she did it well. Her heels clicked softly against the floor as she approached my desk, carrying a file in one hand and a flirtatious smile in the other.

"Busy, Mr. Eros?" she asked, her voice silky as she leaned a little too close, brushing the file onto my desk.

I didn't look up. "Always," I muttered, uninterested.

She pouted, undeterred. "You know, I could always help...relieve some of that stress." Her fingers grazed the desk's edge.

My gaze flicked to her briefly before returning to the skyline. "I'm good, thanks."

Her smile faltered for a half second, but she recovered quickly, the professional mask sliding neatly back into place.

"Ms. Troy has requested your presence in her office," Vanessa said, tone crisp now. "Says it's urgent."

I sighed, rising from my chair with the kind of ease that came from centuries of this sort of thing.

"Of course it is." I ran a hand through my hair and let out another slow breath. "Tell her I'm on my way."

Vanessa lingered, casting one last glance my way—maybe searching for a reaction I had no intention of giving.

When the door clicked shut behind her, I adjusted my jacket and muttered to myself, "Showtime."

Ms. Troy.

To everyone else, she was Stella Troy—the impossibly poised founder of Arrows Align, the record-breaking matchmaking empire built on an algorithm she claimed could outmatch fate itself.

My...mother.

Aphrodite.

Goddess of love. Of beauty.

When I stepped into her office, I wasn't even pretending to be surprised. She sat behind her desk, fingers flying over a sleek keyboard, the picture of modern power. She didn't bother to look up.

"I've been summoned," I said, letting the drama curl around my voice like smoke.

Still typing. "Is it done?"

Of course it was done.

"She's out of your way," I replied, leaning casually against the doorframe. "But you already knew that, didn't you?"

Finally, she looked up.

Cool, calculating eyes met mine. Her platinum hair—glossy, immaculate—framed her face in perfect waves. Dressed in a tailored steel-gray suit, she looked more like a luxury brand ambassador than a deity.

"Fine," she said, her tone flat. Unbothered. Icy.

The irony was never lost on me—that the goddess of love could be so entirely devoid of it.

I rolled my eyes. "You're worried she'll ruin your precious launch event?"

She didn't blink.

But I felt it—that shift.

"Careful," she murmured, her voice low and precise. "You're too wrapped up in your...playthings."

Careful.

I stiffened, just slightly. The Command pressed down on me like a dog reacting to the sudden tug of its leash.

Still, I smirked. "You've always loved my games."

Her eyes flickered, daring me to push further. I could practically hear the unspoken *try me.*

"You're not here to play with your food," she said coolly, each word deliberate, razor-sharp. "You're here to be useful—unlike your siblings."

She stood slowly, smoothing down the front of her suit, then met my gaze head-on.

"And..."

A pause—just long enough to ensure she had my full attention.

"I expect you to escort me," she continued. "To the Titanomachy celebration, and the launch event later tonight."

There it was.

The real reason for this little performance.

I arched an eyebrow, a slow smile tugging at my mouth. "Couldn't ask Hephaestus?" I said, bringing up my father's name with just the right amount of bite. "I'm sure the two of you could use some...quality time. For appearance's sake, of course."

It landed.

I watched a flicker of tension ripple through her. Her posture straightened.

But before she could respond, the office door swung open without warning.

Vanessa burst in, pale and visibly rattled, as if she'd sprinted through a hurricane to get here. "Ms. Troy," she breathed, trying to compose herself, "Mr. Mars has...arrived."

And just like that, as if conjured by conflict itself, he appeared.

Ares.

He strode in like the world owed him a kingdom and he'd come to collect. Every step radiated his ever-present arrogance.

Tall. Broad-shouldered. Muscles. Even his hair seemed to cut like weaponry.

He didn't spare Vanessa a glance. His attention was locked on my mother, gaze raking over her like she was the battlefield he wanted to conquer.

"Well, well...if it isn't the beauty herself," Ares drawled as he sauntered closer, eyes drinking her in. Despite our lingering tension, I watched her relax ever so slightly. Her spine eased. Her posture softened in that way it only ever did for *him*.

"Still making men tremble at the sight of your beauty?" he asked, his voice smooth, taunting—far too familiar.

My mother didn't respond right away, but the slight curve of her lips said enough. She held his gaze, her voice dripping honey when it finally came. "Only the ones who deserve it."

Ares chuckled low, a grin spreading across his face. "I'd expect nothing less." He stepped closer, his hand brushing against hers. "Seems I'm in luck, then. Maybe I'll get the chance to earn my place beneath your feet...*again*."

I wanted to vomit.

Ares smirked, clearly enjoying the moment, until his gaze flicked to me. His amusement deepened.

Disgusting.

It wasn't their affair—or even loyalty to my father, Hephaestus—that twisted in my chest. It was the fact that they flaunted whatever this was right in front of me, while my mother refused to free me to love. Me, the god of it, mind you.

"And what about your boy here?" Ares asked, his voice like a blade being sharpened. "Still obeying Mommy like a good little soldier?"

My jaw clenched, anger simmering low and hot in my chest.

Obeying—like I had a fucking choice.

"Enough," Aphrodite cut in. Her eyes flicked between us, her power simmering like heat between our bodies.

Ares lifted his hands in exaggerated surrender, still grinning. "Didn't mean to cause trouble."

Every word dripped with false apology, but his gaze never left mine. He was daring me to react.

"Cupid. Leave us."

My mother's hand waved in casual dismissal, like I was a servant rather than her son.

I didn't wait to see what came next. I turned and walked out before they started producing even more offspring on the desk.

I closed the door behind me, hearing the lock *click*—a sound more beautiful than anything else in the world.

"Titans are stirring again."

Ares's voice stopped me cold.

"Tartarus isn't as quiet as Zeus insists," he muttered, lower now—more serious.

I froze, hand still on the doorknob, my pulse quickening.

I wasn't supposed to hear that.

My mother's voice came next—softer, but edged with tension. "They're just rumors."

Rumors.

All the gods had been hearing whispers of unrest. It wasn't unusual, not as the summer solstice crept closer. The story of Cronus clawing his way out of Tartarus to end the world was practically a bedtime tale by now—a divine ghost story passed around like gossip.

But Ares didn't sound amused.

"It's different," he said, voice grim. "This time, it's not just Cronus. Other Titans are stirring. And we must be ready—especially with our sons being so...volatile."

Our sons.

He meant Phobos and Deimos.

I exhaled slowly.

Aphrodite and Ares—together, they had three children:

Phobos, god of fear.

Deimos, god of terror.

And Harmonia, goddess of unity.

My half-siblings.

Aphrodite's tone sharpened. "I'll handle them."

Ares let out a dry, humorless laugh. "You always say that. But they're just as much mine as they are yours. And you know damn well they'll fight us if it comes to that."

My jaw ticked.

Phobos and Deimos had always pushed limits—twisting Commands just enough to avoid breaking them outright—manipulators of loopholes and technicalities.

And now, somehow, they were tied to Tartarus.

Tied to the rising storm I could feel tightening in my blood.

A low roll of thunder echoed in the distance.

Phobos.

Deimos.

Cronus.

Nothing about this was a coincidence.

Rumors weren't enough.

I needed more.

More reach.

More ears.

The wind was always listening.

Zeph was always listening.

Maybe more than even he realized.

CHAPTER FIVE

SKYE

Maybe I needed to check the caffeine levels in these teas.

I dropped the bags onto the counter and made my way to the mirror above the sink.

One more time.

I ran my fingers over my skin, pressing lightly just below my collarbone. But there was nothing—no cut, no mark, no sign that anything had happened.

No, Skye. Stop. It was just the tea...right?

My mind was desperate for any kind of excuse to explain what had happened.

I. Wasn't. Stabbed. I'd repeated that who knows how many times since waking up last night.

I slumped onto the couch, cradling my head in my hands.

Marnie must've sensed my nerves. She leapt into my lap, purring like a small, fuzzy engine pressed against my chest.

"Thank you," I murmured, kissing the top of her head and holding her close.

The sun was already blazing by the time I finally left the apartment and headed down to the shop. It was so hot, I could feel my sunscreen melting off my face.

I cringed, already dreading how long the AC would run today—and how high the electric bill would be because of it.

I was rounding the corner when I nearly collided with someone.

"Oh—sorry!" I blurted, reaching out instinctively.

It was my neighbor—the one with the tiny dog whose name always escaped me. My gaze dropped to the pink sparkly collar.

Lola. Right.

The second my fingers brushed her bare arm, my eyes were no longer seeing the same—my neighbor was suddenly rushing out of a store, clutching Lola inside her jacket like she'd stolen her. The shock made me yank my hand back as if I'd touched fire.

What the hell?

"Are you alright, dear?" my neighbor asked, eyeing me with concern.

I couldn't answer. My heart was racing as I stepped back, shaking my head.

"Sorry—just running late," I mumbled, wincing at the now high-pitched ringing in my ears.

Um, what...was...that?

Cullen's face popped into my mind like my brain was trying to show me a cue card with the answer on it.

Nope. Nope. Nope.

I picked up my pace, practically skipping as I neared the door to Mystic Soulstice—like it was a portal that could shield me the second I stepped inside.

I reached for the doorknob. It was warm, almost hot from the sun. I braced myself.

The bell above barely made a sound as I slipped through the door, half-expecting to find some sort of crime scene.

But...everything was exactly as I'd left it.

Nothing seemed to be stolen. Everything was still. Undisturbed. Like Cullen had never been in this store to begin with.

I lingered in the doorway, the door bumping gently against my back as I scanned the room. I searched for something...anything that would prove I wasn't losing my mind. But there was nothing.

Absolutely nothing.

My fingers drifted across the counter, cool and smooth under my touch. For a heartbeat, I let myself believe that maybe last night had been a caffeine-induced fever dream.

But the pressure in my chest said otherwise.

I felt as if, at any second, Cullen would walk back in here, lock his eyes on mine, and take my very soul with him.

Why...did that not scare me?

THE REST of the day I forced myself to focus on the shop—anything to shake the thought of visions from my head.

It was just as busy as ever. No one mentioned Cullen. It was like he hadn't even been here. Which made no sense. Someone like him was... unforgettable. So why did it feel like he'd never existed at all?

I shook my head and turned to the plants, watering them a little too thoroughly. I adjusted the stained-glass lanterns hanging from the ceiling, straightened bowls of quartz and moonstone, and wiped down the already spotless counters.

Keep moving.

Don't stop.

"These are quite beautiful."

I turned to see an older man studying the display of crystal pendants. His fingers carefully caressed the glossy stones before settling on a delicate amethyst wrapped in copper wire.

I set down my towel and offered him a warm smile.

"Perfect for my wife's birthday," he added, handing me the necklace and his card. Our fingers touched briefly as I took it—

And then the world tilted.

I was now standing in a dimly lit corner of a living room, lit only by the flicker of a TV. Sat beside it, a life-sized blow-up doll dressed in what looked like couture—his wife. Her plastic eyes stared blankly ahead. One stiff hand rested on his knee, and he leaned in close, whispering something, gently tilting her head to nuzzle his.

I gasped and recoiled, heart pounding.

Gone. The vision was gone now.

The man blinked at me, concerned. “Is something wrong with the necklace?”

“No—not at all,” I said quickly, swallowing the nausea. “I’m just a bit lightheaded.”

I forced a smile, though the room still swayed.

“Everything is fine.”

I said it more to myself than to him.

When the bell jingled behind him and the door clicked shut, I rushed to the back room.

I closed the door and leaned against it, trying to catch my breath. I pressed my fingers to my temples, forcing slow, steady breaths.

What is happening to me?

Lydia had always been the *gifted* one. Her readings were more like friendly conversations, as if she guided people through their own over-thinking.

But this...was...different.

I dropped into the nearest chair, staring blankly at the floor as thoughts swirled like a current I couldn’t escape.

If this was real—if I was actually seeing things—why now?

I buried my face in my hands. If this was what having powers felt like, I wanted no part of it.

I needed to close the store. Yes, just shut it down and maybe see a doctor, a therapist, or both.

I stood, gathering my things in a daze.

Outside, the sun had already begun to set, and no other customers were around to witness my mental unraveling. So I’d just close a little early.

I reached for the front door—only to freeze as it moved on its own.

The bell above chimed, the door swinging wider.

Crap. Bianca.

I had completely forgotten about our appointment. But judging by the way she burst inside, phone already in hand, she hadn’t forgotten hers—or her livestream audience.

She didn’t even glance at me. With her phone out, moving around to capture every inch of the shop, she looked like she was arriving at a photo-shoot, not a modest little psychic shop on the corner.

“Hey, everyone!” she cooed, spinning her phone back to herself to get her best angles. "We're back at Mystic Soulstice today, and I'll be going live soon for my reading! So, standby—you won't want to miss this." Her voice dripped with sugary sweetness.

It physically hurt to make a half-hearted smile, feeling the rising anxiety in my chest, desperate to get out of here.

The words felt like syrup as I spoke. "Nice...to see you again."

Her bright, bubbly expression shifted the moment the camera clicked off. She practically skipped over to the counter, leaning against it to make herself more comfortable.

"So, it looks like my fans are really paying off for you."

I swallowed hard, the butterflies in my stomach turning into wasps.

She leaned in closer, her perfectly manicured nails tapping against the counter. "Well, I've done my part—made you relevant. Now—"

"I haven't forgotten, and I will pay you," I said, cutting her off.

Bianca straightened up, her smile widening. "Good. I'd hate to see things get...complicated between us." She surveyed the shop, eyes gleaming with satisfaction.

She tossed her hair back and tapped her phone screen, not waiting for me to respond as she strolled toward the reading room, expecting me to follow her.

"Lydia..." I glanced around the shop—my place of refuge. Now, a house of straw waiting for the lie to blow it all away.

Forgive me.

Bianca set up her phone on a little tripod, angled it just right, and settled into the chair across from me.

"So, Skye, I actually did get back with my boyfriend—because you were right, he *did* need to refill my cup." She laughed, winking at her phone before continuing, "Now my followers want to know when he's going to propose!" She giggled, eyes sparkling as she looked into the phone's camera.

I glanced at the stream on her phone, and the comments were rolling in like rapid fire.

She's so pretty!

When's the wedding?!

Where did you get your outfit?

I forced a smile, trying to calm the growing unease in my stomach. "Let's see what the universe has in store."

I hesitated as I reached for her hand. The last time I touched someone's hand...

I shook my head. I had done hundreds of these readings. Just focus on the energy—the feeling.

"Ready?" she asked, flashing the camera another perfect grin.

I nodded and took her hand. The moment our fingers touched, I fell.

Visions crashed into my mind—like the rush of wind when you roll down a car window too fast. I saw her tangled in bed with a man—but something was off. They whispered about not getting caught, about how the man's brother would kill him if he found out.

This...wasn't...her...boyfriend.

The images shifted—bodies pressing together in a heat so intense my eyes burned. I reached up, grabbing at them, making sure they weren't actually on fire.

I forced myself back. The words came out before I could stop them.

"You're sleeping with his brother."

I didn't realize how loud silence could be.

Her smile froze in place, the blood draining from her face as if I'd just slapped her. The livestream comments exploded, one after the other, like popcorn kernels popping in a hot pan.

WHAT DID SHE SAY?!

NO WAY!

LMAO! Cheater!

I blinked, trying to clear my head. What...did I?

Her nails clipped my skin as she jerked her hand away and stood abruptly, chair scraping loudly against the floor.

"What the hell did you just say to me?"

I opened my mouth to apologize, to explain something—but the words wouldn't come. The vision hadn't left. It was still flashing behind my eyes, refusing to let go.

Bianca grabbed her phone and yanked it off the tripod. The livestream was still running as her followers spammed the chat.

"FUCK...YOU."

She drawled it, annunciating each syllable to make sure I got it.

Then she turned and stormed out of the reading room.

I stood there, stunned, before my legs moved on instinct, carrying me after her. But by the time I reached the door, it had slammed shut behind her—our deal going out the door with her.

I was alone.

Alone.

My hand flew to my chest, fingers clutching at my cotton shirt. I knew this feeling. Too well. Too often.

Breathe, Skye. Breathe.

Three things. Name three things around you.

One...moonlight streaming through the window.

Two...a wooden chair leaned against the wall.

Three...the front door, still shaking slightly from Bianca slamming it shut.

I moved toward it on autopilot.

My hands trembled as I reached up and flipped the sign on the window to *Closed*—the only thing I could do at this moment.

I needed control.

I needed to get out of here. *Now.*

CHAPTER SIX
CULLEN

I stood at the rooftop's edge, wings unfurled to their full span, casting long, moonlit shadows across the tiles. The feathers shimmered faintly—pure white with an iridescent sheen. Every subtle movement sent a ripple through them—powerful, yet light as air.

Mortals couldn't see me like this. Up here, high above the city, I could watch without interruption.

And I was watching her.

Through the wide front window of Mystic Soulstice, I saw Skye pacing the shop floor. She kept fidgeting with her hands, twisting her hair up only to let it fall again—over and over, like she couldn't find comfort no matter what she did.

She...wasn't broken.

There was tension in her, yes—but she was upright. Moving. Enduring. Stronger than I'd expected. And that stirred something in me.

Each curse worked differently depending on the target, and this one seemed to trigger every time she touched someone's skin.

Interesting.

Not that it mattered—she could still touch me. The curse wouldn't affect me; it was part of me.

Maybe if I disguised myself, I could—

A sharp breath escaped me.

Touch her?

Why was that even crossing my mind?

No. I couldn't risk another encounter. If Aphrodite found out Skye wasn't curled up in a padded room...she'd want more. More suffering. More destruction.

I needed to keep her off my mother's radar. As long as Skye didn't seem like a threat, Aphrodite would eventually move on—find something, or someone else, to destroy.

I shifted my wings, the night air cool against my skin—but it did nothing to temper the heat coiling low in my chest.

Still...how was she still standing? Still fighting?

I'd cursed her. Marked her. She should've shattered.

And yet...she pulled at something deep inside me, something I thought I'd buried centuries ago.

She *possessed* me.

Every part of her sank beneath my skin. I wanted—gods, I wanted—to be the only reflection in those eyes. To make her look at me and see no one else. To feel her pressed against me, lips parted, breath trembling, saying my name like it belonged to her.

I couldn't want her—*not like this.*

Still...her eyes.

That color—forget-me-nots.

An impossible blue, like spring breaking through frost. They stared right through me, soft petals hiding thorns—ready to cut if you got too close.

And I hated how I longed for them.

How I longed for *her*.

Whoosh.

I didn't need to look to know—Zeph had arrived, materializing from the swirling air. He landed lightly beside me, his long hair and robes settling with him like the wind itself had taken human form.

When I turned, his signature grin was already in place.

"You've got a look," he said, amusement threading through his voice. "Mesmerized by this one, are we?"

I shot him a warning glance but said nothing.

"Oh, come on," he pressed, folding his arms like he was settling in for a show. "I've never seen you this invested in one of your mother's assignments."

Assignments. He meant victims—but he never said that part out loud. He knew I preferred to treat it like a game. I couldn't get attached. I couldn't disobey an Olympian Command.

"She's strong," I said finally, keeping my voice even—though the possessiveness creeping in wasn't exactly subtle. "Stronger than the others."

Zeph raised a brow. "Strong, huh? But wasn't she supposed to break? That's what your mother wanted, right?"

"She'll get what she wants," I muttered, letting the words hang. "No one's ever beaten the curse before."

There was a pause, then Zeph gave a low chuckle, shifting his weight as he leaned against the rooftop ledge.

"Well, I'd say you've got your hands full with this one." He nudged my shoulder with a smirk. "Honestly? I like it. You, flustered over a mortal woman."

I shot him a dry look. "Do you have actual business, or are you just here to meddle in my game?"

His grin faded. The shift in his demeanor was immediate.

"As a matter of fact, I do." He paused, eyes scanning mine. "They're close."

They.

Phobos and Deimos.

My muscles tensed.

Of course they were. And just when things with Skye were starting to get...complicated.

Their cruelty wasn't like mine. I played. I teased the line. But they... they fed on suffering.

The only sliver of hope? Harmonia.

Or Harmony, as she called herself now.

Of all Ares' children, she was the only one I didn't mind calling a sibling. Hell, I even liked her. She was the only one who tried to keep this dysfunctional family from burning everything down.

She never liked how our mother treated me. She never said it outright —there was no point, not with the Command—but I saw it in her eyes.

Soft. Steady. Like she recognized the pain I carried. She couldn't stop it, but at least she saw it.

And that meant I wasn't alone.

She tried. Gods, she tried.

She'd pull Phobos and Deimos back from the edge when no one else could. Step into the chaos, speak—and somehow, peace would prevail.

But even Harmony had limits.

Phobos and Deimos didn't like being leashed. They never leave without wrecking something first.

Just knowing they were nearby made my skin crawl. I rolled my shoulders, resisting the urge to crack my neck. Reckless. Dangerous. Every time they came, it ended the same.

With me cleaning up the aftermath.

"Already stirring up trouble before the Titanomachy celebration," I growled, imagining how short my mother's temper would be if they caused a spectacle.

Zeph nodded. "You know them. If there's even a sliver of opportunity to get into your mind, they'll take it."

My fists clenched. My wings twitched, agitation running through every feather.

I didn't have time for their obsession with getting in my head. Not now. Not when my attention was fixed on Skye. But ignoring them? That would only make it worse. That would make them want to find something —someone—I cared about.

And torment it.

I exhaled sharply, my gaze drifting over the glittering sprawl of the city below.

"Fine," I muttered through clenched teeth. "I'll monitor only at the celebration."

I'd escort my mother, make an appearance for the Olympians, and disappear before anyone got the urge to play neurosurgeon.

My jaw tightened as I stepped back from the edge, Ares' words about the Titan unrest still lingering in my mind. "Any other whispers on the wind? Tartarus? Phobos and Deimos?"

There was a pause—then a breeze curled around my neck, like Zeph was testing the air again.

He exhaled. "Nothing new on the west winds. Phobos and Deimos are close, but they're clever—they know exactly where my reach ends and stay just beyond it. Just far enough, I can't hear whatever they're plotting. Annoying bastards."

A breeze curled around my shoulders, thoughtful.

"As for Tartarus..." Another pause. "There's movement, yeah. But when isn't there? Especially on the solstice."

His voice dropped a degree. "Zeus hasn't told Hades to reinforce the gates. So either he's not worried...or he's doing a damn good job pretending."

I stared out for a beat, the city lights blurring beneath me.

"Keep listening," I said at last. "I want to know the second Phobos or Deimos try anything."

"You mean..." Zeph hesitated. "Are you worried about the mortal?"

I didn't answer.

Instead, I stepped off the rooftop. My wings spread wide, catching the wind, lifting me above the skyline.

Below me, she was still pacing inside Mystic Soulstice—my little reader—unaware of the gods circling overhead.

As if watching her could somehow keep her safe.

"Zeph," I murmured. "Stand guard."

CHAPTER SEVEN

SKYE

I had no idea how long I'd been pacing.

When my knee smacked into the counter, I actually thanked it—for snapping me out of whatever spiral I'd been caught in.

Clutching my knee, I sucked in a breath and forced it out slowly, trying to manage the pain. Once it dulled to something tolerable, I slid to the floor, huddled behind the counter with my back pressed against the cool wood. My legs felt like jelly, and my brain ached. I wasn't sure how much more I could take.

I considered going to a doctor. But what would I even say?

They'd ask when it all started. And I'd have to tell them...what? That a stranger strolled into my shop and then—

Did what?

Drugged me? Hypnotized me?

I didn't have answers. And I wasn't in the mood to be looked at like I was crazy. Or high. Or worse—told it was all in my head or blamed on "hormones."

I ran my hands through my hair again, cringing at the oily texture. I'd been doing that too much lately—a nervous habit.

At least the shop was closed for the night. I could head upstairs to the apartment. Try to sleep.

I shifted to stand—

Jingle. Jingle.

The sound froze me.

The front door handle rattled. Metal scraped against metal, far too loud in the silence.

Was someone trying to break in?

My heart thundered, each beat pumping fresh panic through my veins.

Cullen. Was it him?

My breath caught at the thought—those golden eyes holding mine like he already owned every piece of my soul.

The door rattled again, harder this time. Someone was testing the lock.

A cold prickle swept across my skin. I scanned the room for a plan—anything. A weapon. A phone. A hiding place.

God, why hadn't I kept something behind the counter?

Slowly, I crouched low, pressing my back against the wood, my breath shallow and fast. The dark felt heavier now, like it was settling on my chest.

Then—I heard it.

Click.

The lock gave way.

The quiet shattered with a groan of rusty hinges as the door swung open. Footsteps followed—soft, unhurried. Like whoever it was already knew precisely what they were walking into.

My gaze snapped to the antique mirror on the wall, its surface warped and cracked. I held my breath, eyes locked on the distorted reflection of the door.

A figure appeared.

Tall. Feminine.

Something about her tugged at the edge of memory...familiar.

A chill threaded down my spine as she stepped further into the room. That's when I saw it in the mirror—red-tinted glasses, the lenses glowing faintly in the dark.

"Relax. I'm not here to hurt you," she said, each word laced with irritation. "Believe me, I didn't want it to come to this. I shouldn't even be involved." Her arms crossed tightly over her chest, muttering that last part more to herself.

Her glasses caught the light as she turned her head, and our gazes met in the mirror.

"You want answers, don't you? About what's happening to you?"

I blinked, my hand rising instinctively to my chest as recognition flared. The bar. The woman with the blood-red glasses.

My fingers curled against the thudding beat of my heart as I slowly rose from behind the counter. Fear still hummed in my veins, but curiosity began to burn through the panic. She didn't move—just stood there, watching me.

She was slim, a long leather jacket wrapped around her like armor. Her jet-black hair was tucked into the collar, sharp and clean. And those red glasses gleamed in the dim light, casting her in shadow—less a person and more a vision from some gothic noir fever dream.

"I remember you," I breathed, the words tight and unsure in my throat. "From the bar."

Her lips tugged into a humorless smile.

"Name's Euryale," she said, slow and deliberate. "Eu-ry-a-le."

She spoke like she expected me not to get it—that I'd need it spelled out.

I swallowed hard. My nerves were frayed, but I forced the words out anyway.

"What...what is going on?" My voice wavered despite the effort to hold it steady.

Euryale didn't answer right away. She stepped forward, her boots silent against the floor. The counter now the only thing separating us.

"I think I know the curse," she answered carefully, as if testing the words in her mouth. "But I need to be sure."

Before I could react—before the instinct to move or even flinch reached my body—her hand shot out and clasped mine.

A jolt tore through me, like static prickling across my skin. The shop blurred at the edges. The city lights outside the window bent and warped around us.

Then everything disappeared.

I was at a funeral.

Aunt Lydia's.

The scent of stirred earth and sunbaked dirt filled my nose. White flowers drooped in the heat. Murmured condolences floated around me like ghosts.

And in the back—partially hidden in shadow—her.

A woman with red glasses. Watching.

The scene rippled.

Suddenly, I was back in Mystic Soulstice—but years earlier. Lydia sat at a small round table, laughing. Across from her sat Euryale. The two of them sipping tea like...friends.

Then it shifted again.

A stretcher. Flashing red and blue lights. Euryale stood on the sidewalk, arms wrapped tightly around herself as the paramedics loaded Lydia into the ambulance. Her head turned away, like it hurt too much to watch.

I wanted more. To stay inside the vision, to push deeper into whatever this was—but then Euryale let go.

Everything vanished.

Mystic Soulstice snapped back into focus. I stumbled, clutching the counter for support, my breath ragged.

"What...what was that?" I gasped, my voice shaking.

She hesitated, like she was gauging how much truth I could take.

"What did you see?" she asked, her tone probing but not unkind.

I swallowed hard, trying to pull myself back into the moment.

"You were there...when Lydia died?"

She nodded, lips pressing into a thin line. "Anything else?"

My heart pounded as I straightened, despite the tremble in my legs.

"You knew her," I said. "You were friends. You were at the funeral."

A sharp pain sliced through my skull, sudden and searing. I grabbed my head, staggering a step.

"So...the visions trigger based on the person's thoughts," Euryale murmured to herself, more observation than explanation.

Something flickered in her expression—restraint, maybe. She took a slow breath and gave a reluctant nod.

"Yes," she replied quietly. "I knew Lydia."

I blinked, stunned.

Her words pushed the throb in my skull into the background. It wasn't the pain I was focused on anymore.

"What did you do? What's happening to me? Who...are you?"

The questions spilled out of me. I wasn't even sure which one I wanted answered first.

Euryale tilted her head slightly. "I know you have questions about Cupid—"

"Wait. *What*? Cupid?" I cut in, my voice sharp, like the name alone had snapped something in me.

She didn't flinch. Just nodded.

"Yes. Cupid. God of love and desire. Son of Aphrodite. You know the story—the fat baby in a diaper with wings, floating around with a bow?" She twirled her fingers in the air, mimicking flight. "Yeah, well...he's not a baby anymore. And those arrows? They don't just make people fall in love. They crawl inside your head. Twist your will. He goes by Cullen now."

My mouth went dry.

Her words were like pieces of a puzzle I hadn't even realized I'd been putting together.

"So...what he did to me—"

The stabbing—its memory surged up.

There hadn't been pain. But something had shifted. Something inside me had...opened. My breath hitched. I remembered his eyes—

And then it was gone. The memory slipped away, like water through my fingers.

Euryale's voice cut back in, colder now.

"You're not the first person he's done this to. And you won't be the last. But most people..." Her jaw tightened. "Most don't survive it."

The words sank into my skin like ice, and dread pooled deep in my stomach.

"Why?" I whispered. "What did I do?"

Something shifted in her face—just for a second. Her fingers flexed, slow and tense, like they remembered something her mouth refused to say.

"Cupid's cursed, too, in his own way," she murmured, softer now. "I'd bet anything his mother had a hand in it."

"His mother," I echoed, the way she said it, like she was so familiar with them.

I narrowed my eyes at her.

"You're cursed, too, aren't you?" I asked, my voice low. "What did he do to you?"

Her hand twitched, hovering near the rim of her glasses—but she didn't take them off. Her jaw tightened, like she was swallowing something jagged.

"Not the time," she clipped. "Listen...I've been watching over you—for Lydia's sake," she hissed. "And now, with everything that's happening... she wouldn't have wanted you to face this alone."

Watching over you.

The words barely had time to settle before something in me cracked.

I laughed—short, disbelieving. "Are you kidding?"

All the grief I'd been carrying, the loneliness, the confusion—it roared up at once.

"You don't get to say that," I snapped. "You don't get to just show up out of nowhere and claim you've been watching over me like some guardian angel."

My hands curled into fists before I even realized it. "Lydia never mentioned you. Not once." I swallowed hard, throat tightening. "And now you're saying you knew her?"

I moved out from behind the counter.

"Where were you when I was planning her funeral?"

My breath caught, the edges of my anger fraying with the ache I hadn't let myself feel in weeks. "You say Lydia wouldn't want me to face this alone?" I took a step closer, my voice low and shaking. "Well—I already am."

Still, she didn't interrupt. Just stood there and took it, her silence more infuriating than any excuse she could've offered.

"Watching over me..." I muttered again, shaking my head. "Unbelievable."

Euryale tucked her hands into her pockets. Her gaze drifted—anywhere but me. "I'm sorry about Lydia." The words came low, careful. "I know that isn't enough."

A pause. Her fingers twitched in her pocket. "Losing her..." Her jaw clenched. "It's not right. She still had so much life to give this world."

I shifted, flinching at the sound of her name on her lips.

"So what now? You show up, tell me I'm cursed, and that's it? There's nothing I can do?"

She didn't answer right away. Instead, she moved slowly across the room. For a moment, I thought she might leave. She paused near the door, one hand brushing a nearby shelf like she was steadying herself—or lost in a memory. Then, she turned back to face me.

"We're going to get the arrow back," she said, her tone hard and resolute. "And I know exactly where Cupid will be tonight."

"Why should I trust you?" I asked, narrowing my eyes.

Euryale's hand dropped from the doorknob as she stepped closer, closing the space between us.

"Because I've seen what happens to the others," she replied, her voice like ice. "They end up hollow. Just...shells. Alive, but barely. Waiting for their bodies to give out. You're stronger, Skye—but you won't last much longer if we don't act."

So...this was a death sentence?

My gaze dropped to my trembling hands. "I can't...I can't touch people's skin," I whispered, the words tasting like shame. "Every time I do, I see things."

Euryale studied me silently, then reached into her coat and pulled out a pair of worn leather gloves. She offered them without a word.

"Looks like it causes pain, too," she said simply. "These should help."

I slid them on, the leather stiff but comforting, grounding me. But just as she drew her hand back, something on her wrist caught my eye—a thin bracelet of pale blue and silver crystals that shimmered faintly in the low light.

I froze, breath catching in my throat.

"That bracelet..." The words were barely more than a whisper.

Euryale followed my gaze, glancing down at her wrist like she'd forgotten she was even wearing it.

"Lydia gave it to me," she explained, voice quieter now. "Said the crystals would help keep me calm." Her fingers brushed the smooth stones, slow and reverent.

"Blue lace agate," I murmured, memory surfacing before I could stop it. "It's meant to soothe emotions."

I could still hear Lydia saying it, her voice full of quiet certainty as she clutched that same bracelet on one of her bad days. She always wore it when things got hard—like armor no one else could see. I hadn't seen it since the funeral. Seeing it now, on someone else's wrist, twisted something sharp and aching in my chest.

"She was the closest thing I had to family for a long time," Euryale added, her voice drifting, wrapped in something fragile.

A lump rose in my throat. I wasn't the only one who'd lost her.

I still didn't fully trust Euryale. But maybe...

Maybe it was enough that Lydia had.

I drew in a shaky breath, trying to steady myself as the pieces shifted inside me. She knew more than I did. And if there was even the slightest chance of surviving whatever this was—of fighting it—I needed answers.

"Let's go," I said, squaring my shoulders.

Euryale's lips twitched into something faintly satisfied.

"We'll need to move fast," she said. Then her gaze dropped, and even though her eyes were hidden behind those blood-red lenses, I could feel her sizing me up.

"But first"—she nodded toward my outfit, deadpan—"you'll need to change."

CHAPTER EIGHT

CULLEN

I walked beside my mother, the winding path to Mount Olympus stretching before us like a bridge spun from light. The air here was thinner, purer. Even the deep blue sky seemed nearer—because it was.

Olympus rose above the mortal realm, perched atop a mountain peak veiled in cloud and guarded by enchantment. Towering marble halls, flame-lit temples, and rivers that shimmered like starlight—all hidden in plain sight, beyond mortal comprehension.

There were many ways to reach Olympus. Gods could summon a direct path—so long as they declared, "*Zeus is King*"—and Zeus's lightning would flash them to the summit. Others flew, rode the winds, or used the goddess Iris's rainbows as bridges through the sky.

But of course, Aphrodite preferred the most dramatic entrance possible.

A golden chariot drawn by winged Pegasi.

They were only visible if they allowed it—pristine creatures, sparkling like diamonds in the moonlight. Their hooves struck the clouds, which shifted beneath them like splashing puddles, parting and swirling in reverence.

It was beautiful, like watching nature in its most divine form.

My mother moved with effortless grace, in a crimson gown that matched her lipstick exactly. The gown shimmered in the torchlight, reflecting on the waterfalls like blood on water. Her golden hair fell in flawless waves down her back, each strand artfully placed, hand resting lightly on mine as I escorted her. A show for the others, as always.

"It's an honor to escort me," she said, her voice slicing through my thoughts like I had no right to be glaring at her.

"Of course. How dare it be perceived otherwise," I muttered, glancing at her and pasting on a perfect smile.

She arched a brow, unconvinced, but didn't argue. Instead, her gaze turned forward, toward the towering gates of Olympus. The divine gathering had already begun. Laughter and conversation drifted on the wind, mingling with the soft music of lyres and flutes. Gods and goddesses, cloaked in shimmering robes, glided between marble columns with nectar-filled goblets.

The Titanomachy celebration was always a spectacle. Held on the summer and winter solstices, it honored the Olympians' victory over the Titans—a grand display to solidify their claim to power.

Their triumph.

Their thrones.

Their right to rule gods and mortals alike.

And, of course, to honor the nectar.

Twice a year, during the solstices, the waters of Olympus shimmered gold—liquid divinity winding through fountains, sacred pools, and carved channels like veins of light. A gift born of war. A prize earned.

One sip—

That's all it took to become immortal.

And time bowed to you.

Yet we still gathered. Still drank.

Not out of need.

But for ritual.

For tradition.

So I'd be there, right where I was forced to be...at my mother's side—wearing the right mask, saying the expected lines, playing the dutiful son.

Pretending I wasn't thinking about a mortal girl pacing her little shop like the world was ending.

While Olympus drowned in gold.

As we neared the Grand Hall—the pulsing heart of Olympus—

columns loomed overhead, etched with runes. The marble beneath our feet was inlaid with intricate mosaics of gold and lapis. At the center, a massive eagle spread its wings across the floor, talons gripping thunderbolts, feathers crafted from slivers of mirrored glass that caught the light with every step.

At the far end of the hall stretched the Olympians' table—long, imposing, carved from black obsidian veined with molten gold. It looked like lightning frozen mid-strike, held captive in stone.

And at its head stood Zeus.

His robes shimmered like molten sunlight, gold and silver woven so finely they looked poured into his broad frame. His hair, a deep gray slicked back to his shoulders, gleamed beneath a jagged crown of gold.

Hera was at his side, his bonded wife, peacock feathers rising from her gown and threading through the dark coils of her hair like living ornaments.

Athena—goddess of wisdom and war strategy—stood still as stone to their right, feeding the owl perched loyally on her arm. Across from her, Poseidon twirled his trident like it weighed nothing, the metal catching the light in steady, ceaseless motion—like the tides.

Further down: Apollo, Demeter, Artemis, Ares, Hermes, Dionysus, and Hephaestus.

The Twelve.

The ones who ruled Olympus.

And the ones who never let anyone forget it.

Below them, the lesser gods—still mighty in their own right—drifted along the lower tiers of the hall, orbiting in silent reverence. Close enough to admire. Never close enough to threaten.

My mother cast me a sidelong glance, offered a curt nod, and released my hand. She moved toward her seat beside Hephaestus; neither exchanged a look.

Not surprising.

I didn't follow her. Instead, I slowed my steps, slipping into the press of the lesser divine bodies—my kind—content to become a shadow in their light.

Better a ghost among gods than a pawn at their table.

Zeus rose from his seat at the head of the Olympian table, the motion alone enough to hush the room. Light from the chandeliers caught on his golden chalice, setting it aglow as he raised it high, commanding silence without a word.

Laughter died instantly, as if the very air had been ordered still.

"Brothers, sisters, children of Olympus!" His voice thundered through the hall, every syllable echoing the memory of ancient battles. His eyes burned—not with warmth but with the fire of conquest, the Titanomachy still smoldering behind them. "Today, we celebrate our greatest victory—the day the Titans fell, and Olympus was born!"

A roar of approval shook the hall. Goblets lifted, nectar spilling over golden rims. I raised my own cup—but my gaze kept moving, sweeping the crowd, searching for my half-siblings.

Then Zeus's tone shifted.

"We must remain vigilant," he said, his voice dropping lower.

Just four words—and the atmosphere cracked like ice.

The gods stilled. You could feel it—that subtle shift in the air, the way the laughter shriveled and died. Everyone recognized that tone. I forced my expression to remain neutral, but I knew where this was headed.

"The prison of Tartarus still holds," Zeus continued, words laced with warning. "But we cannot forget the power that once rose against us."

The silence that followed was heavier than stone, colder than the highest peaks of Olympus.

"It is through our continued strength and vigilance that the Titans remain where they belong. Tartarus holds because we Command it to. The chains that bind our enemies are forged by Olympus itself."

He raised his chalice again, and the look in his eyes said it all: this victory—this peace—was because of him. Because of Zeus. And no one should forget it.

Another cheer rose—more performative than passionate. Golden nectar sloshed over goblet rims as the gods toasted themselves, their supremacy, and their eternal reign.

But beneath the gold and glory, there was fear.

And maybe...rightly so.

The formalities ended, and the celebration roared back to life. Music swelled, laughter spilled like wine, and feasts resumed—as if the rumors of the Titans were nothing but noise in the blur.

Goblets clinked in exaggerated cheer. Toasts rose—not to unity or peace—but to themselves. Gods praising gods. Power congratulating power.

Nymphs and muses wove through the crowd like ribbons, their laughter light as they danced and sang for the gods they worshipped.

I stayed at the edge, watching, pretending not to notice how they eyed each other's thrones more than their faces. It was always like this—glitter on rot.

But Olympus loved its *distractions*.

I leaned back in my seat and exhaled quietly.

No sign of Phobos or Deimos.

I couldn't tell if that was a good thing or not. Maybe Harmony was handling them.

At least it meant I could slip away.

I was halfway to slipping out for some air when a voice cut through the noise—sharp, familiar.

"Cullen Eros."

I smiled before I even turned. I'd know that voice anywhere.

"Still gracing us with your presence at these family functions?" Harmony asked, her tone light and amused. "I thought for sure you'd vanish before the toasts."

I turned to find her slipping effortlessly into the seat beside me, her gown catching the chandelier's glow—blue and silver silk flowing around her like moonlit water.

"Well, you know how it is," I said, leaning in with mock solemnity. "I just couldn't wait to hear one of Zeus's *compelling* speeches."

She snorted, rolling her eyes. "Careful. If Hera hears you, she'll incinerate you before dessert."

I gave a theatrical shudder. "Terrifying goddess. Remind me to stay out of smiting distance."

Harmony smirked. "But seriously—you? Still here...why? Looking for chaos?"

Her eyebrow arched, like she'd already guessed my intentions.

"Maybe I missed your sparkling company," I replied, lifting my glass toward her.

She laughed, but her eyes saw past my attempt at flattery.

I took a slow sip of nectar, letting the sweetness and burn settle at the back of my throat. My gaze drifted across the hall again—searching faces, noting absences.

Then I set the goblet down, casual but deliberate.

"Actually...I *am* here for chaos," I said, glancing at her. "Do you know where Phobos and Deimos are? Controlled?"

Harmony's expression shifted—subtle, but not subtle enough for me to miss. "Controlled?" she echoed, one brow lifting. "They're Phobos and Deimos. When are they ever controlled? I spend most of my immortal life making sure one doesn't flatten a city just because they're in a mood."

She popped a grape into her mouth, chewing as she scoffed. "It's a full-time job, believe me. But why the interest? Is this about the mortal girl I've been hearing whispers about?"

Of course she'd heard.

"And knowing you," she added, "it's more than just whispers."

I rolled my eyes. "Gossip is the world's most efficient communication system, especially when gods have nothing better to do."

"Please." Harmony leaned her elbow on the table, chin resting in her palm. "You know I'm not judging. I just want to know how you're doing."

Harmony. Always asking, always watching. Less like a sister and more like the mother I never had—the kind who didn't have an agenda.

I opened my mouth to respond, but the hairs on the back of my neck stood on end before a word left my lips.

Trouble was closing in.

I didn't have to turn. The air shifted—sharp, cold, crawling with dread.

Phobos and Deimos.

They never walked into a room—they arrived, like a shadow spilling across the floor, devouring the light in its path.

Phobos reached us first. His skin was flushed, as if he were always burning from the inside out. His eyes—bloodshot and darting—moved with the frenzy of someone reliving their worst nightmare on loop. Every twitch, every breath, radiated fear.

Beside him, Deimos looked almost translucent, like a ghost given shape. His wild black hair shifted around him, distorting like a heat haze rippling through the air. His smile was razor-thin—sharp enough to strip away hope and leave only terror in its place.

"Cupid," Phobos drawled, voice slick as oil. He leaned in too close, the sour stench of fear clinging to him like perfume. "Heard about your latest...interest."

Deimos didn't bother with pleasantries. "Aphrodite's been talking again," he said, grin curving like a blade. "She always has the best gossip."

Phobos snorted, his sunken gaze fixed on mine. "What was it like," he murmured, "watching her mind and soul unravel before you?"

I clenched my jaw, carving my expression from stone. The worst thing you could give them was a reaction. They fed on discomfort like wine—swirling it across their tongues and savoring every drop.

So I gave them nothing.

"Must be fun," I said flatly, lifting my glass, "being so invested in my personal life. Almost makes me feel important."

Harmony shot me a warning glance: *Don't let them bait you.*

Too late. I was already bracing for it.

Sensing the tension, Harmony shifted in her seat, tone velvet-smooth with a sharpened edge. "Boys," she said, eyes flicking between them, "don't you have someone else to bother?"

Phobos laughed, sharp and grating. "Why would we, when Cupid here is always the most fun at the party?"

Deimos leaned in, his voice a mockery of a whisper. "Think she'll last long? Or will she end up like the others?"

I forced a smirk, though my blood burned beneath my skin. "I don't know, Deimos. Maybe you should ask your last conquest how long she lasted—assuming she's still breathing."

He had compared her to Aphrodite once. Loudly. Crassly. Said his touch made mortals *beg*, just like the goddess of love herself.

She'd smiled at the time, but later gave the order.

And I obeyed.

Harmony's glare said it all: *stop*.

And she was right, of course. The more I spoke, the deeper they'd drag me in.

Phobos's grin thinned into something colder. "Watch yourself, Cupid," he murmured, voice low and curling like smoke. "Wouldn't want anything...*unfortunate* to happen."

"Enough." Harmony's voice sliced clean through the tension. Her eyes flared. "Both of you. Go."

The twins exchanged a look—one of those silent, smug communications that always meant trouble was postponed, not avoided. But they obeyed, peeling away into the crowd like wraiths.

Harmony let out a slow breath, her posture softening only after they were gone. "I swear, they get worse every time. Keep a closer eye on your mortal."

I shrugged, tension still clinging to my shoulders. "It's under control."

"You'd better hope so." She gave me a quick wink, her voice slipping back into that familiar teasing lilt.

Then she rose, smoothing her gown like she was wiping the whole encounter away. "I've made enough of an appearance," she said, brushing imaginary dust from her sleeve.

"Will I see you later? At the Arrows Align launch event tonight?" I asked, lifting a brow.

Harmony's gaze flicked across the hall toward Aphrodite. Her eyes narrowed slightly, taking in whatever fresh performance was playing out. A smirk tugged at the corner of her mouth as she turned back to me.

"No," she answered, voice breezy but edged. "I've been Commanded not to attend. Apparently, our dear mother thinks my presence might ruin the mood—something about disapproval, judgmental stares, and the awkward reality of her still being with my father."

My grip on the chalice tightened.

Olympian Commanded, she meant.

Before I could respond, Harmony pointed a finger at me, her voice slipping into that mock-lecture tone—soft, amused, dangerously close to smug.

"Be careful tonight, Cullen. Dionysus has been experimenting with drinks again. I hear his new concoction is...hallucinogenic."

I scoffed out a laugh. "Noted."

Harmony gave me a final look—something thoughtful flickering behind her eyes—then swept off into the crowd, her gown trailing behind like a silver whisper.

I watched her go, unease pooling quietly in my gut. She'd left too suddenly. She never left suddenly. And that look just before she turned away...she was holding something back.

Still, I knew better than to chase after her. Harmony didn't speak until she was ready—no point in trying to pull the truth from her before she decided to hand it over.

I downed the rest of my drink and leaned back in my seat, letting my eyes scan the hall again.

And there they were—Ares and Aphrodite. Trading glances. Painfully obvious.

They'd been playing this game for centuries, pretending they weren't entangled in each other's schemes and sheets.

I rolled my eyes.

My father, Hephaestus, didn't stay. No surprise there. He rarely left his forge anymore. The Underworld had become his refuge—his workshop, his prison, his solitude.

I might've pitied him if I cared.

But I didn't.

He left the moment he learned the truth. The moment he discovered Aphrodite and Ares's affair. Slipped into his forge and never looked back.

Once, he tried. Said something to me as he walked away.

"You look like her."

The last words he ever said to me.

Then he left me behind. Left me to serve her.

Fuck him.

With Harmony gone, I figured I'd made enough of an appearance myself. Phobos and Deimos were here—not in the Underworld, not making a move in Tartarus—so I could turn my attention to more important things.

She was waiting.

The thought of Skye tugged the corner of my mouth into the ghost of a smile. I wanted to check on her. See how she was holding up with everything the gods had so graciously hurled her way.

I was halfway to the exit when I felt it—that low, crawling sensation of being hunted.

Deimos. Of course.

"Leaving so soon, Cupid?" His voice was thick, every syllable sticking like sap. "Not before we have a little fun."

I turned slowly. Met his eyes with a calm I didn't feel. "Fun," I repeated flatly, already done with this.

Behind him, Phobos emerged like a shadow peeling itself off the wall, his presence heavier, more suffocating than his brother's. He looked amused. That was never good.

"One game," Phobos said, his tone deceptively light. "Just one. Let's make it interesting. Archery. You versus Deimos. Three rounds. Your favorite, isn't it?"

I stared at them both. "You want to challenge me to archery?" I didn't laugh. I wanted to, but the heat simmering beneath my ribs wouldn't allow it. "You sure that's wise?"

Deimos just shrugged, indifferent. "It's a way to pass the time. Unless, of course..." His smile twisted, sharp and cruel. "You're scared. Like the rest of the gods around here."

The rest of the gods—none of them interacted with Phobos and Deimos. Not just because they were the products of an affair, but because...who wanted to linger around fear and terror? The others were repulsed by something they couldn't control.

I might've pitied them if they weren't such assholes.

I didn't blink. "You must be bored."

Phobos's grin stretched wider, feeding off the rising tension. "Bored? No. Just in need of...stimulation. Unless you've still got *errands* to run for Mommy?"

I didn't bother to hide the disgust that flickered across my face.

"What's in it for me?" I asked, even though I knew I wouldn't like the answer.

Deimos stepped in closer, his voice turning cold, serrated. "Winner gets to play with your little mortal girl. Loser finds a new toy."

My jaw locked.

The silence spread like a shockwave. The crowd stilled—some pretending not to listen, others watching with open hunger. Gods and goddesses leaned in, breathless.

They wanted a reaction.

They were about to get one.

I met Deimos's gaze head-on. "You're out of your depth."

Phobos chuckled, the sound a soft, serpentine hiss. "Am I? You may have the skill, Cupid—but fear...fear is a powerful thing. It clouds the mind. Shakes the hand. Are you sure you don't have a problem performing under pressure?"

I felt a flicker of irritation, my fingers curling slightly at my sides. This was their game—to poke and prod—but I wasn't sure if ignoring them would de-escalate things or make it worse.

Might as well get it over with.

"Fine," I said, cool and steady. "Pick a target."

Deimos's eyes lit up as he scanned the hall. "The chandelier," he declared, nodding toward the grand fixture floating overhead. Its glowing orbs pulsed softly, suspended midair. "First to hit three orbs without breaking the chain wins. Three shots each. We alternate."

I offered a humorless smile. "This 'fun' won't take long."

Already, the gods were gathering like spectators in an arena, their eyes gleaming with anticipation. Even Zeus, usually above such displays, paused mid-sip from his chalice, attention sharpening.

A nymph approached, offering us standard arrows—no magic, no tricks.

Deimos picked one up, spinning it between his fingers with a wicked grin before glancing at me.

"Wouldn't want Cupid wasting his own arrows on this," he said, voice dripping with mockery. "Hard to win when your target falls in love instead of hitting the mark."

I chuckled darkly, feigning amusement. "You think it's just my arrows? If you're worried about the target falling for me, you'll need to help me cover up...heard my ass is pretty dangerous, too." I smirked and clicked my tongue at him.

Around us the nymphs and goddesses stifled giggles, probably assessing my claim for themselves.

Deimos rolled his eyes, clearly not amused, but said nothing. He stepped forward like a specter, drew the bowstring tight, and released in one smooth motion. The arrow struck the first orb cleanly, sending a soft glow cascading through the chandelier.

The crowd murmured its approval.

I watched him from the corner of my eye, noting the way he held his posture. He was good. But then again, I was better.

Let him have his moment. It wouldn't last.

I stepped up next, hands steady, the bow an extension of my will. The familiar tension in the string was grounding—a reminder of who and what I was. I released the arrow, which struck the orb dead center, splitting the light with surgical precision.

One for one.

Deimos notched his second arrow, drawing back with deliberate slowness.

From across the hall, Aphrodite's voice floated—silken but edged. "Careful, Deimos. I'd hate for you to embarrass yourself when my *son* will undoubtedly hit the mark."

Fuck—this was not the time for her to show favorites.

A muscle ticked in Deimos's jaw. The bowstring quivered against his fingers.

He released.

The arrow clipped the edge of the orb, leaving it spinning but unbroken. A ripple moved through the crowd—uncertain, not quite disapproving, not quite impressed.

His glare slid toward me, all heat and venom, before snapping back to the target as if he could burn it down with a look.

I stepped forward again, confidence trailing behind me like a cloak. The bow fit naturally in my grip, a weapon I'd mastered long ago. But as I drew back the next arrow, I felt it—a creeping, corrosive unease disturbed the air around me.

Phobos.

Of course. He couldn't resist. Cheating was his essence.

I felt him prying at my concentration, a shadow lurking just beyond reach. His gaze wrapped around me like a noose—suffocating.

I tried to push past it, but it was already too late. My fingers slipped on the string, releasing the arrow half a breath too early. It veered off course, missing the orb by inches.

The crowd gasped, the sound echoing like thunder through the hall. I could feel their stares—expectant, hungry for weakness.

I clenched my jaw, heat flaring as I tightened my grip on the bow. Across from me, Phobos grinned, basking in the disruption he'd caused.

Damn him.

His voice slid in behind me, smooth and venomous. "Losing your touch, Cupid?"

I didn't answer. Didn't even look at him.

Deimos stepped up for his final shot. The hall fell silent as he drew his bow and released.

The arrow soared—but just before it struck, the orb bobbed ever so slightly. The shot grazed it, spinning it in place but leaving it unbroken.

My hand drifted toward the bracelet at my wrist, ready to arm it in a heartbeat for his inevitable outburst—

But it never came.

Instead, Deimos lowered his bow with a calm so out of place it snagged my attention. His jaw was set, but his expression stayed level, almost...accepting.

That wasn't like him.

What were they up to?

The crowd stirred—impressed, but not quite satisfied.

My turn.

I locked my gaze on the target, the rest of the hall blurring into shadow.

My fingers tightened around the bowstring as I nocked the last arrow, its shaft smooth and cold beneath my grip. I drew it back slowly—each inch a defiance against the whispers clawing at the edges of my mind.

Phobos's voice still echoed there, dripping doubt, daring me to miss.

I silenced him with a single thought—

Arrows know no fear.

The arrow flew straight and true, striking the orb dead center. Light shattered in a brilliant burst, scattering across the hall like a thousand stars. The crowd erupted in applause, gods roaring their approval.

I turned to the twins. "Looks like I win."

Phobos began to clap—slow, mocking. His eyes gleamed with manipulative contempt. Just like our mother.

"Impressive," he said. "Truly. Very *lucky* shot."

"Luck had nothing to do with it," I replied, spine straight, leaning against one of the marble pillars. The cool stone at my back grounded me. I met his gaze without flinching.

Then I let my voice drop. "Touch her—and I'll make sure fear finds you before you even see me coming."

The crowd stirred, but their noise felt far away—muted, like a dream. The world had narrowed to the space between the three of us. Phobos's smirk twitched, faltering for a heartbeat, but the sharpness in his eyes didn't waver.

Around us, the gods grew bored. Their attention slipped, drifting back to wine and laughter. But Deimos stayed alert, arms crossed, eyes gleaming like he was waiting for the next act.

The silence stretched taut, the muscles in my neck and shoulders tightening.

Then—shift.

A breeze stirred above, brushing past me, lifting the edge of my collar.

Zeph was here.

"Cullen."

His voice cut through the murmur of conversation.

"We need to talk. Now."

CHAPTER NINE

SKYE

"It will do."

Euryale's words echoed in my head as we walked down the dark street. I couldn't even remember owning this dress—it was just the first thing I'd grabbed while scrambling through the maze of half-unpacked boxes in the apartment. Black, with lace sleeves and a high collar. The humidity clung to it like a second skin, and I kept tugging at the hem, which was shorter than I remembered—something the honking cars made sure to remind me of.

The noise didn't seem to faze Euryale. She kept moving. Head down, I was practically out of breath trying to keep up.

I wasn't sure what to make of her, but when she'd followed me up to the apartment, Marnie—usually standoffish with strangers—had purred and rubbed against her leg like they'd known each other forever.

Cats can sense things in people, right?

Euryale had crouched down, surprisingly gentle, her fingers gliding through Marnie's fur with a soft smile. It was oddly sweet—like watching a storm cradle a flower.

I jogged slightly to match her long strides. "So, where will he be?"

She didn't slow or look at me. Her head stayed forward. "He's at this event tonight—celebrating that app thing, what's it called, Align something, whatever his mother created. The perfect distraction for us to find where Cupid might've stashed the arrows."

I nearly tripped. "Wait—he works for Arrows Align?" My voice jumped in disbelief. "You're telling me *gods* are out here promoting dating apps?"

Euryale stopped in her tracks, giving me a long, measured look.

"And I thought I was the one living under a rock. He's one of the faces of the app—some playboy bachelor everyone's obsessed with. Haven't you seen his face plastered everywhere?"

I rolled my eyes. "I have better things to do than keep up with whichever god is trending on social media."

She muttered something under her breath. "I've known him long before any of this Arrows Align nonsense."

Long before? She didn't look much older than me. Was she also some kind of god?

We continued through the dimly lit streets, puddles from the earlier rain dampening my ankles.

I glanced sideways at Euryale. Her jaw was set, expression unreadable behind those ridiculous red glasses she never seemed to take off.

Why?

"You never answered me," I pressed, partly out of curiosity, partly to break the silence. "How do you know Cullen? Were you guys...um, together?"

She shot me a glance but kept walking. Her lips twitched. "If only it were that simple."

Suddenly, she stopped, and I nearly bumped into her.

A neon green sign blazed the word IVY. A long line of people snaked down the block, dressed in some chaotic fusion of high fashion and Renaissance-fair cosplay. The bass from the music pulsed through the sidewalk like it could knock me off my feet. The entire building throbbed with energy.

Dark windows loomed above the entrance, reflecting the wild scene below. I moved instinctively toward the line, trying to blend in.

Euryale's arm shot out, blocking me.

"No chance we're going in that way," she muttered, scanning the area. With a subtle nod, she steered me toward the back of the building.

The alley was narrow, shadows clinging to the brick walls. We passed a couple tangled together before stopping at an unmarked door. It looked like a service entrance; bussers and staff slipped in and out without so much as a glance in our direction. Without hesitation, Euryale pulled it open, revealing a dimly lit passageway.

"After you," she said, her voice low, like we were slipping into another world entirely.

The moment we entered, the world exploded around me. The music was deafening—a pounding rhythm that reverberated through my chest. I braced for the smells of sweat and smoke, but instead the air carried the rich, unexpected scent of a summer vineyard.

Euryale didn't bother shouting over the noise. She flicked her wrist, gesturing upward.

Up we go.

I followed, weaving through the dense sea of bodies. The space was far more massive than it had looked from outside. The ceilings stretched impossibly high, disappearing into shadows, while the air shimmered with electric energy, as if lightning itself had RSVP'd.

At the center of the room, a towering waterfall cascaded into a glowing pool. Neon blues and greens shimmered through the water, casting ghostly reflections on the crowd. It didn't look real—more like something out of a dream.

People danced around it as if they were made of water themselves, rippling in time with the music. Others lounged on plush velvet couches, drinks in hand, their laughter drowned beneath the relentless beat. Along one wall, the bar stretched endlessly, gleaming under the lights like a river of glass and liquor. Opposite it, a raised DJ booth pulsed with the Arrows Align logo, sending out a neon heartbeat that lit the room.

Euryale moved through the chaos with surprising ease, her slim frame slipping between bodies. She glanced back at me once, then pointed toward a narrow staircase tucked at the side, leading to a more secluded level.

I followed carefully, keeping my gloved hands close, weaving through without letting my skin brush anyone. Each step was a struggle against the shifting ground, like walking on wet sand.

When we reached the upper level, the roar softened, though the music still pulsed like an insistent heartbeat. From the balcony, the entire club stretched out beneath us—a swirling sea of bodies and light. The waterfall gleamed like liquid electricity, casting an otherworldly glow across the room.

It was impossible not to get drawn in.

Euryale's gaze swept the room.

"He's not here yet," she muttered, voice tight with frustration and a trace of impatience.

My stomach twisted. The thought of seeing Cullen again—after everything—made my chest tighten. The memory of his hands on me...

"You're scared," Euryale said flatly, not even glancing my way.

"No," I snapped, forcing steadiness into my voice.

"Good." Curt. Dismissive. She wasn't about to coddle me.

I turned back to the chaos below, trying to find some numbness—anything to keep the pressure in my chest from crushing me.

"We'll wait, then," Euryale murmured, scanning the room through her ever-present glasses.

I shifted, uncomfortable, watching the ebb and flow of the dancers. "So...Lydia. How did you know her?" I asked, both curious and desperate for distraction.

Her expression softened—barely. "Lydia had a way of getting involved in...things." A faint curl touched her lips—something between a smirk and sigh. "Let's just say our paths crossed when we both needed each other most."

I opened my mouth to press for more, but a sudden horn blast cut through the club, shifting the atmosphere in an instant.

The waterfall—once a mesmerizing backdrop—parted cleanly down the middle. Water cascaded to either side like a grand curtain being drawn. The crowd erupted as a figure stepped onto a raised platform at the center, his entrance perfectly timed to the spectacle.

He was impossible to miss.

Radiating extravagance, he wore an opulent gold suit that shimmered like a walking disco ball, embroidered with emerald vine patterns curling up his sleeves. His shirt hung open at the collar, revealing a tangle of gold chains. Tousled dark hair framed a face that was—

Wait. Was that a tiger?

An actual tiger paced at his side, its sleek orange fur rippling with every step. I pressed a hand to my chest, swearing I could feel the faint vibration of its massive paws through the platform—insane, given the music was pounding hard enough to rattle the walls.

The man grinned, teeth flashing as he raised a microphone. His voice thundered over the beat.

"Welcome, my friends, to the night of nights!" He paused, letting the cheers wash over him. "We're here to celebrate a new era of Arrows Align! Here's to a whole lot more fun!"

At his gesture, staff began moving through the crowd as if assembling a flash mob.

"What the hell?" I muttered, leaning forward.

I nudged Euryale, my eyes wide. "Is that...a real tiger?"

She pressed her fingers to her temples, unimpressed. "Yes. That's Dionysus. God of wine and festivity."

My jaw dropped. "And...tigers, apparently."

Euryale crossed her arms, gaze steady on the stage. "Among other things. He owns this club—and a dozen more. Of course he'd make a dramatic entrance. And he talks too much. If Cupid's anywhere nearby, he'll know."

Her voice slowed on the last words, focus drifting far past the flashing lights.

I followed her gaze, still reeling. A god running nightclubs and hosting events for a dating app? Have they always been here—living among us, turning our lives into entertainment?

Onstage, Dionysus ended his performance with a flourish, lifting a glass high.

"To Arrows Align—and all the love it brings!"

Before I could absorb it, a waitress appeared with a drink. Her shimmering green uniform clung like a second skin, making her look almost inhuman.

The glass itself was surreal—shaped like the twisted stem of a leaf, delicate and alive. Inside, liquid shimmered between shades of green and gold, as if plucked from another realm.

I reached—

Euryale's hand shot out, knocking the glass aside. "Don't," she snapped, voice sharp, body tense. "Drink nothing here."

She pulled me back by my gloved hands.

Startled, I blinked. "What's in it?"

Her jaw tightened. "More than you can handle."

I recoiled slightly, glancing at the trays still circling the crowd. My stomach churned. I looked back to the stage just in time to see Dionysus exit, the tiger padding beside him like a well-trained shadow.

Euryale's gaze tracked them as they disappeared behind a velvet curtain that led to a VIP section.

That's when I saw her.

The most beautiful woman I'd ever seen.

Even under the pulsing lights, her features glowed with sculpted perfection—impossibly symmetrical, too flawless to be human. But something else lingered, sharp and dangerous. Looking at her felt like staring into the sun—you knew it would burn.

Dionysus dipped into a bow. She inclined her head, lips moving to form words I couldn't catch. He bowed again, then slipped past her.

Beside me, Euryale stiffened. Her entire body went rigid, a predator catching a scent.

She turned sharply, jaw tight, and gave a curt gesture toward the balcony. "Stay here."

I instinctively stepped forward. "What's going on? Where are you—?"

"Just stay." The words came quiet but firm. She hesitated, then exhaled, as if deciding I deserved at least a little more. "Like I said—Dionysus talks too much. And it looks like he's unaccompanied at the moment. If I'm gone longer than thirty minutes, go back to the apartment. Speak to no one."

Her attention had already shifted to the crowd, her body angled toward it.

I opened my mouth to question her again, but something about the way she moved stopped me. Pushing her wouldn't get me anywhere. She disappeared into the crowd, swallowed by the chaos as if she'd never been there at all.

Suddenly, the lights felt too bright, the music too loud. I couldn't tell what was pounding harder—my heart or the bass vibrating through the floor.

And just like that, I was very, very alone.

"Hello, beautiful. You need a drink just as lovely as you."

Another waitress appeared at my side, more persistent than the last.

She pressed the drink toward me again, her voice smooth and coaxing. "Just one sip," she urged, each word dripping like lust.

I felt...drawn to it.

The longer I stared at the swirling liquid—green and gold and glimmering like liquid magic—the more it called to something deep inside me, like it held the answers to everything I'd ever wanted.

I reached for it.

No.

My hand jolted back. I swatted the glass away. It flew from the waitress's grip, shattering on the floor in a burst of shimmering spray. But before I could fully process what I'd done, a single drop landed on my lips.

It was enough.

Something shifted inside me.

The fear. The tension. That suffocating weight I'd carried for so long—it was gone. Like someone had opened a window inside my chest. I inhaled, and my lungs filled in a way they never had before, like I was finally breathing real air.

My feet moved on their own, light and confident, like a dancer slipping into muscle memory. I was already walking—no, gliding—into the crowd. The bodies around me swayed like seaweed in a tide. The bass pounded through me, syncing with my heartbeat until it was all the same rhythm.

I knew there was something I was supposed to be doing. Something important.

But it was slipping.

Dissolving under the beat.

Swept away with each pulse of music.

I spun, laughter bubbling out of me before I even knew why. I twirled between strangers whose eyes glittered under the strobe lights. Hands grazed my waist, fingers brushed against the fabric of my dress, sending a shiver of heat through me. I didn't care who they were. I didn't care what they wanted. I just kept moving. Free.

Whatever thoughts I was supposed to hold onto—whatever pieces of myself mattered—were falling away like petals in the wind. That small voice in the back of my mind, the one trying to warn me, to ground me, was fading. Drowned by the music, smothered by the heat, the noise, the rush.

And then it was gone—my glove.

I didn't even feel it slip off my left hand. I only noticed when cool air kissed my bare palm. I reached for it, startled—but it was already lost, swallowed by the crowd.

Then came the flashes.

Each brush of skin against mine sent a jolt through me—surges of images, memories, thoughts. But they weren't mine. Faces I didn't recognize. Lives I hadn't lived—desires I didn't want.

Please...make it stop.

I stumbled. My breath caught, vision blurring. I tried to pull away, to escape the tide of bodies pressing in from all sides. But the crowd wouldn't let me go—heat, movement, hands—all of it closing in.

And the visions kept coming. Harder. Faster.

Slamming into me like waves.

Drowning...I was drowning...

Then—hands.

Firm, sure, gripping my wrists and pulling me in.

And the world stilled.

The visions stopped.

I clung to the touch, desperate, my only anchor in the chaos. The grip was steady. Strong. And in that instant, everything else fell away. The pounding noise, the heat, the pressure—it all dissolved.

There was only the feel of my heartbeat and the person who held me.

My breath hitched. My body froze as recognition surged through me like lightning.

I looked up, eyes locking with his.

One hand gripped my bare left hand with an unyielding hold. The other moved slowly from my still-gloved right hand, sliding down to rest possessively on my waist, fingers curling as if letting go wasn't an option.

Cullen had found me.

CHAPTER TEN
CULLEN

The descent from Olympus to the mortal world felt longer than it ever had.

She's not alone anymore. Zeph's warning echoed in my head, each repetition tightening the knot in my chest. Every instinct screamed to abandon everything—find her, now—but my mother's Command still bound me: escort her to the Arrows Align event.

I couldn't leave.

I'd gripped Zeph's shoulder, my voice steady only because it had to be. "Stay with her. Close enough to see her. Not close enough to be seen."

He gave a sharp nod and vanished into the wind.

"That *game* was an embarrassment." Aphrodite's gaze cut across the chariot to me as she reapplied her lipstick, each stroke like a weapon.

I sighed, resting my chin against my fist. "Really? I didn't realize winning was an embarrassment to you."

She scoffed, tilting her head just enough to reveal the faintest curl of a smirk. Her lips parted, ready to deliver the killing remark—

—but the chariot jolted as it touched down on the roof of IVY. The wheels hissed against the landing pad, the *thud* reverberating up through my shoes. Dionysus's den—though tonight, it hosted the kind of event where manipulation wore the mask of love and fulfillment.

Before she could speak again, I unlatched the chariot door and stepped out. Cool night air sliced through the lingering perfume. My shoes hit the rooftop first, solid and grounded. The Pegasi adjusted their stance, then went still, as if sensing their master.

I reached up to offer my hand. She accepted without hesitation, her gaze searching mine—reading far too deeply for my liking. Whatever she saw, she kept to herself, gliding past with the kind of elegance that almost made you forget she was dangerous.

I fell into step behind her, matching her pace as we moved toward the entrance.

The moment I stepped through IVY's doors, it hit me.

At first, it was nothing more than a faint flicker of warmth at my wrist—easy to mistake for the heat of the crowded club. But then it sharpened and deepened, pulsing in steady waves from the bracelet. The magic was unmistakable.

Skye's arrow.

My chest tightened. She was here.

I instinctively scanned the room, catching flashes of strangers, glitter, and light in the crowd. The bracelet's heat surged, almost impatiently, as if it, too, wanted me to close the distance.

She's close.

Every muscle in me tensed with the urge to move—to push through bodies, rip this place apart until I found her, and make sure she never left my sight again. But that would be unwise. My mother's eyes were everywhere tonight, and I couldn't let her know Skye was here.

No. The dominoes had to fall in perfect order. One wrong move, and they'd all come crashing down before I could get to her.

Domino one: make an appearance.

Domino two: find Skye.

Domino three: slip away before my mother decided I was worth summoning...again.

Which meant I needed a distraction—something loud, something chaotic, and, most importantly, something that wasn't me.

The Arrows Align event was...something. A celebration of the app's latest milestone—yet another of my mother's schemes, dangling the promise of *true love* in front of humans like bait on a hook.

We reached Dionysus's VIP room—spacious, secluded, perched at the top of a waterfall with a balcony that overlooked the glittering chaos below. Inside, gods and mortals mingled freely, with even a few Olympians among them. I slowed my steps, catching sight of Athena on the dance floor, moving as if she didn't care who watched. Her owl, Nyctimene, perched nearby, fixed me with a stare sharp enough to suggest she knew I was up to something.

Heads turned as soon as we stepped in. All eyes on Aphrodite—drawn, ensnared, worshipping without even realizing it. Simply breathing the same air as her felt like a privilege they hadn't earned.

"Cupid," she said, her voice smooth as glass, laced with that quiet, unshakable control.

"Mother." My reply dripped sarcasm as I waved over a passing waitress with a tray of drinks—Harmony's warning about them still fresh in my mind.

She leaned in, waves of her hair falling onto my shoulder. Her tone sank lower. "You've been distracted. Distant." Her eyes narrowed, gleaming with something colder. "Where's my gleeful obedience?"

I'm so done with this.

All of it.

"Nothing's changed," I answered, turning away to scan the crowd, feigning interest in the celebration swirling around us. But my eyes betrayed me, drifting again—searching through the glittering chaos for one face. *Skye.*

She was out there, somewhere in this maze. I needed to find her before anyone else did.

Aphrodite's gaze followed mine, her expression tightening. She always knew when my attention slipped—especially when it wasn't on *her.*

"If I didn't know better," she murmured, "I'd say something—or someone—is pulling your focus."

I forced a smile as I turned back to her. "I'm here, aren't I?"

"Yes," she replied, calm and unimpressed.

I tipped my head back, stretching the tension from my spine. "I'm always here."

But she wasn't convinced. Her fingers brushed my arm, hovering somewhere between maternal, as if she were testing out what the word meant. But still...the force of it was a reminder.

You belong to me.

"See that you are, my son."

Just like that, she turned and melted into the crowd that worshipped her. I stood there momentarily, exhaling slowly, the weight of her words pressing down on me. Not a Command, but a weight nonetheless.

I needed to move. Keep looking. But not *too* obvious.

I slipped back into motion, letting my gaze sweep across the club again.

Before I could get far, a cluster of siren giggles erupted beside me—clinging like squid to a ship. They pressed closer, angled bodies promising what they could offer. My gaze slid over them—flawless skin, lips glistening as if they'd just run their tongues across them, like I was a meal waiting to be devoured. Lust and temptation clung to every curve of their bodies, heavier than the fabric of their dresses.

Once, I would have indulged. I would've drawn it out—teased them to the edge, wrung every gasp from their throats, left them cursing my name when they realized no one else could match it.

But when my eyes met theirs...the illusion broke. Pretty, yes. Perfect, even. But their eyes were wrong. None carried that impossible shade of blue—forget-me-nots in full bloom. None burned with that wild, untamable spark that danced in hers.

They weren't her. They could never be her.

One leaned in too close, trailing a finger down my arm like a whisper. "So handsome," she purred, voice sweet and practiced. "Like an angel."

The words rang empty.

"Not interested," I muttered, brushing them off.

With a flick of my wrist, they slipped back into the crowd, a trail of disappointed sighs echoing in their wake. I barely had time to breathe before the air shifted—subtle at first, like the drop in pressure before a storm.

The music didn't change, but everything else did.

The atmosphere thickened, charged with something heavier. Darker. A weight that settled over the room like a warning, coiling in the air, pressing at the edges of every breath.

Perfect timing—hello, domino number three.

Ares.

He didn't just enter the room—he claimed it, claimed every pair of eyes the moment they landed on him.

Phobos and Deimos flanked him, one on each side. The resemblance to their father was unmistakable—

The gods of war and chaos had arrived.

My mother reappeared at my side, as if love and war were magnets.

I didn't move my head to look at her. "What are *they* doing here?"

"They won't cause any trouble tonight," she said simply.

I almost laughed. That wasn't reassurance—that was delusion. I didn't trust them for a second.

But I trusted them to do exactly what I needed: cause a scene loud enough to cover my exit.

"Mother."

Phobos's smile curled as he stepped toward her, voice smooth, but laced with venom. "Congratulations. Wouldn't dream of missing your big night."

Her gaze slid lazily to him, a smile curving her lips.

"Of course you wouldn't," she purred. "It *is* my night, after all. And I won't have any of you ruining it. You will behave."

Behave.

Phobos's grin faltered at the Command—but only for a heartbeat. He smoothed it back into place, masking whatever flicker of irritation had sparked beneath the surface. Before he could respond, Ares stepped forward, his massive frame cutting cleanly through the space as he moved closer to Aphrodite.

"I already told the boys—no fighting," Ares said, voice low and rough, his hand brushing her arm in a deliberate, lingering gesture.

Aphrodite didn't flinch. She met his gaze with steady, unshaken confidence.

"Oh, I'm not worried about them," she replied coolly. "They wouldn't dare defy me. Not tonight."

Ares chuckled—dark, amused, clearly enjoying the bite in her words.

Without breaking eye contact, Aphrodite stepped past him, her gown trailing like liquid fire. As she moved, she brushed his shoulder with effortless precision.

"Come," she murmured, her tone soft but unmistakably commanding.

He followed without hesitation, a glint of mischief in his eyes.

"Don't have too much fun without me, boys," he called over his shoulder.

Together, they disappeared into the crowd—like gods retreating from their thrones, the world parting to let them pass.

The moment they were gone, the air between us snapped taut. Sharpened.

Phobos turned to me, his grin still in place—but now edged with something venomous.

"Cupid," he drawled, stretching the name like a threat. "Must be exhausting, being Mommy's personal errand boy."

Deimos laughed quietly beside him, stepping in just close enough to tip the air into something tense.

"It's funny, really," he said, voice slick, laced with mockery. "All that power, and yet—still tethered."

I met their stares without blinking, a smirk tugging at my lips.

"Still bitter about the contest, are we?" I asked, every word a provocation.

Phobos's grin faltered—just briefly—a flash of irritation before he smoothed it over with his usual smugness.

"Lost a battle," he said, voice tightening, "but we'll win the war."

Deimos shrugged and leaned in slightly, his voice dipping low. "Imagine it, Cupid. No more constraints. No more Olympian Command keeping you on a leash."

Their eyes met briefly—a small, practiced signal. A test. A lure.

They wanted more. They always did.

"Careful," I said, my tone light but edged with steel. "Wouldn't want to choke on the leash you're so desperate to snap."

Phobos stepped closer, his voice smooth, but the danger in it pulsed like a viper.

"Honestly," he pressed, "don't you ever wonder what it'd be like—to be the one in control?"

I clenched my jaw. I knew what they were doing. This wasn't just bait. It was recruitment.

I held their gazes a beat longer, letting them think I was considering it, that I was listening.

Then I smiled. Mischief was in my blood.

"Maybe," I said slowly. "Shame we can't talk more about this. Shame I'm stuck here on Aphrodite's Command."

I began to pace, just slightly enough to sell the drama. Then I glanced back at them, the glint in my eye deliberate.

"Ares said no fighting."

A pause. A grin.

"But I don't recall anyone forbidding...*demonstrations.*"

That got their attention.

Phobos tilted his head, intrigued. Deimos's grin widened—sharp, feral.

I leaned in slightly, my voice low and conspiratorial.

"Accidents happen."

I turned, pressing my back against the bar's counter, already mapping the fastest route to vanish before their fireworks began.

Phobos's voice trailed after me—low, amused, edged in darkness.

"Now that sounds more like Cupid."

Deimos followed, his tone like a blade sliding from its sheath.

"You always were the clever one. Play now. Talk later."

I gave a single nod. And just like that, they were gone—springing free as if I'd unleashed a plague into the world.

Perfect.

Let them make a scene.

Let the gods turn their heads toward the wrong fire.

Because even if this whole place went up in flames—

I'd find Skye in the smoke.

I pushed off the bar and moved.

The club throbbed like a living thing—lights strobing, bass pounding against my ribs. Faces blurred, smearing together in the chaos.

Find her.

Find her.

Find her.

I cut through the riptide of bass and bodies, every step pulled by instinct alone.

And then—

I saw her.

Skye.

She was on the dance floor, lost to the rhythm, spinning like the world belonged to her alone.

The violet and gold lights cascaded across her skin, catching on the wild edges of her movement.

Her hair, loose and untamed, whipped around her like a dark halo, alive with every beat.

In that moment—

She was everything.

Unrestrained.

But then—

I saw it.

The tiniest flicker. A split-second crack in her expression.

Panic.

The crowd was closing in—too fast, too close.

Hands. Too many of them. Grabbing. Grazing.

Hands I pictured pinned to the floor with my arrows so their owners could watch them bleed for daring to touch her.

Her body stiffened. Her rhythm faltered.

She wasn't dancing anymore—she was struggling to breathe.

To escape.

To survive.

She was drowning in the curse I gave her.

And I—

I saw red.

Whatever restraint I'd been clinging to shattered.

I moved without thinking. No hesitation. No mercy.

People stumbled out of my way—or I made that choice for them.

All I could see was her.

Skye.

In a breath, I was at her side.

My hands closed firmly around her wrists—one bare, the other gloved. She'd hidden her hands beneath the leather, careful not to lay her skin against anyone else.

She understood.

A spark of pride curled in my chest—*clever girl*, already learning to guard against her curse.

I drew her toward me. She stumbled, startled, but I caught her—anchoring her in place.

Her body trembled—just faintly, but enough. Enough to feel the heat radiating off her skin, the thrum of her panic echoing in the space between us.

But all I could think about was how perfectly she fit against me. Like the universe had carved her for this—this exact moment.

I drew her in closer.

Close enough to feel her heartbeat crashing against mine.

My mouth found her ear. "You're alright," I whispered, low and steady, the words slipping beneath the music. "I've got you."

Her breath hitched. Her heart pounded against my chest.

And for one suspended second—

The crowd dissolved.

The lights dimmed to a flicker.

The noise drowned beneath the sound of her breathing.

There was only her.

Pressed to me.

Warm, trembling, utterly real.

And the thing twisting inside me—

That dark, electric pull—

It tightened, clawed deeper, reshaping itself, like it said: *Mine.*

She tilted her face toward mine, just slightly—

And our lips hovered, a breath apart.

Close enough to feel the warmth of her mouth.

Close enough to taste the sweet ghost of Dionysus's wine clinging to the air between us.

She smelled like heat and danger and everything I shouldn't want.

But gods—

I wanted.

The urge to close the distance—

To devour that final inch.

To obliterate the space between us and taste her—

Claim her—

Right here. Right now.

A shrill, piercing *screeeaaam* sliced through the air.

There it was.

Phobos and Deimos had started their little "demonstration."

"We need to get out of here," I murmured, my voice rough at the edges.

I slid one hand from her wrist to her waist and then to the small of her back, while the other still held her bare hand, guiding her through the crowd.

She didn't resist.

Didn't ask questions.

Just moved with me, like we were part of the same current.

As we slipped through the chaos, my thoughts raced.

She was in it now—

Tangled in the divine threads of my world.

And I didn't know if I wanted to shield her from it—

Or drag her down with me.

CHAPTER ELEVEN

SKYE

The effects of the drink had long worn off, leaving only the sharp edge of adrenaline to keep me grounded. My heart pounded in my chest, and I wasn't entirely sure why I'd followed Cullen. Maybe it was the look in his eyes—or maybe instinct had kicked in before I had time to think.

Where was Euryale?

Cullen was leading me—dragging me—by my bare wrist through a maze of corridors, his grip firm but not painful. I stumbled after him, barely keeping up as we twisted through hallways, taking so many sharp turns that I had no idea where we were anymore.

At last, we stepped into a dimly lit lounge. The heavy door shut behind us with a definitive *click*. The room was sleek but lived-in, filled with dark leather furniture and a large desk at the center, its surface cluttered with stacks of papers. Above us, a glass ceiling revealed the night sky—the moon a new moon, casting a pale silver glow over everything.

I stood frozen, breath catching. Cullen walked to the desk without a word, turning his back to me. He planted his hands on its edge, shoulders tense, as if holding something back—as if trying to regain control of himself.

Silence thickened between us. My pulse thundered in my ears as my gaze flicked to the door. An escape plan formed rapidly in my mind.

Could I make it?

I took half a step toward the door—

"Go ahead," he said, still facing away. His voice was calm but still sent a chill down my spine. "But you wouldn't get far."

I froze, swallowing hard. My mind raced for a response, but all I could do was stare at the back of his head, trying to gauge how serious he was.

"What...am I your prisoner now?" I asked, trying to make my voice sound more threatening than the fear twisting in my chest.

He finally turned. "Not a prisoner," he said, a faint smirk curling at the corners of his mouth. "More like...a guest."

A guest. Right.

Every nerve in my body screamed to run—but something in the way he looked at me made me hesitate.

"Funny way of treating a guest," I muttered, flexing my wrist where his grip had been.

Cullen's eyes flicked to my hand. The smirk vanished, replaced by something harder to read. He stepped away from the desk and toward me. "We needed to move. You heard them, didn't you? Felt it—the fear flooding that room?"

Was that what it was? That awful sound—like someone dying.

I didn't answer, but my silence must have confirmed it, because Cullen's eyes sharpened with interest. He took another step closer. "You weren't wrong to follow me, Skye."

The sound of my name on his lips sent a strange shiver through me.

I hated that it affected me. But it did.

I crossed my arms, trying to project confidence—even though my pulse still hadn't settled since the moment he dragged me in here. "Cupid, right?" I asked, meeting his gaze with as much defiance as I could summon.

His expression shifted, a flicker of amusement sparking in his eyes. He let out a low chuckle. "Look who's the stalker now," he said, the smirk returning. "Cullen. *Cupid* is my ancient name."

I clenched my jaw, unwilling to let him get under my skin.

But my eyes betrayed me, drifting over him despite myself. His dark suit was tailored to perfection—sleek, understated, expensive. The charcoal fabric shimmered faintly under the moonlight, and the unbuttoned collar of his black shirt revealed a hint of skin. Everything about him screamed control—effortless, dangerous control. Even the shine on his shoes and the glint of his cufflinks felt intentional, like nothing about him was ever accidental.

This was a god?

I'd expected someone old and wise, not someone who looked like he'd stepped out of one of my fantasy books.

Cullen caught me staring. A slow, predatory grin curved his lips as he began to circle me, like he was stalking prey he already owned.

"You think knowing my name means you know me?" he murmured. "But I wonder...do you even realize what you've stepped into?"

"You stabbed me," I seethed, tracking his movements.

His eyes flickered—just for a second. "Stabbed is a bit of an over-reaction."

"What would you call an arrow in someone's chest, then? *Foreplay*?"

He stopped mid-step, pressing one finger to his mouth.

Did he think this was funny?

I closed the distance between us, rage drowning out better judgment. For a moment, I forgot I was standing toe-to-toe with an actual god.

"You cursed me—"

Something shifted in his expression, as if a memory clicked into place. His gaze dipped to my side. "How's that hand?"

I moved instinctively, tugging my lace sleeve over my bare skin where the glove had been lost.

A tight swallow caught in my throat.

When I looked back up, I was caught. His golden eyes had softened—not enough to be safe, but enough to pull me in despite every warning screaming in my head.

Cullen's breath eased out. "It wasn't my intention—"

And then—

A sound.

Crack.

I barely had time to register it before the glass ceiling above us shattered.

Cullen moved in a blur, shoving me out of the way just as shards of glass rained down.

I gasped, bracing for impact—but it never came. The fragments missed me entirely.

Euryale landed between us like a falling shadow. She moved so fast I only caught the glint of her glasses before she lunged at Cullen. In her hand, an expandable baton snapped open with a sharp metallic *hiss* as she swung hard toward him.

Cullen twisted just in time, dodging the blow. The air crackled as the baton sliced through it. His expression darkened, and in one swift movement his fingers brushed the bracelet at his wrist. He gave it a sharp twist, and the metal shimmered—unraveling into a sleek silver arrow that materialized between his fingers. Its tip caught the moonlight above, gleaming like a promise of violence.

"You really shouldn't have done that," he growled, holding the arrow like a blade.

Euryale didn't flinch. She spun the baton in a tight figure-eight, her glasses fixed on him. "You never should've touched her," she snapped. She struck again, aiming for his side, but Cullen parried with the arrow. The clash of metal rang out.

I stood frozen, breath caught somewhere between fear and awe.

They moved like they'd done this before—two ancient forces locked in a dance older than memory. Each blow came fast, precise, impossible to follow. Despite that, neither gave an inch.

My feet refused to move. The air around me felt heavy, as if it had turned to stone. I couldn't look away.

Cullen twisted to avoid Euryale's baton, the sharp clash of their weapons making me flinch. He deflected her next strike effortlessly, spinning the arrow in his grip like it was second nature. The force of the impact sent them both sliding back a few steps, but Cullen straightened without missing a beat, grinning as if none of this fazed him.

"Well," he purred, voice low and mocking, "good to see you. Still as feisty as ever, I see."

Before Euryale could launch another attack, Cullen raised his free hand—his other still tightly gripping the arrow. "Alright, alright. Truce," he said, a crooked grin spreading across his face. "As much as I enjoy our little reunions, you and I know there's no point dragging this out."

Euryale didn't lower her weapon, but her stance shifted. There was something in his tone that made her hesitate.

I stood there, heart pounding, trying to understand where I fit in this standoff.

Then Euryale spoke, her voice low and steady. "Give. It. Back."

Cullen's gaze flicked to her, the corner of his mouth twitching with amusement. "You think that'll be enough? Enough for her?" He scoffed. "Even if I handed it over, it wouldn't break the curse—you know that."

His eyes shifted to me. "Even if I wanted to, that's not how it works."

He brushed glass shards off his shirt as if this were nothing new. "The curse stands," he said simply. Then his expression changed. He tilted his head, and his voice dropped. "But...there might be another way to mitigate things."

Euryale's grip tightened on the baton, her gaze sharpening. "This isn't one of your games."

Cullen's grin went flat, replaced by something else. "You have your reasons for wanting this curse broken. And now"—his eyes locked on mine—"so do I."

Confusion twisted in my stomach.

Why did he look at me like that?

"She's different," he said, eyes fixed on me, a dark gleam flickering in their depths. "And now we're not the only ones who've taken an interest."

"What are you talking about?" I stepped forward.

Euryale mirrored me instantly, moving to stand between us. "What exactly are your terms for this *sudden* interest?" she asked, each word threaded with suspicion.

Cullen's grin widened—sharp, knowing—as he leaned back against the desk. The arrow spun lazily between his fingers, his posture radiating ease.

"Come with me. We'll negotiate properly. But we need to move quickly—before other parties make their move."

My heartbeat spiked.

Go with him? I can't—no. No, that's not—

"You mean Phobos and Deimos are here," Euryale cut in, snapping me out of my thoughts. Not a question.

She sneered. "Afraid of them?"

Cullen's amusement vanished, his voice turning glacial. "Don't underestimate them." His gaze locked on hers. "Even I can't take both of them at once."

Then he turned to me. "And Skye," he said my name like a caress, "would you rather take your chances with my brothers?"

Brothers?

Euryale's eyes darted between us, baton still raised but looser now. She hadn't lowered her guard, yet she hadn't struck again either.

"I wouldn't expect you to trust me," Cullen went on. "But you have a choice—keep fighting me...or keep her alive long enough to feed her cat."

My chest tightened. The room felt too small, the walls closing in as Euryale shot me a sideways glance, her jaw clenched. I braced for another clash.

Instead, she exhaled through her teeth and stepped back with a frustrated growl. Her reluctant nod met mine.

It would seem we had no good choices.

"Fine," I said, the word escaping before I could think better of it.

The devil you know is better than the ones you don't. But he was still a devil—and I knew nothing about the kind of hell this one was offering.

Cullen's mouth curved, a spark of satisfaction lighting his eyes. His gaze slid to the office door, where the shadows stretched long and dark—like the opening jaws of a trap.

"Shall we?"

Cullen led us through the winding hallway onto the club's main floor. I kept my bare hand tucked beneath the lace sleeve as much as possible, shielding it from any accidental touch. Music still pulsed faintly in the distance, but the space around us felt different—like we were being watched.

He glanced over his shoulder at Euryale and me.

"I just need to call—"

"Leaving so soon?"

Cullen turned slowly. I followed his gaze.

I couldn't tell which of them had spoken—their voices overlapped, layered like a broken radio signal, tones bleeding into one another. It was like listening to two discordant songs at once.

"Not going to introduce us...Skye, is it?"

The way their eyes swept over me made my skin crawl—like they already knew exactly who I was, why I was here, and what I feared most.

Their faces were nearly identical, both wearing the same unnerving smile.

One was lean and tall, his jet-black hair spiked like obsidian shards. The other was shorter but broader, his build taut with caged strength, his hair pulled back in a severe knot that sharpened the hard planes of his face.

But their eyes...

Gold.

Not the soft, sunset gold of Cullen's gaze. This was molten—liquid metal alive and burning, a window to the fire raging within. My stomach dropped.

These were Cullen's brothers.

I recalled Euryale's voice: *Phobos and Deimos are here.*

And now I was staring straight at them.

They began to move toward me, their steps deliberate, savoring the fear radiating off me.

Before they could get too close, Cullen and Euryale stepped forward in unison, forming a not-so-human wall between me and them.

Cullen's stance went taut, his hand flicking upward. A quiver of arrows shimmered into existence across his back in a flash of light. Beside him, Euryale shifted, her baton catching the pulsing glow—gleaming silver, its sheen almost sentient, as if aware and ready to strike.

The brothers froze. Their grins didn't waver, but a flicker passed through their eyes as they glanced from Cullen to Euryale. Assessing. Calculating.

For a moment, no one moved, as if we were chess pieces waiting to see who would make the first move.

Cullen took it.

"Phobos," he said evenly, "have you forgotten our deal?"

Phobos tilted his head, as if weighing the thought. "Deals are only binding if they amuse us." His gaze slid to the one I assumed was Deimos, who gave a slow, solemn nod.

"And we're no longer amused."

Deimos stepped forward, his eyes pinning me in place. "Using us as a distraction," he said in a mockingly fond tone. "I'm almost proud. She must be something special." His smile stretched unnaturally, like it wasn't made to fit a human face. "Hand over the girl. Or maybe...we let Mother in on this little secret."

"No."

Cullen's word cut through the air like it carried its own gravity. Even the flickering lights seemed to falter.

The twins exchanged a look, their grins widening in unison.

"Oh well," Phobos murmured, his tone dipped in delight. "I think it's time for another *demonstration*."

The light shifted. Darkness twisted around us as if it were alive.

Then came the screams.

Soul-splitting. Primal.

People dropped to their knees, clawing at the floor, at their own faces, at *nothing*. A wave of pure terror surged through the room—like everyone's worst nightmare had ripped free and taken shape.

The twins just stood there.

Watching.

Enjoying.

The ground rippled beneath my feet, trembling as if it wanted to shake us off. Shadows crawled up the walls, stretching long and grotesque, twisting into figures that weren't just monsters—fear itself made flesh.

Demonic forms oozed from the corners of the room, slithering across the ceiling, taking shape with every heartbeat. Teeth. Claws. Eyes that glowed red in the dark.

I couldn't breathe.

The music still pulsed, pounding against my ribs like a second heartbeat.

Tables flipped. Glass shattered.

Euryale edged closer, her body taut, baton angled to strike. Her gaze darted from shadow to shadow, desperate for something solid to lock onto. But there was nothing. Just fear. Everywhere.

"Stay with me." Cullen's voice cut clean through the noise. His gaze flicked between me and Euryale.

I nodded quickly, forcing down the panic clawing at my throat.

Then—movement.

From above, a shadow lunged. A clawed limb shot toward me. I stumbled back with a gasp, my hand flying out instinctively—grabbing Cullen's arm like it was the only solid thing left in the world.

He moved without hesitation, shifting in front of me like a shield. His muscles tensed. “Euryale,” he barked, urgency cracking through his voice, “any time now would be great.”

I turned to her, confused, my breath too shallow, too fast.

She didn’t answer immediately—but her hand was moving.

To her glasses.

“Shut your eyes!” she snapped.

I obeyed without question, squeezing my eyes shut just as I saw her lift them.

Somewhere in the dark, a voice slithered through.

“Well, well, well,” Phobos drawled, thick with amusement. “A Gorgon. Welcome to the party.”

Gorgon?

Then—a different kind of sound. Not screaming, but groaning. Growling. Like something was struggling.

“You do remember we’re immortal, right?” Deimos snarled. “You won’t hold us for long.”

“Don’t need long,” Cullen muttered, still shielding me. “Just enough.” Then, to Euryale: “Hold them as long as you can.”

Deimos cut in, his voice tight but dripping venom. “How’s the family? In the Underworld, aren’t they? So fortunate...for them.”

SCREEEEE!!

Something screeched in answer—high, grating, inhuman.

The twins laughed. Hollow. Cruel. The kind of sound that said they already knew how this would end—and relished dragging it out.

I squeezed my eyes shut until it hurt. Air whipped past me in sudden, violent bursts, as if something massive were circling close enough for me to feel it brush my skin.

“Please,” I gasped. “Tell me what’s happening—”

Cullen’s breath hit the back of my neck.

“Euryale has a hold on them—for now. But they’re breaking through. And they won’t think twice about bringing this whole place down with them.”

Then a snap: “Step left. Now!”

I moved instinctively, lunging sideways as something slammed into the floor where I’d been.

“Down!” Cullen grabbed me, yanking me toward him. I ducked

beneath a rush of air—something fast slicing through the space I'd just occupied.

Another wave of energy crashed through the room, shaking the ground so hard it buckled under my feet. I would've fallen if Cullen hadn't pulled me back up instantly.

"Move right. Keep low." His grip was unshakable, guiding me through the chaos like we were dancing with death. I followed every order, clinging to him like a lifeline—because that's exactly what he was.

Then—a scream. *Her* scream.

"Euryale!" I shouted, reaching out into the blackness.

But before I could take a step, Cullen's hand wrapped around my wrist. Not rough. Not gentle. Just absolute. He pulled me back with a force that stopped me cold.

"I'm fine!" Euryale's voice rang out—cracked, but unbroken. Fierce. Still fighting.

"Feeling a bit *unstable?*" the twins taunted in unison, their voices soaked in malice—like the sound of something dead and decaying learning to speak again.

Then came a growl. Low. Guttural. Not human.

"Keep your eyes shut," Cullen ordered, and somehow his voice cut through everything—calm and commanding, like it was just the two of us even in the middle of hell.

I nodded, but panic surged, searing through my chest like acid. I needed to help. I needed to see.

Aaaaahhhh!!!

Euryale screamed again. Louder. Broken. Agonizing.

And my terror shattered into action.

My eyes flew open.

Just a sliver. Just long enough to see flickers of something moving—black, spindled, impossible—

But Cullen's hand snapped up, grabbing my chin and yanking my face toward his before I could see anything clearly.

"No." His voice was low, feral. His fingers gripped just tight enough to hold me still, his eyes boring into mine. "Eyes on me."

I froze.

Wings.

They exploded from Cullen's back in a blaze of light—like a sudden starburst, as if the very sky had ruptured.

They unfurled with a sound like a hundred sails catching wind, then curved inward, folding around me.

My breath caught—it was like standing before an angel.

I couldn't move. Couldn't speak.

They were beautiful, though *beautiful* didn't quite capture it. Arcs of white rose above my head, each feather dusted with the faintest shimmer, as if stardust had settled upon them. They tightened around me, his quiver shifting and adjusting with the movement as though wings and weapon were born of the same breath.

A living cocoon. A prison and shelter all at once.

And within...there was us.

His grip loosened slightly. "Just...look at me," he repeated, softer now, almost like a plea—but still layered with that same unshakable command.

I locked onto him, struggling to breathe through the pounding in my chest. I fixed on his golden eyes as a sound like the world collapsing roared behind him.

Growls twisted through the air, like something demonic was straining to tear through reality itself.

Closer. Closer.

Cullen moved, and his wings moved me with him, pulling me out of its line of sight.

They unfurled for the briefest heartbeat—just enough for a blur of motion and sudden blaze of silver-blue light: the glow of his arrows. He loosed them with deadly precision, every shot striking its mark.

The shadows screamed, their cries twisting like steam, recoiling from the light.

He turned back to me.

I reached for him—

—and my vision darkened.

Something hit me.

Hard.

Air exploded from my lungs as I was thrown to the ground, the shock ripping every thought from my head.

Pain tore through my knees and palms as I hit the floor, my body twisting on impact. My hair whipped across my face, blinding me. The club spun—walls, lights, people, shadows—all a blur.

For a second, I didn't know which way was up.

Through the curtain of tangled hair and pain-blurred vision, I glimpsed something that seized the breath in my chest.

Euryale.

She stood impossibly tall, green scales glinting beneath small, bleeding cuts. Her hair wasn't hair at all.

It was alive.

Writhing, hissing serpents coiled atop her head, glistening with venom and rage, shifting like they could taste blood in the air.

The power radiating from her was like a wall—a force that didn't just hold Phobos and Deimos back. It fought them.

Their steps faltered. Parts of their bodies hardened into stone, only to crumble away—then reform, freeze, and break again, over and over.

Like they were wading through a river made of stone.

This...this was her curse.

My lungs locked, the air thick in my throat as our eyes met—glowing red. Piercing.

And then, for a heartbeat—

One.

Her eyes softened.

Like she hadn't wanted me to see her like this.

Like it broke something inside her, too.

But then—

Cullen.

His hand closed around my arm, fast and firm, yanking me to my feet. His gaze swept over me, searching for damage I might not have felt yet.

"Interesting," Phobos drawled, dragging our attention back to the chaos. His voice curled through the air like smoke. Beside him, Deimos tilted his head, grinning with too many teeth. "Didn't think she'd actually look."

I barely registered what they meant—until Phobos raised his hand.

Darkness rippled from his palm, condensing into a jagged spear wreathed in red-tinted shadow. The air warped around it, bending as if the weapon were eating the light.

My stomach dropped.

Then—he threw it.

The spear sliced through the chaos like an eclipse.

Euryale turned—

Too late.

The shadow struck her square in the side.

It didn't lodge—it dissolved on contact, vanishing like smoke.

But the damage was done.

Euryale cried out, the sound raw and furious as blood spilled from the wound. Her knees buckled, her strength collapsing beneath her. She crumpled, one hand clutching her side, the other clawing the ground as she hissed in pain.

"Euryale!" I screamed, lunging forward, hand outstretched—

But I didn't make it far.

The ground split beneath us.

A *boom* thundered through the club, rattling my bones. The floor cracked, and something—someone—dropped from above.

He stood in the epicenter, the ground beneath him shattered in a spiderweb of force. His arrival sent a shockwave through the air, toppling chairs, splintering what glass was left, and dragging silence in its wake.

He was tall, his frame burning with muscle and fury. But his face...he was smiling. Smiling like he enjoyed the chaos, the destruction.

Like this was exactly what he was made for.

Phobos and Deimos stepped back.

The suffocating fear that had clung to the room evaporated, as if it had never existed.

The man didn't even look at them.

His voice rolled through the club like tearing metal: "Enough."

The air shifted.

Power flooded the space in a single crashing wave.

Phobos. Deimos. Cullen—frozen.

But I wasn't.

I ran toward Euryale, heart pounding, vision narrowed to a pinpoint. She lay in a spreading pool of blood, her green skin paling with every second. The serpents in her hair were retreating, curling back into dark, limp strands. Her face—so fierce only moments ago—looked heartbreakingly human now.

"Come on," I whispered, dropping to my knees beside her. I pressed my gloved hand into the wound, stacking my bare hand on top, desperate to stop the bleeding. "Stay with me. Please. Please..."

Her breath was shallow. Fragile.

But still there.

"Ruining my night."

My head snapped up.

Above us, on a balcony, stood a woman—the woman. Behind her, the once-majestic waterfall was a cascade of fire and floating debris. She stood like a queen, surveying the ashes of her ruined empire.

Her icy glare swept over the chaos with surgical precision. Then her eyes landed on Cullen—and froze.

She gripped the railing, knuckles white. "All of this," she said, her voice low and lethal, gesturing vaguely at the glass, the bodies, the carnage. "And for her?"

A breath of silence.

And then—

"Looks like *they* found a loophole," the man rumbled, his eyes flicking between Phobos and Deimos with something like reluctant admiration—until the woman turned that blistering glare on him. Then his face tightened, jaw clenched.

"Mother," Cullen said, stepping forward, his voice tight.

My breath caught.

Mother?

No. No, that wasn't—

That was Aphrodite?

The woman on the balcony narrowed her eyes, lips curling as if the very sight of me was an insult. "You're all disappointments," she spat.

Her gaze flicked to me again. She let out a breath like she was bored, then began tapping furiously on her phone, utterly unfazed by the destruction.

"This will take a lot of work to clean up," she muttered, her tone calm and businesslike, already spinning the narrative without ever lifting her eyes from the screen.

She sighed and slowly lowered her phone, her gaze locking on Cullen.

A cruel smile spread across her lips.

"Cupid," she said, voice silken and sharp. "Enough of your games."

Then, flatly, with terrifying finality—

"Dispose of her. Now."

Her voice turned my blood to ice.

I didn't move. My hands stayed clamped desperately over Euryale's wound—slick with blood, trembling. My breath came in shallow gasps as I stared at Cullen.

He stepped forward.

Slow. Mechanical. His wings dragged, catching on chairs and sending them toppling with dull *thuds.*

His face was blank. His eyes...dulled, as if someone had reached inside and extinguished the fire.

What...what did she do to him?

A cold dread uncoiled in my stomach. Each step he took seemed to reverberate up through my bones.

He crouched in front of me, his gaze locking onto mine. I clung tighter to Euryale, curling my body over hers to shield her from whatever was coming. My heartbeat was so loud I could barely hear anything else. Her blood seeped through my gloves—still warm. Still alive.

"Cullen...no."

His golden eyes stared back at me, but there was nothing inside them. Just a void. An absence. And in that emptiness, I knew—*he* was gone.

He raised his hand.

I reacted on instinct. Wrenching my bare hand free, I swung wildly to stop him, to do something.

He caught my wrist.

And the moment his skin touched mine—

Something inside both of us shattered. A pulse of energy surged between us.

Cullen jerked, gasping. His entire body locked up, trembling as if lightning had torn through him. I felt the tremor in his grip. Then—his eyes.

They blinked, unfocused at first...then widened, searching. Confusion flickered there, followed by dawning recognition.

The emptiness was gone.

He saw me.

For a breath, neither of us moved. I watched him—like he was coming back from somewhere far away. His fingers tightened around my wrist, not in restraint but as if anchoring himself to me.

"We're leaving," he said, his voice rough and cracking, each word fighting its way out. "Now."

Above us, Aphrodite flinched. Her mouth parted, but she didn't speak.

Phobos and Deimos stood perfectly still, their bodies poised like statues.

And then, in eerie, reverent unison, they spoke.

"Praxis."

The word echoed through me.

Praxis.

It rang inside me—like something I was supposed to know.

From above, Aphrodite's voice cut through the air.

"Cupid," she hissed, fury blooming across her face. "You dare—"

The club doors exploded open as if struck by invisible hands, a violent gust howling through the space. Glass rattled. Dust lifted from the floor. A gale tore through the wreckage like the world itself had exhaled.

I staggered, nearly knocked back—but Cullen's hand never let go.

His wings beat once, and the world shifted.

Air spiraled around us in a wild protective current.

Then he moved—scooping me forward with one arm and bending to lift Euryale with the other.

We were airborne. I held tightly against him, the wind roaring in my ears.

Heat radiated from his body, wings curving to shield us from the chaos still raging behind.

When he glanced down at me, that spark of his flickered back into his eyes, a small smile touching his lips.

"Our ride's here."

CHAPTER TWELVE

SKYE

I'd never seen so many shades of gold.

I sat up slowly, my body sinking into the softest mattress I'd ever felt. My fingers grazed the sheets—silk, smooth and cool against my skin. Marnie was curled against my side, purring softly—

Wait.

Marnie?

I rubbed my eyes, still groggy, and looked down at her. She was curled into a perfect ball, completely unbothered—her tiny chest rising and falling with each steady purr. I reached to pick her up, and she gave a slight, confused shake of her head, like she wasn't sure what I was doing.

I moved her gently, inspecting her like I expected something to be wrong.

She looked fine. Healthy. Safe.

But why was she here—and not at the apartment?

My gaze swept the room, and my heartbeat quickened as fragments of last night surged forward. The club. The chaos. Euryale—and then Cullen.

There was wind—Cullen's arms.

Then—nothing.

A tightness clamped around my chest. I instinctively pulled Marnie closer.

"Where are we?" I whispered, my voice barely steady as I forced myself to take in my surroundings again.

This wasn't my apartment. Not even close.

High arched ceilings soared above me, and every surface shimmered as if freshly polished. It was a room from a children's story—a real-life King Midas myth, where everything he touched had turned to gold.

I shifted Marnie in my arms and lifted one hand to block the sunlight streaming through a set of windows. White lace curtains billowed gently in the breeze.

What the—?

The leather gloves Euryale had given me were gone, replaced with satin ones. They were beautiful—delicate, pearlescent. Just another question to add to the long list I was collecting.

With Marnie snug in my arms, I swung my legs over the side of the bed and stood. The cool marble floor sent a shock through my feet, chasing away the last fog of sleep.

But that wasn't the only thing to hit the floor.

Something brushed against my legs—soft fabric pooling at my ankles.

I looked down.

A dress.

A white gown, to be exact—lace, straight, ribbons down the side. It looked like it belonged on some storybook princess wandering through moonlit gardens. Not me, currently clutching her cat like a weighted blanket.

I held Marnie tighter, trying not to spiral at the thought of *someone* dressing me while I was unconscious.

Nope. Not thinking about that. Not going there.

I tore my gaze from the bed and focused on the room instead—searching for a distraction, for answers, for anything that made sense.

But the space felt...off. Not fully lived-in, not completely empty either. Like someone was either moving out—or just moving in.

I crept toward the door, my steps cautious, the marble cool beneath my feet. Pressing my ear against it, I strained for any sound—voices, footsteps, *anything*—but nothing.

Somehow, the quiet made my heart race faster.

I reached for the doorknob, half-expecting it to resist, to confirm my worst suspicion—that I was trapped.

But it turned. Smooth. Effortless.

They didn't lock me in?

A dozen questions surged at once, but I shoved them down and took a steadying breath. Slowly, I eased the door open. It didn't creak. Not even a whisper.

Marnie shifted in my arms but stayed tucked close as I stepped into the corridor.

And then—I froze.

The hallway was breathtaking.

It seemed to stretch endlessly. I'd traveled with my parents growing up—seen palaces, museums—but this? This made Versailles look like a starter home.

Mirrors lined the walls, scattering light in every direction. Gold-pillared ceilings arched overhead, intricate and boundless. Grand windows and doorways blurred the line between inside and out, as if boundaries didn't quite exist here.

I moved closer to one of the windows. Outside, clouds drifted by—soft, slow, and close enough to touch.

No.

No, this place couldn't be real.

"Impossible..." I whispered.

Still, I walked. Marnie nestled close, and my bare feet made no sound on the marble. The silence pressed tighter with every step.

Am I...alone?

I caught glimpses of myself in the mirrors, flinching each time I turned a corner and met my own startled reflection—as if the place was playing tricks on me.

Fuuuckk.

I sucked in a breath and looked down. A thorn, no bigger than a sewing needle, peeked out from a stray rose branch curled along the floor. It had nicked my ankle. A small bead of blood welled up, bright against my skin.

Roses?

I looked up—and stopped.

The hallway had opened into something else entirely—a garden.

I inhaled slowly, deeply, trying to steady myself, only to be overwhelmed by a wave of scent—floral, citrusy, sweet, and wild all at once.

I'd dealt with all kinds of incense and oils before, but nothing I could compare came even close.

Sunlight poured in from above, golden and soft. Fountains bubbled along the path, their waters catching the light and scattering it like a thousand tiny diamonds. At the center of the nearest one, a statue stood mid-pour, elegant and still, water flowing endlessly from its marble hands.

I blinked.

Maybe I was dead. Maybe this was heaven.

I was about to take a cautious step forward when Marnie suddenly shifted in my arms, tensing.

"No—Marnie, wait—"

But it was too late.

She wriggled once, twice, then twisted free in a flash of warm fur and darted out of my grasp. Her paws hit the grass, and she took off down one of the garden paths like a shot.

"Marnie!" I cried, my voice echoing through the air, bouncing off rose-laced walls and flowering hedges.

I lunged forward, chasing after her—heart racing, breath tight, bare feet sinking into the cool, dewy grass. The garden blurred around me in a haze of motion and panic. Statues, fountains, petals—it all became a smear of color as I sprinted after her.

I turned a corner—and stopped dead.

There, beneath the sweeping branches of a tree heavy with pale blossoms, sat a man I didn't recognize. He rested on a carved stone bench, calm as could be. And curled up in his lap, of all things, was Marnie. My cat. Purring like she'd never known stress in her life.

He stroked her fur with one hand, long fingers moving in slow, absent-minded circles. She leaned into his touch like he was hers.

The man looked up, his eyes catching mine with unnerving ease. He was tall—even while sitting. His silver hair fell over his shoulders in silky, straight strands. His clothes were relaxed, draping around him in soft folds, and one sleeve bunched like a blanket over Marnie's back.

A grin tugged at his mouth. "I'm not much of a cat person," he said casually, voice warm with amusement. "But for some reason, they just can't resist me."

I blinked, still breathless, trying to make sense of the scene. "Wh-

who...are you?" I asked, my voice more air than sound as I took a cautious step forward.

The man smiled, unbothered. "Zeph," he replied, like that name alone should explain everything. He leaned back on the bench, entirely at ease, fingers still drifting through Marnie's fur. "Cullen's out at the moment, but he should be back soon."

Cullen.

He knew Cullen. He was part of...all of this.

If he knew Cullen, then maybe—

I stepped forward, my voice catching in my throat. A wave of worry, so intense it shocked me. "And Euryale? Is she okay? Where is she?"

Zeph's expression shifted instantly. That calm ease faltered, just for a second, replaced by something more careful. He tilted his head, tone softer now. "She's alright. Just resting," he said gently, like he knew I needed more than words. "You'll be able to see her soon, I promise."

Relief washed over me, and I pressed a hand to my chest, trying to steady the frantic rhythm of my heart. But it wasn't enough—not when a thousand questions were still circling like vultures in my mind. I drew in a shaky breath, trying to piece together what little I actually understood.

"Where am I?" I asked, my voice low, uncertain.

Zeph chuckled softly, like I'd just asked the most obvious question in the world. "You're safe. That's what matters," he answered, expertly dodging the heart of it.

Safe. That's all he was going to give me?

I stepped back and crossed my arms, eyes narrowing as I studied him. How was I supposed to trust anything this guy said?

"So what are you—some kind of bodyguard?" I asked, sarcasm laced through my words, hoping to get actual answers.

Zeph arched an eyebrow, clearly more entertained than offended. "I wish. Those guys get way more action."

He actually winked, which only added to my confusion, but he didn't give me time to dwell on it.

"I get it—you're not big on trusting people right now. I don't blame you," he said, standing and gently moving Marnie off his lap. She stretched lazily, then padded over to the now-empty bench and curled up, utterly unbothered.

Zeph raised his arms in a casual stretch, like this was just another typical day for him. "But if you want, I can show you around. You might even spot a few good escape routes while we're at it." He gestured for me to follow, as if this were no big deal.

I didn't move. My arms stayed crossed, eyes locked on him. "You're not human, are you?" The words came out barely above a whisper—half a question, half me just trying to make sense of any of this.

His smirk deepened, clearly amused by my suspicion. "What gave it away?" he asked, voice laced with mock innocence.

I rolled my eyes. "Let me guess—you're some kind of god, too, right?"

Zeph spun beneath the blooming tree, grinning like I'd just delivered the punchline he'd been waiting for. "Guilty as charged." He gave an exaggerated bow, sweeping one arm out with theatrical flair. "Zephyrus, at your service—god of the west wind, bringer of gentle breezes and cloudless skies."

I scoffed. "West wind? What, is there a whole set? North and south, too?"

"And east," he added, shifting his weight like he was settling into a long-told story. "My brothers. Though, between us, I'm definitely the most fun." He flashed a smile—dimples and all—and I hated how effortlessly likable he was.

With a flick of his wrist, a soft breeze stirred the air. Petals lifted from the nearby flowers, caught in the current like tiny fragments of light. They swirled around us in a delicate spiral, shimmering in the sun as if the scene had been pulled from a dream.

I paused, watching the petals dance, completely forgetting my present circumstances. "Beautiful," I murmured, unable to hide the awe in my voice.

Zeph's gaze flicked to me, his expression shifting—surprised, maybe, by the compliment. A slow, satisfied smile curved his lips. "I do my best to please," he said smoothly, already turning down the path without checking if I'd follow.

"Come on now. You're meeting Sara—she'll get you to Euryale."

"Who?" I asked, not realizing that question was all it took to get me moving after him.

"She runs this place when Cullen and I aren't around. Best to stay on her good side—she might look like sunshine and rainbows, but she won't hesitate to toss you off the edge if she thinks you're a threat to Cullen."

He must've sensed my hesitation because he gave me a sidelong glance.

"Really? After Phobos and Deimos, I thought you could handle anything."

Phobos and Deimos...

Images of shadows and the monsters spilling from them clawed at the edges of my mind. My brain was still processing the fact that something like that could even exist.

"What they did—"

"Gods of fear and terror," Zeph cut in. "They live up to their names—I'll give them that."

Gods. Gods...

How many were there?

Zeph stopped and turned to me. "You're safe."

He repeated it, softer this time.

His eyes were gold like Cullen's, and it made me think maybe all gods carried a trace of gold in them—but Zeph's held faint white lines, swirling like tails of a cloud. They looked like what I imagined touching the endless sky might feel like.

My heart clenched. Lydia had taught me how to read people, not gods.

But something in me believed he was telling the truth about me being safe. And somewhere in this place, Euryale was here.

"So...escape routes, huh?" I said, starting down the path again.

Zeph let out a low, amused chuckle. "I like you."

To my surprise, I found myself half-smiling back.

As we walked, he gestured casually to our surroundings, like he was giving a private tour. That's when I realized—we were suspended high in the sky, the world far below us, veiled by clouds.

Good thing I wasn't afraid of heights.

The deeper we went, the more the garden seemed to stir. It was no longer the quiet, eerie place I'd first woken up in. Now, it felt alive.

Graceful figures began to appear between the trees and flowerbeds, strikingly beautiful. They moved as if they were part of the gardens themselves.

Some knelt to tend the flowers with near-reverent care. Others danced in soft spirals, their gowns trailing like mist. A few played by the fountains, their laughter ringing like tiny bells. As we passed, some waved, a few smiled—and one or two even bowed.

"Nymphs," Zeph explained, watching me watch them.

"They serve Cullen," he added.

A surge of disgust twisted in my gut. "He has slaves?"

Zeph let out a short laugh. "Gods, no. Nymphs are loyal to the gods, but their service isn't forced. Yes, some gods mistreat them, use them like servants—or worse. But Cullen? He simply offered them a place to stay. They're creatures of nature, and here, among the clouds and gardens, they thrive. They care for the palace out of respect and gratitude."

For a brief second, I felt the smallest flicker of approval for Cullen. But I forced it away, shoving the thought aside. I couldn't afford to forget who he was—or what I was to him now.

I paused, still unsure of the dynamic between them. "How do you know Cullen?" I asked, curiosity slipping through.

Zeph shrugged with easy nonchalance, his tone light. "The gods' circles aren't as wide as you'd think."

I raised an eyebrow, clearly unconvinced. He caught the look but only smirked, refusing to elaborate.

"But unlike Cullen," he added with a grin, "I'm actually a lot more popular."

A laugh slipped out before I could stop it. "Is that so?"

Zeph chuckled, visibly pleased with himself—but before he could deliver a comeback, a smooth, slightly mocking voice cut through the air: "Glad to hear you're running a little PR campaign in my absence."

I turned—and there was Cullen.

His presence shifted the atmosphere instantly, like the whole garden knew who had arrived. He stood at the entrance, arms crossed over his chest, the soft light catching the sharp lines of his jaw. A plain dark T-shirt clung to him, and fitted jeans hugged him in a way that lit a slow, dangerous fire in my body. I'd only ever seen him in suits, so seeing him like this...yeah, my brain went blank for a second.

From the corner of my eye, Zeph caught my very obvious stare and arched one brow.

I rolled my eyes and tore my gaze from Cullen.

Zeph gave a soft, knowing snort before turning back to him. "Well, that was fast. Zeus must've been preoccupied."

Zeus. A name I actually knew, pulled straight from old stories—Zeus, king of the gods.

Cullen's eyes narrowed at Zeph, the kind of look that said he'd already revealed too much.

Unfazed, Zeph stretched lazily, arms arching over his head exaggeratedly. His grin widened as he glanced between Cullen and me.

"Well," he drawled, "as much as I'd love to stay for this delightful exchange, I've got winds to blow and all that."

The sigh that followed was pure theater. I was starting to realize Cullen must be used to it, because he didn't so much as blink.

Just as Zeph turned to leave, he paused, tossing a look over his shoulder. "Oh, and Cullen? I assume you'll need time to prepare for the ceremony later?"

I blinked. *Ceremony*?

Cullen's jaw tensed—a flicker of irritation crossed his face, quickly masked by dry amusement. He looked one sarcastic remark away from an eye roll.

Zeph caught it and smirked, shooting me a final wink. "You two should...catch up," he said with a chuckle, then strolled off. "You kids behave now."

Just before he turned the corner, I cleared my throat. "Zeph..."

He paused, glancing back with one eyebrow raised.

"You..." I said slowly, the memory clicking into place. "You're the one who...saved us back there. At the club."

I flexed my hands, the satin of my gloves digging into my palms.

"Thank you," I added, hoping the words carried what I couldn't fully express.

His grin softened. "Anytime," he murmured warmly. "Not every day I get to save two beautiful women...and Cullen's pride."

He gave a final wink before disappearing down the path.

"Thanks for that," Cullen called after him, watching him go.

I narrowed my eyes slightly, aware of how convenient Zeph's exit had been. The moment he was gone, what had felt like a wide, sunlit garden now felt smaller, more enclosed—like the hedges were inching closer.

"No one can come here without my permission," Cullen said, breaking the silence. "That includes Phobos and Deimos. They won't be able to touch you while you're here."

I should've felt relieved. Safe. But instead, the palace struck me as something else entirely—a beautifully made cage.

"Where am I?" I demanded.

"My palace," he replied, folding his arms across his chest. Then, almost as an afterthought—like he was weighing how I'd take it—he added, "In the sky."

The sky...fucking hell.

"I want to leave," I said quickly.

Only his eyes moved then, tracing slowly down my body, as if deliberately ignoring my words.

"I hurt you...that was not my intention."

That threw me off.

Cullen took a step closer.

"At the club, my mother Commanded me. And as one of the Olympian gods, she's...not someone I can disobey."

I frowned. "Then why did you stop?"

His hand raked through his hair, the motion more frustrated than casual. His gaze cut back to me, sharp. "Why indeed."

It felt like he was searching for something in me, like he believed the answer to his question was written beneath my skin.

I scoffed, crossing my arms like the motion could shield me. "So what, you just expect me to stay here until you figure it out? I have an apartment. A shop—"

"They'll both be taken care of. I'll have reports sent to you."

I stared at him, heat and disbelief flooding through me. "So I *am* your prisoner," I muttered, folding my arms tighter.

He closed the space between us in an instant.

"No," he said, quieter this time. "How many times do I have to say it? You're not my prisoner."

But there was something else in his voice—anger.

Why did *he* sound angry?

Shouldn't *I* be the one who's angry?

I swallowed hard, my throat tight, ready to lash out.

Then his hand lifted.

It hovered between us, fingers flexing slightly—like even he wasn't sure if he should touch me. The hesitation made it worse.

And then—he reached.

His fingers brushed the ribbon dangling from my dress. Just a breath of contact, silk against skin, but it sent a jolt of heat through me.

My breath hitched. He didn't let go.

Instead, he held it between his fingers, dragging the delicate fabric slowly through them as if it were fragile. Precious. Like he was savoring the feel of it...and maybe imagining the feel of *me*.

My pulse pounded. I couldn't move. Couldn't speak. Anger melted into something heavier, molten, dangerous, coiling low in my belly.

Say something. Pull away.

But I didn't.

And neither did he.

He lifted the ribbon—slowly—to his lips. His breath brushed over it first, warm and maddeningly light. Then his mouth closed around it.

Soft. Intentional. Lingering.

It felt like he was kissing me directly. Heat flared beneath my skin, blooming in my chest and spreading low, stealing the strength from my legs.

I stood frozen, breathless.

Somehow, I forced a step back. But the space did nothing to break the current pulsing between us.

"This—" I began, my voice faltering, thin and unsteady.

I looked away, forcing down the chaos clawing at my chest. "It doesn't matter," I said tightly, though I wasn't sure whether I was speaking to him or to myself.

Another step back. The ribbon slipped from his grasp.

"You might have carried me off from the club like some princess," I continued, tone sharper now, "but let's not pretend you're some kind of hero."

Something flickered across Cullen's face—raw, exposed—before he smoothed it away like someone recovering from a slap.

"So that's how you see me," he said, voice low and dangerous as he stepped forward again, reclaiming the space I'd tried to put between us. "You're right—I'm no hero. And you're no princess in need of saving."

He paused. His head tilted slightly, gaze burning into mine.

"But here we are. And I'm offering to help the cursed princess."

I swallowed hard. "Help me?" My voice cracked again, traitorous. "How?"

His golden eyes roamed over me slowly, deliberately—taking in the intricate lace at my neckline, the satin gloves on my hands. He didn't hide the heat in his gaze, and I hated how it made my skin burn in response.

Then that slow, knowing smile curved his lips.

"What," Cullen drawled, "you don't recognize a wedding dress when you see one?"

CHAPTER THIRTEEN
CULLEN

I gripped my mouth as hard as I could, holding in the roar of laughter. Her expressions—gods help me, I could stare at them for the rest of my immortal life.

"Please don't mind me," I said as a few nymphs paused in their work to glance my way.

I exhaled, straightening again.

Preparations moved swiftly. Nymphs glided in and out, silk banners unfurling, flowers placed with care, trays of food and drink drifting past. My palace seemed to breathe, and I couldn't remember the last time it had felt this alive.

Skye.

How would she react when she saw this?

Seeing her in that dress—now I understood why a groom wasn't meant to glimpse his bride before the ceremony.

Because it ruined you. It *wrecked* you.

She was stunning. Radiant.

And for a heartbeat, she looked so beautifully shocked. I saw the widening of her eyes, the parting of her lips, the way realization struck like lightning.

The dress.

My words.

She hadn't even spoken yet—hadn't rejected the idea, hadn't questioned it—when I moved.

Before she could speak, I spread my wings and took to the sky.

A bonding. A wedding in mortal terms. *Ours.*

And I needed everything.

Every truth, every secret. Every *inch* of her.

Her touch.

With one graze of her skin, I resisted an Olympian Command.

I'd never known control like that.

Never craved freedom like this.

The sound of the orchestra tuning instruments shook me from my thoughts. Their notes reverberated across the ballroom, filling the grand space.

My gaze drifted to the arched windows, the gardens stretching below. She was no longer where I'd left her, but I wasn't concerned. She wouldn't go far. The ceremony was nearly ready.

And soon, so would its bride.

The rhythmic *clack* of footsteps echoed off the marble floor, pulling my attention back. The nymphs stilled, their eyes darting toward the sound. Curious glances flicked between me and the approaching figure, tension rippling through the room.

I shifted, casting them a glance—a silent warning. One by one, they lowered their gazes and returned to their tasks.

The footsteps grew louder. Sharp. Purposeful.

"What in all the levels of the Underworld is going on, Cullen?"

I didn't need to turn to know who it was.

Harmony.

Because what's a wedding without a little family drama?

I sighed and turned. She stopped just short of me, arms crossed, irritation radiating from her like heat. I met her glare without flinching.

"Careful," I said, voice low. "You're here as a guest."

She rolled her eyes, arms tightening across her chest. "You might be interested to know about the *mess* you left behind at the club. They're still cleaning up the stone statues."

Euryale. A surprise—but not an unwelcome one. She was no threat to Skye. If anything, she might prove useful.

Harmony pressed on, narrowing her eyes, sensing my distraction.

"Oh, and there's more. Rumors are flying about some girl. A few guesses on who she might be."

I let her words hang, turning back toward the nymphs. They'd lingered again, curiosity gleaming in their eyes. This time, I let them feel the full weight of my gaze. They scattered like leaves in a gust of wind, returning to their work.

"Anything else?" I asked, voice edged with dry sarcasm. "Or did you just come to offer wedding advice?"

Harmony sighed, exasperated.

"You're out of your mind if you think this is going to work."

I ignored the bite in her tone.

"Zeus has been pressuring me to marry for centuries," I said, cool, unbothered. "Politically, it suits him—me bonded, no longer something my mother can parade around. Less turmoil in his precious kingdom."

Harmony didn't buy it. Her brows knit, skepticism carved deep.

"There's something off about her..."

She wasn't wrong.

Skye was different.

She resisted my curse.

Her touch had broken through an Olympian Command—something no mortal or god should have been capable of.

She was more.

More than I could explain.

And I needed to understand why.

But I wasn't handing Harmony that thread to pull. Not yet.

Instead, I smirked and brushed the thought aside.

"Wouldn't a marriage keep Olympus entertained?" I offered lightly. "Give them something new to gossip about?"

Harmony's expression hardened. She wasn't amused. "This isn't a joke. Aphrodite is pissed, and when she's pissed, we all suffer for it. And Phobos and Deimos?" Her voice dropped, edged with warning. "They'll be far too interested in her."

My smirk faded. The thought of those two setting their sights on Skye twisted something deep in my gut. Keeping her here—keeping her away from them—was the entire point. The only reason I had brought her to my palace.

I'd had Zeph stir the winds around the palace, letting in only those loyal to me. There were, of course, a few exceptions—Zeus among them—but I'd made sure they were distracted. I'd sent nymphs to deliver Dionysus's newest wine, boasting about its contents until curiosity did the rest. They wouldn't be able to resist.

I cast Harmony one last glance before turning back to the preparations.

My voice was low and firm, but I cut it with something colder.

"Let them try."

Harmony opened her mouth to respond, but another irritation strolled into my ballroom before she could speak.

"Well, well. If it isn't Olympus's favorite bachelor, turning into a groom."

Hymenaeus strode in with all the pomp and self-importance I'd come to expect. He was draped in fine robes the color of freshly spilled wine, carrying himself like he was the most vital god in Olympus. For the purposes of this ceremony, he unfortunately was. As one of the gods of marriage and unions, no bonding was truly sealed without his blessing—a formality, but an unavoidable one. The only reason I had allowed him into my palace.

He eyed me with the kind of scrutiny that suggested he was savoring my predicament. "You should be thanking me, Cupid. Without my presence, this little union of yours would be meaningless."

I didn't bother dignifying that with a response, but Harmony tilted her head, feigning thought. "And yet, your presence is so forgettable. Strange, isn't it?"

Hymenaeus stepped closer, a smirk curling his lips as his gaze dragged over Harmony. "A goddess like you, unclaimed? A tragedy. But don't worry—I'd be more than happy to correct that."

Harmony didn't even pretend to entertain him, offering a saccharine smile that didn't reach her eyes. "Oh, I'd hate to waste your time. I hear rejection is devastating for a god of your...*delicate* stature."

His smirk twitched, just for a second, before he smoothed it back into place. "You wound me."

She shrugged, utterly unbothered. "Not deep enough, apparently."

I stifled a laugh, disguising it as a cough. Hymenaeus shot me a glare, but I only raised a brow, silently daring him to say something. He didn't.

Harmony huffed, rolling her eyes. "Well, since I apparently have to get ready for a wedding, I'll leave you to it." She turned on her heel without another word, muttering something about pompous windbags as she strode out.

I envied her for leaving.

Hymenaeus chuckled, though there was an edge to it. "Your sister—always so *titillating*. Anyway, we have much to discuss. Ideally, the ceremony would've taken place during the winter solstice. The nectar could have completed Skye's transformation—made her fully immortal. But since you're clearly in a rush to be bonded..."

His eyes swept over me, thick with judgment.

"Technically," he continued, "the nectar isn't required for the bonding. She'll just need to be in Olympus by the solstice to receive immortality."

Creeaakk.

The tall windows groaned open, letting in a gust of wind that stirred the edges of the silk curtains.

"And you can't have a ceremony without your best man. I know, I know—you didn't ask. Thought I'd save you the trouble."

Zeph strolled in, unbothered and grinning.

Hymenaeus's jaw tightened, his patience thinning.

"I'll take my leave and handle the rest," he said coolly before turning on his heel and stalking off.

I watched him go, smirking.

"I'll have to pay for that later," I muttered, throwing Zeph a crooked grin.

"Still can't believe it," Zeph said, shaking his head. "After all these centuries, you're actually getting bonded. And we don't even get time for a proper bachelor party."

"Well, first..."

I stepped forward slowly, raking a hand through my hair as the thought settled over me.

"I have to give my bride-to-be the *proper* motivation to agree."

CHAPTER FOURTEEN

SKYE

I recognized some of these herbs.

My fingers reached into a brown bowl, rolling over the sprigs and buds.

Bowls were scattered everywhere—some even hung from the exposed roof beams above me, bundled in twine and dried in clusters.

But this wasn't Mystic Soulstice.

I was in some kind of medical wing, surrounded by white walls traced with golden lines that pulsed faintly in the light.

Nymphs—at least, that's what Zeph had called them—moved silently. Up close, I noticed their eyes, each a different shade of green, catching the sunlight as it slanted through the windows, shifting toward sunset. They tended to Euryale, who was still sleeping, her glasses resting over her eyes. The snakes and green scales I'd seen before were gone—as if they'd never existed at all.

I sat at her bedside, I didn't know for how long, trying to make sense of everything that had happened.

She had snakes.

I could still see them—writhing, coiling—burned into the backs of my eyelids.

She had snakes.

And she had fought without hesitation.

She had snakes...

And she had protected me.

I glanced at her again. Gorgon, they called her. Most people would've been afraid—maybe I should've been—but I wasn't. I saw strength there. Unapologetic strength.

I wasn't used to people getting close to me—except Lydia. She was the only one who'd ever pushed through my walls. And now, sitting here, I finally understood why she and Euryale had been friends.

And then Cullen had saved us both.

Ugh. Cullen.

He'd flown off with that irritating, arrogant face—right after making some smug comment about the dress I was wearing. A wedding dress.

What the hell had he even meant by that?

Was he planning to force me into some kind of marriage? I'd sooner have thrown myself off this floating palace and taken my chances with the clouds.

I should burn this dress, I should—

Someone approached, pulling me from my thoughts. A nymph moved to check Euryale's blood pressure. She was the same one who'd brought me here. Her movements were quiet, precise, her focus sharp—like an artist painting on a grain of rice.

I stayed silent, not wanting to break her concentration. She finished, scribbled something onto a clipboard, and quickly slipped away, the pale yellow of her dress swishing softly behind her.

My heart clenched, unable to form words, afraid to know whether it was good news or bad. I looked back at Euryale.

Still...who—or what—exactly was she?

If I could just read her mind...

The thought hovered at the edge of my consciousness, tempting, dangerous.

There was a way to find out.

I hesitated, glancing down at Euryale, weighing the risk.

I hoped she would forgive me for what I was about to do. Guilt crawled beneath my skin—it felt invasive, wrong—but I needed answers. Answers that might help her, too.

Slowly, I tugged at the satin of my gloves, peeling them off one finger at a time until my hands were bare. I looked down at her—so still, so peaceful. Her face seemed almost fragile in the soft, golden light.

I took a steadying breath, reached out, and touched her hand.

Her skin was cool against mine.

And then—

I was no longer in the room.

Swirls of color lifted and danced around me—emerald greens, deep violets, molten reds—twisting together like an autumn forest reflected in a river. My fingertips grazed them, and I could feel them humming with life, carrying me forward. It felt like I was stepping consciously into a dream...or a memory.

I stood in a sun-drenched meadow, wildflowers swaying in the breeze. In front of me were three women—the only one I recognized was Euryale—laughing. She seemed so different here.

The sisters were beautiful, not just physically, but with a light in them, a kind of innocence.

"Medusa, Stheno, look!" Euryale's voice was full of love and laughter as she called out to them.

Medusa. Stheno.

Their names echoed through the memory.

I watched, feeling like an intruder, powerless to stop the flood of images.

Then the scene shifted.

I blinked, bracing myself—

Now I stood inside a darkened temple. At its center, a massive, towering statue seemed to hold up the entire structure with its sheer size.

Aphrodite.

This was her temple—built for worship, for prayers and peace.

But it didn't feel like one now.

Now, it felt just a place of judgment.

Euryale stood beside her sisters, their faces shadowed with confusion and fear as they clung to one another.

Then Aphrodite appeared.

Her golden form shimmered with a light so blinding it almost forced me to look away, but there was no warmth in it—only cold fury simmering beneath flawless perfection.

"You dared to let a god defile my temple," she hissed, circling them like a predator. “You let your beauty tempt Poseidon himself. You thought yourselves worthy of my favor—and invited ruin upon me. This is a punishable act.”

My fists clenched.

Tempt. The word burned through me. Why were they being blamed for his crime? Why were victims always made to carry the shame and guilt, while their aggressors walked free—as if leaving their sins on our bodies could wash them from their own?

I dropped to my knees beside them, the fabric of my dress scraping against the stone floor, anger flaring hot in my chest. This wasn’t justice—it was jealousy. It wasn’t about what they had done but about what they were. Beautiful. Threatening to a goddess who couldn’t stand the thought of competition.

Medusa trembled, reaching forward. “We never—”

“Silence!” Aphrodite’s voice cracked like thunder, her eyes blazing with fury.

“You will serve as an example of the temptation of beauty and what it brings.”

She raised her hand.

From the shadows, Cullen stepped forward—bow in hand, arrows gleaming with silver-tipped ends—and my heart clenched. He looked the same. And...not. It was as if he’d severed his emotions, detaching himself because it was the only way to survive.

He moved slowly, almost reluctantly, drawing one arrow. I knew what those arrows could do. I’d felt it myself.

For the briefest moment, his eyes met Euryale’s. Something flickered between them—hesitation...maybe even guilt.

But then Aphrodite’s power surged behind him, her voice sharp and commanding: “Cupid, now!”

Cullen released the first arrow. Then the second. Then the third.

The curse struck like a tidal wave.

The sisters gasped, bodies convulsing as if the very air had turned to poison. Silken hair coiled and split, warping into writhing serpents that hissed and snapped at the air. Flawless skin hardened into jagged scales, the curse creeping across their faces like a spreading disease. Their eyes flared a burning blood-red—no longer human.

They were being rewritten, their beauty torn apart and rebuilt into something the world would fear. Gorgons.

All because the goddess of love chose willful blindness over justice.

Aphrodite smiled, cruel satisfaction gleaming in her gaze as she looked upon their suffering.

"Let this be a lesson to all who serve me. I am not one to be compared to."

Cullen stood motionless, bow lowered. His face gave nothing away—but I saw it. A flicker of regret, buried deep beneath the weight of obedience. He'd done as she Commanded.

But he hadn't wanted this.

Why did that stir something in me?

Before I could stop myself, my hand reached toward him, fingers half-lifted, like I could close the distance between us. Like I could touch the part of him that felt. The part that regretted. But before I could take a single step—

The vision vanished.

The temple's warmth disappeared. In its place was a cold, dark cave.

The air was thick with damp earth and dread. Shadows clung to the jagged stone walls like they were alive, watching. In the distance, the echo of armored footsteps bounced through the tunnels—relentless, closing in.

Euryale crouched beside her sisters, breath shallow, trembling. Medusa and Stheno flanked her, their bodies forming a shield. Euryale's smaller frame pressed into Medusa's side, clutching at her as if safety could be held by force. They looked as though they'd been running for days.

Medusa stood at the mouth of the cave, eyes glowing faintly in the dark. The serpents in her hair hissed and writhed, tasting the air, sensing danger on the wind. Beside her, Stheno gripped a bloodstained spear scavenged from a fallen soldier. The cursed sisters had become warriors—yet they were still hunted like monsters.

"They're coming," Stheno growled, her voice echoing off the stone. "We need to be ready."

Euryale's heart thundered. I could feel it—the sharp edge of her fear. She wasn't like her sisters. She wasn't built for battle, couldn't stare down death with the same iron resolve.

"I'm sorry," Euryale whispered, her voice cracking as she clung to Medusa's arm. "I'm not strong enough. Just...leave me."

Medusa turned toward her, the fierce glow in her eyes softening. Her serpents calmed as she cupped Euryale's cheek, voice steady and low.

"We're sisters. We protect each other."

The *clang* of armor grew louder—closer. Soldiers shouted, their leader's name echoing like a battle cry.

Perseus.

Then, the cave entrance exploded with light as the army stormed inside.

Stheno roared, charging first, spear raised high. Her monstrous strength sent the first wave of soldiers crashing backward like they were nothing. Medusa followed, her eyes burning with vengeance. One by one, the men who dared meet their gaze turned to stone—frozen mid-scream, terror etched into their features as if by a sculptor's hand.

Euryale stood paralyzed, watching as her sisters fought with everything they had. Their curses—once cruel punishments—were now their weapons against a world that had cast them out. She wanted to help. She wanted to be strong like them. But all she could do was hide, clinging to the cold stone walls of the cave while the battle unfolded before her eyes.

The clash of metal, the shouts, the cries of the dying—it was all deafening. Still, the soldiers kept coming.

Even with all their power, Medusa and Stheno were outnumbered. Their strength, though formidable, was fading.

Euryale's heart cracked as she saw it—Stheno struck by her own stolen spear, her body collapsing to the bloodied stone floor. Medusa roared, a cry of pure rage and heartbreak, but she couldn't hold them off forever. With one final, defiant look toward Euryale, Medusa met her fate—cut down by a man cloaked in the title of hero, as though that word alone excused every atrocity committed in its name.

They had fought and died for her.

Tears streamed down Euryale's cheeks as she stood alone in the shadows. She'd been protected—but at what cost?

Everything.

Everyone.

The world around me shattered, the vision dissolving like smoke.

I gasped, lurching upright in my chair. My hand ripped away from

Euryale's as I stared at her, heart pounding. My fingers trembled at what I had just seen.

Euryale didn't deserve any of this...and maybe neither did Cullen.

I looked around. The room was silent now. The nymphs were gone. Only Euryale remained, breathing softly, glasses still perched on her nose.

Then I felt it—warmth on my upper lip.

I reached up.

Blood.

This...wasn't a good sign.

"Careful, my little reader. Doesn't look like you can touch many more people much longer."

I whipped around.

Cullen stood on the balcony, casually leaning against the doorframe like he hadn't just crept up on me. His outfit had changed—back into a sharply tailored suit, designed to draw the eye to his infuriatingly perfect frame. He tilted his head, gaze locked on the blood still dripping from my nose.

Instinctively, I wiped it away, my fingers trembling.

"Funny," I muttered, heat rising to my cheeks. "You find this funny?"

He didn't answer. His eyes shifted to Euryale, still sleeping soundly. He said nothing. Just stood there, watching her.

I wasn't sure what he was doing.

I wasn't sure of anything anymore.

"You didn't want to curse them, did you?" The question slipped out softer than I intended. But...I needed to know.

Silence. Cullen didn't confirm or deny—didn't take his eyes off Euryale.

"I know what it's like," I continued, my voice low. "To have parents who expect everything. To always be a disappointment. It's exhausting." I wasn't sure why I was admitting this to him, of all people, but the words spilled out before I could stop them.

Cullen stepped closer, his warmth radiating beside me—so close I could almost feel the gentle brush of his breath against my hair.

"Euryale has the best care," he murmured, voice softer. "The wound was extensive, but she'll recover in time. You don't need to worry."

There was no teasing in his words. Maybe that's why I believed him.

Either way, I let out a slow breath, tension draining from me as I gave a slight nod.

But, of course, the moment couldn't last.

Cullen turned, moving toward the balcony again.

My stomach tensed. I hated how my pulse jumped.

"Flying off again?" I asked, trying to keep my voice uninterested, my gaze fixed down.

Cullen paused at the edge, turning back with that maddening smirk.

"Well," he said, unfolding his wings in one graceful motion, sunlight catching along the golden edges—

"Not alone this time."

He extended his hand toward me. That grin only widened.

I blinked, staring at him like he'd lost his mind. "No way," I said, shaking my head. "No way am I flying off with you."

Cullen raised a brow, clearly entertained. "Oh, really?"

He lowered his hand, but didn't walk away. Instead, he reached into the inside of his jacket and pulled something out—long, slim, glinting in the light.

I squinted, my stomach sinking before I even made it out.

He twirled it between his fingers. That maddening smirk never left his face.

"I thought," he drawled, voice smooth and infuriatingly casual, "you might want this back."

In his hands, he held my arrow.

CHAPTER FIFTEEN

SKYE

So much for claiming I wasn't some princess.

Cullen cradled me against his chest like I weighed nothing. One arm supported my back, the other beneath my knees, steady even as we soared high above the palace. My hands clutched at his shirt, fingers curling into the fabric to steady myself—though the warmth of his body and the closeness between us did nothing to calm my racing heart.

From this height, the palace was truly breathtaking. Perched among the clouds, it looked like a fusion of several villas and a castle, archways and terraces shimmering with golden brick. Slender towers stretched toward the sky, and grand balconies opened onto endless blue. At the far edge, a waterfall spilled from the grounds and disappeared into the mist below, as if the entire structure hovered at the world's edge.

We landed with barely a sound—the descent so soft it felt like stepping onto sand. Cullen's hands lingered at my waist as he set me down, his touch sending a ripple of heat through me that made my breath catch and my legs momentarily falter.

As he stepped forward to open the grand, ornate doors, my eyes caught on his wings—still partially unfurled. Pure white and impossibly soft-looking, each feather appeared to be spun from clouds. I had feathers in my shop, but none compared to these.

"If you keep looking at me like that," Cullen said, glancing back with a smirk, "I might start thinking you like what you see."

Heat rushed to my cheeks. I quickly looked away, muttering, "I was just wondering how you manage to fit through doorways with those things."

He chuckled, low and deep, as he pushed the door open.

"Tightly."

I hesitated, but then shook off the thought.

If he meant to hurt me, he would've already done it.

So I followed him—no, I followed my arrow, still captive in his hand.

The door opened...into a garden? No, not quite.

It was a room, but a massive tree stood at its center, branches stretching upward and curling along the walls, as if holding the space together. Embedded in the trunk was a full-length mirror, its surface shimmering faintly, as though the tree had grown around it—claimed it.

Cushions and raised platforms surrounded the base, and scattered across them were makeup brushes, fabrics, bits of lace, and ribbon.

Wedding dress, Cullen's voice echoed in my mind.

A flutter of nerves stirred in my chest.

"A cage is still a cage, even if it's dressed up like some pretty room," I said, forcing confidence into my voice despite the sudden thundering of my heart. "I thought you were the god of love, and you thought this would—"

The door closed behind us with a quiet *click*, cutting me off. I looked up.

Cullen's smirk deepened. His wings folded in, feathers dissolving into his back with a faint shimmer.

"I am the god of love and desire," he purred, drawing the words out like a reminder of exactly who he was. He leaned back, pressing one boot against the door as if to seal us in. "You humans are just so full of feelings. I can taste them—your obsessions, what draws you in...and what drives you away."

The thought of him being inside my head made heat prickle across my skin.

"I feel your heart recoil at the thought of a cage." His gaze lingered, piercing. "I feel your loneliness—"

He stopped. The silence stretched, heavy. He drew in a sharp breath, then let it slip out slowly through his teeth, the sound almost a hiss.

His hand rose to his collar, unfastening the top button like the fabric was stifling. The motion exposed the lines of his collarbone, a defined, ghostly curve etched in the shadows. My eyes betrayed me, following the movement.

"Tell me, Skye..." His voice dipped, smoother now, more dangerous. "Do you truly think me so heartless?"

His eyes softened as he asked, but their intensity still stole the air from my lungs. My pulse pounded hard enough that I was sure he could hear it.

Was I supposed to answer?

He didn't give me the chance. He shifted, sliding his foot from the door and tilting his body closer. His arms crossed over his chest, as if he would take his time watching me unravel.

"My proposal."

I raised an eyebrow, suspicious. "For the arrow?" I asked, my tone sharp as I nodded toward him.

He uncrossed his arms and tapped the side of his jacket pocket, a small, smug smile tugging at his lips.

"It is for the arrow...and more."

I shot him a skeptical look that would've made Lydia and Euryale proud. He only chuckled—a sound that seemed to vibrate right through me. And I wondered if I'd ever stop being unnerved by him.

He took a slow step closer, his hand brushing the branches of the tree, his eyes never leaving mine. "I also can give you the nectar of the gods," he said, slowly unfolding each word. "It would rewrite you. Free you from the curse. Make you immortal."

He paused, letting the promise settle between us.

"No one would dare touch you again."

I blinked. "Immortal?"

He nodded, studying me intently. "The nectar is a drink—an elixir. It's only available during the solstices. We've just passed the summer solstice, so the next one won't come until winter."

My hand shot out to the wall, bracing myself. "What...winter? I'd have to stay here for months?!"

A quiet beat passed. When he spoke again, his voice had shifted—softer now, almost cautious. "Yes...and there's also a condition."

He let the silence stretch before finishing, his lips curving slightly.

"For the nectar to be yours, we'd need to be bound," he said. "Officially."

Bound. The word echoed in my head, over and over—*bound, bound, bound.*

I pressed my fingers to my temples, the satin gloves sliding uselessly over clammy skin.

"To get this nectar...I have to be bound to you?" My voice cracked.

My gaze slid to the mirror, then dropped. "Is that—Is that why I'm wearing this dress?" My eyes darted around the room, confirming what I already dreaded. This...this *was* a bridal suite.

"This is a wedding?"

A short, disbelieving laugh escaped me—one that didn't quite mask the rising panic in my chest. "You've got to be kidding me."

Something flickered across his face before he straightened, his voice smoothing over.

"Once we're bound and receive the nectar, you'll be free to live however you choose. Even now, you can walk away—face the curse alone, if that's what you want."

His tone was steady, almost calm, but underneath it...something was testing me.

I tore my gaze from him, my head throbbing.

Dress.

Wedding.

Bond.

If I stayed, I'd be trapped here. With him. For months. Until the winter solstice. Married to him.

But if I didn't—if I left—I'd still be cursed. Unable to touch anyone again. Still losing my mind, piece by piece.

Cullen seemed to sense my hesitation. Without a word, he reached into his jacket and drew out the very arrow that had cursed me.

"In the meantime," he said, holding it out, "this will keep the curse at bay until the nectar is ready. It's not a cure, but it'll slow the effects." A faint, wry smile tugged at his lips. "Euryale...she ate hers when she was in her Gorgon form. It gives her some control. With her eyes shielded, her true form stays hidden—hence the glasses."

He studied me carefully, as if waiting for the question I hadn't yet asked. Then, without pushing, he extended the arrow again, holding it a hair's width from my hands.

I hesitated, then slowly turned my palms upward. He placed the arrow gently across them, his fingers brushing mine—long enough for me to feel their strength.

"Yes," he murmured, catching the question in my eyes. "I gave Euryale her arrow back. Zeus was tired of the bloodshed between the gods and the Gorgons. I returned it as a peace offering—on the condition she abandon her revenge. She agreed."

I glanced down at the arrow gleaming in my hands.

"Why?" I asked quietly. "Why not just let the curse end me?"

When I looked up, I had to tilt my chin to meet his gaze—he really was that tall.

"Skye," he said, voice low. His eyes darkened. "If you haven't figured it out by now...you're different. And I intend to find out everything about you."

Restless, I started to back away. His eyes tracked me, a faint smirk tugging at his lips, as if he knew exactly what effect he had.

Part of me screamed to run.

Another part—reckless, curious—ached to understand everything about him, too.

I stopped, just as his lips parted to speak.

I cut him off before he could.

"Fine," I clipped, the word fast—like if I didn't spit it out quickly, I'd choke on it. "I'll agree to this...arrangement. But don't think that means I'm willing to be...bound to you in other ways. Like *that*."

His eyes flared—just slightly—and a twitch of amusement pulled at his lips as he brought a hand to his chin, as though the motion were the only thing keeping him from laughing.

He knew *exactly* what I meant.

Then, with infuriating calm, he tilted his head and murmured, "Oh? Already picturing me in your bed? I thought we were just talking logistics."

I blinked—then sputtered. "That's not—I didn't—"

My gaze snapped away, jaw clenched, willing the heat in my cheeks to cool.

Focus. Focus on literally *anything* else.

I cleared my throat.

"When—how do we...bind this?"

Without hesitation, he lifted his hand. A subtle flicker of sparks danced from his fingers as he snapped them, almost as if the deal I'd just made had already been sealed.

If it were possible to die from pure, blindly innocent light, it would be at the hands of nymphs.

They swept into the room in a flurry of laughter and motion, their voices surrounding me, their energy seeming to bounce off the walls.

Cullen lingered just inside the threshold, his eyes tracking their every move. Then, as if satisfied with what he saw, he slipped into the adjacent room. A wall separated us now, but I could still feel him somehow.

The nymphs guided me onto a plush platform and got to work, layering fabric over my gown with the kind of focus that made me nervous to move too much. Embroidery bloomed across the bodice and sleeves like magic, threads and pearls shifting over my skin. Soft layers floated down to the floor in rippling waves, making it hard to tell whether this was still a hostage situation or my dream dress.

They tugged at my hair, weaving in pins and tucking loose strands into place. I coughed as a puff of powder hit my nose, earning a chorus of apologetic giggles.

Finally, they stepped back, hands clasped in satisfaction, their eyes bright with pride. After exchanging a few excited glances, they parted, revealing the full-length mirror set into the tree.

I took one look and barely recognized the woman in the reflection. Sure, I knew the face—my cheekbones, my eyes—but everything else felt...different.

A gentle nudge from one of the nymphs pulled me out of my daze. "He's waiting," she whispered, her voice tinged with excitement.

I took a steadying breath and let her guide me.

The nymphs led me through an arched doorway into a wide, open space. Cullen was already there, seated with his hands interlocked, posture tense, leaning forward as if patience were a foreign concept.

The second his gaze landed on me, heat bloomed in my cheeks. His golden eyes roamed over every detail of the gown. I felt pinned in place—it wasn't just the dress he was seeing, but the way my body moved with it...and beneath it.

He didn't speak. His jaw clenched. And just like that, I found myself standing taller, torn between wanting to disappear and a strange, unshakable urge to possess his attention.

I shook off the thought and looked down at the arrow still resting in my hand. A soft, nervous laugh slipped out as my thumb brushed the sharp tip. The awkwardness made the arrow feel like both a shield...and a question hanging silently between us.

"So, I'm just supposed to...hold this forever?" I asked, aiming for light-hearted but landing somewhere between dry and uneasy.

Cullen moved almost instantly, like he'd been waiting for the question. Without a word, he reached over and snapped the tip off the arrow. The break was quick, clean—like he'd done it before. "You only need to bear the arrowhead," he said simply.

He drew a slender chain from inside his jacket—dark silver, sleek. Without a word, he took the arrowhead from my hands and fastened the chain to it.

Then, holding it lightly between his fingers, he stepped behind me. He paused, hovering close, his breath brushing the back of my neck as if waiting for permission. I gave a small nod.

His movements were soft, deliberate. His fingers brushed lightly over the nape of my neck as he gathered my hair to one side, and I inhaled sharply—startled by the graze of his touch. He slipped the chain over my head, letting it fall until the arrowhead came to rest against my chest, cool metal against warm skin.

But the heat of his touch lingered.

"This," he murmured, his voice a low thrum against the quiet, "will grant a bit of reprieve—for you...and for me."

He stepped back in front of me, his gaze dropping to the arrowhead. Slowly—almost hesitantly—he lifted his hand, fingers brushing along it as if placing a protective spell. *For you and for me*. The words echoed in my mind. There was something in his eyes—as if my pain somehow hurt him more than it hurt me.

"You won't need the gloves anymore," he breathed, then paused. "May I?"

I nodded, my voice caught somewhere between my chest and throat.

Speechless. Breathless. Stupid.

His fingers found the edge of the satin and began to peel it away—slow, careful. The fabric slipped down my arm, and his touch, light as it was, sent a shiver racing up to my shoulder. He repeated the motion with the other, his eyes never leaving mine.

Where else might those hands touch...

Before the silence could stretch too far, one nymph cleared her throat, a soft smile tugging at her lips. "It's time," she said gently.

"Now?" I echoed, panic creeping in as the reality of what was about to happen settled in.

Cullen didn't respond. He only extended his arm.

I hesitated, then slipped my hand into the crook of his elbow. His steady warmth grounded me as he guided us down an expansive corridor lined with towering pillars and flickering torches. Shadows danced along the walls, swaying with each flame, as though the hall itself were bowing to us.

I DIDN'T BELONG HERE.

"Skye." Cullen's voice cut through my thoughts as he stopped abruptly, tugging me to a halt in front of a closed door.

He exhaled, irritation flickering across his face. "Were you not listening to a single word I just said?"

I matched his tone, sharp and biting. "Oh, I'm sorry if I'm a little distracted by the fact that my life is gone now—and that I'm about to get fucking married."

Cullen tensed, pinching the bridge of his nose. "There will be an altar, and the officiant, Hymenaeus, will say a few words. Then we exchange an offering."

"Blood?!"

His head snapped back, recoiling as if I'd insulted him. "No. We're gods, not fucking vampires." His eyes slid down, lingering deliberately at my neck. He leaned in, voice dropping to a mock whisper. "Unless...that's something you're into."

I shot him a flat look, hoping my expression conveyed exactly how unamused I was.

A discreet cough broke the moment. A nymph approached, bowing slightly. "Divine Cullen, it is ready."

My stomach tightened, nerves crawling under my skin.

"You're beautiful, if I haven't mentioned that already," Cullen whispered, standing beside me as we lingered just inside the threshold.

My breath caught as the doors eased open.

At first, I saw only light. Moonlight poured through towering windows that opened into clouds, spilling across the marble floor in a silver wash.

A single rose petal drifted from above, grazing my shoulder before spiraling to the floor. The delicate touch made me pause. I tilted my head back—and forgot how to breathe.

The ceiling rose above us like a living sky—paintings of gods and monsters twisted together. It looked alive, like it was breathing, watching my every step—all those golden eyes staring back at me.

Then Cullen's fingers found mine.

Though my arm was already looped through his elbow, he reached across his chest with his other hand to brush mine. The contact was light, almost hesitant, but it jolted something inside me.

His touch was warm. He didn't pull; he didn't need to. My feet moved on their own, drawn to him despite the alarm in my head.

We descended the grand staircase together, hand in hand. Our steps echoed softly through the marble halls, steady as a heartbeat. Below us, at the chamber's center, an empty dance floor gleamed beneath the moonlight—polished to a mirror's sheen.

Around us, figures were draped in opulent robes and gowns. Some had horns curling from their temples, while others stood on the cloven hooves of goats, their faces hidden behind elaborate beards braided with ribbons. No number of fantasy novels or tarot cards could've prepared me for seeing it in person. Gods—because that's what they had to be—I was sure of it now.

They turned in unison, like spectators at a tennis match, and I was the ball.

I caught a flicker of green eyes—familiar ones. Some of the same faces who'd helped me with my dress and hair were now among the guests. They were in exquisite gowns woven with sunlight and flowers. Cullen hadn't treated them like servants or slaves; they were equal to his other guests.

Their gazes slid over me, curious but softened with smiles, dipping respectful nods toward Cullen and me.

But none of it—none of them—rattled me nearly as much as the subtle way his thumb moved over the back of my hand.

Euryale was going to kill me.

Cullen's grip remained steady as he led us to the center of the floor. He leaned in, a murmur against my ear. "The ceremony begins with a dance."

My heart stuttered. "I-I don't know how to dance like this."

A smirk ghosted across his lips as he leaned closer, his breath brushing my skin. "Put your feet on mine."

The warmth of his breath made my back arch toward him. I turned my head slightly. The gods were watching—whispering. I could feel the weight of their stares on every inch of exposed skin.

But I turned back to him. Slowly, I stepped onto his shoes.

His arm slid around my waist, pulling me closer until my chest pressed against his. My breath hitched. The fact that he was the most handsome man I'd ever seen was of no help in this situation.

I almost forgot we had an audience until the music began.

Cullen moved like he'd been born for this—smooth, powerful, completely in control. He guided me easily, every step confident, every turn perfectly timed. I followed instinctively, moving my body with the rhythm, with him.

His hand at my waist tightened, pulling me into a slow spin that brought me flush against him again. My fingers curled at his shoulder, not for balance—but because I didn't want to let go. I was dancing with fire, and a part of me wanted to lean in closer, to see how much heat I could take before I burned.

When the final note faded, Cullen didn't release me. He guided me into a deep, graceful dip, one arm supporting me with effortless strength. Applause swelled around us, but it felt far away, like a murmur at the edge of a dream. His eyes held mine, hand still firm at the small of my back, as if daring me to trust him.

Slowly, Cullen pulled me upright.

The motion brought our bodies flush, my breath catching as we stood there, chest to chest, my heart pounding against his like a bird trapped between cupped hands.

"See? You are quite the dancer—"

Cullen froze.

His body went rigid beside mine, the change so abrupt I felt it before I saw it in his eyes.

I squinted up at him, confused.

The applause faltered, fading like a wave pulling back from shore.

Above us, the chandelier trembled, swaying as if stirred by distant thunder—like a storm had crept into the walls, shaking the foundation itself and drawing every gaze upward.

I followed Cullen's line of sight to the top of the sweeping staircase just as a blinding flash of lightning split the room—illuminating two towering figures standing shoulder to shoulder.

They looked like what absolute power would wear if it dressed up as royalty. The man had silver hair that brushed his shoulders and a golden wreath on his head. His robes shimmered as though spun from raw starlight, and the way he held himself seemed to command the space around him—as if gravity itself had to ask his permission.

He was, without a doubt, a king.

The king extended his arm to the woman at his side, guiding her with practiced elegance. She was beautiful, undeniably, with a golden wreath on her head and a dress strung with purple amethysts along its piping neckline. But it was her eyes that caught me. She never once looked at him. Not when he moved. Not when he offered his arm. It was as though she didn't need him at all, but allowed him to escort her anyway.

Gasps rippled through the room.

Cullen shifted beside me, slow and tense, as though even a breath too loud might trigger something.

"Hera," he murmured. "Zeus."

Another bolt of lightning cracked across the sky, lighting up the hall as their gazes swept over the crowd—and then landed, unmistakably, on me.

CHAPTER SIXTEEN
CULLEN

Zeus and Hera.

The king and queen of Olympus.

I gritted my teeth. *So much for Dionysus's wine being a distraction.*

"Well," Zeph murmured just behind me, low enough that only I could hear, "this should be interesting."

I didn't turn. *Interesting* wasn't the word I'd have chosen.

Dangerous.

Catastrophic.

Those felt closer to the mark.

Olympians rarely attended weddings outside the Twelve—especially not Zeus. And Hera, goddess of marriage and family, was even less likely to waste her time on unions she deemed beneath her.

Now...they were here.

Each step they took down the stairs echoed through the chamber, a cadence set to the low rumble of thunder outside, as if the storm were punctuating their arrival. He held his hand out, palm up, and Hera's hand hovered above it—a charged space between them, as if physical touch were a concept they had transcended.

A ripple of murmurs swept through the crowd before breaking into silence. Then, one by one, they fell to their knees in reverence.

I instinctively straightened, drawing Skye closer. My hand found the small of her back, and to my relief, she didn't flinch or pull away. If anything, she leaned into my touch.

She tilted her head up toward me, eyes asking silently: *Do we just stand here?*

I gave the faintest shake of my head. *Stay still. Say nothing.*

As they descended, Zeus's gaze swept the room like a monsoon, pressing down on everyone.

My most devoted attendant, Sara, offered him a golden goblet brimming with ambrosial wine. He accepted it with a flourish of his hand, never sparing her a glance.

But then, his eyes locked onto us—me and Skye.

I'd already secured his approval for the marriage—or what passed for it. He'd been too engrossed in Dionysus's wine to focus.

"Do what you like, boy," he'd said with a wave, never even looking at me.

But now...he was paying attention.

Fuck.

Zeus raised his goblet high, voice booming through the hall with effortless power. "Please...let the bonding continue!" he declared.

A ripple of polite applause followed, but I felt the tension beneath it—stiff, coiled, waiting to snap.

"Tonight, we celebrate a union most...unique," Zeus continued.

It felt less like a celebration and more like the beginning of a test.

"And what better way to honor such an extraordinary moment," he said, the corner of his mouth curving slyly, "than with the blessing of Hera herself?"

I slowly turned my head to Zeph. His eyes moved, and I followed them into the crowd. I found Hymenaeus standing stiffly, a flicker of rage briefly shadowing his features.

Hera...offering the blessing. That was Hymenaeus's domain—for bonds outside the Twelve, for mortals. This was his role. His blessing.

But he didn't protest. Didn't speak.

He simply turned and faded into the crowd.

A low murmur rolled through the hall as the weight of Zeus's words settled. A blessing from Hera...for a mortal. Not even god or a hero. A mortal.

This was—unprecedented.

What the hell was Zeus playing at?

Hera stepped forward, her gaze sweeping over us. She wasn't just looking—she was evaluating, weighing the worth of this union down to the marrow.

I clenched my jaw and forced a smile, nodding in acknowledgment as the guests broke into fresh applause.

Skye stood beside me, spine straight. When I looked at her, she met my eyes. If she was scared, she didn't show it.

Then Zeus's gaze shifted—past me, landing squarely on her.

"And this," he murmured, more to himself than anyone else, "must be the mortal bride-to-be."

I opened my mouth to answer, but before I could speak, Skye stepped forward.

"That's correct," she said, her voice steady.

Both Zeus and I froze for an instant, caught off guard by her boldness. Zeus's brows lifted, his surprise fleeting but evident, replaced by something resembling curiosity. His lips quirked into a small, sardonic smile, as though amused by her nerve.

I felt my pride stir. She hadn't waited for me to shield her. Instead, she'd met the king of the gods on her own terms. It was reckless, dangerous—and utterly intoxicating.

Zeus's lips curved into a smile that didn't quite reach his eyes. He stepped closer, his towering frame casting a shadow over her.

"You're bold," he drawled, the amusement in his voice failing to hide the sharp edge that made my teeth clench.

He reached out a hand—not to touch her, but to gently tuck a stray curl back into place. She froze instantly.

"I hope you're as strong as you are bold, little one. You'll need it."

My hand tightened at the small of her back, trying to tell her in some way...

You're not alone.

Zeus's smile widened as if he'd caught the gesture. "Well," he said, turning back to the altar, "let's not keep Hera waiting."

As we moved, I leaned in, my lips barely grazing Skye's ear. "Do exactly what I do," I whispered. Her body tensed, but she still managed a slow, almost unnoticeable nod.

The altar stood at the far end of the ballroom, elevated for all to witness. Steps wound upward to a stone platform where a single brazier burned at its center—its flames danced in hues of green and purple, casting a flickering light across the polished floor and the towering columns that flanked the space.

Hera waited there, poised and statuesque, her figure framed by the glow of the fire. The scent of burning myrrh curled through the air as the crowd's murmurs fell to silence.

She stepped forward, lifting her hands high. The entire audience hushed as if the palace itself held its breath.

"By the threads of the Fates, by the nectar, and by the blessings of Olympian power," Hera intoned, her voice echoing through the chamber, "I bind two as one."

Two nymphs approached, stepping between Skye and me. They carried a golden, translucent veil, which they carefully draped over us. The sheer fabric shimmered in the firelight, catching the glow like liquid sunlight—pulling us closer, even if my bride might've wished to tear it away.

But she didn't.

Skye stood unflinching beneath it, her hand warm and steady in mine. I had braced for resistance—for trembling fingers—but none came. Instead, her chin lifted, eyes gleaming beneath the veil. No fear. No pleading. She stood before the gods as if reading their destinies, daring them to challenge her.

My little reader—now, unmistakably, *mine.*

Then came the offering.

Hera extended a shallow bowl toward us, resting it in my hands. Inside lay a piece of bread and pool of sacred oil—symbols of sweetness and sustenance, union and endurance.

Skye's eyes darted to mine, questioning, but I gave her no sign of concern. I accepted the bowl from Hera.

I tore the bread and dipped it into the oil. The green liquid rippled with movement, catching the light. Turning to Skye, I met her gaze—and held it—as I lifted the offering between us.

Not blood, I mouthed, exaggerating the words just enough for her to catch them, letting a slow, wicked smile curl my lips.

She scoffed, but her lips parted.

She leaned in and accepted the bread, her mouth brushing my fingertips. The touch was fleeting—yet it seared through me, a jolt of heat sparking straight to my core. Connection. Fire. I searched her eyes, and for a moment, I saw it—a flicker of something that mirrored the fire spreading through me.

Then it was her turn.

Without hesitation, she tore a piece of bread, dipped it in oil, and brought it to my lips. I leaned forward, deliberately letting my mouth graze her fingers as I accepted it, the warm taste of her skin like spiced cider on my tongue. Her breath hitched, but she didn't pull back. Her eyes held mine, daring me to be the first to look away.

Around us, I felt their eyes—but it all fell away.

Until there was only her.

Only us.

Then Hera's voice cut through the silence, the altar fire rising around her.

"The bond is accepted."

Skye turned toward the goddess, her eyes reflecting the brazier's flame, each flicker rivaling its burn. She stood before beings who could end her existence with a second thought...and she didn't shrink away. I didn't know whether to curse her boldness or fall deeper into it.

Gods, I wanted more—I wanted all of her. Her strength. Her words. Her eyes—the way the fire danced in those forget-me-not blues.

She'd agreed to the bond, but she didn't yet understand what it meant—what she had given me. Not fully.

But I would make her see. Make her *feel* it.

And when she did—

When she craved it in return—

There would be no undoing us.

Zeus stepped forward, dragging my attention back. He lifted his hands and placed them gently atop our veiled heads.

"May the Fates continue to weave their threads, and may this bond bring strength, honor, and prosperity to all," he intoned.

The brazier's flame shot upward in response, glowing across every surface.

Applause erupted, a wave of sound echoing off the walls. I turned to Skye.

She stood motionless beneath the veil, cheeks flushed, but her gaze burned with something deeper. Fiercer.

She was a survivor. A fighter.

The clapping began to fade, but the tension in my blood did not. Not even close.

The sacred veil lifted. Skye had barely drawn a full breath before a whirlwind of nymphs descended on her, their laughter like wind chimes in a storm.

They were everywhere at once—silks, flowers, ribbons swirling around her like living confetti. In the space of a heartbeat, they'd swept her away from my side.

"Come, new bride Divine!" one of them called. Another draped a garland of jasmine around Skye's shoulders, tugging her gently forward as petals rained around her like snow.

I took an instinctive step forward, but Skye didn't resist. She let the nymphs lead her toward a corner of the ballroom where their laughter mingled with the music and flowers fell around her, their vibrant colors stark against the polished marble floor.

Though she seemed surprised, she wasn't afraid.

I tracked her until the dancing nymphs obscured her from view, my every instinct on edge. Only then did I feel the presence behind me.

"Zeus," I said, keeping my tone level as I turned to face him. "An unexpected honor to have you here tonight. Do tell—how was I so worthy of Hera's blessing?"

Zeus sipped from his goblet, swirling the liquid as though considering my words. "Does the king of the gods need a reason to bless a bond such as this?" His voice was calm, even amused, but the undercurrent of menace wasn't lost on me.

I kept my expression neutral. "Of course not. Forgive me—it was a generous gesture. I would've just expected both of my parents in attendance for such an occasion." I let the words hang, watching for any crack in his mask. "It's unusual for tradition to be overlooked."

Zeus's smirk faded, his golden goblet lowering slightly. "You should be grateful for my restraint. Consider it a gift that I didn't *insist* on their presence."

The breath stilled in my chest. *A gift.* That's what he called it. As though sparing me from my mother's meddling—and whatever she might've done to Skye—was something I should thank him for.

I forced my voice to stay steady. "Of course," I replied, though the words tasted bitter. "I'm grateful for your consideration."

Zeus's gaze locked on mine—as if deciding whether to punish the edge in my tone. After a moment, he straightened, and a slow, smug smirk curled his mouth.

"You'd do well to enjoy this night," he murmured. "After all...Skye is very special."

The way he said *special*—like he already knew everything about her—made my jaw tighten until my teeth ached.

Before I could respond, Hera appeared beside him, every step poised and regal, as if the floor bowed beneath her heels. She didn't spare Zeus a glance.

"Come," she said—her voice quiet but laced with unmistakable command.

She paused.

"I want to leave this"—a flicker of disgust crossed her face—"place."

The silence that followed landed like a slap.

Zeus chuckled under his breath and cast me a sidelong look.

"Wives," he muttered. "You'll see soon enough, I'm sure."

I bowed, lowering my back in a deep, theatrical curve.

He extended his arm, and Hera took it with the grace of someone enduring poison—her fingers curling slightly, as if bracing for contact.

Then Zeus raised his free hand. A flick of his fingers—

Lightning split the air.

And they were gone.

I didn't move. I just stood there, eyes fixed on the space where they'd vanished.

The tension in my chest didn't ease.

It coiled tighter—like the storm he carried hadn't truly left, only changed shape.

Without turning, I tilted my head slightly, my voice pitched low—meant for one ear alone.

"Zeph," I murmured. "Be watchful tonight."

The air shifted at once. A subtle brush of wind ghosted past my ear—Zeph's answer. Silent. Assured. He'd heard me.

I lingered at the threshold, eyes catching on a lone figure slipping into the night's embrace.

Skye.

Her silhouette moved through the moonlight, and I followed, drawn to her like the tide to the moon.

I stepped onto the balcony, the crisp night air scented with the faint perfume of the gardens below. Skye stood at the railing, her back to me. My gaze caught on the embroidery of her gown, shimmering with jasmine petals as it flowed down the elegant curve of her spine.

I didn't move. Not at first.

I watched.

And in that stillness, she looked like she belonged—like the stars had carved out this world just for her. The wind toyed with the loose strands of her hair, lifting them gently, and her breathing rose and fell in rhythm with the hush of the night.

She wasn't running.

When I stepped forward, it was slow—each footfall quiet against the obsidian stones that gleamed under the moon's pale glow. She didn't turn, but I saw the faint twitch of her fingers curling tighter around the cold metal of the railing.

She knew I was there.

And she didn't pull away.

"Escaping the nymphs already?" I asked, half-teasing as I came to stand beside her.

Skye glanced over her shoulder, the corner of her mouth curving into a smirk.

"I didn't realize bonding came with such...*enthusiastic* guests."

A low chuckle rumbled in my chest.

"I wonder—was it the nymphs you were fleeing, or were you testing the boundaries of this bond? Not that I'd mind chasing you. I'd enjoy it, actually."

Her smile vanished.

She turned to face me fully, her eyes sharp.

"Testing boundaries?" she echoed, voice cold. "You think I'd waste time running from you?"

She laughed—a short, bitter sound.

"You cursed me. And now you've bound me. Why would I choose to run? I'm already caught." Her voice cracked on the last word, anger warring with something quieter, more uncertain.

My hands clenched at my sides.

"You still have choices," I replied, stepping closer, letting the heat between us build. "And you made one. You stayed. You're here."

Her laugh came again, harsher this time.

"I stayed because I need to break the curse," she snapped.

But her gaze lingered—too long for someone only seeking escape.

She stepped closer, craning her neck to meet my gaze. "Don't mistake desperation for a choice," she said, her voice strained as if holding back her anger. "I don't belong to you, no matter what this bond says."

I didn't move. I held her stare, the fire in her eyes dragging me under. I leaned in, close enough to steal the next breath from her lips. Her composure slipped.

My voice dropped to a growl.

"You can tell yourself that. That it's only the curse keeping you here." I tilted my head, just enough for her breath to catch. "But you know better. And I plan to show you exactly what you do to me."

Her head snapped toward the horizon. She gripped the railing like it was the only thing keeping her grounded.

My eyes followed the curve of her neck, the flutter of her pulse beneath skin I had to resist tasting.

I eased back—barely.

"Skye," I murmured, saying her name like a caress.

She froze.

She heard it—the way I said her name—like it was mine to claim, like it belonged in my mouth, whispered against her throat in the space between breath and desire. Her grip on the railing loosened. She turned to meet my gaze.

And this time, it wasn't anger staring back.

It was a flicker. A crack in the fortress she'd built around herself, and I saw it. I wanted more of it. Again and again. I wanted to watch her choose me—not because she was bound, but because she wanted to. Even if that choice came wrapped in fury and fire.

"I'll keep my word," I said softly. "I won't force anything on you. All I ask is that you stay—at least until you've received the nectar."

She didn't answer, but her eyes didn't leave mine. Her shoulders tensed, then softened just slightly. Her breathing quickened. Her lips parted—just enough to draw my gaze, to test every shred of restraint I had left.

My fingers twitched against the wrought iron, fighting the urge to close the space between us. To reach for her. To claim what some part of me already considered mine.

I leaned in.

She didn't move.

Just one touch. Just one—

"Cullen."

Harmony's voice cut through the moment like shattered glass, splintering the heat between us into jagged shards. Skye startled, stepping back. I felt the rupture like a snap in my chest, the sudden severing of something that had just begun to take shape. Her walls slammed back into place.

I turned, jaw clenched, fighting the growl rising in my throat.

Harmony stood at the balcony's edge, tension etched into every line of her frame.

She wasn't alone.

Zeph.

And beside them—Hermes.

He hovered in the night, winged sandals beating the air, as if untouched by the weight of the world. One of the Twelve. A messenger of Olympus. In his hands, he carried a small box wrapped in black silk ribbon.

"I bring a message," Hermes said, his voice smooth and glinting like a blade.

He held out the box.

"From Phobos and Deimos."

My instincts flared. I didn't move at first.

Hermes drifted forward, package outstretched, as if he didn't care what it contained—or what it might mean.

I took it slowly, every muscle taut. The box was light.

Zeph and Harmony drew closer.

Their wariness said what none of us voiced.

Phobos and Deimos.

It could've been anything in that box—a message, a threat, a severed head.

I slipped the ribbon free.

The silk fell like a whisper to the obsidian floor.

I lifted the lid, and on top was a glossy card: *For our Skye.*

I moved the card aside, my eyes fixed on the contents nestled in a bed of black satin.

A pair of golden scissors.

My eyes trailed the long blades.

At the pivot where they met, a serpent devoured its own tail—an ouroboros—cast in the metal. Its eyes were tiny rubies, glinting like embers in the night, locked in an eternal cycle of creation and destruction.

The scissors of the Fates.

A cold fury settled in my chest, my hand crumpling the message. For Phobos and Deimos to possess these...

Harmony's hand found my arm. "Cullen," she murmured, her voice steady. "Don't."

I could feel a vein on the verge of bursting, the pressure sharp behind my temple.

I looked at Skye. She didn't know what was happening, couldn't see what was inside.

I turned back to the box.

"They think they can threaten her?" My voice dropped to a growl, low and dangerous. "Then they'll get their war."

CHAPTER SEVENTEEN

SKYE

Why was it so loud?

I stumbled through the crowd, gasping for air as faceless figures crushed in around me.

Too close. Too close.

"You thought you could escape this, didn't you?" a voice hissed above me.

I snapped my head up, but the mass of bodies only pressed tighter. Phobos and Deimos emerged from the shadows, their long fingers stretching toward me.

"You are marked, Skye," Phobos breathed, his voice echoing everywhere and nowhere at once.

I shoved forward, desperate, but the floor rippled beneath me—tiles melting into quicksand. My feet sank. A scream tore from my throat but made no sound.

And then I was falling.

I hit hard. No sound, no breath. Just silence.

Cullen's palace.

My stomach lurched as I staggered to my feet. The grand halls were fractured, chandeliers dripping molten gold that sizzled and spat against the warped checkerboard floor. Vines crawled across the walls like veins of a dying beast. Death itself felt alive.

"Home sweet home," Phobos sneered, his words sliding into my ears like oil.

I staggered back—and collided with something solid.

Relief sparked hot in my chest as I spun and saw him.

Cullen.

But when my eyes lifted to his—my relief froze. His eyes were black. Not just the pupils. All of it—his entire eye swallowed in darkness.

Behind him, his white wings stretched wide, but streaks of dark green marred the feathers. I could see the edges fraying, the rot spreading slowly from the tips inward, like spilled ink bleeding across paper.

"Cullen," I whispered, reaching for him. "Please..."

He didn't move. Didn't even look at me.

"Even he can't save you," Deimos snarled.

A flash of lightning ripped through the room—a bolt of searing white.

And then Phobos and Deimos lunged.

Sunlight hit my face, blinding me as I jolted upright. I gasped, trying to find a rhythm to my breath, but the scream from my nightmare was still lodged in my throat. I grabbed my chest, fingers digging into the silk of my shirt as I pressed a trembling hand over my heart. I pounded it, trying to numb the phantom sensations still clinging to me.

It wasn't real.

But it had felt so—

I squeezed my eyes shut, willing the memory away. My hands shook as I exhaled slowly, forcing my body to calm down. The oxygen helped. I felt it grounding me.

When I opened my eyes again, my gaze dropped—drawn to the soft gleam resting against my chest.

The necklace.

Cullen's arrowhead.

Its silver point was a comforting warmth against my skin, like a cup of tea on a rainy autumn day. It felt like a shield over my heart that the nightmare couldn't touch—and that alone made me feel safe.

A faint hum emanated from the silver, a low vibration I felt when I ran a fingertip along its edge. It was the same subtle energy I'd felt from the crystals at Mystic Soulstice.

My eyes started to blur.

My shop. My home.

It had only been three days, but when I closed my eyes, washed-out images appeared as if they were someone else's memories. And when I opened them, I was here. In Cullen's palace. I kept repeating that fact in my head, trying to convince myself this was real. That this was mine now.

My golden cage.

Well, it certainly earned the name. The bed alone could've housed a family of four.

I swung my legs over the edge and let out a shaky breath. Somehow, all my things had found their way here.

How I missed the simplicity of jeans and T-shirts. The gown I'd worn during the bonding ceremony, stunning as it was, made me feel like a prized exhibit. Finding my own clothes tucked neatly inside a carved wardrobe had been the first moment of real relief I'd felt in days—like getting back a tiny piece of myself.

I stood and moved toward the vanity. There, on top of a stack of books I'd planned to read months ago, rested the deck of tarot cards Lydia had given me years ago—as if she'd always known I'd need them.

I reached for the deck, searching for any kind of guidance. I pulled a single card, letting it fall faceup onto the vanity with a whisper of paper on wood.

The Tower.

On the card, a stone tower split down the middle by a jagged lightning bolt. Flames licked from the windows, and tiny figures tumbled headfirst into the void below. The card meant sudden upheaval, destruction, and forced transformation. Basically, my life was tearing apart.

"Yeah," I muttered to myself. "That tracks."

For three days, I'd unraveled any sense of normalcy I'd managed to cling to.

The memory of the bonding ceremony clung to me like a virus I hadn't shaken. Standing before...gods—I was still processing their existence. My legs had trembled beneath the folds of my dress, and if Cullen hadn't been holding me, my knees would've surely given out.

His hand had warmed mine during the ceremony, and now, here I was, bound to him.

I'd expected something to happen after Hera proclaimed us bonded. I'm not sure what—maybe I'd be able to read his mind, or my eyes would change from blue to gold. But nothing. I'd willed myself to feel something, to sense the connection, but all it did was twist my emotions into knots. I wasn't sure if that was the bond or just me.

No...I shook my head. I'd felt this way even before the bond. Maybe it was the arrow, or his power as the god of love and desire. Because the desire was certainly there...

When he'd said my name.

Skye.

The way he said it—curling around each syllable as though he were tasting it. The sound reverberated through me, and for the first time, my name didn't feel like mine until it came from his lips.

His eyes pinned me in place, seeing every hidden thought, every doubt, every trembling piece of my soul. He saw it all—and he didn't look away.

He stepped closer, his hand brushing near mine, close enough to feel the heat radiating from his skin. The chill of the air couldn't touch me, not with him that close. My heart raced, each beat pounding like a slow, heavy bass note, and I knew he could hear it.

And then he'd leaned in.

His gaze flicked to my lips. My thoughts scattered, every rational part of me gone. I didn't move away. If anything, I'd leaned closer, drawn to him like water to a parched earth.

Then the spell shattered.

If someone hadn't interrupted, I wasn't sure what I would've done—or worse, what I would've let him do.

I slapped my cheeks lightly, trying to shake off the thought. *Get a grip,* I told myself. *He's the reason you're in this mess in the first place.*

I exhaled slowly. Fresh air. I needed fresh air.

Pulling on a simple pair of dark jeans and fitted black tank top, I tied my hair into a tight ponytail, keeping it away from my face. Changing my clothes made me feel a little more in control, even if everything else felt like chaos. As I leaned over to lace my boots, the weight of my necklace hovered in the air, reminding me of its previous owner.

It didn't matter how confused I felt about Cullen. He wasn't around—and hadn't been since the moment we were bonded.

Ever since...some god had handed him a strange box.

The moment Cullen opened it, his face went stone-cold. His fingers curled around the edges of the lid before he snapped it shut. I didn't see what was inside, but his reaction said more than enough.

I could almost *see* the anger radiating off him—like heatwaves, like a color I didn't have a name for. And I didn't read auras.

Since then, the study doors—slammed shut.
Him—gone.
Just me.
Just me here, in this place I don't understand.
And my brain—hell, my brain won't stop:
Fuck Cullen for leaving me here.
What was in that box...?
Fuck Cullen.
That box.
Fuck.
Cullen.
Box.
Cullen.
Fuck.

I BARELY STEPPED out of my room before coming face-to-face with a bright-eyed nymph.

She stood in the hallway like she'd been waiting for me—slim and petite, with short blonde hair streaked with green, cut into a pixie style that shimmered in the high-window light. Slightly pointed ears peeked through the strands. I froze, startled for half a second, until recognition clicked.

"Sara," she said, offering the name like a gentle reminder.

But I knew her name. I was surprisingly good at names and faces—it used to annoy my sisters that I could remember guests at our parents' parties when they couldn't. And Sara wasn't exactly forgettable; she had this distinct energy, sharp and bright. What I didn't know was if she was here as Cullen's spy.

So I just nodded.

Sara smiled as if nothing about this was awkward. "Divine Cullen will be in his study today. You're free to explore the palace and grounds as you wish."

I nodded again.

As if pleased by my stellar communication skills, she clasped her hands and gave a graceful bow. "Divine Skye, do you require anything presently?"

"Divine?" I repeated, lifting a brow. "Just Skye is fine. And no, I'm good...but thanks."

She smiled warmly. "Divine is the proper term of respect for gods and goddesses. And while you're not yet a goddess, you are bonded to one—so the title still applies. But if you insist...Skye, it is."

She did this, I noticed—dropping little tidbits about the world I'd been thrown into. Who the gods were. The Olympians—the Twelve. Like a governess training me to be queen. Only she clearly hadn't gotten the memo: once I got the nectar, I was gone.

I started walking, and she fell into step beside me as we moved down the corridor, her presence so light it almost reminded me of a fairy. "The kitchen staff has just finished preparing fresh bread," she said conversationally, her voice lilting like wind chimes. "And the rose garden is more vibrant than ever. It's quite the sight, if you feel like visiting."

Her cheerful updates washed over me, barely registering as I moved on autopilot through the corridors. My body kept walking, but my mind was somewhere else entirely.

When we turned a corner and Cullen's study came into view, my steps faltered.

The grand doors loomed ahead. My pulse quickened.

I'd been told I could explore the palace freely, but what would I even say if I walked in there? Every time I passed by, I'd only seen attendants moving in and out—quick, quiet. Once or twice, I'd glimpsed Zeph slipping through the doors. He'd smile, calm as ever, like nothing was wrong, but he never stopped. Not a word.

"Skye?" Sara's gentle voice pulled me back.

I blinked and looked over at her. Her wide eyes were bright with curiosity, though she said nothing—just waited.

"Sorry," I murmured, forcing a smile. "You were saying?"

I turned away from the study and kept walking, heading toward the wing where Euryale was still being cared for. Sara resumed her updates with the same soft energy, trailing beside me like a breeze.

Still, I couldn't help but glance over my shoulder, back toward those doors.

Whatever Cullen was doing in there, I hoped it had nothing to do with me.

Because now, the countdown to the nectar had begun.

Even after just a few days, I'd started forming a routine. Routine was good. Keep things mundane—though calling anything about this place ordinary felt like a stretch. The palace was vast, so massive I doubted even months would be enough to explore it all.

A sigh slipped out of me. *Months*. I'd be here until the winter solstice.

For all its beauty, the palace felt eerily empty. My footsteps echoed through the halls, and somehow the silence here was louder than any solitary confinement.

Most of my time was spent with Euryale. Helping the nymphs care for her gave me something to hold onto. Her condition had improved—breathing steadier, skin less pale—and just yesterday, I'd even seen the faintest flicker of her fingers. The nymphs whispered excitedly that she could wake at any moment.

Marnie, of course, had made herself at home by Euryale's side. She was curled up on the edge of the bed, her content purrs blending with the soft murmurs of the nymphs as they worked. They were absolutely smitten with her, taking turns feeding her bits of fish or stroking her fur. Marnie, ever the opportunist, basked in the attention.

I found myself slipping into their rhythm, my hands moving instinctively as I helped prepare herbs for Euryale's care. Their work was meticulous, almost poetic, as they crushed leaves and mixed them into pastes.

It reminded me of my days in the shop, blending teas and herbal remedies with Lydia. I could almost hear her voice—steady and warm—walking me through each step, just like she always did.

"Gentle pressure, Skye," she would say, her hands over mine, guiding. "You want the oils, not the pulp."

I traced the edge of a rosemary sprig between my fingers, its sharp, earthy scent cutting through the cloud of memory. My chest tightened at the thought of Mystic Soulstice...and Lydia's apartment. Sara had said the day after the ceremony that she would have news soon, but how long would that take?

I wiped my hands on a cloth and glanced toward the grand doors leading back into the palace. A sigh escaped my lips.

I needed a walk.

Leaving the room, I wandered through the vast halls until I stepped onto one of the many balconies scattered throughout the palace. The warm summer breeze felt amazing. *I'll have to thank Zeph later.* I leaned against the cool iron railing, letting the wind swirl my hair out of my face.

A soft bumping sound drew my attention downward. A window stood slightly ajar, nudging rhythmically against the wall across the courtyard.

I froze.

Through the window, Cullen stood at a large table. His hands gripped the edges, the veins in his forearms standing out as his muscles tensed. He leaned over, studying something with razor-sharp focus.

The breeze caught in his hair, tousling it just enough to make him look ruggedly disheveled. His sharp jawline, kissed by the golden light of the setting sun, drew my gaze down the curve of his neck and the way his shirt clung just a little too well to his frame.

Fuck. He's attractive. And he knows I know he is.

I hadn't expected to feel anything but pure rage. After all, he'd been a ghost since the bonding ceremony, locking himself away like I didn't exist. But now...

As if sensing my gaze, Cullen turned.

Panicking, I ducked—crouching behind a tall potted plant near the balcony's edge. My heart raced as I pressed my back against the cool ceramic, cursing myself for being utterly ridiculous. *What am I doing? He's going to think I've been spying on him.*

"Don't be ridiculous," I muttered, shaking my head.

I waited a few seconds, then dared to peek over the planter. My gaze darted back to the window, but he was gone.

The room beyond was empty now, the breeze catching the edge of a paper on the table where he'd stood moments before. I lingered for a beat, unsure whether I felt relief or disappointment.

With a huff, I straightened and leaned back against the planter, letting the breeze wash over me again. Whatever he was doing wasn't my concern—or at least, that's what I was going to tell myself.

I stepped off the balcony, cheeks still warm. *Hiding behind a potted plant—really?* I shut the glass door behind me and smoothed my palms over my jeans, trying to shake off what I'd just done like a sour taste in my mouth.

A blur of motion—and suddenly, I wasn't alone anymore.

My back hit the cool wall, and before I could react, his arms caged me in, braced on either side of my head.

My breath caught as I tilted my chin up to face him. And gods help me, I wasn't prepared. He was even more devastating up close.

"Enjoying the view?" His voice was low and teasing, lips curving into a slow smirk that felt like a challenge.

I swallowed hard, my mouth suddenly dry. "No...and what—what are you doing?" I managed, though it came out more jumbled than intended.

"Checking on you," he said smoothly, as if pinning me to a wall were the most natural thing in the world. His gaze flicked over me, lingering in a way that made my skin heat. "You've been exploring, haven't you?"

"You've been spying on me?" I shot back, my pulse hammering.

"Observing," he corrected, his voice a near purr. "And I've noticed a few things," he added casually. "Like the way you keep finding excuses to wander near my study. Hoping to see me, were you?"

The nerve. The sheer arrogance. I glared at him, determined to hold my ground—even though his proximity was doing all kinds of inconvenient things to my brain.

"Narcissist," I muttered, though the bite I meant to have came out more like a breathless accusation.

His smirk deepened. He leaned in, his voice brushing my cheek like a secret.

"Sorry—no relation to *that* Narcissus," he murmured. "I don't waste time staring at my own reflection"—his gaze flicked pointedly to my lips—"not when there's something far more tempting standing in front of me."

My brain short-circuited.

"And unlike him," he said, almost as an afterthought, "I know how to give as *well* as receive."

My knees felt weak.

"Let me go," I demanded, but the words lacked the conviction I needed—they came out far less convincing than I'd hoped.

He didn't budge. Instead, he angled closer, chest brushing mine in the faintest touch that somehow felt like a spark set loose under my skin. I shifted, trying to duck beneath his arm, but he moved effortlessly, cutting me off in a single fluid step.

"Tsk, tsk." His tongue clicked, amused, like he'd expected me to try.

That amusement lit his eyes, gold flecks catching like fire, and my cheeks flared hotter the longer he looked. His smirk deepened, head tilting, one brow lifting in a silent dare for me to try again.

He was so...so infuriating.

"Why are you here?" I snapped.

"What do you mean...little reader?" His voice slowed, tongue tracing the edge of his open lips.

I groaned. "Why do you call me that?"

"You read my palms the first night we met. I haven't forgotten." His voice dipped lower, arrogance radiating off him like heat. "Neither have you."

Heat shot up my neck. "You've been gone three days."

His brow arched; he actually had the nerve to look surprised. "Have... have you been counting?"

"Yes," I seethed. "Like a jail sentence. Nectar should be down to...what, a hundred and eighty days?"

I expected anger, but instead, he exhaled slowly, the warmth of his breath brushing my skin and drawing an involuntary arch from me. "You're not my prisoner." His voice softened, but his body still caged me in, holding me just as captive as his words. His gaze lingered on my mouth before returning to my eyes. "Tell me how to convince you of that."

My breath quickened, my chest rising against his. He was too close—close enough I couldn't look away. I could see every fleck of gold swirling in his irises, like glitter suspended in a snow globe.

And then there was his mouth—

If he kissed me right now...

"Cullen," I breathed—quieter now, almost a warning, almost a plea.

"Yes...?" he drawled, all smug confidence, like he knew *exactly* what he was doing to me.

I shook my head, trying to steady myself, trying to cool the heat rising in waves beneath my skin. My hands came up, pressed lightly against his chest—I debated whether to use whatever strength I had to push him away...or not use any at all.

His body was solid under my palms, his thin shirt doing nothing to hide the muscle beneath. It was practically decorative at this point.

He groaned softly at my touch, the sound rough in his throat. His lips dipped dangerously close to my temple—so close I could feel the whisper of his breath against my skin.

Closer...closer...closer—

Then, air.

Cullen leaned back with visible effort—just enough to meet my eyes.

"Have dinner with me."

It wasn't a question.

"What...?" I asked, thrown off by the sudden shift.

"Dinner," he said again, stepping back to give me room to breathe. "Tonight."

Before I could argue—or say something I might regret—he turned and walked away, leaving me still pressed against the wall.

Gods help me. What have I gotten myself into?

CHAPTER EIGHTEEN

SKYE

I stood with my back to the full-length mirror, hands on my hips, surveying the battlefield of fabric strewn across the room. Dresses, skirts, blouses—hell, even a pair of sweats—were draped over every available surface like my closet had straight-up exploded. I sighed, eyeing the wreckage before dragging my attention back to my reflection.

"What am I even doing?" I muttered.

"Have dinner with me," Cullen had said.

After days of silence and secrets, now he suddenly wanted to talk? Over dinner? The pure, unbelievable audacity.

Part of me wanted to go—throw on sweats, act like it was nothing, and demand answers. Answers like what was in that damn box that turned him into a self-imposed recluse.

But another part—the one currently elbow-deep in a pile of little black dresses—was far less logical.

I shifted off the heap, a dress slipping to the floor as I did. Snatching it up by the hanger, I held it out. Red. The shade of matte lipstick, cut low at the neckline with a slit that climbed scandalously high. Lydia had given it to me for my twenty-first birthday, right after my boyfriend dumped me because, apparently, I tempted men with my revealing clothes; I should be ashamed.

Lydia had laughed and, quite graphically, told me exactly where she'd like to shove his shame. *People get to dress however the hell they want*, she'd said. *We are not responsible for anyone else's emotions about it.*

It was by far one of the most daring outfits I owned. But daring...sexy... that felt dangerous.

My fingers traced the fabric, and my mind betrayed me. Suddenly, it wasn't me holding the dress—it was Cullen's hands. One slid firm against my hip, nails grazing my side, while the other drifted lower, slipping through the slit to coax my leg up, pinning me against him.

I swallowed hard, dragging myself out of the fantasy as heat coiled low in my stomach. Dangerous. Definitely dangerous. *What the hell was wrong with me?*

I paced the room. Sure, Cullen was infuriating, arrogant, and entirely too full of himself.

But he was also...captivating.

The memory of him leaning over the table flashed in my mind—the way his muscles flexed, the quiet strength in his arms. Arms that looked more than capable of holding me. Positioning me...

I shook my head. *No. Stop. Bad idea.*

And still...the thought of testing his self-control sent a thrill racing down my spine. His image lingered, taunting, as I reached for the red dress.

If Cullen wanted to play games, maybe I'd play, too.

I slipped into the dress. Smooth material glided over my skin, hugging every curve just right. I adjusted the slit a little higher—just enough to make someone wonder if I was wearing anything beneath.

I wasn't.

Not in a dress like this.

Then I reached for the chain and centered the arrowhead between my breasts. Cold metal. His curse. *His.*

I wouldn't deny that there was something between us. Heat. Chemistry. Lust. I felt all of it.

And he felt it, too—the way he looked at me, like he wanted to devour me with every breath I took.

But that didn't mean I wasn't still angry, or confused about everything I'd gotten myself tangled in.

I caught my reflection in the mirror and held my own gaze.

I didn't have to go. I could let him sit there, brooding and gorgeous, waiting for me all night.

But the thought of showing up—of seeing his face, of watching him fight to hold on to his restraint when he saw me in this dress?

Yeah...way too tempting.

And anyway, I had questions. Like what was in that damn box.

That's why I'm going.

Yes.

Just a fact-finding mission.

In heels.

"Okay, Cullen," I murmured to my reflection, running my hands over the soft fabric with a little more pressure than necessary. "I want answers."

The corners of my lips curved as I tilted my head, taking in every line of my body.

Let's see who ends up on top tonight.

My mind, traitorously, painted it clearly—me straddling his lap, dress hiked up, his hands locked around my thighs, guiding me as I rode him slow and relentless, over and over, until neither of us remembered who we even were.

Fuck. I needed to get laid, apparently.

I shook my head and slipped into the quiet halls of the palace, my heels clicking softly. The sound echoed faintly. Normally, I would eat alone in an empty dining hall, Sara coming in now and then.

But tonight would be different.

Each step toward the dining hall felt as though something was guiding me toward it.

I smoothed the fabric of my dress one last time. Taking a steadying breath, I straightened my shoulders and fixed my gaze ahead. Whatever awaited me tonight, I was ready.

Or at least, that's what I told myself.

Then I took another step, and the stillness shattered.

Music.

The sound swelled as I drew closer, and when I reached the dining hall, I froze in the doorway.

Cullen stood before the open balcony, bathed in starlight. The curtains behind him moved lazily in the breeze, swaying in time with the music he coaxed from the strings. His violin—carved from dark, elegant wood—gleamed under the soft evening glow.

My eyes tracked the serenity with which he guided the bow, as if the instrument were simply an extension of himself.

He looked...breathtaking. His blond hair fell slightly into his face, his shirt unbuttoned at the collar, and his sleeves rolled up to reveal muscular forearms that flexed with each motion. His eyes were half-closed, as if lost in the melody.

I listened. Cullen curled around the neck of the violin, his fingers pressing firmly, knuckles tightening as though each note physically pained him. Every vibration reverberated through the room—through me—filling spaces I hadn't realized were hollow. His wrist flicked, sharp, the bow slicing at an angle that sent the pitch climbing high—so piercing it lodged in my chest like his arrow had. Then he drew back, coaxing the strings into something softer, lower...a sound that felt unbearably alone.

The way he played, it was almost as if the music *knew* me.

A tear slipped down my cheek. Why did this feel like it reflected more than any mirror ever could? I brushed it away quickly.

Without thinking, I stepped forward, my heels tapping softly against the floor. The faint sound must've caught his attention—because his bow faltered, the melody breaking, and he finally stilled.

"You don't have to stop," I said, the words slipping out before I could second-guess them.

Cullen paused, his brows lifting slightly as surprise flickered across his face.

"Thank you, but the main guest has arrived," he replied smoothly, setting the violin and bow down on a nearby table with meticulous care.

As he stepped back, his hands moved to his sleeves, slowly rolling them back down in a way that seemed second nature.

I swallowed hard, heat rising to my cheeks as I forced my gaze past him, pretending to study the room instead of the man standing in the center of it. But I wasn't fast enough. Cullen's eyes tracked me—starting at the delicate straps of my dress and trailing all the way down. His smirk deepened, and I realized this might've backfired. Badly. I was more affected than he was, and he knew it.

I crossed my arms, a flimsy shield against his gaze. But it was too late

—he'd already taken in every detail. The flicker of amusement in his eyes told me so.

"The food should be prepared soon," he added, his gaze lingering, as though daring me to admit that I'd noticed—and cared—about the way he looked at me.

I shook myself free of the thought and let my eyes drift toward the long table stretching endlessly before me. A pristine white runner flowed down the center of the dark oak, embroidered with delicate gold threads that shimmered under the lantern light above.

Stepping closer, my fingers brushed the surface. The carved patterns swirled and twisted along the wood, resembling vines and leaves, as if the garden itself had been captured and etched into the table.

Out of the corner of my eye, I caught Cullen adjusting the polished silverware, even though it already looked perfectly placed.

Was he...nervous?

Cullen stopped and motioned toward a chair near one end, pulling it out. His eyes flicked to mine, expectant, patient.

I hesitated—but eventually slid into the seat and nodded my thanks.

He lingered for a moment, his hand brushing the back of the chair as he pushed it in just slightly—then turned and walked to the opposite end of the long table.

To sit, I presumed.

Apparently not.

Before I could fully settle in, Cullen reached for what looked like an absurdly heavy chair and carried it across the space like it weighed nothing. He set it down beside me—close.

I blinked at him, confused. He just leaned back in his seat, entirely unbothered.

"I don't follow customary rules," he explained, like it was a fact so obvious he rarely had to say it aloud. As if pretending to be bound by anyone's expectations had never once occurred to him.

Before I could respond, Sara and the other nymphs appeared, gliding in and filling up wine glasses, bringing trays of food that made my stomach rumble at just the sight of it. Dishes were placed delicately before us—seared meats, roasted vegetables, and warm, fragrant bread.

I took a bite and nearly groaned. The flavor was rich, warm, and dangerously addictive. Every meal here had made me taste things I never thought were possible, and I was starting to suspect I'd need to size up my entire wardrobe if I stayed much longer.

But tonight, I was having a harder time enjoying the damn meal.

Every time I lifted my fork, every time food touched my tongue, Cullen's eyes followed the movement as he sipped his wine. It was like the act of my eating was something he had the right to study. Or savor.

Fine. He wanted to play games?

Game on.

I shifted in my seat, stretching. My arms rose slightly as if to adjust my hair, the movement causing the neckline of my dress to dip just enough to hint at the curve of my collarbone. I leaned back slightly, crossing my legs under the table in a slow motion that made the slit in my dress part just a little further.

I knew exactly what I was doing—and judging by the way Cullen's gaze darkened, so did he. His hand stilled on his wineglass, knuckles tightening just enough to betray his restraint.

I remained calm, determined not to let him see the effect he had on me. But...he did have an effect on me. A prickle of heat spread across the back of my neck, and I felt a single bead of sweat trail down between my breasts.

I straightened in my chair, angling my head, pretending indifference —or at least faking it well enough to make him believe I could.

"So," I began, swirling the wine in my glass like I wasn't trying to redirect the heat crawling up my spine, "you play violin?"

My tone was casual. Neutral. As if the question wasn't a desperate attempt to steer us away from the way he'd been looking at me.

Cullen's mouth twitched. "Yes," he said smoothly, leaning back just enough to look casual—and completely in control. "I enjoy activities where I can use my fingers."

I nearly choked.

The wine hit the back of my throat wrong, and I had to fight to swallow it down without coughing up my dignity. My cheeks flared, heat rising fast, and I set the glass down with a little more force than I meant to. "Good for you," I muttered, voice slightly hoarse, still recovering from almost dying via innuendo.

Unbothered, Cullen reached for the bottle and refilled my glass. "Careful," he murmured, low and teasing. "At this rate, we'll run out of wine."

I forced a small, close-lipped smile, lifting my glass again like I wasn't two seconds from combusting. Like I hadn't just imagined those fingers on something...else.

"What were you playing?" I asked quickly, feeling steadier once the wine touched my lips again.

Cullen swirled his practically empty glass slowly. "Not something constructed by a mortal, if that's what you mean."

"You wrote it yourself?" I said, surprised.

He paused mid-swirl, his eyes flicking up to mine before a half-smile curved his mouth. "Any feedback?"

I tried not to look too impressed, feigning thought instead. "It was..." I let the word hang, then added, "You said you could feel desires—and the lack of them. Was that what you were playing? Someone's loneliness?"

For once, Cullen was silent. No teasing comeback. He looked at me as if in a game of hide-and-seek, I had found him just as the game began.

I smirked, satisfied.

I was right.

"Something like that," he finally answered, reaching for the now mostly empty wine bottle and refilling his glass. He then leaned forward slightly, resting an elbow on the table. "Do you play an instrument?"

The question caught me off guard; I could almost feel the genuineness in his voice.

I let my fingers trail along the cool stem of the glass, stalling. "No," I admitted, giving a small shrug. "I took piano lessons when I was younger, but stopped."

His brow arched. "Why?"

I shifted in my seat, the question stirring something I hadn't expected. "My parents didn't see much value in it for me," I replied, my voice softening. "They preferred I smiled pretty for pageants instead."

The words slipped out more easily than I meant them to. I hadn't thought about that in years. But just mentioning it brought back the sharp scent of hairspray and metallic taste of lipstick.

Cullen's expression darkened. His jaw clenched, tongue pressing to his cheek like he was biting something back. "They made you stop doing something you enjoyed...just to parade you around like a doll?" He said *doll* like poison leaving his mouth.

I blinked, surprised by his intensity. "It wasn't a big deal," I said quickly, brushing it off. "Lots of kids stop lessons. And it's not like I was any good."

His gaze cut through that flimsy excuse like a blade. "That doesn't make it right," he growled. "You deserved better than that. They should've supported you—encouraged you. Not used you for their shallow image."

I stared at him.

Maybe it was the wine, or maybe I was just buzzed on the fact that he actually listened—not just heard me, but *saw* me.

I found myself leaning in, just slightly, caught in the gravity of him.

But then came the soft shuffle of footsteps—an interruption wrapped in silver trays and sweet smells.

The nymphs returned, placing a polished platter in front of me. One of them lifted the lid with a flourish, revealing an array of decadent desserts, each more extravagant than the last. But I barely registered them.

My eyes landed on it.

Chocolate mousse. Dark and glossy, topped with a perfect swirl of cream.

Before I could stop myself, my fingers curled around my spoon, reaching for it.

"Your favorite," Cullen said smoothly, as if impressed with himself. "Regarding my recent absence, I see now that it was...an oversight. One that will be rectified immediately."

I froze, spoon hovering midair. My gaze snapped to him. "What?"

He leaned back slightly, the faintest smile tugging at his mouth. "I make it my business to know your favorites."

Heat crept up my neck. I narrowed my eyes. "Oh, so you think getting my favorite dessert makes everything just...go away?"

"Hmm." He tilted his head. Setting his glass down, his fingers traced the rim in a lazy circle, the faint hum resonating between us.

"I see you require more groveling," he murmured, his voice dipping lower, the corner of his mouth tugging upward. "Shall I feed you the mousse on my knees, little reader?"

Clank.

The head of my spoon hit the plate, my fingers still gripping the handle. I forced my gaze back to the glossy swirl of chocolate, rolling my eyes as if the gesture might cover the heat burning in my cheeks. No way was I giving him the satisfaction.

"And what?" I shot back, recovering. "You don't do dessert? Is that above someone like you?"

He lounged deeper into his chair, utterly relaxed. "Desserts are not above gods. I simply don't like sweets."

"You don't like sweets?" My brow arched. "You do realize you're basically the mascot of Valentine's Day, right?"

I twirled the spoon in front of him with mock flourish. "Wait, wait, let me guess...you're already *sweet* enough."

Oh yeah. I was definitely drunk.

I blinked, momentarily stunned, as his entire face lit up. A rare, genuine smile curved his lips, dimples appearing on either side of his mouth like an ambush. Unfairly attractive. And for a second, I forgot whatever clever thing I was supposed to say.

"Well," he said, his laugh fading but the warmth lingering in his expression, "you can have my share."

I rolled my eyes but didn't argue. *Gladly*.

"I don't know if I can be bonded to someone who doesn't like sweets," I teased, reaching for the mousse.

But before I could take a bite, his hand shot out—fast.

Fingers curled around mine, firm but careful.

He guided the spoon to his mouth in one smooth motion, lips parting as he slipped the mousse in.

His gaze never left mine.

My breath caught.

The way his tongue dragged slowly over the edge of the spoon, flicking it just so, made me think of a nature documentary—the kind where a flower blooms in slow motion.

My flower was definitely blooming.

And still, like an idiot, I clung to the spoon.

Cullen's smirk deepened.

His fingers lingered, brushing against mine before finally pulling away.

He leaned back with lazy confidence, placing a finger to his lips. His tongue darted out, slow and unapologetic, to catch the last trace of mousse at the corner of his mouth.

"You know..." he drawled. "This is payback."

Payback?

Cullen didn't give me time to ask. "You didn't wear that dress just for dinner."

He leaned forward slightly, elbows resting on the table as his eyes swept over me—undressing me with a look. "You wore it for *me*," he continued, voice dropping to a murmur, "didn't you?"

I raised a brow, determined not to give him the satisfaction of seeing me flustered. "Wow," I said coolly, reaching for my wine. "Someone's confident tonight."

The corner of his mouth curved—just a twitch—but there was a glint in his eyes now. "Oh, I'm right," he purred, his tone carrying that dangerous mix of arrogance and amusement. "You wanted my attention, Skye. Congratulations—you have *all* of it."

Desire coiled low in my stomach, tightening until it was hard to breathe. My fingers twitched against the glass, suddenly too aware of every inch of skin he could see. He looked at me like he was already undoing me—devouring me—piece by piece.

And then, with maddening slowness, his hand moved.

His fingers hovered just above my leg, so close I could feel the heat radiating from them. My breath caught as he traced the air along the edge of the slit in my dress, following the line of my exposed skin.

"You wore this," he murmured, his voice deeper than I'd ever heard it, "knowing what it would do to me."

I should've pulled away. Should've said something. But I didn't.

My skin leaned into him before the rest of me even had a chance to catch up.

"Say it, Skye," he continued, hand still resting just barely beneath the fabric, eyes locked on mine. "Admit that you want this."

I swallowed hard. "It wasn't for you," I shot back, my voice steadier than I felt.

His grin widened, a dark glint of triumph flashing in his eyes. "Liar."

Say something, anything.

"What about the box?" I blurted, my voice desperate to shift the focus away from me—and from the ache building in my chest.

His smirk vanished.

Slowly, painfully, he withdrew his hand, his touch leaving a trail of heat in its absence.

He straightened. "The box?" he repeated, his voice controlled. His hand—which had just moments ago been tracing fire along my skin—now rested casually at his side, as if he'd never touched me at all.

"Yes," I went on, my words spilling out in a rush. "The one from the bonding ceremony. Is that why you've been gone?"

He didn't answer for a moment, his eyes locked on mine as though weighing what to say. Then, slowly, he stood. The scrape of his chair against the floor sent a jolt through me, but he moved with an eerie calm, picking up his glass and turning his back.

With a steady hand, he poured more wine, tilting the bottle slightly as it emptied. "Skye," he said at last, his voice impossibly smooth. "It's being handled."

"That's not an answer," I snapped, irritation bubbling up, threatening to spill over.

He turned, wineglass in hand. "No. It's not."

The refusal only fanned the fire my chest. My nails dug into the table's edge, and the wood was no match for the frustration building inside me.

I stood. "This—"

The dining hall doors burst open with an echoing *bang*.

"Absolutely not!"

Euryale's voice thundered through the room.

I turned in shock to see her striding in, wrapped in a dark robe that looked hastily thrown on. Her hair was disheveled, and her glasses sat firmly on her nose. Behind her, a small cluster of nymphs fluttered nervously, wringing their hands and pleading for her to slow down.

"Lady Euryale, please," one of them whimpered, "you mustn't exert yourself!"

Euryale ignored them entirely, her fiery gaze locked on Cullen. "You think I don't know what you're doing?"

Cullen leaned lazily against the table, swirling the wine in his glass as if her fury were nothing new. "Well," he said smoothly, draining the last of his drink, "I see you're feeling better."

"Don't you dare patronize me!" she snapped, jabbing a finger in his direction. "You had no right to bond her to you!"

My mouth fell open as I glanced between them, my head spinning.

But what struck me most wasn't the anger or accusations—it was the fact that she was standing here at all.

"You knew she was awake?" I demanded, whipping my head toward Cullen.

He didn't even flinch, his gold eyes sliding to mine.

"Yes."

CHAPTER NINETEEN

CULLEN

Zeph was already lounging in the corner of my study when I walked in, one leg draped lazily over the arm of the chair. His fingers tapped idly against the wooden frame, like he'd been waiting there...all night.

"So," he drawled, "how'd the big date go? Romantic moonlit strolls? Serenaded music? Did you share dessert?"

I slammed the door shut behind me, the echo punctuating the dark look I shot him—one that could make lesser beings reconsider their existence.

Zeph, of course, wasn't a lesser being. He just grinned wider.

"Ah, that good, huh?"

I didn't respond. Words would only give him more ammunition. Instead, I crossed the room to the nearest shelf and poured myself a drink. I doubted even Dionysus's latest concoction would ease the frustration in my chest, but it was worth a full glass to try.

I'd been so close—so *fucking* close.

For a fleeting moment, Skye had let me in.

At first, I'd been curious about her—about her ability to resist the curse, to defy an Olympian Command. And yes, she was beautiful, and yes, the way her leg leaned into my touch made it clear we were drawn to one another. But it went deeper than that. The way she responded to my music.

When I played the violin, I reached for her emotions. I pulled her loneliness into the strings—the ache she carried so quietly no one else seemed to notice. How long had she lived with that weight? Believing the only person who'd ever truly loved her was gone. The grief was so unbearable that she'd rather lock herself away than risk feeling it again.

I *felt* that.

Her loneliness mirrored my own so perfectly that it hollowed me out.

I wanted to take that pain from her, wrap it in chains, and bury it inside myself. Make her ignorant of that kind of hurt forever.

It was then I realized the walls I'd spent centuries securing were breaking *with* hers. They were collapsing into one another—until hers became mine, and mine became hers.

And then she'd brought up the damn box.

My jaw clenched as I stared into the amber liquid swirling in my glass. That fucking box. The second I avoided the question, the fragile trust she'd started to offer me shattered like glass. I could almost feel the walls slamming back into place—taller, thicker than ever—and this time, I wasn't sure I could break them down again.

And by perfect *fated* timing, Euryale had chosen that exact moment to make her entrance.

I downed the rest of my drink in one swallow. The burn in my throat wasn't enough to simmer the one in my chest. My hand tightened around the glass.

Sara had told me Euryale was awake hours before dinner. I could've told Skye immediately, ending our night before it began. But I didn't.

No, I made a choice. I'd asked Sara to lace Euryale's drink, just enough to keep her under until morning. I'd worked too hard, chipped too carefully at Skye's defenses, to lose the fragile sliver of trust she'd finally started to give me. If adding something into Euryale's veins bought me more time, so be it.

But it hadn't been enough. The concoction wore off sooner than expected, and Euryale had stormed in like a lioness defending her cub.

Skye hadn't said a word. I wanted her fire—I wanted her to curse me—but she just left. She left me with silence. The same silence I'd lived with all my life.

The glass cracked in my hand under the pressure of my grip, the sound yanking me out of my thoughts.

"Watch it," Zeph chided. "Those are antique."

I exhaled sharply and set the fractured glass on the desk, its jagged edges catching the moonlight like teeth. My hand raked through my hair, a useless attempt at restraint.

"You need to leave."

"Do I? Not before I give you my excellent romantic advice," Zeph said, his tone deceptively light as he straightened in the chair. "You created *all* of this by keeping her in the dark. Fix it. Tell her."

I didn't respond. He was right.

I hadn't planned for this. I hadn't planned for *her*.

This had spiraled into something I couldn't control.

Zeph rose to his feet, robes falling slowly at his sides. "Personally, I'd love to see you sulk for a few more hours—it's endlessly entertaining—but that's not going to solve anything."

I leaned back against the desk. Fixing this wouldn't be simple—but I wasn't about to let her slip through my fingers.

Not now. Not ever

The crackle of the fireplace reverberated through the room.

Zeph said nothing, but I could feel his patience waning as I stared at the corner of the desk. My eyes drifted to the small box sitting atop it. Flickering in the firelight, its contents seemed to burn brighter than the fire at my back.

Inside: the scissors.

The Fates were their rightful wielders. The blades themselves seemed ordinary, but they weren't made to cut thread or cloth—they severed life. One cut, and it could end a being's entire existence. Their future, gone.

They had no place in mortal or divine hands—yet here they were, sitting in mine.

Zeph finally broke the silence, his voice dry. "You going to keep staring at it? I'm starting to think you enjoy this whole tortured immortal act."

I shot him a glare but relented. "She asked about them."

He shrugged, unbothered. "We've been over this. I don't know why you're not grasping that Phobos and Deimos are trying to rattle you. And, judging by your face, they're succeeding."

"It's not just about rattling me," I countered, getting up from the chair.

"They likely struck a deal with the Fates. If they've been granted insight into the future, they're a threat."

Zeph tilted his head, considering. "A deal would come with strings. And I'd wager those strings are looped tightly around Phobos and Deimos's necks."

I didn't respond. Phobos and Deimos had always been unpredictable. Over the past few days, I'd done everything I could to fortify the palace—strengthening its barriers, assigning nymphs to guard Skye's apartment and shop, instructing them to gather any whispers they heard.

Nothing. Not a single hint of a plan, a movement, a crack in the silence. That only made it worse.

Creaaaak.

"Are you still cooped up in here?"

I turned to see Harmony push open the study door and stroll in—not that she ever waited for an invitation.

"Well, well," Zeph purred as he rose, every ounce of him lighting up at the sight of her. "If it isn't the goddess of unity herself."

He closed the distance in a few bold strides, wind stirring as if it bent to greet her, too. Harmony's hair whipped across her face, and with an exasperated flick, she tossed it back into place.

The two of them together...I was never bored.

Harmony had relegated Zeph to the eternal, unbreachable category of *brother's best friend* eons ago, but that never stopped him. He'd hurl himself into the pit of Tartarus if he thought it might earn her a smile. I almost applauded the effort.

She rolled her eyes, utterly unfazed. "You're as observant as ever."

"Thank you, princess," he said with a grin.

Harmony ignored him and turned to me. "There's still no word from Phobos and Deimos, and Zeus won't act without concrete proof of a threat."

By now, Phobos and Deimos would have a list of demands. They'd be baiting mortals with fear and paranoia, starting wars and instigating chaos—anything to force my hand.

War. Chaos. Fear.

All of it would be a prelude.

They wouldn't touch me first. No...they'd go after Skye.

They'd tear apart everything she loved and make her watch it fall, just to see me shattered.

Harmony stepped closer, her voice calm but firm. "The Fates cannot leave the Underworld, and Phobos and Deimos will have cursed themselves for seeking them. Everyone knows it's a bad omen to see the future."

"So," Zeph interjected, "they're banking on you doing something stupid."

I shot him another glare, but Harmony nodded. "He's not wrong," she admitted, though the words clearly pained her—as Zeph grinned like a cat given cream.

She stepped back from him, putting more space between them, then continued. "Phobos and Deimos thrive on chaos. They're waiting for you to overreact, to make the first move so they can twist it to their advantage."

I turned back to the fire. Doing nothing felt like surrender. But acting too soon—too rashly—could be just as dangerous.

Leaning back against the edge of my desk, I crossed my arms and fixed my gaze on Harmony. "So what do you suggest I do, then?" The bite in my tone was hard to soften.

Zeph stepped in front of Harmony, all casual mischief, tossing a glance my way. "Oh, I don't know," he drawled, voice thick with mock innocence. "Maybe take advantage of the...*benefits* of being a newlywed."

His grin widened, savoring the thought. "You know—indulge in a little divine consummation. Lucky you."

If Zeph had been anyone else—*anyone*—he wouldn't have finished that sentence. There'd be an arrow through his heart and another through his eyes for daring to speak about *that*.

"Watch it," I warned, eyes narrowing with lethal precision.

Zeph raised his hands in mock surrender. "Message received," he said lightly, though the corner of his mouth twitched with the faintest hint of a grin.

Harmony pushed him aside. She brushed a strand of golden hair behind her ear and sighed.

"Ignore him. Focus on the fact that if Phobos and Deimos were planning something immediate, you'd already know. Which means there's still time."

She paused, then hesitated, her lips pressing into a thin line. "Unless..." she began, rolling her eyes as if the next words physically pained her, "you could always talk to Aphrodite."

Even Zeph stayed quiet.

The mere suggestion scraped against every nerve.

"Talk to her?" The words left my mouth in a slow, venomous drawl, each syllable wrapped in as much hate as I could muster. "You think that's the solution? After...everything?"

"I didn't say it was a solution," she corrected evenly, as if explaining something to a child. "If anyone knows what our brothers—or the Fates—are planning, it's her."

I stared at her, the thought of returning to the goddess who called herself my mother twisting something deep inside me. I'd rather walk into my arrows. Repeatedly.

"Like I said, there's still time." Harmony didn't wait for a reply. She crossed the room to the window, drew back the curtain, and glanced outside as if searching for something.

She turned back to me with a slight smile. "Now...as for Skye," she said, pausing as her grin widened. "I think you just need to sweep her off her feet."

CHAPTER TWENTY

SKYE

I'm so tired.

I'd spent hours—stretching into the morning—telling Euryale everything.

Everything.

About Cullen. About the bonding ceremony. About knowing her past. We wandered along the paths outside while she listened. She didn't interrupt, just listened.

As we walked, her gaze drifted to my chest, where the necklace Cullen had given me rested—its arrowhead catching the morning light. Without a word, she reached out, her fingers brushing the delicate chain. Her touch was gentle, almost cautious, like she was confirming a suspicion.

I tensed out of habit, bracing for the rush of visions that used to come whenever someone touched my skin. The nymphs had grazed me a few times, triggering nothing, but I didn't know if that was because of the necklace—or because they weren't human. I had no idea what to expect with someone like Euryale.

But now, as her fingers brushed my skin—nothing.

Euryale released the chain. "So," she murmured, intrigued, "it works."

I let out a shaky breath, as if confirming it for myself. "Yeah," I breathed. "Looks like it."

Her lips quirked, though it wasn't quite a smile. "Good," she muttered, more to herself than to me.

I gave a small nod.

She resumed walking, and after a beat, I followed.

"I despise this," Euryale said suddenly, like she was biting back the full weight of her frustration. "You being bonded to him."

"I don't love it either," I replied, running my fingers over the soft petals of a nearby flower as we passed. "But...being here and waiting for the nectar feels like the only thing I can do right now."

Euryale's sharp gaze cut to me. "I don't trust Cullen."

I almost laughed, but it came out as a tired sigh. "You think I do?"

Dinner with Cullen kept replaying in my mind like a video I couldn't skip. For all his infuriating arrogance, there had been moments that felt... nice. His smile. The warmth in his golden eyes when he looked at me. Against all logic, I'd started to let my guard slip—to believe that maybe, just maybe, there could be something.

But then I had to go and ask about the box.

His smile vanished. He didn't lie, but he didn't trust me enough to tell me the truth.

And that—*shit*, I couldn't even think straight.

How was I supposed to make sense of my feelings when he couldn't trust me with the truth? My hands curled into fists at my sides, nails digging into my palms.

Euryale stopped and turned to face me fully. "He may have claimed you as his," she said, her voice steady and calm, "but don't forget who you are. Don't let him—"

"I won't," I cut in, my voice sharper than I intended. I couldn't handle another lecture about Cullen right now—not when I was still trying to figure everything out myself.

Her lips pressed into a thin line, but after a beat, she gave a reluctant nod.

She started walking again but then froze, her body going rigid.

I frowned, glancing at her. "What?"

Euryale's jaw tightened. She tilted her head toward the clearing ahead.

"That one," she muttered.

There, nestled in a sunny patch of the garden, was a small table set for two. Plates of breakfast were already laid out, steam curling from the warm dishes. And standing beside the table was Sara.

"That nymph drugged me," Euryale hissed, each word low, coiled, like her snakes were readying to strike.

I blinked, startled, my gaze snapping back to Sara. She wore a frilly pink gown, like she'd bloomed straight out of a tulip. Compared to her, Euryale and I looked ridiculously underdressed—me in a white halter top and jean shorts, her in a black tank and cargo shorts. And still, Sara only smiled, as if no thought troubled her.

"You're sure?" I asked, skeptical, trying to picture someone that airy being so deceptive.

Euryale didn't hesitate. "Positive."

Sara spotted us and waved, her smile widening as if she were genuinely delighted to see us. "Good morning!" she chirped. "I thought you might like breakfast in the garden. Isn't it such a lovely day? Tea should be ready momentarily."

Euryale didn't respond, her glasses fixed on Sara like she was deciding whether or not to turn her to stone.

"Thanks, Sara," I said, breaking the awkwardness as we approached the table.

"Oh, it's no trouble at all," Sara replied, smoothing the tablecloth. "You two enjoy. I'll be back with the tea." She beamed at us again, then turned and walked toward the palace, her dress swishing with every step.

Euryale watched her go, expression unchanging. "She's up to something."

"She looks harmless."

"That's the point," Euryale said darkly, sitting at the table with a scowl. "The ones who smile like that are always the most dangerous."

Euryale leaned forward in her chair, tracing the rim of her empty teacup with one finger as if inspecting it.

"How are you feeling?" I asked, glancing at the faint scar peeking from the collar of her top.

Euryale followed my gaze and shrugged. "It's healed enough." Her tone was dry, but there was a flicker of sincerity beneath it. "I've had worse."

I raised an eyebrow.

Her lips twitched, almost forming a smile. "I've been around a long time. That barely made the list."

Despite her attempt at nonchalance, her voice tightened my chest. "You didn't have to do that, you know. Risk yourself for me."

Euryale's gaze sharpened, piercing in a way that made me straighten. "Yes, I did. Lydia would've done the same. And since she's not here anymore..." Her voice softened, expression shifting. "Well, someone has to look out for you."

My throat tightened at the mention of Lydia—an open wound that refused to heal. The grief came in waves, and in my mind, I saw the tarot card of the *Five of Cups*: a figure staring down at three spilled goblets, ignoring the two standing behind them. The message was to focus on what remains, not what's lost. But...it was hard not to stare at those empty cups.

"Why didn't Lydia tell me about you?" I asked quietly.

Euryale's head turned, her glasses catching the light as she stared toward the rolling clouds. "I asked her not to," she answered, voice low. "My world is dangerous. I didn't want to pull anyone else into it unnecessarily." She paused, a flicker of something—regret, maybe—crossing her face. "I didn't even want Lydia involved, but she was...persistent. Stubborn as hell."

A faint, bittersweet smile curved her lips. "She never let me push her away." Her voice softened further, as if the words themselves were hard to process. "She was one of the few mortals who treated me like a person, not a monster."

Her voice wavered, and without thinking, I reached for her hand.

"She always treated me that way, too," I said gently. "Like I mattered. Like I was more than what people expected of me."

Euryale nodded slowly. "That's why I can't fail you. Not after I couldn't save her—"

I tightened my grip on her hand. "It wasn't your fault." I spoke each word with truth, willing her to believe it. "Her heart gave out. I'm just glad she wasn't alone."

She squeezed my hand in return. "You're not alone either. You have me."

I smiled and nodded, as if she were gripping the other end of the weight crushing my chest, keeping it from collapsing.

Shifting in my seat, I tried to find the right words. They swirled in my head, tangled and uncertain. *How did I even begin to ask this?*

"So...gods," I said finally. The word felt strange and clumsy on my tongue, like it didn't belong in my mouth at all.

Euryale arched a brow, but said nothing, so I pressed on. "I mean, I know what you are—different..."

A Gorgon who could turn people to stone.

I chose my words carefully, trying to ask without offending her. "I'm not afraid of you. But I don't understand—your eyes can turn people to stone, so why can I look at you and nothing happens? What about the gods?"

Euryale let out a slow breath. "I figured there'd be questions. No—gods don't turn to stone. I can slow them down temporarily, though." She paused, then added, "As for you...I've been wondering the same. I never tried it with Lydia, so I don't know if it's unique to you or something in your bloodline. Maybe you've got demi-blood—half god, half mortal. It's possible."

I raised an eyebrow. "It would be tempting to try it on my sisters..."

Euryale scoffed at my teasing and continued. "Cullen's library might have answers. He's been hoarding rare texts for centuries—more than I've ever seen in one place. Have you looked into anything there yet?"

I shook my head. "No. I've been too busy sorting through herbs and making sure you don't..." I trailed off, the words *bleed out* hovering unsaid.

She huffed a quiet laugh. "Fair enough."

Meow.

A streak of orange fur leapt onto Euryale's lap.

Euryale froze as Marnie settled herself comfortably, purring loudly. She blinked down at the cat, clearly caught off guard. "Is this normal behavior for her?"

I laughed. "Not really, but she's been by your side while you've been recovering. Looks like you've stolen my cat."

Euryale raised an eyebrow, her lips curving into a half-smile. "Clearly, she has good taste."

"*Clearly*," I said, rolling my eyes but unable to suppress my grin.

Marnie kneaded her claws into Euryale's lap before curling up again.

Euryale sighed. "Well, I suppose she can come with me to the library."

"Tea is ready."

Euryale and I both turned at once. Neither of us had realized how quietly—or how quickly—Sara had returned to the table.

"It is already at the perfect temperature," she said, her movements smooth as she poured the tea, gesturing lightly toward the sugar and cream.

Euryale frowned after taking a sip, holding her teacup at arm's length like it was foul. "What is this?" she muttered, her nose wrinkling.

I blinked at her, puzzled. "You don't like tea?"

She set the cup down abruptly, porcelain clinking. "It tastes like a rotten lemon."

"Lemon?" I echoed and took a sip, tilting my head in confusion. "There's no lemon in this. Just chamomile and honey."

Her gaze dropped back to the cup, expression darkening. For a moment, I thought she might hurl it across the table.

"Skye..." Her voice cracked, hand trembling violently around the handle.

"Euryale?" I leaned forward, panic rising in my throat.

Before she could get another word out, her body slumped forward, her face hitting the table with a dull *thud*. The teacup slipped from her hand, spilling its contents across the white cloth. I froze, eyes wide, heart lurching.

"Euryale!" I scrambled up, grabbing her shoulders and shaking her. She didn't stir. Her breathing was steady, but she was completely out.

A soft voice sliced through my rising panic. "Oh dear. Apologies for the dramatics."

I turned to see Sara, perfectly calm, shifting her gaze from me to a group of nearby nymphs. "Everyone, make a note to adjust the dosage next time," she ordered, lifting Euryale's hand and letting it drop limply back to her side. "That was clearly too much."

The nymphs nodded and jotted down notes without hesitation, as if this were all part of a bizarre science experiment.

"What the hell did you do?" I snapped, moving closer to shield Euryale.

Sara tilted her head, confused by my raised voice. "Nothing harmful, I promise. It was simply...necessary. Cullen would like to have a word with you."

I barely had time to process her words before a sudden rush of wind engulfed me.

Strong arms wrapped around my waist, lifting me effortlessly from the chair. "What—!" I yelped, twisting instinctively—but I already knew who it was.

"Hold on," Cullen drawled.

I barely managed to grab his shoulders before the ground vanished beneath us, and we shot into the sky. The gardens blurred below, fading into a patchwork of green and gold as we soared higher and higher.

"Cullen!" I shouted, glaring at him. "Put me down!"

He smirked, ignoring my protest as his grip tightened around me. "I will...I just need a moment."

Wind whipped past us, tugging at my hair, and the sheer height stole the breath from my lungs. I wrapped my arms around his neck and legs around his waist, clutching him as my heart hammered against my ribs.

I glanced down—and immediately regretted it. The palace gardens were now a distant smear of color far below, and my stomach flipped. With a final, powerful beat of his wings, Cullen's grip tightened at my waist as he steadied us midair.

"There," he said casually, his voice condescendingly calm. "Better?"

"No, not better!" I retorted, pushing against his shoulders to look at him. "Put me down!"

"Not yet," he chided, his arms firm around me. "We need to talk—without you running off."

"I wasn't running off!" I spat back. "And you didn't have to drug Euryale *again* to talk to me!"

His expression flickered with confusion, like he hadn't thought of that. "She's fine," he assured, attempting a disarming smile. "Think of it as...an extended nap."

I narrowed my eyes at him. "Not funny."

"Come on, just a little funny?" he teased, a faint smirk tugging at his lips.

I shot him a look that answered his question.

He sighed, shaking his head like a scolded child. "Fine," he muttered, his tone laced with annoyance. "I won't drug your precious friend again. Apology accepted?"

I stared at him. "That...that was an apology?"

"Yes."

I scoffed, rolling my eyes.

His jaw tightened, and a harder edge crept into his tone. "I don't need to be apologetic for being who I am. You—"

"Me?" I interrupted, taken aback by his audacity. "I'm not the one flying people into the sky and throwing them into existential crises."

"Yes, you," he drawled, his tone shifting—quieter now, but more dangerous. "You can't even admit what you want."

"What are you talking about?" I asked, trying to keep my voice steady, though the intensity in his eyes was beginning to rattle me.

"You know exactly what I'm talking about," he replied, his presence suffocating. His gaze held mine captive. "You feel something for me."

I stared at him, my mouth a dry line. "What?" The word cracked on my lips as disbelief poured through me.

"You know what I am talking about," he repeated, leaning in slightly, his voice dropping to a near growl. The corner of his mouth curved. "Say it."

I glared at him, my temper flaring. "And if I don't?" I shot back, my voice sharp. "What are you going to do—drop me?"

His grin slowly grew. "Now that," he said, his tone almost a purr, "sounds like a challenge."

Cullen's grip shifted immediately. One of his hands left my waist, and before I could process what he was doing, his arm swept beneath my knees. With one smooth motion, he lifted me against his chest, my breath catching as I realized—I was cradled in a full princess carry...again.

"Ten seconds," he commanded.

I froze, my pulse hammering against his thumb where it brushed my wrist. "Wha—what?"

His golden eyes burned into mine. "To tell me how you feel," he growled. His grip on my wrist tightened just slightly—not enough to hurt, but enough to make a point. "Don't lie," he added, his gaze dropping pointedly to where his thumb rested on my pulse. "I'll know."

I gasped, wrenching at his grip. "You're insane!" I yelled, the edges of my voice fraying with panic.

"Ten," he said, his tone eerily calm, like he wasn't counting down to the worst thing imaginable.

"Nine."

"Cullen, stop—" My voice broke as I yanked against his hold, but it was like trying to pull free from a nightmare.

"Eight." His grip tightened just enough to send a cold jolt through my veins.

"Seven...come on, Skye," he hummed slightly.

"Fucking ass!" I screamed, my chest heaving as panic swelled.

"Six. And such words...don't tempt me," he teased.

"I don't—" My words dissolved into a half-sob. "I don't know!"

"Five."

"Four."

My pulse pounded beneath his hand. "Mon...ster." I dragged the word out like a curse, my lips aching from the pressure of forming the *m*—as if even speaking it hurt.

"Three."

His lips curled into a faint, almost cruel smile. "Monsters don't give second chances."

"Two."

"I don't trust you!" I shrieked, hurling the words like a blade, desperate to wound him the way his calm shredded me. "You leave me. You hide things from me. And you won't tell me anything!"

That stopped him. His grip didn't loosen, but something flickered behind his eyes.

"Trust," he repeated, tasting the word like he was trying to understand it for the first time.

"How can I trust you?" I said, slower this time.

He froze, his lips pressed into a thin line.

"No more secrets," he murmured suddenly, his voice softer. "I'll tell you everything. But you have to give me something. *Anything*."

My chest heaved, and I hesitated.

His eyes darkened, the vulnerability hardening back into something cold. "One second more, and I'll take your silence as your answer."

"I—" The word caught in my throat, panic cutting me off as I tried to speak.

"One," he rumbled, his voice dropping like the final stroke of a bell.

"Wait!" I screamed, but my plea was swallowed by the rush of wind as his hand opened.

And then—I was falling.

The air ripped past me, howling in my ears, a brutal roar that drowned everything else. My stomach twisted. My limbs flailed, searching for something—anything—to hold onto. But there was nothing.

Just me.

Alone.

Falling.

The clouds blurred past like ghosts. I couldn't breathe. Couldn't think. Only feel.

Helpless.

I was back in every moment I'd been abandoned. Every time someone I trusted had let go. Every time I'd had to claw my way back from nothing.

My heart pounded. I squeezed my eyes shut.

This is it.

Then, just as the darkness began to swallow me, warmth closed around my body—solid. A force that stopped the fall.

Pulled me back from the abyss.

I gasped as Cullen's arms wrapped around me, his grip firm, wings beating powerfully against the air.

My breath hitched as I opened my eyes and met his. They were like opalite catching the sun, so bright and intense that I couldn't look away.

Cullen's voice was low but carried over the wind like an oath. "You never have to be afraid to fall. I will *always* catch you."

He drew a breath, his neck stretching toward the sky above us, as if releasing every ounce of restraint he'd been holding inside. When his gaze returned to mine, it had softened—yet there was something pained in it, too. "I don't want to keep things from you anymore. I've spent too long in silence, too long—" His voice caught, rougher now, as if the words resisted leaving him. "I don't want that life. Not for you."

I couldn't look away from him, couldn't form words, couldn't do anything but focus on the man holding me.

His grip tightened slightly, as if he feared I might slip away even here. "I will earn your trust, no matter how long it takes. And when I do—you will *never* be alone again. Neither of us will."

Maybe it was the sting of the wind still lingering on my skin, or maybe it was the rush of adrenaline fogging my brain, but nothing else seemed to matter in that moment. My fears, my doubts—they all fell away, replaced by the overwhelming need to be closer to him.

I didn't think. I didn't second-guess. I curled my fingers around the back of his neck and pulled him down to me, crashing my mouth against his.

It wasn't soft. It was raw, breathless—like I'd been drowning and he was the only oxygen left in the world.

For a heartbeat, he stilled, as if surprised. But then—he claimed me.

His arms tightened, locking me to him as he kissed me back, deep and devastating. His mouth moved against mine like he'd been starving for it—for me. One hand fisted in my hair, tilting my head back, and his mouth trailed lower—along the corner of my lips, the edge of my jaw—before returning to my mouth, like he couldn't bear the thought of leaving it.

It was just me and him—and the way we fit together, like we'd done this a thousand times before.

Like he'd been made to find me in freefall.

And for the first time, being caught didn't feel like surrender.

It felt like freedom.

CHAPTER TWENTY-ONE

SKYE

Euryale's room mirrored mine across the hall.

I sat cross-legged on the floor near her bed while she slept off whatever Sara had dosed her with. My tarot cards were spread out in front of me, lantern light flickering across them as I shuffled for what felt like the hundredth time tonight. Each spread told me the same thing: *stop denying your feelings.*

I stared at *The Lovers* card, glaring at it as if I could will it to change. Two figures stood in a lush garden, their eyes locked on one another. In the background, a serpent coiled around a tree while an angel hovered above them, watching. The card was about choice—about remembering to listen and honor your deepest desires, and to choose the path that resonates with your soul.

My soul...

My fingers grazed my lips. I could still feel *him* on them. It had been... unlike anything I'd ever felt before. I couldn't imagine anyone else being able to compete with that kiss.

I was so absorbed in my thoughts that I almost didn't hear the sharp intake of breath.

Euryale's bed creaked as she sat bolt upright, moving like some reanimated corpse brought to life.

"Euryale?" I said cautiously, setting my tarot cards aside.

Her head jerked around the room spastically before finally locking on me. "That nymph," she spat, saliva glistening on her lips, "will be praying for death."

"Wait—just calm down," I murmured, rising to my feet, hands lifted in a steadying gesture.

"She dared to drug me *again*," she hissed, her fists clenching so tightly her knuckles went white.

"Euryale, please," I pressed, my voice firm but gentle. "I don't agree with what Sara did, but she wasn't trying to hurt you. She was just being stupidly loyal to Cullen. She didn't think—"

"That much is obvious," Euryale seethed, her fury barely contained.

Before I could say another word, she stormed past me, moving fast.

"Euryale, wait!"

I raced out of the room after her, my heart pounding. I had to catch her before she did something she'd regret—or worse, something she wouldn't.

I FINALLY CAUGHT up to Euryale, nearly colliding with her back, and looked up. I squinted—another ballroom. *Seriously, how many did this place need?*

This one resembled the ballroom from the bonding ceremony, but instead of flowers and ribbons, a massive wooden table dominated the center, surrounded by oak chairs, leather cushions, and plush benches.

"You," Euryale growled.

I turned to follow her gaze.

Sara stood at the far end of the room, clipboard in hand. Her cheerful smile widened as we approached. "Good evening, Lady Euryale, Skye," she said warmly—as if she hadn't drugged Euryale into oblivion hours ago.

Oh fuck.

Euryale closed the distance in a few strides and thrust out her hand. A gust of wind followed, knocking Sara's clipboard from her grip and sending it clattering across the floor. Sara's smile didn't falter, though her eyes narrowed ever so slightly.

"Drugged. Me." Euryale spat each word like a verdict from an executioner.

Sara tilted her head, lips curving into a serene smile. “You look well rested.”

Oh fuck, fuck, fuck.

Euryale lunged, her movements a blur—hair snapping like whips, black strands trailing behind her like ink drawn across paper.

But Sara didn’t flinch.

She sidestepped the attack as though she’d seen it coming. She wasn’t just dodging—she was gliding through Euryale’s strikes, like water slipping through cracks in stone. Every step, every twist, every turn seemed rehearsed, as if she were performing some elegant, deadly dance.

“Both of you, stop!”

I tried to move, tried to wedge myself between them, but they were too fast.

Euryale struck again and again. Sara evaded every blow, her light footsteps barely whispering against the polished ballroom floor.

Euryale’s momentum sent her crashing into the table, fingernails gouging deep scratches into the heavy wood. Sara leapt onto the surface, landing light as a feather. She spun, dodging another strike as Euryale followed, the table trembling beneath the force of her landing.

Sara moved as if this were simply another task on her daily checklist. She ducked under a wild swing, her smile never fading.

Is she enjoying this?

Euryale swiped directly at Sara’s midsection. But Sara vaulted backward, flipping off the table, her dress fluttering around her like a cape. She landed in a low crouch—perfectly balanced—and smirked as another nymph tossed her something. Sara caught it without looking.

“Want this to help you?” she asked, holding up Euryale’s baton. Her voice was sweet, but the glint in her eyes was anything but. She twirled the weapon lazily between her delicate fingers.

Euryale froze, her gaze locking on the baton. Her body tensed like a coiled spring, and I knew she was about to explode.

“Enough!” I shouted. But it was useless. They were too far gone.

The air thrummed as the two of them squared off, ready to collide.

And then—

A powerful gust of wind tore through the room. It roared to life like a living thing, slamming into them both. I threw my arms up to shield my face as it howled around us, whipping my hair and sending loose pages from Sara's clipboard spiraling into the air.

When I dared to lower my hands, I saw Zeph standing at the center of the chaos. He held out one hand lazily, the wind coiling around him like an obedient pet. Euryale and Sara were forced apart, the gust pushing Euryale several feet back, her feet scraping against the floor as she struggled to resist. Sara staggered only slightly before the wind pinned her against one of the heavy wooden chairs.

The air between them churned, creating an invisible barrier that kept either from moving closer to the other.

Zeph tilted his head as he surveyed the scene. "Unbelievable," he drawled, the wind still howling softly around him. "Out of all the things I could be doing tonight, I'm stuck breaking up a girl fight." He sighed dramatically, though he clearly seemed to enjoy this.

Before Euryale or Sara could react, Cullen appeared beside Zeph—along with the woman from the bonding ceremony.

"The night's still young," Cullen said smoothly, his lips curving into a faint smile. "If you ladies are done..." He paused as his eyes swept over the wreckage. "We have business to discuss."

This felt uncomfortably like a work conference. Cullen stood at the head of the massive wooden table, commanding the room like a CEO about to launch into a presentation. The rest of us were scattered around, each claiming our own corner of space.

Euryale paced near the door, arms folded tight across her chest. Sara, as far away from her as possible, sat perched on the edge of a chair at the opposite end, clipboard balanced neatly on her lap—as if nothing about this situation was unusual.

Zeph lounged against the windowsill, his gaze fixed on the woman from the bonding ceremony, who now stood beside Cullen, speaking quietly to him.

I pieced it together—this was Harmony. Sara had mentioned during one of her lessons after the ceremony that she and Cullen shared the same mother, Aphrodite, which also made Phobos and Deimos her brothers.

Somehow, I'd ended up awkwardly wedged in the middle, sitting stiffly in one of the leather chairs along the table's side.

I tried not to fidget, but my eyes kept drifting toward Cullen.

Our kiss.

We hadn't talked about it. And the way he looked so unfazed made me question if it had even happened.

Harmony walked away from Cullen as he prepared to speak. She was beautiful—long golden hair, radiant skin—it was easy to see Aphrodite in her. She seemed close to Cullen in a way that made my stomach twist uncomfortably. If she wasn't his sister—

Wait—weren't Zeus and Hera related?

I shook my head quickly, trying to dislodge the thought. No, I was not going there. History class had already taught me enough about the *messed-up* family trees of Greek mythology.

"Skye."

I blinked and found Harmony watching me as she glided toward the unoccupied chair beside mine.

"I want to apologize..." She lowered herself gracefully into the seat, crossing her legs. Her pencil skirt shifted, and I realized her legs were about the length of my entire body.

She spoke again, snapping me out of staring. "I should've introduced myself properly. I'm Harmony. Our first meeting should've been...better."

Her words caught me off guard. I hesitated, then managed, "Oh." My eyes flicked to Cullen, who didn't seem to notice us—absorbed by the nymphs clustered around him, one pressing something into his hand. "Uh, thanks. It's—well—it's been a lot."

Harmony leaned in slightly, the tilt of her head making her look almost sympathetic. "You've handled it well."

Before I could decide if that was a compliment, Cullen's voice cut through the room like an alarm. "Let's get started."

Harmony exhaled sharply, rolling her eyes as she sank back into her chair. I looked up—and found only myself reflected in Cullen's golden irises.

"As promised," Cullen began, "I'm going to tell you everything."

I straightened, pulse quickening—wanting, *needing*—to believe him.

Then my gaze slipped downward, tracing the line of his arm to his hands.

He was holding something.

A small black box.

My breath caught—*that* box.

Cullen took a single step forward and placed it on the table before him.

THUD.

For such a small object, the sound reverberated through the room like a shockwave.

"This," he said, voice steady but low, "was inside the box you saw me holding at our bonding ceremony. The scissors of the Fates."

The box seemed to hum in the quiet, its etched patterns catching the soft light as though alive.

Cullen flipped the latch and slowly lifted the lid. I craned my neck to see inside, holding my breath. Nestled on a bed of dark velvet, a pair of golden scissors gleamed, a faint serpent coiled in a circle etched into the handles.

Without hesitation, Cullen reached in and lifted them, balancing the weight carefully between his fingers.

"The Fates," he explained, "are beings of the Underworld who see all—past, present, and future." He turned the blades slightly, and the light seemed to bend with them. "These are the very tools they use to sever the threads of life. They hold the power of destiny itself."

A chill rippled through me. I instinctively leaned back. "Should you even be touching them?"

Cullen's mouth curved faintly, but the smirk didn't reach his eyes. "Only the Fates can truly wield them," he said. Then, as though a shadow passed over him, his expression hardened. "The scissors aren't just theirs—they *are* them. A fragment of their soul. Phobos and Deimos couldn't have stolen them. They were given."

And then—without warning—he slammed the blades down against the table.

I flinched as the force shook the wood. The ancient blades embedded themselves deep into the surface, standing upright like Excalibur in its stone.

Zeph let out an exaggerated sigh, shattering the tension. "Such a shame," he drawled, shaking his head. "That was a really nice table."

Cullen rolled his eyes but didn't break stride. "If Phobos and Deimos have seen visions of the future, they'll plan to exploit it."

Harmony leaned forward, her hands clasped lightly. "Or," she said gently, her gaze flicking to me, "like I've told Cullen before...this could all be nothing."

Euryale tilted her head, her tone careful. "Regardless of their intent," she pressed, stepping closer to Cullen, "if there was a vision—do you think Skye is part of it?"

Cullen's jaw flexed, muscles tight. "Phobos and Deimos have been trying to break the bond since the dawn of the Twelve. And now their interest in Skye..." His gaze flicked back to the scissors, lingering.

Harmony rose from her chair, eyes shifting to Euryale. "She could be the target...or the threat to their plan. We don't know yet."

Heat pricked my chest. My fingers fumbled with the chain around my neck, curling around the arrowhead like it might shield me. I pressed it tight, shut my eyes, willing the faint vibration against my skin to do something—anything. *Why were they talking about me as if I wasn't even here?*

The tap of a footstep drew me back. I opened my eyes to find Cullen standing over me, his shadow spilling across my chair.

"I think everyone in this room can attest that you're different, Skye," he rumbled, voice low but certain. His golden eyes fixed on me, unblinking. "Whatever connection you have...it's far beyond anything we can explain."

Without another word, Cullen turned, gripped the scissors, and drew them from the wood. He slipped them back into the velvet, closed the lid, and pressed the latch until it clicked. Straightening, he handed the box off without hesitation.

"Store them in the armory," he ordered. The nymphs bowed and carried it away. His gaze returned to me, answering before I could speak. "It's the most secure place in the palace."

My head dropped into my hands. The weight of it all pressed in, my thoughts sliding apart like I was trying to read a language I didn't know.

The silence stretched until Euryale's voice cut through it. "I'll search the library," she said firmly. "Anything that ties the Fates, Phobos, and Deimos—we'll find it."

Zeph moved next. “As always, I’ll listen. If Phobos or Deimos so much as stir near the palace, we’ll know.”

Cullen gave him a sharp nod, then turned to Harmony.

Her eyes met his without wavering. “You can’t keep avoiding her, you know.”

He didn't answer. He simply crossed his arms, using his silence as a wall between them.

Harmony’s jaw tightened, but she sat back down. “Fine. Then I’ll speak to the others, see if there’s any news. We’re going to need allies.”

Cullen’s gaze broke from hers. “We don’t need anyone else. We handle this ourselves.”

Harmony’s lips pressed into a thin line, but she didn’t argue further.

I shifted in my seat. “I want to train.”

The words tumbled out before I’d fully thought them through.

Every gaze swung toward me, but I pressed on. “If this is about me—if I’m the one they’re targeting—I won’t just sit here. I don’t want to be powerless. If I have to fight, I will.”

A slow, satisfied grin spread across Cullen’s face. He tilted his head back, considering. “Then I’ll be in charge of your training.”

My mouth fell open, a retort sparking on my tongue, but before I could get a word out, he clapped his hands lightly.

“Let’s get to work,” he commanded. Then, with one last look in my direction, he added, “We’ll start tomorrow.”

Just like that, the meeting was over.

As the others began filtering out, I hesitated, my gaze flicking toward Cullen. He hadn’t moved from his spot—still leaning against the edge of the table, arms crossed, as if waiting for the room to clear. My pulse quickened.

I needed to say something, anything. I stood and moved away from the table. “Cullen—”

A light touch on my arm jolted me. I turned to find Sara beside me, her voice low. “Skye, do you have a moment? I have that report on Mystic Soulstice.”

From the doorway, Euryale gave an audible huff. She shifted her weight, restless, and for a heartbeat, I braced for another clash between them.

I forced a smile, trying to cut through the tension. "Euryale, I'll meet you in the library."

Her jaw tightened, but after a pause, she gave a curt nod. "Fine."

She strode out, and I let out a silent breath of relief. The last thing I needed was for them to start arguing again.

Sara stepped closer, all business, as if I were just another client on her roster. "While you've been here, a team of nymphs has been overseeing your apartment and Mystic Soulstice, handling their care spectacularly."

I stiffened. *Their care?* My stomach twisted. I grimaced, picturing nymphs fussing over shelves I'd painstakingly arranged. "What *exactly* are they doing to my shop?"

Sara smiled, clearly unbothered by my growing concern. "They've kept it presentable, managed the influx of customers, and ensured the business continues to thrive. Your neighbors, I assure you, are none the wiser." She moved to show me her clipboard, filled with graphs I didn't understand, and continued. "Financially, Mystic Soulstice is seeing significant improvement. We've streamlined operations, increased online engagement, and diversified income streams to minimize reliance on foot traffic."

I blinked, impressed by the string of business terms I barely understood. "I...didn't realize things were going that well," I admitted, feeling both relieved and oddly disconnected from Mystic Soulstic.

Sara nodded, her expression unwavering. "We've also terminated any association with the influencer you previously worked with. Her tactics didn't align with the image you're cultivating."

That snapped me out of my daze. "Wait—what?"

Before Sara could respond, I turned to Cullen, narrowing my eyes. "Terminated?"

He rolled his eyes, tone almost exasperated. "No need for hysterics—nothing drastic occurred. I simply paid her off. Silence and discretion go a long way."

"You didn't have to do that," I said quickly, heat rising to my face.

Cullen shrugged, his smirk faint but teasing. "Sure, I did. You're my wife."

My breath caught, the word landing like a stone in the pit of my stomach. *Wife*. He hadn't called me that before.

I could only stare.

Sara gave a polite bow, then slipped a hand into the folds of her dress. A faint glow lit her face.

I squinted. "Is that a phone?"

She glanced up with a small smile. "Of course. The service here is excellent. We may avoid most modern technology in the palace—too much electricity can be terrible for nature—but phones were deemed essential." Her fingers flew across the screen, clearly not an amateur.

I thought of my phone, lost at the club—not that it mattered. Who would I have called? My family hadn't spoken to me since they'd practically shunned me; they wouldn't have even noticed I was gone.

"Now, if you'll pardon me." Sara slid the phone away and inclined her head. "Goodnight, Skye. Divine Cullen."

She bowed slightly and disappeared down the corridor, leaving just... us. Alone.

Wife still echoed in the silence.

I shifted my weight, smoothing my hands over my shorts as if that might steady me. My gaze darted anywhere but at Cullen—first to the table, scarred with Euryale's nails, then to the floor where scraps of Sara's paper still clung—before finally, reluctantly, finding him again.

"Thank you...for telling me everything," I managed at last.

His gaze slid to mine, something softer flickering in his eyes. "You deserved to know."

I nodded quickly, biting the inside of my cheek. The air between us stretched thin. I should say something else...

Cullen moved suddenly, leaning further against the table, arms braced behind him. The motion lifted his head slightly, exposing the line of his throat and sharp angle of his jaw. He tilted his face toward the ceiling, moonlight catching the hollow of his neck and making him look every bit the god of love people claimed him to be.

How could I ignore the kiss? How could I ignore him?

My gaze betrayed me, tracing over him—and I bit my lip when his voice broke the silence.

"Be careful looking at me like that," he murmured, his tone low, a warning threaded with heat.

I froze, warmth flooding my cheeks. He'd caught me. But instead of retreating, something inside me shifted. I moved closer.

Each step was hesitant at first, but the pull toward him—toward the quiet gravity between us—grew stronger. By the time I stopped, only a breath separated us.

I couldn't hear anything anymore. It was as if the world itself had gone still. My gaze lingered on the rise and fall of his chest, each breath drawing me closer without a single touch.

My gaze climbed slowly—past the line of his throat, where a pulse flickered, up the sharp edge of his jaw, until at last I met those sunset eyes.

They burned into me. He leaned in, his voice dropping to a growl that ignited every nerve in my body.

"Skye," he whispered, "I can't hold back anymore."

My back hit the table with a soft *thud*.

His hands caught mine, pressing them above my head, wrists pinned beneath his grip. The cool surface beneath me, the warmth of his body above—I was caged, caught, completely at his mercy.

But I didn't want to run.

My breath hitched as my legs shifted, parting instinctively, shamelessly—inviting him closer, aching for contact. I felt like prey tangled in a web, not struggling but offering myself to the predator above me.

He dipped lower, his breath brushing the side of my neck. Desire chased across my skin, my chest rising and falling too fast. Heat licked through me, curling tight in my stomach.

"Cullen," I breathed, barely able to form the word.

He didn't answer.

Instead, he buried his face in the crook of my neck and inhaled—slow and deep. The sound was rough, almost primal, sending a shiver straight down my spine.

"What...?" I tried again, voice trembling as I struggled to catch my breath—let alone slow the chaos building inside me.

His lips brushed just beneath my ear, the heat of his voice curling around me. "You shouldn't be so surprised," he murmured, his breath hot against my skin. "I've seen the books on your nightstand—the underlined passages, your little notes."

He dragged his teeth along the shell of my ear, catching the lobe between them.

A sharp gasp tore from me when he bit down—quick, stinging—only to soothe the ache with the slow sweep of his tongue.

"I found them," he went on, his voice darker now, "very *insightful*."

The words barely registered. My body had gone still, as if calibrating, fine-tuning my senses to focus solely on him. My pulse hammered everywhere: in my throat, at my wrists...between my thighs.

I shuddered as he pressed closer, his hips slipping between my parted legs. My body betrayed every rational thought, arching toward him even as my mind screamed that this was insane.

"I—" The word fractured on my lips, useless, drowned out as his mouth traveled down the column of my throat.

His teeth grazed the tender hollow where my shoulder met my neck. This time, the sound that broke free wasn't a gasp but a moan that made my lips tremble.

He lifted his head, just enough for his mouth to brush my ear again.

"If you're worried about someone hearing..." His smirk curved against my skin. "Then you should focus on being very, *very* quiet."

He pressed his hips into mine, drawing another gasp from deep inside me as my body arched instinctively to meet his.

His lips trailed lower, brushing the slope of my collarbone. "Though..." He paused, lifting his eyes to meet my gaze. They shimmered mischievously. "I doubt you'll manage that."

Then his mouth was back on me—open and warm. Every kiss was a brand, each one marking a new place that now belonged to him. I writhed, desperate for more, but his grip on my wrists only tightened, pinning me to the table, forcing me to feel every torturous second.

A whimper slipped from my lips—soft, helpless.

He stilled, lips brushing over my skin. "That didn't sound very quiet," he murmured, his voice a breath against the heat he'd left behind.

My eyes locked on his. I arched a brow, offering a slow, daring smile—one that challenged him to try to keep me quiet. Then I wrapped my legs around his waist and yanked him down, grinding my hips against his in a slow, devastating stroke.

He pushed himself up, gaze darkening instantly. The smirk vanished. Hunger consumed him.

He growled low in his throat, his mouth crashing back to my neck with unrelenting force. His teeth scraped over my pulse, then his tongue followed—slow, hot, and utterly possessive.

When his lips sealed over the hollow beneath my jaw, the suction was deep and sharp. I cried out, twisting beneath him, and when he didn't stop, I fought against his hold until one hand tore free—sliding into his hair and anchoring him harder against my throat.

"Cullen," I gasped, breathless and shaking, needing him—*everywhere*. I rocked my hips against him again, the table creaking beneath us.

He groaned into my skin, the sound vibrating against me in a way that made my thighs shake. His free hand slid down, gripping my thigh and spreading me wider. His fingers dug into my skin—claiming, demanding—and the hard press of him against my core sent a fresh wave of heat crashing through me.

His mouth dragged down my chest, and his hand slid beneath my shirt—rough palm over soft skin—until it found my breast. He teased the sensitive peak with a slow, lazy circle of his thumb.

"Don't stop," I begged, breath ragged, voice broken with ache.

But then—

Everything stopped.

CHAPTER TWENTY-TWO
SKYE

Sleep was impossible.

The palace was too quiet, too still, and I lay there staring at the carved ceiling like it held answers, groaning softly as I turned onto my side.

Cullen.

I sighed and threw an arm over my eyes, trying to block out the faint golden light leaking through the curtains. But it was no use. I could still see him—in my mind, his hands on me...and his mouth.

"Not...yet," he'd growled, his breath hot against my neck, as if restraining himself took everything he had.

He hovered over me, the heat from his body practically burning through my skin. "Once I take you," he murmured, fingers tracing fire along my cheek, "I won't be able to let you leave my side. Ever."

His thumb brushed lightly over my lower lip, as if making a silent promise to return to them. I parted my lips, breath catching—but instead of kissing me...

He pulled back.

"But not now," he said, voice tight, jaw clenched like it physically hurt to stop. "Your training comes first."

He gathered me in his arms, the tension between us thick enough to choke on. "As much as I want to lose myself in you right now..."

His lips brushed my cheek—*my cheek*—and then he was gone.

Now I was lying in this stupid, extravagant bed. Sexually frustrated. And alone. Again.

I let out a long, throaty groan and threw my arm back over my face. How was I supposed to survive in this palace if he was capable of that?

At least life is consistent in screwing me—just never in the way *I* want.

My internal frustration was interrupted by the door slamming open.

"Good morning!" Sara called, aggressively cheerful as she marched in and yanked the curtains open. Light flooded the room, stabbing into my retinas.

I groaned louder. "Sara," I muttered, sitting up and shielding my face. "Is everyone this painfully awake in the morning?"

She grinned, utterly unfazed by my annoyance. "Not everyone. Just the competent ones." She pointed to herself like she was awarding herself a gold star before giving me a once-over.

"You look..."

"Thanks." I deadpanned.

"Like hell," came a voice off to the side.

I turned my head.

Euryale leaned casually against the far wall, her silhouette framed by morning light. Arms crossed, dressed in a fitted black collared top with matching leggings—like she'd just come back from a workout. Marnie was weaving around her legs, purring.

"That was uncalled for," Sara chided, shaking her head. She set a bundle of forget-me-nots on the table—tiny blossoms with pale blue petals and bright yellow centers, like they were smiling. With a flick of her hand, the flowers straightened, sparkling faintly as if delighted by the attention.

I was still in awe sometimes—Sara really was a nature nymph.

Wait a second.

I blinked, glancing between the two of them—genuinely surprised they weren't at each other's throats. I raised a brow at Euryale, silently asking the question. She glanced at Sara, who met her look with equal coolness. Then Euryale rolled her head and waved a dismissive hand, clearly not in the mood to explain.

Before I could push, Marnie leapt away from Euryale's feet, flicking her tail as she padded across the room. She sprang onto my bed, nuzzled the covers, and began to knead them with her tiny claws before settling down.

"What is everyone doing in here?" I asked, reaching down to scratch Marnie's belly.

Euryale's eyes flicked to my neck—her lips pressed into a tight, knowing line.

"Careful, Skye," she drawled slowly, like a warning. "You're playing a dangerous game."

"What are you—" I began, but the rest of the sentence died in my throat when I followed her gaze to the mirror across the room.

There it was.

The faint purple-blue mark on my neck—*Cullen's mark.* My cheeks flamed, and I yanked the blanket up to my chin like that would somehow erase it.

Sara tilted her head, a delighted sparkle lighting up her face. "Divine Cullen is quite handsome," she said sweetly. "I'm overjoyed that love has come to you both so soon."

"No," I snapped, sharper than intended as it sliced the air between us. I didn't even want to think about that.

Euryale held up a hand, a silent request for me to listen. "Not judging. Just...be smart."

Sara, of course, looked thoroughly entertained by it all. "Well, this is already shaping up to be a wonderful morning."

"Out," I ordered, grabbing a pillow and launching it at her. She dodged easily, laughing as she slipped toward the door.

Euryale turned to go as well. "I'll be in the library. There are some old journals I want to go through—"

"Oh! I can help!" Sara popped her head back in, all too eagerly.

Euryale hissed softly, a warning sound more instinct than speech. Her fingers curled in irritation, but she didn't object.

I sat up, still gripping the blanket around me. My mind spun, reaching for anything—something—I could contribute. Something useful.

"There was...something," I said slowly. "Back at the club, Phobos and Deimos—they called me a name."

Both women paused.

My voice dropped to a murmur, as if saying it too loud might summon something. "Praxis."

Sara tilted her head, confused. Euryale's expression didn't change, but her posture stiffened ever so slightly.

"Do you know what it means?" I asked, glancing between them.

Sara gave a slight shake of her head—no.

Euryale thought for a moment. "I'll see if I can find a reference," she replied at last, stepping toward the door, with a quiet Sara trailing behind her.

I nodded to myself, the word *Praxis* lingering on my tongue like a burn.

Euryale paused in the doorway, glancing back over her shoulder. "Focus on training today," she quipped, pointing a sharp finger at me.

"Yes, Mom!" I called after her with a grin.

Without missing a beat, she flipped that finger into a middle one as she disappeared down the hall.

THE COOL MORNING air bit at my cheeks as I jogged across the sprawling palace grounds, each breath escaping in soft white puffs against the pale dawn. Wisps of mist curled along the horizon; it still hadn't fully hit me—endless clouds surrounded this place. The sky stretched on forever, streaked with shades of pink and orange. Beautiful...but isolated.

Then again, given the circumstances, maybe isolated was safer.

Dew clung to the grass, dampening the hem of my leggings. Sweat slicked the back of my neck, sticking my racerback tank and the arrowhead to my skin. My hair, pulled into a loose ponytail, bounced with each step, though a few stubborn strands clung to my damp face.

The brisk air should have kept me grounded, but my thoughts kept spinning—Phobos. Deimos. The Fates. It was like they were taking turns juggling knives in my brain.

And then there was Cullen.

Every stray thought of him felt like a phantom touch—like the ghost of his hand wrapping around mine, pulling me back into the ballroom, refusing to let me go.

I tried to focus on the rhythm of my breathing and the steady pound of my feet against the earth. But my body was heating up—and not just from the run.

And then—*oh shit*—my foot caught on a dip in the ground, and before I could catch myself, I tumbled forward, hitting the ground with a graceless *thud*.

I hit hard, the cool blades slick against my back. Above me, the clouds swirled lazily, almost like they were laughing.

I stayed there for a moment, letting the damp seep into my clothes, grateful for the stillness.

"Falling for someone already?" a familiar voice teased from above.

I groaned, rolling onto my side and propping myself up on my elbows just as Zeph strolled over, hands tucked casually into the pockets of his robes. His long hair fluttered behind him, stirred by a breeze that brushed my skin.

"Looks like we've got a long way to go if you're this unbalanced already," he remarked, crouching beside me with a smirk that nearly rivaled Cullen's.

"Should I fetch Cullen? I hear he's quite good at satisfying women when they're on their backs."

Heat rushed up my neck. I sat up quickly, brushing grass from my hands in a futile attempt to mask my embarrassment. "Hilarious," I muttered, rolling my eyes to hide the traitorous blush creeping across my face. "And why are you here? I thought Cullen was supposed to be training me."

Zeph placed a hand over his heart, his expression a picture of exaggerated heartbreak. "Wounded. Truly. And here I thought we were becoming friends," he said, his voice dripping with theatrical sorrow.

I stared at him, incredulous. "Really?"

He extended a hand to help me up, his smirk deepening when I hesitated. For a moment I just stared at it, debating whether I even wanted the satisfaction of taking it. Finally—reluctantly—I slid my hand into his, letting him pull me to my feet.

I immediately crouched and re-tied my shoelace, fumbling with it a moment longer than necessary to procrastinate meeting his gaze.

"That disappointed, huh?" he teased, clearly enjoying himself. He leaned in, dropping his voice to a conspiratorial whisper. "Don't worry—today's just a warm-up. Cullen had to...cool off." He paused dramatically.

"Cold shower, I think. Seems like something—or someone—has him just as distracted as you are."

Without thinking, I yanked off my shoe and hurled it at him with all the force my indignation could summon.

Zeph didn't even blink. With a lazy flick of his wrist, the shoe froze midair, reversed direction, and flew right back at me. I stumbled but managed to catch it.

"Feisty. I like it," he said with a hearty laugh. "That might actually help you survive today."

I crossed my arms, leveling him with what I hoped was a properly intimidating glare. "Are you done?"

His grin only widened, turning wicked. He stepped back and motioned for me to follow.

"Done? Oh, sweetheart, we're just getting started."

Then, in a sharper tone: "No more distractions. You want to learn to fight? Show me what you've got."

I followed him toward an open field, set up like some kind of divine Olympic training ground. Nymphs bustled around, moving equipment and setting up stations—though a few looked panicked as they tried not to damage the grass in the process.

Well, let's go.

Zeph pushed me harder than I expected. We started with basic drills—laps around the grounds, weaving through makeshift obstacles, and footwork that left my legs trembling.

"Balance is everything," he explained, demonstrating a defensive stance with a fluid grace that made it look effortless. "You lose your footing, you lose the fight."

He flicked his hand, and a sudden wind swept me off my feet, sending me crashing to the ground. At this rate, the dirt and I were becoming very well acquainted.

Zeph waited as I picked myself up, bracing for another round.

"Ready yourself," he warned.

I gritted my teeth, adjusted my stance, and nodded.

Another sharp movement from Zeph's hand, and the wind slammed into me again—stronger this time. I hit the ground with a groan.

"Again."

I flopped down with theatrical exhaustion. "Great. Just great. *Again* is officially my new least favorite word. Right up there with *moist*."

Zeph chuckled, standing over me with his hands on his hips. "Get your moist ass up and do it."

"If you've got a statue of yourself somewhere, I'm carving the word *again* on it," I said, breathless but grinning.

"Flattering," he replied with a grin, tossing a water flask to me. "Now, guess what?"

I stared at him in horror. "No."

"Again."

By the time we finished, the sun hung low in the sky, casting golden light and long shadows across the field. My body felt like it had just run five marathons back-to-back.

"Not bad for a mortal," Zeph noted, pausing to take a long pull from his flask.

I managed a tired smile as I bent down to grab my water bottle.

When I looked up, Zeph had tucked the flask away and drawn something from inside his robes. With a flick of his wrist, two small, gleaming objects spun through the air before landing neatly in his palm.

"One more thing..." he said, tone casual but eyes sharp. "I found these in the armory. Lightweight, and they'll cut through flesh like butter. So don't go slicing your fingers off—or I'll never hear the end of it from Cullen. Start working them into the stances we covered today."

He stepped closer, extending his hands. Resting there were two daggers, forged of blackened steel. Small enough to vanish into a palm, their slender blades tapered to a needle-like point. Crimson leather wound tightly around their hilts, the color seeming to bleed into the dark metal itself. At the base, diamond-shaped pommels glinted faintly, like compressed stars caught in the dying light.

I set my water down and cautiously picked up the daggers. I'd never held a weapon like this before—the closest I'd come was the suit of swords in my tarot deck. I shifted my grip on the hilts, testing their balance. They were shockingly light.

With a flick of Zeph's hands, the air shifted and whipped around my legs, carrying something with it. Threads of dark leather wove together midair, forming twin brown harnesses that clung to my thighs. The straps tightened against my skin, snug but not uncomfortable, and settled into place with a final snap of pressure.

I slid the daggers into their sheaths, the blades vanishing into the leather with a soft scrape of metal.

"Thank you," I murmured, my eyes lingering on the daggers a moment longer, as if by staring hard enough I could believe they actually belonged there—on me.

Zeph stretched with a groan. "I think we can call it for today. I've got a date tonight," he announced, looking far too pleased with himself.

I arched a brow, smiling at him.

He crossed his arms, grin widening. "Harmony needs an escort to Olympus. So...date."

They're together?

I rolled my eyes as I lifted my water bottle. "Does she know that?"

With a smug grin, Zeph flicked his hand—and the bottle flew right out of mine.

"Hey!"

"And to think," he said, all mock regret, "I was going to glide you back to the palace so you didn't have to walk."

"Wait!"

He made an over-the-top motion with both hands, like a stage magician silencing an audience, then pushed off the ground and began to hover.

"Enjoy your walk," he called, giving one last teasing jab before soaring into the sky.

I threw my hands up. "Wha—the f—" But laughter broke through before I could finish.

Fair enough.

I DRAGGED myself back to the palace, every muscle screaming in protest. The thought of sinking into a hot bath was the only thing keeping me going—like a shimmering oasis at the edge of a desert.

The tub, an oversized basin of smooth porcelain, sat nestled atop a pedestal. Like everything else in this place, it looked as though it were floating. It shimmered through a soft haze of steam that curled upward in lazy tendrils. The water, infused with fragrant oils of lavender and jasmine, rippled gently as I stepped in, the arrowhead around my neck sinking into the water with me.

The moment I fully submerged, the tension in my body began to dissolve. Heat enveloped me, easing the deep aches in my limbs and unraveling the knots that had settled in my shoulders. My head rested against a silk pillow perched at the edge, and I let my eyes flutter closed, the quiet hum of the faucet blending into the stillness.

Knock, knock.

I winced, muscles snapping taut once again.

"Skye," came Cullen's voice from the other side of the bathroom door.

I froze, sinking lower into the water. The delicate lace of bubbles no longer felt like much of a shield.

I said nothing.

"Really? Silent treatment...?" he drawled, his voice dipping low, almost a caress. I heard the faint *creak* of the door and knew he was bracing his hands against it, leaning his weight closer...closer to me.

"I didn't realize," he murmured, letting the words linger, "that missing training would earn me a punishment this...severe."

I swallowed hard, fingers tightening around the edge of the tub, knuckles turning white.

"Don't worry," he added, his tone dropping to a velvet growl. "I'll make it up to you tomorrow. *Thoroughly.*"

Heat surged through me. I squeezed my thighs together beneath the water, trying to ignore the traitorous pulse blooming between them.

He was still on the other side. The door remained closed.

He wouldn't actually come in...would he?

Why did that thought thrill me?

I stared at the door, watching the slow shift of his shadow. Maybe it was the steam. Maybe it was him—so close, just inches of wood separating us.

I let my hand slip beneath the surface, breath catching as my fingers trailed down my inner thighs to their apex, brushing over the sensitive skin. The warm water lapped gently around me, but the tension coiling inside me only grew tighter.

I kept my eyes locked on the door, on the shape of him lingering just beyond it. He was always doing this—teasing me, edging me.

I guess I'll have to take things into my own hands...literally.

I hummed as my fingers found that spot, circling, teasing. Every stroke sent a ripple through me, and my body ached for me to move faster.

My eyes fluttered shut as I pictured him—his weight pressing me against the table, his breath at my ear, his hands pinning me down.

I bit down on my lip to stifle the sound that threatened to escape me.

Fuck. I'm already so close. Just thinking of him...it was enough to completely undo me.

"Skye," he said suddenly, his voice a silken murmur. "Still silent?"

I froze. My hand stilled beneath the water.

"Don't take too long," he continued, his tone darker. "Or I'll start thinking you're imagining me in there."

A soft whimper slipped out before I could stop it. My hand flew to my mouth, and the water shifted with a betraying splash.

Silence followed.

When he spoke again, his voice was rougher—tight, like he knew exactly what I was doing. Like it was taking everything in him not to push open the door.

"You should come out soon," he muttered, almost to himself. "Before I stop caring that there's a door between us."

A beat of silence. Then—

"Besides...I've got something for you."

And just like that, his shadow disappeared.

I stayed still for a moment, heart pounding, the air thick with what hadn't happened. Then curiosity overtook hesitation.

Barely pausing to dry off, I threw on the nearest clothes and ran a towel quickly through my damp hair, which still clung stubbornly to my neck.

"Cullen?" I called, stepping cautiously out of my bedroom.

Silence.

I glanced both ways down the corridor, then began walking toward the main hall.

As I reached the open room at the end of the hallway, I stopped. Cullen was standing there, and beside him was the most exquisite piano I had ever seen.

Its ebony surface gleamed like a polished mirror, clear enough to catch the flush rising in my cheeks. The piano's curved legs ended in clawed feet, reminiscent of a lion's paw—or, given the world I was in now, perhaps something even more deadly.

"What..." I started, my voice catching as I stepped closer. "What is this?"

"A gift," Cullen said simply. "You mentioned you used to play." His voice softened. "I thought it was time you played again."

My fingers trembled as I reached out, brushing the smooth keys with a feather-light touch, half-expecting the whole thing to vanish like a dream. "It's beautiful," I whispered, my throat tightening.

"It's yours," he replied, stepping closer.

I turned toward him, my thoughts tangling beneath the surface, wondering how true he was.

"You deserve something that's yours," he said gently. "Something no one else can take from you."

Before I could second-guess myself, I closed the space between us and wrapped my arms around him—an embrace that felt reckless and... perfect.

Cullen stiffened for a moment, as if he'd never been hugged like this before. Then, slowly, his arms came around me, drawing me close to his chest.

"Thank you," I breathed.

His hand cradled the back of my head, fingers threading through my still-damp hair. "You don't need to thank me," he murmured. "I just want to be of service to you."

There was something in his voice, as if he didn't quite believe he deserved to give me anything at all.

I pulled back slightly to look up at him, my breath catching at the intensity in his gaze. Then, without a word, he dipped his head and pressed a lingering kiss to the crown of my head.

"Go on," he whispered, nodding toward the piano. "Play something."

With one last glance at him, I turned and approached the piano, settling onto the bench and placing my fingers lightly on the keys. The first tentative notes floated through the room—a melody I hadn't touched in years, slowly coming back to life.

And somehow...I was coming back to life with it.

CHAPTER TWENTY-THREE

SKYE

I think I could've played that piano all night.

Cullen had stayed with me the whole time, smiling contentedly as he watched me. He never corrected me, never interrupted—just let me rediscover it at my own pace.

I still couldn't believe he'd done that for me.

I was falling for him.

Falling for this place.

Falling into his world.

Now I just had to survive it.

Which meant more training.

Which meant, once again, no sleeping in.

I looked up. The library's ceilings stretched ridiculously high, with shelves upon shelves of books and scrolls climbing the walls. Their spines shimmered with gold and silver script, as if they were bound in jewelry. Not a single speck of dust in sight—the nymphs really did take care of every inch of this place.

At the far end, a massive domed window framed the cloud-filled sky. The air carried a warm, oddly comforting scent—like an old whiskey barrel, aged and rich. It was the kind of smell that made the room feel like it was quietly savoring its own silence.

And there I was, cross-legged on an uncomfortably firm cushion, groaning into the early morning hush while Harmony sat beside me, practically radiating peace like we were on some sort of wellness retreat.

"You know it's too early for this, right?" I grumbled, voice muffled by my hands as I rubbed the sleep from my eyes. The faint scent of lavender from the incense Harmony had lit only made me sleepier.

"Quiet your mind, Skye," Harmony said gently, her golden hair catching the first light of sunrise spilling through the window.

"Quiet my mind?" I muttered under my breath. "My mind needs coffee."

Euryale, seated beside me, let out a soft huff. "You mortals and your dependency on caffeine supplements."

Before I could fire back, the library door swung open and in walked Sara, holding a tray of glasses. "Good morning, sunrise squad!" she sing-songed. I think I must've been tired than I thought, because it looked like tiny stars were faintly dancing around her head as she smiled. "I brought reinforcements."

Is that...are those...mimosas?

I bolted upright from my cushion.

Harmony arched a brow. "Really? During meditation?"

"Of course," Sara replied, setting the tray down with a flourish. "How else are they supposed to find inner peace?"

I snorted, reaching for a glass. "Finally, someone who gets me."

Harmony sighed, her lips twitching with a teasing smile. "Fine. But I'm taking two as punishment for the interruption." She skillfully grabbed a pair of glasses, winking at me as she did.

Euryale took a glass, tilting it slightly as if inspecting the bottom for tampering—not that I could blame her.

Sara smiled at her, and after a moment of scrutiny, Euryale slowly took a sip. Satisfied, Sara moved on to offer drinks to the other nymphs scattered throughout the library.

I took a sip of my mimosa, the bubbles tickling my nose. "You and Sara seem awfully civil lately."

Sara overheard and practically lit up. "Oh yes! Amends have been made—just like the other night—"

Euryale's hand clamped over her mouth. "I'll need *much* more to drink before you reveal...anything," she muttered, though the faint twitch of her lips betrayed a smile.

Sara swatted her hand away and shot me a conspiratorial grin. "She's just shy. But all is well."

I raised a brow but didn't press. Instead, I sat down and leaned against the cushion, letting the warm sunlight and quiet *clink* of glasses lull me back toward meditation. For a second, I almost forgot about the chaos waiting beyond these clouds.

Then I froze mid-sip, eyes flicking to the rising sun. Oh no. "What time is it?"

Harmony glanced over her shoulder at the window. "Clearly after sunrise."

I jumped to my feet, heart sinking. "I'm late!" In a panic, I chugged the rest of my mimosa. The bubbles fizzed violently on the way down, hitting my throat like tiny citrus grenades.

Euryale smirked as I staggered upright, glass still in hand. "You're going to regret that."

"I already do!" I croaked, clutching my stomach as the citrus burned.

Groaning, I shoved the empty glass onto a nearby table and scrambled to collect my things.

Fantastic. First training session with Cullen, and I was going to show up smelling like I'd just gotten hungover from brunch.

Their laughter followed me as I bolted for the door, but I couldn't help the small smile tugging at my lips as I ran. Life here was anything but ordinary—but moments like this? They made it feel like maybe, just maybe...this place was becoming home.

Don't trip.

Don't trip.

Don't trip.

I repeated the words like a mantra as I practically jogged down the winding path toward the fields below the palace.

I launched off the last step and skidded to a stop at the edge of the clearing.

And there he was.

Cullen stood in the center of the field, drawing back the string of his bow as if testing its strength. His hair was tousled, windswept like he'd just been flying, and when the sunrise caught it, the light turned it into a golden halo. He really did look like an angel—even with his wings tucked away.

My gaze slipped lower, over the curve of his shoulders and down to his chest. Bare, gleaming with a thin sheen of sweat. Each pull on the bow made his muscles shift and tighten, the movement so fluid that the bow and his body seemed to communicate—constantly in sync.

I froze mid-step. Seriously? Who trained shirtless at this hour? How was I supposed to focus when he looked like the literal cover of a romance novel?

I realized I was just...standing there. Staring. *Great.*

Snapping myself out of it, I forced my legs to move, pretending I hadn't just mentally undressed him three times.

Cullen looked up as I neared. "You're late."

Just chugged a mimosa like a college freshman, and I'm honestly impressed I made it here without dying.

"Well, some of us need breakfast," I replied, aiming for nonchalance. Unfortunately, the breathlessness in my voice completely betrayed me. Even worse, my eyes flicked to his chest before I could stop them.

Nope. Focus. Eyes on his face. Or better yet, the ground. Yes—staring at the ground seemed much safer.

Cullen didn't respond. He simply held a bow out in front of me. It wasn't his, but a simpler, more traditional one.

"No enchantments. No curses. Just wood and string," he said, as if reading my thoughts. "If you can master this, we'll move on to mine."

He placed it gently in my hands. His fingers brushed mine—barely a second, but a ripple of heat shot through me. I shook my head, forcing myself to focus on the bow. It felt lighter than I expected, almost like it had been made for me. I ran my fingers along its curve, trying to get a feel for it—just like getting to know a new crystal, feeling every groove and indentation.

"Why not just start with yours?" I asked, focusing very hard on sounding normal, even though his proximity made the air feel warped.

"Because relying on divine power alone is a weakness," he explained, his voice dropping to a calm, firm tone. "You need control. Precision. Discipline."

I nodded and tightened my grip on the bow, adjusting my stance toward the circular target with concentric rings of black, blue, red, and yellow at the far end of the clearing. I'd seen enough movies to fake it—feet shoulder-width apart, back straight, inner turmoil...optional.

Then Cullen stepped behind me.

Close.

Close enough that I could feel the faint heat of his skin brushing my back. My heart gave a traitorous lurch, as if it wanted to personally bridge the distance between us, and I had to mentally slap myself.

"Stand like this," Cullen instructed, his hands brushing my shoulders to adjust my posture. I tried—really tried—not to melt under his touch.

Then he pressed gently against my back.

"Archery isn't just about strength or precision," he murmured. "It's about focus."

As he spoke, his hands moved to my hips, correcting my stance with unnerving calm.

"Phobos and Deimos won't just come at you with brute force," he continued, voice darkening. "They'll try to unravel you from the inside—fear, doubt, anger...that's their true power."

I nodded, probably a little too fast, as his fingers drifted away from my hips, the ghost of his touch still searing through me.

"Start with your grip," he said, stepping back into full-on instructor mode. His arms were behind his back, and his posture was straight—like this was a perfectly normal morning in the world of gods.

I adjusted my grip and immediately fumbled the bowstring. *Shit.*

"Here." Cullen stepped in again, his hands firm but patient as they guided mine into place. "Move with the bow, not against it. This isn't about forcing it—it's about balance."

He repositioned my fingers with care, and I sucked in a breath, willing myself to focus. But every light brush of his skin had my nerves jangling in all the wrong—or maybe right—ways.

"Now, draw back slowly," he said. "Feel the tension between the string and bow. Let that guide you."

I pulled the string back. It quivered under my fingers, tension humming in my arms. The arrow's soft feathers brushed my cheek, a cool contrast against the warmth of my flushed skin.

"Good," Cullen murmured, close again. "Now aim. Take your time."

I tried. Gods, I tried. One half of my brain focused on the target—the other was completely occupied with how unfairly good he smelled.

"Your breathing's off," he corrected. "In through your nose, out through your mouth."

I exhaled slowly, grounding myself in the motion. The target blurred and sharpened. I released the string. The arrow flew fast and landed in the blue ring—two colors out from the center.

"Not bad," Cullen drawled, a faint smile tugging at the corner of his lips.

I turned to him, pride rising in my chest, and met his gaze.

Then—slowly—he reached up, his hand pausing midair as if giving me the chance to pull away. I didn't.

His fingers brushed a loose strand of hair from my cheek, trailing softly behind my ear. The warmth of his touch lingered. I felt every graze, every shift of his skin against mine.

And just like that, I forgot how to breathe again.

My hand lifted almost without thinking, fingers barely grazing his as he pulled away.

"Don't hesitate next time," he said, his voice low. Then, after a beat: "And relax your shoulders. You're too tense."

"You're making me tense," I muttered under my breath, fumbling with the bow again.

But he heard. Of course he did.

Cullen's chuckle was low, dark, and far too amused. "Is that what's distracting you?" he purred, stepping closer. "Am *I* distracting you?"

I wouldn't even dignify that with a response.

From my silence, his gaze dropped—slow and unapologetic—as it tracked the sweat clinging to my skin, like he wanted to follow each drop with his mouth.

I didn't shy away. I let him look. Let him see what he was doing to me.

I tilted my chin, shifted slightly—arching my back just enough to lift my breasts higher. Daring him.

His eyes darkened, the sound that slipped from him more growl than breath.

I bit the inside of my cheek, suddenly very aware of how little space there was between us—and how easy it would be to close it.

I was starting to enjoy this. The game of it. Teasing him. Tempting him.

So I pivoted, letting my hips sway as I turned away. My focus shifted to the quiver, though I felt the weight of his stare like heat against my back. My fingers grazed the arrows one by one until I found the right one, then forced my barely steady hand to twirl it, as though it were nothing more than a casual gesture.

"How long have you been...doing this?" I asked, turning back to face him and lifting the arrow slowly, almost like I was dragging it up the length of his body. My voice was light, teasing—like *I* was the one in control now.

But even as I turned toward the target, I could still feel him behind me.

Watching.

Still very much a distraction.

A different smile tugged at his lips. "Centuries," he answered, as if he, too, was pretending he didn't notice what I was doing. "But I suppose I have a slight advantage."

He raised his hand, revealing a sleek silver bracelet around his wrist. With a fluid motion, he twisted it, and a soft golden light flared to life.

I'd seen that light before but had never made the connection—until now.

In an instant, his bow materialized in his hand, a stark contrast to the one I held. A matching quiver and arrows appeared across his back.

"It was from my father," he said, turning the bow over in his hands. He held it out so I could see the carvings, each line etched with a craftsmanship that looked like it had taken lifetimes to perfect. "He ensured that the bow, the arrows, and their enchantments would only obey me—and those I willingly give them to."

He hesitated, as if sifting through his thoughts. "He said it would ensure that I, and anyone I cared for, was never unarmed, no matter the circumstance."

I hesitated, unsure if I should ask the next question. "What's he like? Your dad?"

Cullen's expression shifted, something guarded flickering in his eyes. "Hephaestus. God of fire, metalworking, and craftsmanship."

He let out a dry laugh. "He creates. But it was my mother who broke him. Her open affair with Ares humiliated him—again and again. Eventually, he left Olympus and retreated to the Underworld, to his forge, alone." He paused, his voice quieter now. "He wasn't around after that. Not in any way that mattered."

"I'm sorry," I said softly—and I meant it. There's a particular kind of ache that comes from being let down by your parents. They're supposed to love you unconditionally. They're meant to be the safety net fate chose for you. But when they're the ones who cause the hurt, it feels like nothing is safe. Like there's nothing you can truly trust.

And from the look in Cullen's eyes, I could tell he knew exactly what that felt like.

He shook his head, a wry smile curving his lips. "You can't really hate something that was never around. And...he left me this." He gestured toward the bow, his fingers tracing the carvings absentmindedly.

I stepped closer. "It's beautiful," I murmured, reaching out to touch it lightly. The golden light beneath the surface pulsed faintly—warm, almost alive.

"Does it always come when you call it?"

"Yes," Cullen replied, his voice softening. "And now you'll know how to use it...if the need ever arises."

I met his gaze. He wasn't just training me to defend myself—he was entrusting me with something deeper: knowledge about his past, his lineage...about him.

Then, without another word, Cullen twisted his bracelet. The golden light flared, and in an instant, the bow and quiver vanished.

He cleared his throat, breaking the moment. "Alright," he said, determination back in his tone. "No more stalling. Let's see if you can hit the target again—this time, without me fixing your stance."

I groaned dramatically and rolled my eyes. "Great. Parental trauma and archery lessons. What a day."

Still, I reached for another arrow, drawing back the bowstring. This wasn't just about learning to shoot—it was about proving to myself that I wouldn't be a willing chess piece in someone else's game.

I inhaled deeply, my lungs expanding, and let the breath leak out slowly. My grip loosened just enough, and my shoulders softened. The string stung my fingers as I released.

The arrow cut through the air, slicing forward in a straight, precise line. For a heartbeat, I thought it might veer, but then—*thunk*. It struck, quivering right on the thin line separating the gold and red rings.

I...I did it. Not perfect, though—

"Better," Cullen said, as if interrupting the thought before it could fully form.

I turned toward him, catching the faintest smile tugging at his lips. There was something almost tender in his expression, and it sent a ripple of warmth through me.

"Thanks," I murmured, my voice softer now as I reached for another arrow.

"Ready for part two of the lesson?"

"Two?" The feathers of the last arrow still quivered in the target behind me, but my eyes were already back on him.

"Archery's about precision," he explained, closing the distance between us. His hand slowly brushed my shoulder, fingers drifting down my arm, stopping just above where my own gripped the bow.

"It's about control," he continued, the word hanging heavy between us. "Trust yourself to hit the mark—but sometimes, it's also knowing when to let go."

His hand covered mine, warm and steady, guiding my fingers to release the bowstring. The bow slipped from my grasp, clattering softly against the ground.

The wind shifted, swirling around us. The soft brush of the arrow's feathers against my wrist startled me—and Cullen noticed, like he noticed *everything*. His fingers found my chin, tilting my face toward him as his eyes locked onto mine.

"Did you feel that?" he asked, voice dropping to a hushed growl. "How something as small as a feather can steal your focus? Make your heart race?"

I nodded, wordless. He looked at me like he was trying to read every thought I'd ever had. His thumb traced my jaw—

"Focus," Cullen repeated, his voice softer now but no less commanding. His head dipped, lips hovering just beside my ear.

I shifted slightly. "I am—"

Cullen smoothly took the arrow from my hand. He trailed its feathers along my skin, starting at my wrist and slowly dragging upward—along the curve of my shoulder, over the line of my neck, to the hollow of my throat. The exact spot he'd marked before. *His* mark.

My eyes drifted shut before I could stop them, my pulse quickening beneath the delicate scrape of feathers.

He pressed closer, his other hand sliding to my waist to guide me, positioning me to face the target again. He tipped my chin upward while the arrow's feathers lazily drifted from my neck to my collarbone.

"You're distracted," he murmured, lips grazing the shell of my ear. The low vibration of his voice sent a shiver down my spine, leaving my knees barely holding me upright. "And...what an interesting scent. Do you always start training with a liquid breakfast?"

My cheeks flushed. Of course he'd caught that. "It was one mimosa," I muttered, glaring at the target to avoid his eyes.

Cullen leaned in, inhaling softly near my hair, as though he were memorizing the scent—mimosa, citrus, and something distinctly me. His expression shifted slightly, like he was storing it away.

"When you can hit the center of the target," he drawled, a hunger audible in his voice, "I'll consider your training *adequate*."

He stepped away, putting distance between us as he began walking toward the edge of the archery grounds.

"Now," he said over his shoulder, not bothering to look back, "I think it's the perfect time for a run."

My mouth was dry, heart thudding. "What happens after that?" I asked—meaning, *after my training is adequate.*

Cullen stopped mid-step. His head turned just enough for me to see the glint in his eye.

"My priorities"—he let his gaze roam over me—"will shift."

He angled his head.

"Now run."

CHAPTER TWENTY-FOUR

CULLEN

I need this to be ice.

Water crashed over me in unrelenting sheets—sharp, punishing, but not cold enough to drown out the thoughts clawing at the edges of my mind. My palms pressed hard against the slick obsidian stone of the shower walls, muscles taut, fingers curled into fists as the cascade pounded down from above.

The top of the shower was open to the night sky, exposing me to the silent judgment of the stars. I tilted my head back, letting the freezing streams carve their path over my skin like penance.

This had become a ritual—cold showers, long, sleepless nights.

Being near Skye...breathing the same air...was temptation personified.

And I couldn't give in.

Wouldn't.

Not yet.

She needed me clear-headed. Focused.

Not undone by the parting of her lips when she concentrated, or the way the sun deepened her freckles. Not the way those petal-blue eyes caught mine like she could see through every carefully built wall.

Her training wasn't just preparation—it was survival.

And I owed her that.

I owed her more than she even knew.

Because the moment I gave in...

I wouldn't just want her.

I'd claim her.

Mind. Body. Soul.

Months—years—centuries wouldn't be enough.

She would become the axis around which my existence turned.

And I didn't trust myself to stop once I started.

I exhaled through clenched teeth and pushed off the wall, letting the water hammer my shoulders for one moment more—trying to will away the image of her with me.

Wet.

Breathless.

Cursing my name.

Fuck—Underworld take me.

I shut off the water, grabbed a towel, and stepped into what would soon be *our* room.

Our room. I didn't do clutter. Everything here had its place, a purpose—down to the last bow hair on my violin. Yet I couldn't stop the slow curl of my lips at the thought of her books spilling into this space...certain ones I fully intended to relive with her—thoroughly.

The walls were dark, not because black was my favorite color—quite the opposite. Through the large arched windows, the rising sun fractured the shadows, showing me that even darkness has its cracks. And now...the darkness in me has been pierced, split open by a single name: *Skye.*

My gaze landed on the neatly folded clothes stretched across the bed, exactly as I'd left them.

But then...

I let my eyes drift.

I pictured her there—stretched across the sheets, bare skin glowing against the dark linens. Her hair tangled, clinging to her flushed skin. Her body trembling. The echo of her moans—mine to draw out, again and again. The thought of her pleasure soaked into the very fabric of this bed, and a slow, aching heat tore through me.

My hand brushed the edge of the mattress, as if I might feel her there—warm from my fantasy.

I swore under my breath.

"Focus," I growled, dragging my fingers through my hair—because if I didn't, I would lose every last shred of control I still had.

I toweled off quickly and dressed, my thoughts still swirling as I caught the faint *clink* of glass from the adjoining lounge and the crackle of the fireplace someone had lit. The soft amber glow of the room spilled out into mine, drawing me toward it.

I shook my head and followed it.

Zeph was perched on the edge of one of the leather chairs, casually pouring himself a drink. He glanced up as I entered, his grin sharp.

"Well...don't you look extra clean." He extended a glass toward me, the amber liquid catching the firelight as it swirled. "You're going to cause a drought with all those showers."

I took the glass without a word, the crystal cool against my fingers.

Zeph leaned back, sipping slowly, eyes glinting with amusement. "You know, this wasn't one of your better ideas. Both of you seem particularly... *tense.*"

I shot him a glare, voice flat. "We need to be focused."

"Sure, sure," he said, lifting his glass in lazy mock surrender. "Focused. Naturally."

"Any news?" I shifted the conversation, settling into the seat across from him.

Zeph tilted his head slightly, eyes narrowing—as if listening to something only he could hear.

"The air's been stiller than usual," he murmured. "The wind is carrying less for me to hear. My brothers would call it unnatural."

He took a slow sip, his gaze drifting toward the window. "Still air means no wind," he added almost absently. "As if someone is holding it back."

The fire crackled sharply, punctuating his point. My gaze lingered on the window, searching for movement I couldn't see. Stillness pressed against the glass, and with it came that creeping sense that something was wrong. My fists curled tight.

"Cullen!"

The tension snapped as my door swung open—impressive, considering it was a heavy fucking door.

Zeph's grin curved sharply. "Ah. That voice...music to my ears."

Harmony shot him a side-eye as she swept across the room. "Cullen," she repeated, breathless this time.

I leaned back in my chair. "Is there a reason everyone feels the need to congregate in my room today?"

Harmony ignored the comment, her gaze fixed on me.

With a sigh, I set my glass on the dark wood side table and motioned for her to speak.

Her lips pressed into a thin line, frustration flickering in the slight furrow of her brow. "I've been trying to instill reason with *them*," she began, her voice edged with exhaustion.

I laced my fingers together. "And?"

"And no one wants to get involved," she said flatly, stepping further into the room like her anger needed space to breathe. "They're all conveniently uninterested."

"Shocking. Truly," Zeph drawled, a loud *pop* echoing as he cracked his neck.

Harmony shot him a sharp look, but he only shrugged, already fixing another drink—and handing her one without comment.

She let out a breath, took the glass from him, and turned back to me.

"You think I don't know how ridiculous this is?" she snapped. "I've been humiliated, ignored, and brushed off by nearly every god on Olympus."

She downed the drink like a tequila shot, her face untouched by the burn.

I leaned forward, my voice cutting through the charged silence. "I told you they would not be reasoned with."

"Really? We're doing *I told you so* now?" she bit back, thrusting the empty glass toward Zeph, who happily took it for a refill. "Because someone had to try, Cullen. We don't have allies up there. It's just us. And you're too damn stubborn to even consider talking to Aphrodite."

Her name landed like a spark on dry kindling.

"Don't," I warned, rising slowly from the chair. I grabbed my glass—not out of thirst, but just to have something to keep my hands busy before they shattered something else.

Harmony didn't waver. She stood her ground, her voice low but unwavering. "You're letting your pride blind you."

“My pride?” I repeated, incredulous.

“Yes. Your self-destructive pride. *Talk. To. Aphrodite.*” Each word was a sharp snip, like the sound of my wings being clipped.

I slammed the glass onto the table. The sharp *crack* reverberated through the room, a jagged punctuation to my rising fury. “Say her name again,” I growled, venom coiled in every syllable, “and it’ll be your last in this place.”

Harmony’s eyes narrowed, but she didn’t back down. If anything, she looked more resolute than before. “You think I *want* to suggest this?” she retorted. “I don’t trust her either. But she has the power to Command Phobos and Deimos to stand down. And whether you like it or not, *you’re* the only person she might actually listen to. The *only* one.”

The only one.

Rage flared hot in my chest.

She thought it was because I was the true heir—the only child born of a bond between two of the Olympian Twelve.

But it was simpler...crueler than that. I was the one Aphrodite enjoyed breaking—because I was *his*: Hephaestus’s son.

The son of the man who dared to humiliate her before the gods, to show the universe that the goddess of love and beauty could be flawed. Imperfect.

Harmony pressed a hand to her chest, as if steadying herself, then stepped closer, reaching for my arm. “We can stop this now, if you would just—”

“Enough!” The snarl tore from my throat as I jerked my arm out of reach. “You’ve wasted days groveling before gods who couldn’t care less, and now you stand here and claim I’m the problem?”

Harmony flinched—but didn’t retreat. Her chin lifted defiantly. “Of course you think this is all about you,” she snapped, voice sharp and unyielding. “It’s bigger than you, Cullen.”

A bitter laugh escaped me. “Bigger than me? Spare me your platitudes, Harmony. Yes, you’re the goddess of unity, yet what are you, really?” The words tumbled out, not even waiting for breath. “Mortals still wage war, still slaughter each other over nothing. Where were your words then?”

Her lips parted. Her composure slipped—surprised.

Zeph stood now.

I was dancing dangerously close to a line he didn't want me to cross—and one he wouldn't let me step over either.

But my control was slipping, and the words spilling from my mouth were no longer just anger. They were something else...wounded, disguised as rage.

"You can't fix this with speeches. Not with your ideals. Not with *you*."

"Cullen." Zeph's voice cut in, a final warning.

Harmony's face stilled.

For a second, I saw it—the flicker of hurt ghosting across her features before she buried it behind that infuriating calm.

"I see," she whispered, voice trembling slightly.

She turned toward the door. Zeph moved instinctively, hand halfway to her shoulder—but she slipped past him without looking back. He didn't try again.

At the threshold, she paused. Her gaze flicked over her shoulder, eyes hard and shining. "When you're ready to stop thinking only of yourself, you know where to find me."

Then she was gone.

The door didn't slam. It clicked shut with quiet finality.

And somehow, that made it worse—made it twist deep in my gut.

Zeph didn't speak. He just stared after her, like part of him wanted to follow but knew better.

I sank into the chair behind me, the fight draining out of me.

Regret coiled in my chest, slow and tight. But I couldn't call her back.

Not now.

Zeph lifted a hand. With a flick of his wrist, the breeze carried the cracked glass from earlier into the fire. The flames hissed, licking the broken edges as if swallowing the tension left behind.

"Nice," he muttered. Just one word, but it made my shoulders stiffen.

He stayed still, watching the fire consume the glass, his gaze heavy, as though searching for answers in the cracks.

Then a long, steady sigh.

"I know," he said, voice softer now but no less sharp. "I know why you don't want to talk to Aphrodite. Gods know the horrors she's dragged you through. The things she made you do."

I kept my gaze fixed on the flames, refusing to meet his eyes.

"But," Zeph continued, stepping closer, his tone shifting to something firmer, “maybe it’s time to face your own demons...before Skye ends up having to face hers.”

My fingers dug into the armrest, knuckles whitening. Still, I said nothing.

Zeph lingered for a beat, giving me one last chance to speak. When I remained silent, he turned, shoulders tense, and walked out after Harmony without a single glance back.

The silence that followed was punishing. Every crackle of the fire sounded like a whip against raw nerves.

I stepped forward and braced my hands on the fireplace mantle, the stone cold despite the heat. My eyes locked on the flames—but it wasn’t fire I saw.

Her image wavered in the smoke and heat, etched in ember and shadow. She was bound to the fire, her eyes wide with fear, searching—pleading—for answers. *Why didn’t I stop this?*

Skye.

I couldn’t look away. Couldn’t blink. Her body writhed against the flickering light, her pain unbearable.

Alone.

Because of me.

Because I didn’t do enough.

Because I wasn’t enough.

Knock, knock.

My head turned toward the doorway.

Sara stood there, her silhouette cut against the low light from the hall, like she’d been waiting for the storm to pass.

Her presence grated against my already frayed nerves.

I leaned back in the chair, dragging a hand down my face. “Be quick,” I muttered. “I’ve had enough theatrics for one night.”

Her voice was calm and steady, but the words were anything but. “Skye’s birth records.”

I pinched the bridge of my nose, exhaling hard. “I’ve already looked into the day she was born. There was nothing unusual about it.”

Sara stepped into the room, her gaze holding me with a silent command to restrain myself. “Her file included a doctor’s recording—one that was never officially documented.”

My patience splintered to a razor's edge. "What recording?" I snapped. I didn't need any more riddles.

She stopped just a few feet from me, then spoke—each word seeming to sway the flames.

"Skye wasn't just born," she breathed.

"She also died."

CHAPTER TWENTY-FIVE

SKYE

Priorities.

The rough translation in Greek was *prôtos*.

I only knew this little tidbit because I'd been helping Euryale in the library translate some of the old Oracle journals—learning, in the process, that Oracles had been priests, scribes, obsessive recordkeepers who documented every divine act of the gods and Titans they worshiped.

And that word—*prôtos*—had been lodged in my brain ever since Cullen said his priorities would shift.

A flash of Cullen's eyes, the intensity in them when he said it, flickered through my mind and refused to let go.

I snapped a journal shut—too sharply, as if I could crush the thought out of existence. The nymphs glanced up from their cleaning, and I mouth a quick *sorry* before reaching for the next book. My fingers trailed over its worn leather cover, hoping it held answers—or anything useful at all.

A sigh slipped out of me.

It had been almost a month now.

A month.

How could that have felt like so much time and nothing at all?

By now, I would've been digging through bins of fall décor for Mystic Soulstice—adding pumpkins to absolutely everything I could get my hands on. The thought made my chest squeeze.

Sara had helped, though. She'd kept me updated with weekly reports, even showing pictures on her phone of the nymphs disguised as humans. They were smiling, holding up items, their arms wrapped around my regulars like best friends. They were truly taking care of the place. A place I loved. That had meant everything to me.

Lydia would've loved it, too.

Honestly, I might actually need to hire them after this...

After this. After I found the nectar.

Would life ever really feel normal again?

I missed the shop, the apartment, *my* life.

But...I was starting not to hate it here.

I was changing. Meditation had begun to calm my mind, and dagger drills and bow practice steadied my hands. I was becoming someone else —someone more connected to my own body.

But that target...I still hadn't hit the *damn* center.

Maybe because part of me was hesitant to.

Because once I did...then what? What would happen to Cullen and me?

The thought sent heat pooling low in my stomach—not helped by the fact that Cullen was constantly shirtless in the training yard, sweat tracing down his abs, muscles flexing with every draw of his bow.

But it wasn't just that he was beautiful.

It was the way he watched me—like he saw something in me I wasn't sure I believed in yet. Like I wasn't a girl pretending to belong in a world of gods, but someone who already did.

Only Lydia had ever looked at me like that—like I could be *more*.

And now he did, too.

I caught myself smiling.

"Found a particularly captivating piece of literature?" Euryale's voice cut through, her tone edged just so, as if she knew exactly what—or rather, *whom*—I'd been thinking about.

I snapped my head up, realizing I'd been staring blankly at the same page. Euryale raised a brow, her faint smirk deepening the twist of embarrassment in my stomach. I scrambled for a response, but my silence only made her chuckle as she returned to another journal.

With a sigh, I leaned back in my chair, pretending to focus on the swirling words in front of me.

I couldn't deny it anymore—I craved simply being near him. Cullen made me feel capable, strong, safe. And lately, I'd found myself wanting to make him feel the same.

I knew we needed to stay focused on training—but something had shifted.

We trained, yes, but that was it.

He didn't avoid me like before, but I could feel the distance in his eyes. It was as if my words were some echo he was only half-listening to. He'd smile, just enough to nod—and it was starting to piss me off.

Was this because Harmony and Zeph were gone? I'd assumed Harmony was still trying to appeal to the gods with Zeph at her side, but what if it was something else?

A flicker of movement snapped me out of my thoughts as an orange tail swiped across my face.

Marnie stretched languidly across the table between Euryale and me, her fluffy tail swishing back and forth. Her eyes narrowed at the papers, focused—as if she were reading along with us.

Cough. Cough.

Two nymphs appeared, disguising their interruption as a cough. They exchanged nervous glances as they approached, eyeing Marnie, who had sprawled out even farther—now with a stray tuft of fur floating free.

"Um," one began, her voice polite but hesitant. "Excuse us, but Marnie...her fur is getting on the books we just finished cleaning—"

The other nymph chimed in quickly, her tone equally careful. "Perhaps she could...rest somewhere else?"

I felt my cheeks flush with embarrassment. "Oh, sorry, I'll—" I pushed back my chair, intent on scooping Marnie up before she could cause more trouble.

Without looking up from her book, Euryale flipped a page. "The cat stays."

The nymphs froze, their wide eyes darting between Euryale and Marnie, who let out a soft, contented purr as if she'd just been declared royalty.

"But—" one of them tried again, only to be cut off by Sara, who had been lingering nearby. She crossed her arms and raised a brow. "You heard her," Sara said, her tone firm but amused. "Move along. Plenty of other shelves need your attention."

The nymphs exchanged another glance, clearly reluctant but unwilling to argue further. "Of course," one murmured, bowing slightly before they both scurried off to another part of the library, Sara following close behind like an escort.

Marnie flicked her tail smugly, her green eyes half-lidded in satisfaction.

"Honestly, she's worse than a spoiled princess," I muttered, reaching over to scratch behind her ears.

Euryale let out a small hum of agreement, not even glancing up. "Unlike some, she knows exactly what she wants and isn't afraid to claim it."

I rolled my eyes, but a small smile tugged at my lips.

Back to translating...though after all these hours, my brain was starting to feel like mush.

I groaned, grabbing yet another journal. I leaned over and pointed. "Euryale, how is this pronounced? *K...k...ômai?*"

"It's pronounced *KOH-may*."

My gaze lifted, and my heart gave a hard, unsteady thump, as if trying to climb out of my chest—just to get closer. Closer to Cullen.

He was actually wearing a shirt this time—casually unbuttoned at the top. And of course, my eyes betrayed me, immediately zeroing in on the dip where his throat met the sharp lines of his collarbones.

"The word means 'settlement,'" he added smoothly, his voice pulling my attention up to meet his gaze.

I managed a nod, forcing my hand to write while pretending I wasn't hyperaware of how close he stood.

"Find anything?" he asked, his tone all business. Not even a hint of flirting—nothing.

"Not yet," I replied, sing-songing the phrase with just a touch of annoyance.

Cullen narrowed his eyes at me. I met his gaze without flinching.

"Well, this is riveting." Euryale sighed. "Should I leave you two to your very studious discussion?"

Heat rushed to my cheeks, and I twisted away, pretending to focus on the stack of books beside me. Out of the corner of my eye, I caught Cullen's slight head tilt—a faint smirk tugging at his lips—but he didn't say a word.

I pushed back my chair, the scrape of wood against wood letting out a high-pitched *shriek* that made me wince. "I'll put these away," I mumbled, scooping up a small stack of books like they were a shield. It wasn't exactly a graceful exit, but at least it got me moving.

I made a beeline for Sara, who was giving instructions to the nymphs about dusting and reorganizing the shelves. "Where do these go?" I asked, lifting the books slightly as I approached.

Sara's gaze flicked from the stack in my hands to something—or someone—behind me, a mischievous smile slowly forming. "Oh, those go in the back hall," she replied, her tone light but just a little too quick. "Down that corridor, third door on your left."

She waved me off, already turning back to the nymphs. "You'll know it when you see it. Can't miss it."

I shot her a wary glance, but the soft sound of footsteps behind me kept me from asking more. I could feel Cullen's presence without even turning around.

"Right. Thanks," I said, hugging the books tighter to my chest as I turned toward the hallway. I needed distance. Space. Anything to get away from the walking temptation shadowing me.

The library was a labyrinth of narrow corridors and hidden rooms, and as I wandered deeper through the dimly lit hall, doubt crept in. Maybe Sara had overestimated my ability to find this place. But just as I was about to turn back, I stepped through an arched doorway—and froze.

The room was breathtaking.

Its domed ceiling shimmered with stars and swirling galaxies, casting a soft, celestial glow. The walls were lined with intricately carved panels, each one capturing a scene that seemed to belong to a much larger story. It felt like I had stepped into the storybook of the gods themselves—an entire world etched in wood and stone.

I set the books on a nearby table and stepped closer to one panel. The first scene showed a massive battle—gods, monsters, warriors. The craftsmanship was so detailed I could almost hear the clash of weapons and feel the tremor of footsteps shaking the ground.

"Impressive, isn't it?"

I jumped, just a little, and turned to see Cullen leaning casually in the doorway, arms crossed. His gaze flicked to me, lingered for a beat, then returned to the panels—like he hadn't just startled me into a minor cardiac event.

"Didn't realize you were following me," I said, my voice steady despite my heart hammering against my ribs.

Cullen stepped inside, his movements slow, like he had all the time in the world to dismantle my composure.

"You didn't?" He hummed, tilting his head slightly, as if considering. He sighed, his shoulders lifting slightly as his gaze swept over me. "Seems like we'll have to extend your training," he tutted, each word laced with mock disappointment. "It's a shame, really. You seem so *ready*...for it to be over."

Heat flared in my cheeks, but I curled my hands into fists at my sides, refusing to give him the reaction he wanted. I was tired of the emotional whiplash—flirty one second, cold the next. So instead, I turned back to the panels, pretending they held the secret to tuning him out.

But the space between us vanished as Cullen stepped closer until he stood beside me. His arm lightly brushed mine, sending a subtle jolt through me. I didn't look at him—just glanced sideways, watching from the corner of my eye as his gaze moved across the wall.

"These panels," he began, his voice soft but weighted, "depict the battle between the Olympians and the Titans. The Titanomachy."

I turned back to the images, my fingers tracing the edge of a carved figure, following a wavelike line that wove through the panel until I noticed something—a cluster of those lines converging toward a single point. "And this?" I asked, pointing to a torch whose flames seemed to shimmer, almost alive.

Cullen nodded. "That's the torch Zeus used against the Titans—forged by my father to siphon their power and bind it to the Olympians. Now it remains imprisoned, out of reach, in Tartarus."

I tilted my head, studying the torch. "Why doesn't someone else take it? Use it?"

His gaze flicked to mine, the amusement from earlier gone. "Because my father forged it so no one—mortal or god—can wield the Titans' full power except Zeus. It would destroy anyone else, even with immortality. I almost wish Phobos and Deimos were stupid enough to try."

A chill ran down my spine at the sound of their names, and I instinctively wrapped my arms around myself.

Cullen stepped closer, and for a breathless moment, I thought he might reach for me. My chest tightened with the expectation—an embrace, a touch, anything to be close to him.

But he didn't.

He stopped short, his gaze dropping. Then, without a word, he turned away, putting deliberate space between us.

The whiplash hit again.

"Did something happen?" I asked, trying to keep the edge out of my voice. He still wouldn't look at me—just stood there, back to me, shoulders so stiff I could practically see the tension in them.

He didn't answer. Instead, he stood motionless, like he was weighing whether to speak at all.

Finally, he turned. Slowly.

His eyes met mine, and for a heartbeat, I saw it—something flickering beneath the gold. Hesitation. Maybe even fear.

"I found out something," he said, his voice quieter than before. "About your birth."

My stomach dropped. "What?" I asked, pulse racing. "What about my birth?"

He watched me closely, his gaze both searching and guarded. "You were...stillborn."

"What?" I repeated, unsure I'd heard him right.

"You weren't breathing when you were born," he explained, the words clipped, as though saying them hurt. "But the doctors resuscitated you."

I opened my mouth to respond, but nothing came out. Lydia had told me it was a complicated birth—but she'd never mentioned this.

"Do you think..." I hesitated, glancing at the panels again before turning back to him. "Do you think there's a connection? Is that why I'm... different?"

Cullen didn't answer. Instead, he reached out, fingers gently cupping my chin, his gaze searching mine like he was trying to read something hidden beneath the surface.

I leaned in slightly. "Is that why Harmony and Zeph haven't been around? They know, too?"

He let go of my chin, his hand falling away. "That's not—" He cut himself off, his voice sharp with frustration. "It's complicated."

"Clearly," I shot back, planting my hands on my hips. "What happened?"

"Harmony...Zeph..." Cullen snapped, his tone defensive, but there was something almost boyish in it, like a kid caught in trouble trying to explain himself. "They—" His voice faltered, the words snagging on something he clearly didn't want to admit. His jaw tightened, fingers twitching at his sides like he needed to grab something—anything—to anchor himself.

I waited, arms crossed, watching as he wrestled with whatever pride or anger was holding him back. Finally, he growled, like he was cursing himself for even bringing it up. "We had words," he said curtly, as if that explained everything.

I raised an eyebrow. "You had words?"

His nostrils flared, but he didn't reply. I sighed, dragging a hand down my face. He was so unbelievably impossible.

"Sit down," I muttered at last, pointing firmly toward the nearest chair.

He hesitated, his sharp gaze flicking to me, like he was trying to gauge my angle. "Why?"

"Because I'm asking you to," I replied, holding his gaze with a pointed look.

For a moment, I thought he might refuse. But then—surprisingly—he relented. With a muttered curse, he crossed the room and perched on the armrest of one of the heavy wooden chairs, as if technically following my request without fully committing to it.

"You're so stubborn," I grumbled, mostly to myself, as my eyes scanned the room.

My gaze landed on a candlestick mounted on the far wall, its soft flame flickering gently, casting a warm glow across the dim space.

Spotting a nearby bench, I climbed onto it carefully, the old wood creaking beneath my weight. I stretched up to grab the candlestick, the heat of the flame brushing close enough to prickle my skin. As I stepped down and turned toward him, Cullen's gaze followed me, his expression equal parts curious and cautious.

"What are you doing?" he asked, brows drawing together as I approached.

I set the candlestick down beside him, my eyes locking with his. "It's time for you to trust me—for once," I said softly, reaching for his hand.

He didn't move. For a second, I considered repeating myself, as if he hadn't heard me. Then, slowly, his fingers brushed mine—strained, as if he were holding onto an anchor and afraid to let go.

"I'm...I'm not going anywhere."

I didn't know why I said it. Maybe because it was true. He wanted me to trust him, and I needed him to trust me, too. That meant being honest with myself. I wasn't going anywhere—I wanted to stay. Here. With him.

Slowly, I closed my hand over his, letting my warmth surround him. I shifted, tilting my grip so his palm lay open in mine, fully exposed, fully trusting me to hold him. His skin was warm and rough beneath the softness of my hand, and I felt his breath hitch slightly, a tremor of tension traveling down his arm.

And then the tightness began to ease, inch by inch, like a rope uncoiling. The anchor he'd been clutching loosened, and for the first time, he let someone support him above the weight he'd been carrying alone.

His lips curved, that maddening smirk of his making an appearance. "Didn't know you were so kinky."

"Shut up," I shot back, rolling my eyes in an attempt to keep my composure. "I'm trying to help you, not...whatever it is you're *imagining*."

"Whatever I'm *imagining*?" His smirk deepened, voice dropping just enough to send a jolt of heat up my neck.

Ignoring him, I tipped the candlestick, letting a thin stream of warm wax drip onto his open palm. He flinched slightly, a low hiss slipping through his teeth as the wax landed on his skin.

"Skye," he seethed, his voice tight as his eyes narrowed at me. "I'm immortal, not undead."

"I have had old ladies complain less than you," I teased, shaking my head but smiling.

"Just hold still," I added gently, using my fingers to spread the warm wax across his palm. His hand flexed slightly beneath mine, but he didn't pull away. The wax softened quickly under my touch, and I began to massage it into his palm, my thumbs working in slow, firm circles.

"My aunt taught me this," I explained, focusing on his hand rather than his face. "The heat helps release tension—it melts everything you're holding on to."

Cullen tilted his head back, his eyes fluttering shut as he exhaled a deep breath. "She taught you well," he murmured, voice quieter now.

For a moment, I let myself watch him—really watch him. His face had softened, and his shoulders relaxed, melting under my touch. He looked... beautiful.

The realization slammed into me. This wasn't some client appointment. This was intimate. Too intimate.

What was I doing? My hands stilled, and I pulled away.

Before I could step back, though, Cullen's fingers wrapped around my wrist, holding me in place. His eyes opened, and the way he looked at me —like I was the only thing in the world that mattered—sent my heart tumbling over itself.

"Don't," he said, low and firm, his eyes locking onto mine.

I didn't know what to say. I wasn't even sure I could speak.

Cullen's fingers tightened around my wrist, his grip firm but careful, and before I could think or breathe, he brought it to his lips. The brush of his mouth against my skin sent a shiver racing up my arm, scattering my thoughts like leaves in the wind.

It was impossible to pull away—not that I wanted to. Instead, I felt myself leaning closer, like he was some kind of gravity I couldn't escape.

I shifted my weight between his legs, his warmth enveloping me as he sat there, looking up at me like I was both the answer to all the universe's questions and the source of all his torment.

"Tell me to stop," he murmured roughly—but I didn't miss the way his thumb brushed softly over the inside of my wrist, betraying the steady restraint he was clinging to.

I swallowed hard, the words catching in my throat. I couldn't say it—didn't want to say it. Instead, I stood there, daring him silently, my breath shallow and uneven.

"Skye," he half-pleaded, half-growled, his head tilting forward just slightly, lips brushing my skin again. "Tell. Me. To. Stop."

My chest tightened, and the boldness rising surprised even me. "No," I whispered.

Cullen froze for half a second, then let out a dark, low laugh that sent heat straight through me. "You have no idea what you're saying."

A smirk tugged at my lips, the teasing instinct kicking in despite the wildfire growing between us. "Maybe you're the one who can't handle me." I tilted my head slightly, enjoying the flicker of something darker in his gaze. "After all, I haven't heard any complaints from others."

His expression shifted in an instant. His hand tightened around my wrist, not hard enough to hurt, but enough to make my breath hitch.

"Say that again," Cullen growled, low and dangerous, each word slicing through the air like a blade. "Mention your past lovers, and I'll make sure their heads are delivered to you as a belated wedding present."

A jolt shot through me—the sheer, unapologetic possession in his voice was...exhilarating.

"I'm yours only," he said, softer now but no less commanding.

I didn't refute it.

The way he wanted me—fierce, all-consuming—burned just as intensely as my own desire. I...wanted to be his.

Cullen laced his fingers through mine and started leading me out of the room.

"Where are we going?" I barely heard my voice over the pounding in my ears.

He didn't look back, didn't hesitate—just pulled me along with him.

"Getting your fucking bow."

CHAPTER TWENTY-SIX

SKYE

I think I might've broken this god's mind.

"What are you doing?" I asked, lowering the bow in one hand and the arrow in the other. A slight tremor ran through my fingers.

Cullen walked with infuriating casualness a few feet ahead of me on the field, like we were on some night stroll. He stopped halfway to the target and turned to face me.

"Giving you extra motivation."

"Motivation?" I scoffed.

He tapped his chest with two fingers. "It won't kill me." Then he stretched his arms behind his head. "But it'll hurt like hell. So...don't miss."

I stared at him, completely stunned. "You're insane."

"Come on, little reader," he coaxed, his grin practically vibrating in the space between us.

Little reader, hmph. I wished I had my tarot deck to hurl at him instead of a piercing arrow.

"Don't blame me if I hit you," I warned, adding a teasing lilt to my voice—though it was more an attempt to steady myself than anything else.

His smirk didn't fade. If anything, it deepened, darkening into something far more dangerous.

"I'm not worried," he murmured, eyes locked on mine. "I've already thought of ways to punish you if you do."

My pulse dipped lower. I tightened my grip on the bow, forcing myself to focus, to shove aside the heat curling through me.

I raised the bow, nocked the arrow, drew the string back, and lifted my chin.

He didn't move. Didn't flinch. Just stood there—between me and the target—daring me. Challenging me.

I shifted, tilting my head, trying to find an angle. But his body blocked too much of the target.

How was I supposed to hit it without hitting him?

"I love watching your mind work," Cullen taunted, like every word was meant to slide under my skin, daring me to look at him.

I refused. If I looked—if I met those eyes—I'd forget the bow in my hands and the target waiting behind him.

I shook my head, my grip slipping. The string burned against my fingers as I released.

Shit.

Whoosh.

The arrow flew, a blur of motion between us. But there wasn't enough distance, not enough curve, not enough space for it to miss him and still strike the mark

Just before it could reach him, Cullen's hand snapped up like a bolt of lightning.

The arrow froze—caught effortlessly between his fingers, inches from his face.

My mouth fell open in disbelief.

"Careful, *wife*," he drawled, his voice dripping with mockery as he tossed the arrow to the ground. "I'm starting to think you want me to punish you."

I rolled my eyes, though the heat in my cheeks betrayed me as I reached for another arrow from the quiver on my back.

He shifted his weight. "Hesitation is a weakness. And you're too good for weakness."

He moved even closer to the target, widening the gap between us. The distance made my chest tighten, and the bow's weight felt heavier in my hands.

"Cullen," I warned, my voice shaky despite my attempt to sound firm.

"Focus," he said, glancing back at me. "Because I'm not catching it this time."

Fuck.

My hands trembled as I nocked another arrow. I shifted into the stance he'd taught me.

Don't hesitate.

Don't hesitate.

Don't hit him.

I drew the string back hastily and—released.

The arrow flew faster this time, with more force than the first. It—

The arrow pierced his shoulder.

"Shit," I breathed, the bow slipping from my hands as I rushed toward him. "Are you okay?!"

"Stop!"

His voice cracked through the air like a whip, freezing me mid-step.

He reached up to his shoulder, gripped the arrow, and yanked it out swiftly—no flinch, no gasp. Where blood should've flowed, there was only a faint shimmer of light, pulsing once before fading. His jaw clenched, a flicker of pain flashing across his features, gone as quickly as it came.

"Cullen, I—"

"Again."

The word cut me off.

I blinked, stunned. "What? No! Are you crazy?" My voice cracked.

Cullen stepped forward, boots crunching against the grass. "Stop hesitating, Skye." His gaze burned into mine. "If this were life or death, you don't hesitate. Not for me. You shoot. You save yourself. Do you understand?"

My chest tightened, breath catching in my throat as tears pricked the corners of my eyes. One slipped free, stinging as it trailed down my cheek.

Around us, the clouds pressed closer, like they were holding their breath with me.

My hands trembled, but I refused to fall apart in front of him. I forced the tears back, swallowing hard as something sharper than fear burned through me—anger. It surged in my veins like fire.

I bent down, grabbed the fallen bow with shaking fingers, and stood.

Cullen stepped back into place—still between me and the target. Still *motivating* me.

I nocked yet another fucking arrow. My breath caught as I drew the string, the tension thrumming through my arms and winding tight in my chest. The bow creaked softly beneath the strain, that single sound snapping any lingering hesitation.

My vision narrowed.

The target.

Cullen.

The impossible line between them.

Cullen.

I exhaled slowly.

Target.

And I let go.

The arrow sliced through the air—a streak of silver against the dark. It flew like it had absorbed every emotion I'd poured into it, matching the force surging through me.

The arrow tore through the fabric of Cullen's shirt at his shoulder, slicing cleanly.

A sharp *thunk* shattered the stillness.

He looked at the arrow, now embedded deep in the yellow center of the target behind him, then down at the torn sleeve of his shirt. A slow, wicked smile curved his lips.

"That's my girl."

Cullen's room was exactly how I'd imagined—pristine, as if order itself was the only thing keeping the chaos in him contained. The lanterns on the walls glowed low and warm, their light catching on blue flowers scattered throughout. Forget-me-nots. The same ones Sara had brought to my room.

Were those his favorite?

But my eyes snagged on the massive bed. It was larger than any king-size I'd ever seen, draped in black sheets tucked so tightly I could've bounced a coin off them. Or, in this case, my ass—

I jumped slightly at the sound of the door clicking shut, every nerve in my body alert to him, to the weight of his presence against the stillness of the room.

"The door isn't locked," he said, unmoving from where he stood against it. His voice was rough, strained. "You can leave anytime."

"Are you trying to give me a reason to leave?" I asked, half hoping he wasn't. Half dreading he was.

His gaze darkened, heat pooling in his eyes. "I don't think you understand...my self-control is at its limits." He stepped toward me cautiously, like any sudden movement might break whatever thread of restraint he still had.

I met his stare, tilting my chin up. "I don't want you...in control."

A muscle in his jaw twitched. His exhale came sharp, like he hadn't expected that. One blink, and he was in front of me.

My legs hit the edge of the mattress, and I stumbled back, landing before I could catch myself—less graceful than I would've liked.

I looked up. He noticed...but he didn't stop.

He wasn't teasing anymore.

Cullen's hands moved to the hem of his shirt. As he pulled it over his head, I couldn't help but watch—the way the lantern light kissed the hard lines of his body, the way his muscles flexed, like they could feel my eyes on them.

Then, with a slow stretch, his wings unfurled, their powerful span taking up space in a way that felt...unbound. Freed.

I swallowed hard, my fingers clenching the silk sheets.

The gods had never given me anything.

But this—watching him like this—might be the one exception.

His hands moved to his belt, removing his pants and briefs—revealing all of himself without a hint of hesitation.

Was I still breathing?

Barely.

Cullen stood between my legs, and I couldn't look away. My eyes went wide at the sheer length of him. Even without touching me, I could feel the heat radiating off his body, seeping into mine.

He reached out, brushing a stray strand of hair from my face. His fingers trailed down until they curled beneath my chin, lifting it gently, leaving me no choice but to meet his gaze.

His eyes burned—like a sun flare. Shifting, flickering, pulling me in, drowning me in heat and light.

His palm pressed into the mattress by my head, caging me in. Instinctively, I shifted back, making room as he climbed onto the bed.

"I can smell you everywhere," he murmured—almost feral.

It was warm...and yet a shiver tore down my spine, straight to my core.

Cullen braced himself on his knees, hovering above me.

I watched as his wings—those magnificent, powerful wings—began to retreat, folding into himself.

No.

I reached out without thinking, grabbing his arm. "No...don't hide them."

He stilled, then let out a low growl—a sound that sent heat pooling low in my stomach—and nodded, as if my words were the only thing keeping him tethered.

His wings flared, stretching wide, arcing toward the ceiling.

I reached up, fingertips grazing the soft, silken feathers. Cullen inhaled, his back arching slightly toward me. I continued, stroking along their length, reveling in the way he trembled beneath my touch.

"Skye," he warned, voice strained, nearly breathless. "You're not playing fair."

I smirked, dragging my fingers lower, watching the way his chest constricted.

Cullen's hand shot out, fingers brushing my wrist before curling around it. "My turn."

My back melted into the coolness of the sheets as his fingers skimmed a slow, torturous path along my thighs, stopping at the hem of my shorts.

I needed him. Now.

I moved for the button on my shorts, desperate to peel away everything between us.

But before I could even slip it free, his hand caught mine—firm but gentle.

"So impatient," he teased, his voice a low rumble sending a ripple through my core.

The room was dark, but I knew—*knew*—he could see everything. Every blush. Every shiver. Every inch of want etched across my skin.

His thumb traced a slow, torturous circle over the inside of my wrist.

"I want to savor every inch of you," he murmured, sliding his hand up my sides, fingers skimming the outer curve of my bra.

I bit down on my lip, my body already arching toward him, desperate for friction—desperate for him.

In one breathless motion, I slipped free of his grip, reached for the hem of my shirt, and yanked it over my head—the arrowhead the only thing left dangling from my neck.

I pushed my hair from my face. "I'm not impatient," I muttered. "I'm just...efficient."

That earned a darker smile from him.

Cullen shifted, lowering his weight until he pressed me firmly into the bed. His eyes glittered in the shadows.

"No more removing your clothing," he said, his tone commanding.

Then his hips rolled into mine—hard.

A gasp tore from my throat.

"Understood?" he whispered, breath hot against my ear.

"Yes," I breathed, the word spilling out on a broken moan.

He caught my chin between his fingers, tilting my face until there was no escaping his gaze. His thumb brushed the corner of my mouth, lingering as if he were giving me the chance to run—before deciding I was his to claim.

"Those eyes..." he whispered, almost like a prayer. "They'll be the death of me."

And then he crushed his mouth to mine, hard and deep, stealing the air from my lungs and strength from my body. His tongue swept into my mouth, claiming me with a hunger I hadn't thought it possible, yet my body—trembling beneath him—clearly disagreed.

Cullen's fingers found the clasp of my bra, and—of course, being the god of love and desire—he unhooked it with ease, freeing my breasts to the cool air and his touch.

Without breaking the kiss, he palmed one breast, his thumb tracing slow, rough circles that made my breath hitch.

I moaned against his mouth, my body arching helplessly into his hand.

I needed to feel him—to make him feel the same fire burning me alive.

I slid my hand down his chest, tracing every rugged ridge of muscle, but Cullen caught my wrist and pinned it firmly above my head with one hand.

"Tonight is only about you," he growled against my lips.

Before I could even think to protest, his mouth found my exposed nipple, sucking hard enough to send a fresh shock of pleasure through my core.

I writhed beneath him, the feeling overwhelming, my hips lifting off the bed in silent plea.

He pinned me harder, his hips grinding into mine, and I could feel the heat of his desire through the thin barrier of my shorts.

A whimper escaped me—desperate.

He bit down just enough to make me gasp, the sharp sting immediately soothed by his tongue, pain and pleasure blending until I was nothing but gasping need.

"Please," I whispered, not even sure what I was begging for anymore.

"Gods, Skye," he groaned, lips closing around one sensitive peak, sucking hard as his hand slid down the curve of my waist.

"Your breasts are perfect."

He moved my arms from where they'd been pinned above my head, guiding them down until my hands cupped my own breasts. His touch lingered, thumbs brushing warm trails over my skin.

"Squeeze them," he murmured. "I want to hear your pleasure."

I nodded, my fingers pressing into the soft curves. A breathless whimper escaped as his mouth dipped lower, tracing a searing path down my stomach.

When he reached the apex of my thighs, he pressed a hand between them, coaxing them apart until I opened for him.

He placed a kiss on my inner thigh, his breath warm and torturous against my sensitive skin.

Higher. Gods, I needed him higher.

"You want me?" he said, his voice low and commanding. "Say it."

"I want you," I gasped. I meant it—without a single thread of doubt.

With a swift, fluid motion, he undid the button of my shorts and slid them down my legs, tossing them aside. He left my underwear on, only pushing it to the side, exposing me to his gaze.

"So wet for me already," he murmured. "And I haven't even touched you properly yet."

Then, with devastating slowness, he peeled away the last barrier between us and lowered his mouth between my thighs—his tongue stroking through my folds with divine precision.

I barely had time to gasp before one finger slid inside me—then another—*fuck*, I lost count. His fingers curled just right, sending shockwaves through me as I clenched helplessly around him.

I cupped my breasts, my nipples tight and aching, grinding against his mouth as his tongue moved in perfect rhythm with his fingers.

He sucked hard, and I cried out, my hand flying from my chest to fist in his hair, pulling him closer.

He hummed against me, the sound vibrating straight through my core, lighting up every nerve ending until I thought I might shatter from that alone.

My back arched off the bed as he devoured me so completely, I swear my soul felt it.

Every flick of his tongue, every feral stroke sent me spiraling higher, the pressure coiling tighter and tighter inside me until I hovered on the edge of release.

"Cullen," I gasped, my voice wrecked and pleading.

He slowed his tongue, teasing my swollen clit with torturous control, each stroke softer—until his teeth grazed it.

Sharp.

I jerked, hips bucking, a strangled sound tearing from my throat. His mouth held me captive, tongue soothing where his teeth had teased—only to do it again.

Then his fingers plunged inside me—deep.

I shattered.

A choked moan burst from my lips as pleasure slammed into me. My body tensed, legs trembling, hips grinding against his mouth, chasing every flick of his tongue.

But he didn't stop.

Even as I writhed beneath him, shaking and clenching around his fingers, Cullen kept going—his mouth locked on me, tongue stroking, sucking, licking through every aftershock, wringing every last wave of release.

Only then did he lift his head, licking his lips slowly, savoring every taste of me. His eyes were dark and wild.

I whimpered at the loss of contact, already aching for more—aching for *him*.

"Now...I want to watch you come for me," he rasped.

Cullen fisted his cock, and I barely had a second to breathe before he found my entrance and thrust into me in one deep, claiming stroke.

"Fuck," he groaned, his voice rough against my ear. "You fit me perfectly."

His lips crashed against mine, the taste of myself on his tongue sending another wave of heat through me. My legs wrapped around his hips instinctively, urging him on, desperate for more.

I was already spiraling again, the pressure rebuilding fast. Cullen's thrusts grew faster, harder, each movement driving me closer to the edge. He lifted his head just enough to watch me, his gaze locked onto my face as I fell apart for him.

"Cullen!" I screamed, detonating around him, my orgasm ripping through me in fierce, relentless waves.

My body trembled violently beneath him, and he never once looked away, his gaze drinking in every second of my release.

"Good girl," he murmured against my lips, his voice thick with satisfied pride as I shuddered in his arms, my breath ragged.

I felt myself start to collapse onto the bed, my limbs sinking into the sheets, but Cullen slid an arm beneath my back, holding me up effortlessly.

"Oh, we're not done yet," he growled, his wings snapping wide.

Before I could catch my breath, he flipped me onto my stomach, hauling my hips up until I was on my knees—open and exposed for him.

The sweep of his wings brushed my back, feathers so soft they sent a shiver racing down my spine. One curved low, pressing between my shoulder blades—not painful, but firm enough to keep me pinned.

Then the other shifted, trailing from my calf and gliding higher along the inside of my thigh until my breath hitched.

"Cullen—" I gasped, my knees trembling as the wing slid higher, feathers brushing the place I ached for him most.

Again.

And again.

My nails clawed at the sheets, certain I'd tear straight through them.

Each stroke dragged me higher, unraveling me until I was on the edge of breaking—

"Are you ready for me?" he murmured, his voice tight with restraint. The sweep of his wing grazed the curve of my ass, lingering there until my skin burned for more.

"Yes," I breathed against the now-damp sheets.

He entered me again, slower—agonizingly so. I gasped, still so sensitive but craving every inch of him.

"Skye..." he groaned, his hand spreading over my ass, "*this* is begging for attention."

His thumb teased the tight entrance, circling with wicked patience until a broken whimper escaped me.

I arched back into him, desperate for more.

"More," I rasped, barely coherent.

He gripped my waist with one hand, anchoring me as his thumb pressed into me from behind—just as his cock thrust deep and relentless inside me.

I screamed, all control gone. I didn't care how loud I was. I didn't care if the gods themselves heard. He'd earned it. Damn him, he'd earned every sound that tore from my throat.

I felt Cullen swelling inside me, his pace rough and frantic now. He was close—I could feel it, every thrust bringing him to ruin.

I needed him to fall with me.

"Come...*husband*."

That undid him.

Cullen cursed, his hands digging into my hips as he drove deep one last time. I felt him tighten, felt his cock throb hard inside me as he let go, pouring into me.

We collapsed together.

He didn't pull out—he stayed buried inside me, chest pressed to my back, breath ragged in my ear.

"My little reader is so fucking unfair," he said, lips brushing the shell of my ear and sending another shiver through me. "You have no idea what you do to me."

A lazy, satisfied smile curved my lips even as I gasped for air.

If this was what it was like...I would never leave this bed.

CHAPTER TWENTY-SEVEN

SKYE

So he *does* sleep.

I watched him, my head resting on his chest, rising and falling with the slow rhythm of his breaths. I could've stayed like this forever—his arm wrapped around me, holding me close—if not for the quiet but persistent growl of my stomach.

I tried to remember the last time I'd eaten—hell, the last time I'd even left this room. Hours? Days? Honestly, I was more surprised that Euryale hadn't kicked down the damn door to check if I was still alive. Then again...she probably could hear us.

Heat rushed to my cheeks at the thought. I pressed my face against Cullen's chest, but a small smile tugged at my lips. Tilting my head back, I took him in.

Unfair. That's what it was—how he somehow looked even more beautiful asleep, like peace itself had chosen him as its sanctuary.

My fingers twitched with the urge to touch him.

Carefully, I brushed a stray lock of golden hair from his forehead. He stirred, his lips parting slightly as he shifted beneath the sheets.

I froze, breath caught in my throat.

If he wakes up now, I'll never live this down. Or—god help me—neither will my body.

But his breathing evened out again, deep and steady. I exhaled slowly before easing out from under his arm and slipping out of bed. Not even a twitch from him.

Huh. That was easier than I thought.

I grabbed his shirt from the floor, loving how the oversized fabric hung on me like a dress. Lifting it to my nose, I inhaled.

Yep. Still smelled like him. How did he smell like the beach when there wasn't even a beach at the palace?

My stomach growled again, louder this time. I pressed a hand to it like it was a broken alarm clock begging to be silenced.

Padding backward toward the door, I glanced over my shoulder one last time.

My back bumped into a small table. It wobbled. Something tumbled off.

Thud.

Shit.

I winced, eyes snapping to the bed. But Cullen didn't stir. He remained sprawled across it, the sheets pooled low around his waist, golden hair a tousled halo against the pillow.

What kind of self-preservation instinct was that? And he said *I* needed training. Apparently, he could sleep through anything.

A smile tugged at my lips before I could stop it. I kept learning things about him—little, unexpected things. And it felt so natural, so easy, like we'd always been this way. Like there'd never been a time I didn't know him.

I glanced down, and my gaze landed on a phone. *Cullen's?*

Crouching, I traced its sleek edges with my fingers, surprised. I'd never actually seen him use one—only Sara ever had a phone. Carefully, I set it back on the table and slipped quietly toward the door.

When I opened it, the hallway was bathed in pale, bluish morning light that stretched long and soft across the marble floors.

What the...?

Just outside sat a silver tray piled high with what looked like breakfast: muffins, apples—but what caught my eye was a small card tucked into a cluster of grapes, marked with a little red heart.

Eat it well—Sara and Euryale

I nearly choked on air. Yeah...I doubt they meant the grapes. I could practically hear those two conspiring as they wrote it. I shook my head with a smile.

Still, I had to hand it to them—they really thought of everything.

I leaned down to grab the tray.

It was heavier than I expected. I shifted my weight, trying to balance it, but an apple rolled off the edge.

Dammit.

I quickly set the tray down and darted after the runaway apple.

Gotcha. I crouched, fingers curling around its smooth skin—but when I straightened, my gaze landed on where it had rolled to.

Right at the clawed foot of the piano Cullen had given me.

I stilled, my chest tightening.

He'd gotten it for me simply because he remembered something I once loved. A piece of my old life, handed back to me in this strange, impossible new one.

Slowly, I set the apple back on the tray, my gaze never leaving the piano.

Step by step, I returned to it, letting my fingers hover just above the keys. My breath slowed, steadying.

I pressed down.

A single note rang out—clear, perfectly tuned. The acoustics in this space were incredible. Every sound seemed to linger, suspended in the air.

I moved to sit on the bench, Cullen's shirt sliding up my side as I settled in. My hands found the keys again, gliding from note to note.

I poured myself into the music—into every press, every chord. My pain, my grief, my fear—all of it spilled through my hands.

Each note became a confession—a diary entry. Proof that being thrust into this chaotic world of gods had led me to something I hadn't even known I was searching for.

Lydia's voice threaded through the melody: *Be the magic you seek.*

And with each echo through the halls, the darkness fractured, falling away to make room for something stronger—

Faith.

It unfurled inside me, as if the song had been waiting to tell me I was never alone.

"You didn't have permission to leave."

I startled, spinning around to find Cullen walking toward me—wearing nothing but a pair of briefs, his golden hair tousled, like sleep still clung to him.

"I wasn't gone long," I said, trying to sound casual. "And you need to put on more clothes before someone sees."

Not that I minded the view.

"Someone stole my shirt," he shot back, eyes glinting as he closed the distance between us.

I smirked and turned back to the piano, my fingers gliding lazily across the keys. "Hmm. Feels like it's mine now."

He chuckled deeply, a sound that curled through my chest and buried itself there.

"I suppose I'll just have to move the piano into our chambers," he quipped. "Then you'll have no reason to leave."

That one word—*our*—sent a warm flush racing through me. I bit my lip, trying and failing to hide the smile tugging at my mouth.

"That's...unnecessary," I murmured, though I wanted it more than I knew how to say.

Cullen stepped closer, his bare skin brushing mine—heat sinking into me, curling deep. I imagined us like two coffee cups side by side, steam rising and intertwining, warm and inseparable.

"Keep playing."

His fingers brushed my hair away from my neck, and then his nose followed—grazing my skin just enough to make me shiver.

His lips came next.

Each kiss traced an unhurried path from the curve of my ear to the hollow of my shoulder, a vivid reminder of exactly what those lips could do.

"You're making it difficult," I whispered, though I didn't pull away. If anything, I leaned into him, craving more.

"Keep playing," he repeated, his voice edged with a teasing warning. "Or I'll stop."

My fingers trembled over the keys, but I gave in, letting the music shift—softer now.

"Skye..."

His lips never stopped their slow, reverent trail across my neck and shoulder.

"You've consumed me."

My eyes fluttered shut as I melted back against him.

With a deliberate slowness, Cullen lifted my left hand from the piano and raised it to his lips. The warmth of his mouth met my palm—a slow, searing heat that curled through me. One by one, he pressed a kiss to each fingertip, each delicate touch sending sparks up my arm, as if he were claiming every part of me as his own.

"I want you to stay," he murmured, each word shaped like a vow. "Not because of a deal. But because it's what you want. Because it's *us*."

My breath caught as something cool slipped over my finger, still held in his grasp.

I turned toward him, my pulse thundering. A small golden ring glinted in the soft light.

"Mortals use rings, don't they?" His lips curved into a faint smile. "Not that I need anything to tell the universe who I belong to."

He shifted, revealing a matching band gleaming on his own hand.

I stared down at mine. Intricate knotwork traced the edges—tiny infinity loops, strong, beautiful, unbreakable.

The nectar, the deal—none of it mattered.

All I could think about was him, and the way he'd rewired every corner of my heart.

I couldn't imagine my life without him. I didn't want to.

I answered him the only way I knew how. Leaning in, I closed the space between us and pressed my lips to his.

The kiss was slow. Deep. Consuming. I poured into it everything I hadn't yet dared to say—every ounce of love I didn't have words for.

His hand came up to cup my cheek, his thumb brushing away a tear that slipped free. Then he pulled back just enough to rest his forehead against mine, our breath mingling in the quiet between us.

"You will want for nothing," he whispered, his hand gliding to the small of my back, pulling me closer again.

I smiled against him.

"I want nothing...but you."

"You're awfully tense, love," Cullen purred, each syllable dripping like the sweat trailing down his skin. His hands slid over my thigh. "Are you sure you don't need a deeper stretch?"

I squinted at him, smirking—because we both knew he wasn't talking about yoga.

Sunrise meditation wasn't quite the same without Harmony, but I wasn't about to complain about my current company. Not when said company had his hands on my thighs, guiding me into stretches that were doing *absolutely nothing* to help clear my mind.

I swallowed hard, my pulse quickening as his fingers traced slow, lazy circles against my skin. Heat coiled low in my stomach.

"I don't know," I said, shifting slightly beneath his touch. "I think you just like having an excuse to put your hands on me."

The movement only made everything worse. His grip tightened, pressing my leg down with controlled strength, a sharp pang of awareness slicing through me.

He scoffed, fingers drifting higher, grazing the sensitive skin of my inner thigh. "Guilty."

"You two make me want to lose my nutrients," Euryale announced from one of the library tables, an open book in her hand and not even bothering to lift her gaze.

Cullen let out a slow breath through his nose, his patience visibly thinning. "You don't have to be here."

"I had to make sure the screams echoing through the palace were actually proof that Skye was still alive." She closed her book and waved him off pointedly.

I groaned, flopping back onto the mat, my face burning. "Euryale—"

"She might've died a few times," Cullen added smoothly, winking at me.

I sat up and smacked his arm. "I honestly can't with either of you."

Euryale sniffed, flipping her book open again. "Just keep it to minimal pleasures. Some of us enjoy reading without the soundtrack of Skye's tragic demise."

I buried my face in my hands as Cullen laughed, the infuriating bastard entirely too pleased with himself.

"Excuse the interruption," a voice said. I turned to see a few nymphs approaching, their hands fluttering nervously as they came to a stop before us.

Sara caught up to them. “It’s Marnie—she won’t come down,” Sara explained, while the other nymphs still looked out of breath.

I raised a brow. “From where?”

“The book racks.” Sara sighed, exchanging a glance with Cullen. “The ones in the...*back*...section.”

I blinked, looking between them like I’d missed something. “Maybe she chased a mouse?”

A collective gasp rippled through the nymphs.

Sara’s eyes went comically wide. “No mouse would *dare* be in the library.”

She said it with such conviction it was as if the very idea were blasphemous.

Cullen raised a hand, a subtle gesture to calm them, then turned to me.

“There’s something particularly strange about that cat.”

Euryale snorted beside me, as if agreeing without hesitation.

I stood, taking Cullen’s offered hand as he helped me up.

“Well,” I said, brushing off my legs, “we should probably go see what the little menace is up to.”

Cullen sighed, rubbing the back of his neck. “Keep close. The back of the library is a bit...different.”

We followed him deeper inside, past towering shelves stacked with pristine, orderly books—until the neatness began to unravel. The further we went, the messier things became.

Books crammed sideways, scrolls poking out at odd angles. It was like the nymphs had given up trying to keep this section under control.

I arched a brow.

“Did the Dewey Decimal system just...give up back here?”

Cullen barely spared the shelves a glance. “We—I—don’t come this way often.”

“Why?”

He exhaled, fingers trailing along the spines of the aging books as we passed. "My library collects more than just scholarly works and scrolls. It has a tendency to...record powerful love stories. Ones steeped in deep, lasting emotion."

He gave me a look—one that said he wasn't looking forward to having this conversation.

"A lot of it is about my mother."

Ah.

Before I could respond, a sharp *mrrrrow!* echoed above us. We craned our necks, and sure enough, there was Marnie—perched on the very top of a towering book rack, tail flicking, green eyes gleaming like she'd uncovered the greatest treasure of her life.

"Marnie," I called, my voice gentle but firm. "Come down, sweetie."

She flicked an ear. Ignored me.

"Clearly, that worked." Euryale deadpanned.

"Okay, you try."

Euryale rolled her head before crossing her arms. "Marnie, get down here before I climb up there myself and toss you down."

Marnie let out a disgruntled chirp but still didn't move.

Cullen sighed, rubbing his temple. "This is ridiculous."

I grinned. "She's your cat too now, you know."

"I refuse to claim ownership of a creature with so little respect for authority."

"She's a cat."

"Exactly."

Rolling my eyes, I held out my hands and coaxed softly. "Come on, Marnie. Whatever you found, you can show me down here."

Marnie twitched her whiskers—then, as if deciding I'd suffered enough, finally hopped down from the top shelf. Not, of course, before knocking a book loose with her tail.

I gasped as it tumbled through the air, its worn leather cover flipping open just before it hit the floor with a *thud.*

The impact was heavier than I expected, and the nymphs took a collective step back.

I raised a brow, stepping closer. "That sounded more like a meteor strike than a book."

Euryale bent down and lifted it carefully. The pages had already fallen open from the drop, and the moment her glasses landed on the inked words, something in her face shifted—her fingers tensed around the binding.

She inhaled sharply. "Praxis..."

My brows furrowed. "Praxis," I echoed, moving to look over her shoulder.

"Praxis!" Sara squealed, clasping her hands together like the word alone was sacred.

And then it hit me. That name—*Praxis*—Phobos and Deimos had called me that at IVY.

"What are you talking about?" Cullen asked, stepping closer, his voice almost a growl.

Euryale didn't answer right away. Instead, she carried the massive book to a nearby table. The aged parchment crackled as she carefully turned back to the passage.

Euryale exhaled slowly, then began to read:

I need to finish this.

I moved through wreckage—stepped over shattered armor, over limbs torn from their owners, over the innocent who should never have been caught between Titans and gods. Praxis was a devoted and powerful kingdom, but ruins now—its people slaughtered, its homes reduced to rubble.

Their screams still claw at the edges of my mind.

But their pain will not be in vain.

I knelt at the river's edge, where bodies—some still clinging to life, others long since claimed by death—floated in the murky current. My fingers sank into the water, feeling the power that lingered in their blood, in their essence. This war drained them, but in their final moments, their spirits held the last of their strength. Strength that I can wield.

I took it.

I drew their energy forth, weaving it in the heart of my forge.

There, I bound it to Zeus's lightning and the metal, shaping it into something that will end this torment.

A torch. One that takes from its enemy what they have taken from others. Forged from the very essence of those who suffered. A reckoning. A curse. A justice.

The forge roars around me now as I work, sweat dripping into the flames, pain searing through my ruined hands. But I do not stop. I cannot stop.

I am thinking of you, my love.

Aphrodite—you are untouched by war, by the bloodshed that has stained my hands. You are beauty where there is ruin, warmth where there is cold.

You are love and beauty—but what of vengeance?
What of grief?

If love is the most powerful force in the cosmos, then let this torch—this creation of mine—stand as proof of what love can do. Love does not only heal. It destroys. It burns. It devours.

Let the comet above seal my oath to you: that I will finish this. Perhaps when this war is over, when the bloodshed has ceased, you will see me as something worthy of being bound to you.

Hephaestus

The room was silent.
Praxis...
It was a kingdom.
A kingdom where Hephaestus forged a torch.
A torch fueled with their blood.
Blood.
And Phobos and Deimos—

They must think I come from that bloodline.

Am I?

I turned and saw Cullen, Euryale, and Sara. Their mouths were moving, but their voices blurred into the background—muffled, distant, like they were in a dream. Nothing could cut through the pounding in my head.

Praxis.

Torch.

Blood.

But...something else.

Something missing.

I could feel it—right there, just out of reach.

Yes.

I spun on my heel and ran.

Behind me, I heard Cullen curse under his breath before the sound of his footsteps followed close behind. He didn't call my name or demand an explanation—he just chased me, trusting I had a reason.

I tore through the grand library halls, flying past endless rows of books and towering shelves until I reached it—the panels.

The story of the Titanomachy stretched across the walls, but I barely registered the battle this time. My gaze darted across the painted heavens, searching.

Cullen reached me in seconds, hovering close. "Skye—"

I held up a hand, silencing him as I inhaled sharply.

There was something I hadn't told him.

Not because I didn't want to.

Because I hadn't realized it until now.

I kept my eyes fixed on the panel, my breath shaky as I spoke. "The night I was born...my mother had a dream." My voice softened. "She never told me much. Only that when she woke up, she knew exactly what to name me."

Cullen stayed silent—watching, waiting.

I swallowed hard. "She named me..." My words trailed off as my eyes landed on it.

There, hidden in the painted storm of gods and Titans clashing in the heavens, was something small—a streak of fire, burning red, laced with blue and purple, cutting through the dark sky.

My breath hitched.

And in my mind, I heard my mother's voice again, soft, distant:

"Because it was so beautiful...the sky."

Woven into the panels like a signature from the artist themselves.

"A comet."

CHAPTER TWENTY-EIGHT

CULLEN

"Find any reference to that comet."

My order unleashed chaos. Behind us, Euryale, Sara, and the nymphs were already tearing through the library, their hushed voices overlapping in a chorus of urgency. They scoured every scroll and record, searching for the next time that cursed comet would streak across the sky.

I didn't care about that. Not right now.

Skye hadn't moved. She stood frozen, her gaze locked on the panel like breaking eye contact might make it all real.

I reached for her hand. She flinched—barely—but didn't pull away. Her fingers were cold. I exhaled slowly, guiding her through the winding columns until the noise of the library faded into silence.

I stopped outside the entrance. Turning to her, I brought her hand up to my chest and brushed my thumb across the back of it. "You're thinking too much," I murmured.

She scoffed. "Thinking too much? I'm trying to process the fact that my entire existence is connected to some godforsaken torch of blood and fire—"

Before she could continue, I reached up with my other hand, cupped the back of her head, and pulled her against me. The words died on her lips as I kissed her.

She inhaled sharply, then melted into it, her body softening in a way that sent a ripple of relief through me. My hands slid down her back, fingers pressing just hard enough to keep her there, locked against me.

She sighed against my lips, the sound half-annoyed, half-relieved. "You always do this."

I smirked, dragging my mouth along the line of her jaw. "Do what?"

"Distract me," she muttered, tilting her head slightly as I traced my lips down the column of her throat.

"Is it working?" I murmured against her skin, catching the faint shiver that ran through her.

She huffed, but her grip on my shirt tightened. "Maybe."

I smirked against her pulse, pressing one last kiss there before pulling back just enough to take her in. Her cheeks were flushed, lips parted.

Good. I wanted her focused on us—not bloodlines or torches.

Not when my own mind was already burning with them for the both of us.

A gust of wind swept toward us, twirling Skye's hair like ribbons, making way for an arrival. Zeph materialized before us, the breeze still wrapped around him, holding him midair.

"I hate to interrupt such intimate matters," Zeph drawled, his eyes roaming over us, a smile playing on his lips. "But it seems the Fates are on your side after all."

Skye smiled at the sight of him, like two long-lost siblings reunited.

I shifted, unwilling to show how relieved I was to see him, too. "Zeph... your absence was longer than preferred." My gaze held his for a moment, a silent demand for an explanation. "Care to elaborate?"

Zeph grinned. "Missed you, too. And...Harmony can explain. She brought a gift."

A gift?

The last thing I needed was another gift in this palace.

My fingers tapped a steady rhythm against the wooden council room table —which might as well have been made of glass, given how easily it felt like it could shatter at any moment.

A coldness twisted through my gut—something I'd only ever felt from mortals. *Guilt.*

The words I'd hurled at Harmony were meant to pierce her veil of ignorance, not to become an instrument of infliction.

Harmony sat across from me, arms crossed, silent—as if someone, or some wind god, had dragged her here against her will.

Beside me, Skye shifted in her seat, glancing between us like a witness at a dysfunctional family reunion.

"Is someone...going to talk?" she whispered, cautious, as if afraid the wrong word might set off a war.

Behind us, Zeph let out a sigh and clapped a hand on Skye's shoulder. "I knew I should've brought drinks. There's nothing a few glasses of wine can't fix."

I shot him a warning look. He ignored it with the kind of ease that only comes from centuries of torturing me.

"Maybe a couple bottles of wine," he added, completely unfazed.

I was dangerously close to slamming my head against the table.

Instead, I exhaled sharply and turned my attention to the large sack on the table, tied at one end like a mortal's haul of potatoes. Whatever was inside was rapidly shrinking the margins of my patience.

My gaze snapped to Harmony. "Are you going to tell me what's in the bag, or do I have to start cutting it open myself?"

She didn't even blink. Her focus remained on the sack, her voice a perfect calm storm. "Not yet."

I sucked in a slow breath, rolling my shoulders back. If this were some kind of test in patience, I was about to fail spectacularly.

Zeph pushed off the back of Skye's chair and moved toward the table, planting his hands on the surface as he leaned forward. "I asked Harmony to return in order to—" He hesitated, his usual confidence flickering as he carefully chose his next words.

"You were being a Pegasus's ass," Harmony cut in smoothly.

Heat flared in my chest. My hands curled into fists against the table, but just as I opened my mouth to respond, something soft brushed against mine.

Skye's fingers.

Barely a touch—light, almost absentminded—but it anchored me. My gaze dropped, catching the glint of metal on her hand.

My ring.

Seeing it on her finger sent something dark and possessive curling through me.

"Yes, he was," Skye added matter-of-factly. Then—as if that betrayal weren't enough—she had the audacity to wink at me.

My irritation twisted into something far more dangerous. My eyes dropped to her mouth, then slid slowly back up to meet hers.

"Et tu, Skye?"

Her grin was unapologetic. She leaned in slightly, her fingers sliding between mine with deliberate, teasing ease.

"Always, husband."

Husband. She knew exactly what that word did to me.

A low growl rumbled in my throat, barely restrained. I was seconds away from sweeping her into my arms and carrying her back to our room —to lock the world out and devour her properly.

A pointed cough cut through the room.

"Well...things have certainly changed here," Harmony remarked, her gaze sliding between us with an arched brow.

Skye chuckled, then turned to her with a soft, relieved smile.

The issue between Harmony and me had unsettled her more than I'd expected. Skye looked at Harmony not just as an ally but as something more—a friend, a sister, someone worth protecting.

And for Skye, those connections meant everything.

I exhaled sharply. Apologies were foreign, foul-tasting things in my mouth. Harmony knew that.

And she was enjoying it.

She cut me off with a smirk before I could force the words out. "Before you hurt yourself," she said, waving a hand. "Just say what I want to hear."

My jaw clenched, pride settling like lead behind my ribs.

I could feel their eyes on me.

But Skye's burned the most—silently asking what Harmony meant.

I knew exactly what she meant.

Slowly, through gritted teeth, each word dragging like iron across stone, I spat them out: "I. Was. A. Pegasus's. Ass."

Zeph snorted.

Just like that, I was dragged straight back to adolescence—Harmony scolding me, insisting I repeat those particular words in that exact order. All because I once told her that her hair looked like the tail of a Pegasus.

"Forgiven," she replied, her voice slipping back into the tone I knew too well. "Seems even you can understand that words—mere, useless words—can wound just as deeply as any blade."

My jaw flexed. I had dismissed her as nothing more than a goddess of unity, armed with nothing but speeches. Yet here I was, forced to bow to them.

Skye rose from her seat, sunlight catching her hair as she moved toward Harmony. They clasped hands—fingers lacing together in some unspoken pact—two conspirators bound by victory.

I scowled, barely shifting my glare to Zeph before he clapped me on the back, his grin all teeth.

"Look at you," he remarked, mockingly proud. "Developing empathy."

Screech.

The bag twitched.

The motion was small at first—a slow, dragging scrape against the wooden table, like something shifting inside, testing its surroundings.

Then it lurched.

The twine at the top of the bag strained, the knot pulling tight before, with a sudden, violent jolt, the sack flopped sideways. A sharp, muffled *hoot* burst from within, and frantic movement rustled against the coarse fabric before—

A bird exploded from the opening in a chaotic tangle of wings and talons.

Feathers ruffled, eyes wide, an owl no bigger than a common barn owl spun in the air before making a graceless, spiraling descent onto the table. It landed with an awkward *thump*, its silver-tipped wings glinting as it flailed to right itself.

"What in the name of Olympus is going on?!" the owl snapped, voice sharp with outrage.

Skye blinked. "Is that an owl?"

I dragged a hand down my face, already feeling the onset of a headache. "Not just any owl," I muttered.

Harmony rolled her eyes. "Calm down, Nyx. The drugs haven't worn off yet."

"Drugs?!" She tried to ruffle her feathers but nearly toppled sideways.

"You drugged me, you insufferable little—" She cut herself off, eyes narrowing dangerously. "How?"

Harmony inspected her nails. "Tonic. It worked faster than expected." Then she winked at Skye, adding, "Thanks to Sara, we've got plenty of it around here."

Zeph let out a low whistle—seemingly impressed.

I merely closed my eyes for a long, suffering moment before forcing out, "Are you insane?"

Harmony didn't so much as blink. "You told me words weren't enough. We needed answers."

She said it so simply, as if she hadn't just kidnapped one of Athena's most trusted creatures from Olympus. I pinched the bridge of my nose.

Nyx, meanwhile, had recovered enough to puff up her feathers in fury. "This is an outrage! I will see every single one of you punished for this treason! You will know the wrath of Athena! She will smite you, curse you, cast you into the depths of—"

"Right, I think we got the message," I muttered, patience thinning.

Skye took a step closer, eyes alight with curiosity, but before she could get too near, Zeph casually slid in front of her, arm out like a velvet rope. "Might want to keep your distance, sweetheart."

Skye frowned. "Why?"

I exhaled slowly, my tone edged with impatience as I glanced at the furious ball of ruffled feathers still wobbling on the table. Shadows curled at the edges of my vision, feeding off my irritation.

"She's Nyctimene," I answered, my voice hardening. "Athena's owl of wisdom."

Stepping closer, I let my shadow stretch over her trembling form, my stare cold and unyielding. "And she's going to answer some questions."

Nyx fluffed her wings, her golden eyes gleaming with outrage. "I will not! The wrath of Athena will—"

I leaned forward, smiling darkly. "If you don't, I'll have Zeph whisper in every ear in Olympus about how Harmony outsmarted the great and wise Nyctimene."

Nyx's feathery face scrunched in horror. Her gaze flicked to Harmony, who gave her the most infuriatingly smug smile. The owl's eyes narrowed further.

Her golden gaze then shifted to Skye, tilting her head at an unnatural angle—smooth and eerie, like a predator appraising something small and fragile.

But Skye didn't move.

She met Nyx's stare head-on.

A slow, rasping chuckle scraped from Nyx's beak, her talons curling against the wooden table. "Well, well," she mused, voice thick with mock amusement. "So you're the mortal."

I stepped closer to Skye—not to shield her, not because she needed it—but because we stood together.

Nyx huffed, feathers bristling. "Hmph. Interesting."

I moved again, forcing her gaze back to me. "Phobos and Deimos."

Another dry chuckle rasped from her throat. "Ever since Harmony began her incessant clamor about those two, the gods have done little else but prattle on about you."

She gave a languid shake of her feathers, as though the matter were a dull speck clinging to her wing. "But truly, I fail to see the urgency. Those imbeciles have spent centuries gnawing at the edges of Olympian Command—and not once have they managed to leave so much as a crack in the bind."

"Yeah, well," Skye muttered, crossing her arms. "I'd rather not bet my life on that."

Before Nyx could respond, the doors creaked open. Euryale entered first, walking with purpose, followed closely by Sara, who looked between all of us and—

"Is that—"

"Yes," I said tiredly.

"And was she—"

"Yes."

Sara pressed her lips together and lowered her chin to her chest.

Euryale, unfazed by the theatrics unfolding around her, cast a brief glance at Skye. "You're unharmed," she observed, a quiet assurance rather than a question. Only after Skye gave a subtle nod did Euryale turn her attention back to the table, dismissing the tension in the room as if it were nothing more than background noise.

"We've identified the comet."

The words pulled my attention sharply. "And?"

Euryale nodded, glancing at Sara before continuing, "According to one of the Titans' Oracles, it was named Astraios's Comet—after the Titan of stars and planets—during the Titanomachy. It's returned multiple times since then, but never on a consistent schedule."

I raked my fingers through my hair.

Skye's mother's dream—it couldn't be a coincidence.

Phobos and Deimos waited for the bloodline.

Now...the comet.

I turned back to Nyx. "When is it coming?"

Nyx clicked her beak. "The Titanomachy." A dry, scratching cackle rattled in her throat. "You actually believe Phobos and Deimos can break the bond? They would need the torch. Do you think someone—someone other than Zeus—could wield it and restore the Titans?"

Before I could respond, Euryale moved. She took Hephaestus's journal from Sara and pressed the pages directly into Nyx's face.

"Praxis."

The owl sputtered, stumbling back, her feathers ruffling in agitation. Her sharp golden eyes darted to the text, pupils constricting.

I crossed my arms, watching her reaction carefully as Skye shifted beside me.

"Can a Praxis bloodline affect the torch?" Skye asked, her voice almost hopeful the answer would be no.

Nyx's talons tapped against the table in a slow, thoughtful rhythm. "Hmm. Even if someone of that bloodline could tamper with the torch, a mortal still couldn't wield it."

"The solstice is still months away," Zeph added, as if thinking about the nectar.

Harmony exhaled, the sound heavier than before. "Unless..." Her gaze lifted, dark with realization. "They weren't exactly mortal."

Exactly.

Skye and I were bonded. While she wasn't fully immortal without the nectar, she wasn't exactly mortal either.

My knuckles dug into the table, pressing so hard it felt like my bones were trying to fuse with the wood—anchoring me before the rage swallowed me whole.

I turned back to Nyx, my voice low. Tight. Dangerous.

"Comet."

My grip clenched harder, the wood groaning under the strain.

Nyx's claws extended, gouging into the surface. "I am not the Fates. I cannot see the future—"

"No," I cut in, seething. "But you know the comet's past trajectories. The probabilities of the next one. Calculate it."

She hesitated, humming—just enough to confirm she could. I held her gaze, and with a long, reluctant sigh, Nyx's feathers fluffed. Her eyes closed as if the very mention of it drained her. Then they snapped open, the golden irises rolling back into shadow.

"Days," she murmured, her voice caught in a daze. "Perhaps less."

I pushed off the table, drawing in a slow breath, but the weight in my chest didn't lift. My hands twitched with the need to pull Skye into my arms—to remind myself she was here, still with me, still *mine.*

Because if anything happened to her—if they twisted her into some pawn, some weapon—I would burn Olympus to its bones before I let them take her.

Nyx's golden eyes widened, pupils narrowing to needle-thin slits. Her wings flared, the instinct to flee overpowering the sedative still clinging to her limbs.

"This—this is madness," she snapped, her voice rising, sharp with panic. "If she can wield the torch, break the bind, then she's a threat. To Olympus. To Athena—"

Her beak snapped shut, the sound like steel sheathing a blade.

Then she moved.

Wings spread, talons clawing against the stone and preparing to take flight.

I slid my hand toward the bracelet on my wrist.

I had no intention of letting her leave.

Zeph moved his hands. The air in the room shifted, ruffling Nyx's feathers and sending her flight into disarray.

Harmony exhaled sharply, grabbing her hair in the current. "Oh, for the love of—"

But before Nyx could gather herself, Sara moved—and set down Marnie.

The cat stretched, paws kneading into the wood as she eyed Nyx. Her tail swayed once—intrigued.

Nyx froze mid-motion, wings half-spread, her golden eyes snapping to the feline.

I arched a brow. Nyx was now locked in a silent standoff with a cat.

Sara, beaming, said brightly, “Have you met Marnie?”

Marnie’s tail flicked again—each movement slow, measured, like she was assessing her prey.

Nyx, for all her supposed wisdom, swallowed audibly.

I exhaled through my nose, barely suppressing the smirk threatening to pull at my lips.

“Looks like I’m becoming a cat dad after all.”

CHAPTER TWENTY-NINE

SKYE

Let go...grow.

A simple two-card spread.

First card: Let go—*The Wheel of Fortune.*

A large wheel filled the card, symbols etched across its rim. Figures clung to its edges as it turned—some rising, others falling.

Second card: Grow—*Three of Wands.*

A lone figure stood at the shore, gazing out over an endless expanse of water. Three wands were planted firmly in the ground, anchoring them to the earth. The figure stood tall, waiting, watching for something on the horizon.

Together, the cards revealed: *Surrender control. Move forward.*

How exactly does one move forward? What do these cards expect from me—to reach into my heart, pierced with thousands of glittering shards, and lift them out, one by one, without slicing open my soul?

I sighed, resting my chin on my interlocked hands as I sat cross-legged on the rug before the fireplace. The large, fluffy pillows I'd dragged from my room into Cullen's—*ours*—created a little nest around the glow of the flames. The balcony doors were open, and sheer curtains danced in the night breeze, brushing my arms and the satin of my shorts. My hair lifted and shifted with the wind's gentle fingers, as if even Zeph was trying to tell me not to be afraid.

I stared down at the cards, tracing the outlines of their images before slipping them back into the deck. I shuffled absently, listening to the soft, rhythmic whisper of paper against paper.

I needed something—anything—to make sense of the fact that Phobos and Deimos saw *me* as a weapon.

The floor creaked behind me.

"You know," Cullen drawled, low and warm, "we never did finish our reading."

I exhaled sharply, turning just enough to glance over my shoulder at him. "Hmm. I wonder whose fault that was."

He chuckled and crouched beside me, parting the walls of my pillow nest. His golden hair was tousled, a few stray strands falling across the sharp lines of his cheekbones, as if he'd just run his fingers through it. Dressed in nothing but loose, low-slung sleep pants, the muscles in his torso shifted with each quiet breath.

His fingers brushed lightly over my shoulder, a featherlight touch. "And look where that got me."

He eased the strap of my cami aside and pressed a kiss to the bare skin of my shoulder.

"Hopelessly consumed by you," he murmured. His lips brushed over my skin again, softer, slower. "So...can you read me now?"

Each kiss felt like punctuation, adding weight to his persuasion.

I closed my eyes, letting myself enjoy his warmth. "Fine." I sighed, spreading the deck between us. "But no palm readings this time," I said pointedly.

Cullen hummed in agreement, crossing his legs as he settled across from me. I drew three cards from the deck, flipping them over one by one, my lips pressing into a thin line at what stared back at me.

The Lovers. Judgment. The Hanged Man.

Cullen stiffened beside me. "Well," he said dryly, "that's subtle."

I swallowed. "It's about choice. Sacrifice. Change." My fingers traced the edges of the cards, lingering there.

When I looked up, I found him watching me in silence, his golden eyes narrowed...distant.

He was worried. Worried about Phobos and Deimos. Worried about me.

I didn't want to see him like that.

Leaning forward, I cupped his face in my hands, forcing him to meet my gaze. "Don't," I whispered. "Don't feel anything other than what you feel for me. The circumstances weren't ideal, but I still chose to be bonded to you. And I would choose it again. I would choose *you* again."

His hands came up, covering mine, holding them in place against his skin. His lashes lowered briefly before he turned his face, pressing a kiss into my palm.

I wore his arrowhead. I wore his ring. I'd let him consume me in every way that mattered. But...I'd never spoken the words aloud.

A shaky breath escaped me as I gathered the courage I should've found long before. "I love you." The words trembled from my lips—terrifying, freeing, irrevocable. "I love you, Cullen."

Something flickered in his expression—he moved closer, until there was nothing between us but heat and breath. His hands slid down to my waist, fingers pressing into my skin, anchoring me as if to remind himself I was real—that I was his.

"I've loved you in a thousand ways," he murmured, forehead resting against mine. "Long before I ever had the right to say it."

His lips brushed my cheek, trailing down my jaw with agonizing slowness until his breath warmed the shell of my ear.

"I love you without hesitation," he whispered, "to infinity's end."

His fingers tilted my chin upward, guiding my gaze to his. His golden eyes burned with a molten intensity that unraveled me.

"Just you," he breathed, his lips hovering over mine as our breath mingled.

"Only you."

He pulled me forward with sudden, irresistible strength. A gasp escaped my lips as I fell into him, my hands pressing instinctively against the solid heat of his chest.

I shifted, swinging my leg over him until I straddled his lap, my thighs pressing firmly against his hips, ankles locking behind him. I could feel him—every solid, tempting inch of him—beneath me.

Gods, he's so hard already.

His arms wrapped around me, drawing me closer. I could feel every breath he took, each rise and fall of his chest, his warmth seeping into me.

"Mine," he growled against the shell of my ear, his breath sending shivers down my spine. "You're mine, my little reader."

A quiet sound slipped from me, my body pressing harder against him at his words, desire curling low and deep in my belly. His mouth claimed mine again, his tongue parting my lips, tasting me. I melted into him, fingers tangling in his tousled hair.

I needed this.

I needed *him*.

I needed to be swallowed whole—consumed—anything to quiet the chaos pressing at the edges of my mind.

Slowly, I unlocked my legs and braced my hands against his chest, gently pushing him back.

Cullen shifted, leaning onto his forearms, the pillows pressing firmly beneath him. For a beat, he just stared—brows drawn, lips parted. "Skye?"

I bit my lip, heat rising to my cheeks under the weight of his gaze.

My hands slid lower, tracing the lines of his abdomen—each muscle flexing beneath my touch.

He inhaled sharply, his gaze darkening as he watched my hands trail lower until they reached the waistband of his pants.

"Skye..." His voice was rough, a warning wrapped in want.

But I wasn't stopping. I couldn't.

My fingers hooked beneath the fabric, tugging it down, freeing him.

For a heartbeat, I took him in—this...this was mine.

Then I wrapped my hand around his cock, and a low, guttural sound escaped his lips, a wave of heat surging through me, curling low in my belly.

He was beautiful—thick, hard, his sheer length stealing my breath and drying my throat.

I glanced up, meeting his gaze.

His pupils were blown wide, lips parted, chest rising and falling in ragged breaths.

"Skye." His voice was rougher this time, more growl than word.

Swallowing hard, I lowered my head, lips brushing a tentative kiss against his tip. He let out a strangled sound—a mix between a groan and a gasp—as his hands clenched the rug beneath him.

I pulled back slightly, then leaned in again, slowly swirling my tongue around him, tasting the faint salt of his skin, letting the warmth of my mouth tease him to the edges of his control.

"Fuck, Skye..." he rasped, his voice tight with restraint.

His hands balled into fists, knuckles white, until his restraint snapped. One hand threaded into my hair, gently guiding me into a rhythm.

"You're going to undo me..." he groaned, hips bucking beneath me.

I took him deeper, cheeks hollowing as I slid down further, my throat stretching around him. The sounds he made—raw, broken—sent a rush of heat straight to my core.

He's watching me.

I could feel his gaze burning into me—drinking in every movement, every flick of my tongue, every tremble in my breath.

"You're—*fuck*—you're perfect," he gasped, his voice breaking.

I felt him pulse against my tongue, his faint saltiness lingering on my lips. His body strained beneath me, every muscle taut.

"Skye—" he hissed, jaw tight. Veins pulsed along his throat as he fought for control. "I'm not...going to last long if you keep doing that."

That only made me want to push him closer to the edge.

I gave him one last glance from beneath my lashes, tears streaming down my cheeks as I held his gaze.

I'm his.

And tonight, there was no doubt—he was mine, too.

Suddenly, Cullen's hand shot out, forcing my mouth off him with a strangled groan. I whimpered, but he didn't pause—he maneuvered me with swift, commanding strength, fingers digging into my waist as he pulled me upward, hunger burning wildly in his golden eyes.

"I need to be inside you," he growled, voice husky, thick with desperation.

Before I could catch my breath, his other hand slid between us, yanking my shorts and underwear down in one frantic, fluid motion, baring me completely. I gasped as cool air caressed my heated skin, shivering beneath the intensity of his stare.

He aligned me over him, the thick heat of him pressing at my entrance.

"Cullen—" I barely whispered his name before he thrust up, pulling me down onto him in the same moment.

I cried out, my head tipping back, hands bracing against his chest as he filled me, stretching me to the brink.

A deep, broken moan rumbled from him.

"Fuck," he groaned, thumbs digging into my skin. "You are so tight."

"Cullen," I gasped, my voice breaking as I shifted to adjust to his fullness. But his grip only tightened, urging me faster, deeper.

"Take every inch of me," he growled, hips snapping up to meet mine. "Ride me. Scream for me—I want this palace destroyed with the sound of you falling apart on my cock."

I obeyed, grinding down harder, each thrust sending sparks rippling through me until his name tore from my throat again and again.

His head fell back against the pillows, a guttural groan ripping from his chest. His fingers bruised my hips, holding me down like he couldn't bear the thought of letting me go.

"Fuck yes," he snarled, eyes blazing as they locked on mine. "You're choking me so fucking tight. You love the way I stretch you open, don't you?"

A whimper escaped before I could stop it, my body answering before I could, as pleasure climbed higher. But I didn't want it to end—I wanted to keep feeling this, to keep feeling him.

He chuckled darkly beneath me. "That's right," he coaxed. I know exactly how to fuck you, and I'm not stopping until I feel your slick dripping down my cock."

Then his hand shot up, tangling in my hair—baring my neck to him. His lips ghosted over the exposed skin, breath searing and hot.

"*Wife*," he purred, drawing out the word as I had with him earlier. His mouth lingered at my throat—lips brushing, teeth grazing—before sinking lightly into the soft skin below my ear. A fresh mark. *His* mark.

That was it.

A cry tore from my throat as my orgasm crashed into me—wave after wave rolling through my body, leaving me shaking, breaking apart in his arms.

"Cullen—" I gasped, barely able to form the word.

He roared, thrusting up hard, hips stuttering beneath me as he spilled inside me, his grip tightening as if he could pull me closer, deeper.

We collapsed together, breathless and trembling, our bodies slick and warm against each other.

His forehead pressed against mine, our breaths mingling, his hands still gentle on my waist.

I closed my eyes, leaning into him, my heart still racing, my skin still tingling—utterly consumed. "We need a plan," I murmured against his chest.

Cullen chuckled softly, his hand tracing slow, soothing strokes along my back. "We really need to work on your pillow talk."

"Marnie can't guard Nyx forever." I shifted off him with a tired groan. "And the comet..." I added.

Cullen exhaled sharply, rubbing his temple as if warding off the first sting of a headache. He pushed himself upright, raking his fingers through his hair, then pulled me to my feet with him.

As he released my hand, my eyes lingered on his, feeling the warmth fade as the cool night air took its place.

He moved slowly toward the open balcony doors. The night breeze ruffled his hair as he braced his hands against the frame, staring out into the storm-heavy sky beyond.

"If they're waiting for the comet," he said, voice low but steady, "then we stay put until it passes."

Silence stretched between us—like it physically pained him to say the next part.

"After that..." He hesitated, jaw tightening. "I'll go speak with my mother. She can deal with them."

"I'm coming with you."

He turned, glancing at me over his shoulder, gaze narrowing. "No."

"Yes."

"Skye."

His voice held a sharper edge now—but I didn't flinch.

I crossed the room, stopping beside him. "If I'm with you," I pressed, steady, "her Command won't affect you." I held his gaze. "You know I'm right."

His jaw tightened. He dragged a hand down his face, exhaling like he was holding back an argument he knew he wouldn't win. His fingers flexed at his sides, then curled into fists before he turned fully to me.

His eyes flickered, then his lips quirked into a begrudging smirk. "You're so damn stubborn," he muttered.

Before I could flash a triumphant grin, he closed the space between us in one smooth motion, his hands finding my waist as he pulled me flush against him. A surprised laugh escaped me—only to be swallowed as his mouth claimed mine, fierce and consuming.

My fingers tangled in his hair, and he groaned softly against my lips.

Fine. He could call me stubborn. But he loved me for it.

Buzz. Buzz.

We froze.

Buzz. Buzz.

A sound like...a phone. Cullen's phone.

I felt him stiffen against me.

A knot formed in my stomach.

Slowly, Cullen pulled back, his gaze locking on the glowing screen across the room. His jaw tightened, lips pressing into a hard line. He exhaled—a sharp, reluctant breath—like he was bracing for a fight he already knew he couldn't avoid.

His hand slipped from my waist, fingers trailing across my skin one last time before he stepped away.

I watched him cross the room, each step heavier than the last, like he was walking toward something inevitable.

He paused over the glowing phone.

His thumb hovered above the answer button.

My breath caught.

Don't answer it, a small, desperate voice whispered inside me. *Please... don't.*

He did.

Static.

Then—a voice slithered through the speaker, dark and unmistakable.

"It's time...brother."

CHAPTER THIRTY

CULLEN

I was already moving—grabbing the shirt draped over the chair and pulling it over my head in one fluid motion. Skye was just a step behind, hastily gathering whatever clothing she could, slipping into them as she rushed after me.

We moved quickly through the halls, my senses stretched outward, scanning for any sign of immediate threat. My focus narrowed to the phone pressed to my ear.

"You can't stay in your palace forever," Phobos purred.

Deimos's laugh followed. "How long did you really think you could hide? Mother has missed you."

Mother.

The word felt like a blade in my ear, but I didn't break stride. My free hand curled into a fist at my side, tension building within me. The air around me thickened as the wind picked up—and in the next instant Zeph appeared beside me, his expression dark. He didn't need to ask who was on the other end.

We locked eyes, and without hesitation Zeph fell in beside Skye—another shield between her and whatever was coming.

"You sound desperate," I said into the phone, voice low and controlled, even as rage pulsed beneath my skin.

Phobos gave a theatrical sigh. “Hardly. You’re the one caged in your own home.”

Deimos cut in, voice sharp and impatient. “You could be free. No more Olympus. No more leash around your neck.”

I shoved open the doors and stepped into the garden.

Euryale, Harmony, and Sara were already there, their faces turned skyward. I followed their gaze.

The sky split open.

A streak of white fire tore across the heavens, casting a clawed, sickly glow that bled over everything beneath it.

Astraios’s Comet—like the Titan of stars and planets—had clawed out of Tartarus to deliver the war cry himself.

My stomach dropped—straight into Tartarus with the Titans.

Fuck.

My grip tightened around the phone, the casing groaning under the strain. I forced a dark smile into my voice.

“You want to meet?” I replied, more accusation than question, each word burning with the fire building in my chest. “Fine. How about in a few days?”

Phobos chuckled. “Oh, how generous,” he drawled. “But you see, Deimos and I have pressing matters that simply can’t wait.”

His voice oozed mock sorrow.

“We were truly heartbroken not to receive an invitation to your little bonding ceremony. And no thank-you for our gift?”

Tsk, tsk, tsk—each click of his tongue was a needle sliding beneath my skin.

“So impolite...but alas,” Phobos went on, “we’ve talked it over and still believe family should be together on such important occasions. So, dear brother—”

Buzz.

“We insist—you’ll join us for our ceremony.”

Static burst through the line.

Then—a scream. Ragged. Piercing. Another tore through, overlapping the first. One voice cracked around a sob; the other shredded the silence with a bloodcurdling shriek that made the hairs on the back of my neck stand on end.

Thud. Clang. Scrrraape.

Something—or someone—was thrashing violently against metal or stone.

I turned.

Skye stood beside me, her fingers locking around my arm like a vise. Her face had gone pale, eyes wide—fixed on the phone like it might strike her where she stood.

"Is that...are those...my sisters?" she whispered, terror written across every feature.

I would tear them apart for putting that look on her face.

"Mountains...see you soon," Phobos and Deimos said in unison.

Click.

The line went dead.

Skye didn't move. Her lips parted as if to speak, but no sound came—she was in shock.

I know her. I know her soul.

Even if she wasn't close to her sisters, she wouldn't want anyone to suffer in her place. Not like this. And that's exactly what Phobos and Deimos were doing—not just threatening her.

Substituting.

Her sisters, their blood, were being used—standing in her place for whatever plan they were setting in motion.

And I'd let them.

If it meant keeping Skye safe, I'd trade them in her place without hesitation. But not if it meant the end of everything as she knew it. The end of the world as we knew it.

And that sure as hell wasn't going to happen.

I spun on my heel and stalked back into the palace.

Nyx was still perched on the table, shifting uneasily under Marnie's unblinking stare. The cat's tail flicked back and forth—like a slow metronome, but one that came with claws.

Ffft—

I scooped Marnie up with one arm and pulled her against my chest. She didn't resist—just curled into me like she understood. My gaze locked with the owl's golden eyes.

"Phobos and Deimos will restore the Titans unless the Olympians intervene," I said, leaning closer. "Go to Athena. Go to Zeus. And if he won't act"—I clenched my jaw—"I'll challenge Zeus for the throne."

A sharp inhale sounded behind me.

I turned slightly. The others had followed.

Sara stood frozen, her hands pressed to her lips.

"Cullen..." Zeph's voice came low, uneasy.

I knew exactly what my words meant. Challenging the throne was treason—a one-way ticket to Tartarus. But if I had to drive a stake through the one thing Zeus prized most—his pride—to force him into action? Then so be it.

Nyx studied me for a second longer. Then, with a sharp *whoosh,* she spread her wings and launched into the night. Zeph's winds caught her, a sudden, powerful gust that rocketed her faster until she dissolved into the darkness.

I dragged a hand down my face, forcing a steady breath in and out before turning back to Skye. She was still trembling.

Marnie squirmed in my arms, tense and restless, sensing the energy shift. I exhaled sharply and let her go. She immediately darted toward Skye, but before she could reach her, Euryale intercepted, gently cradling the cat as Skye stood frozen—too deep in shock to react.

Slowly, I pivoted, my gaze finding Sara. She was already upright and alert, waiting for whatever order I was about to give.

"Do whatever is necessary," I instructed, voice low and even.

She nodded, her silent command rippling through the other surrounding nymphs.

Skye blinked as the haze of shock cracked. "Wait—Cullen—"

"Weapons," I interrupted.

"I'm coming," Harmony demanded. Her voice sliced through the tension with such certainty that there was no room for argument.

I gave her a nod.

Skye, however, was not part of the plan.

"Euryale," I called, like a general summoning a soldier.

The Gorgon was already stepping forward, placing herself squarely between Skye and the door. Her hand settled on Skye's shoulder, firm but not harsh.

"No."

Skye shook her off.

The word snapped through the air like a crack of lightning.

"No," she repeated, louder this time. She stormed forward. "I'm going with you."

I turned to face her, meeting her fire with silence. A breath left me, long and deliberate.

"No, you're not."

She stepped closer, one foot in front of the other.

"But you said—" Her voice caught. Her hand lifted, trembling slightly as she jabbed a finger at the arrowhead pendant resting against her chest.

"My heart is cursed," she almost whimpered. "Yours...now belongs to me."

I held out my hands. "Skye—"

She surged forward. Her fingers curled into the front of my shirt, gripping with a ferocity that said everything her voice hadn't. She yanked me down to her.

And the world—

The world vanished.

My hands found her, instinctively, reverently. One slid behind her neck, the other tangled in her hair, gripping like I feared she'd disappear if I stopped. Our lips met—soft at first, then with growing desperation. My mouth parted, deepening the kiss, trying to brand the feeling into my soul before it was ripped away again.

Every protest I'd meant to make dissolved on her lips.

She pulled back just enough to breathe, her forehead resting lightly against mine. Her voice, when it came, was a vow.

"Mine."

I cupped her face, my thumbs gently brushing her cheekbones as if I could soothe the fire blazing in us.

"If you don't want this heart to turn to dust at the mere thought of something happening to you," I rasped, "stay. Please."

She didn't look away. Her eyes searched mine—and I saw everything in them. The fight. The fear. The desperate urge to run with me anyway.

But before she could speak, I reached for my bracelet and fastened it around her wrist. Her fingers closed around it instinctively as her gaze snapped down, confusion knitting across her face.

"What are you doing?" she asked.

I gently lifted her wrist, turning it so she could see the markings and twisting trigger etched into the metal. “Will it with your intent,” I murmured, “and it will obey.”

Skye shook her head, already trying to push it back toward me. “No... you’ll need it. Cullen, that’s your—”

A slow smirk curved at the edge of my mouth, even as my chest tightened. “What? You think that’s my only weapon? I’m kind of insulted.”

She huffed—half scoff, half surrender—but nodded, her eyes never leaving mine. Those lips...gods, they were a temptation I didn’t deserve. I wanted to stay. To kiss her again. To forget the storm gathering at the edge of everything we were building.

But I couldn’t stay—

Not when I knew exactly what my brothers were capable of.

I lifted her hand, threading my fingers through hers, and pressed a lingering kiss to her knuckles.

“Stay put, my little reader,” I murmured, brushing my lips just above hers. “If I have to tie you to our bed to keep you from following me, I will.” My voice dipped lower as I moved to her ear. “And trust me—once I’m through with you, you’ll beg me not to untie you.”

Skye flushed instantly, her breath catching.

“As much as I want tiny versions of you running around this place, best we save the world they’d grow up in first.” Zeph snort-laughed.

Harmony smacked the back of his head, earning a surprised giggle from Sara and even a flicker of a smile from Euryale.

Relief rippled through me as I saw Skye’s shoulders loosen and drop ever so slightly.

My wings snapped open, and in the next heartbeat, I was airborne—gone—before I did something reckless. Like decide nothing, not even the world burning, was worth leaving her.

SWORDS.

Shields.

Spears.

No weapon in my armory could match the power of my bracelet, but each was born of my father's fire—iron forged to face gods, strong enough to cut through the illusions of Phobos and Deimos.

Daggers strapped to my calves. A bow and quiver tight across my back.

And finally, the Roman gladius—a blade I'd taken from Ares himself after one of his *visits* with my mother. Its hilt was wrapped in the impenetrable hide of a Nemean lion. Ares never questioned its disappearance, never pressed my mother, even if he suspected her of the theft. For all his skill in battle, he was blind when it came to her.

Now it was strapped to my side.

Tonight, they all would be tested.

Zeph exhaled sharply, tucking a helmet under one arm. "We ready for this?" he murmured.

"We just need to hold them off long enough for Zeus and the other Olympians to arrive," Harmony said. A spear rested in her grip, but it was her other hand that caught my attention—slipping beneath her collar, drawing out a golden chain.

I froze.

The chain swung like a pendulum, dread ticking with every arc—the necklace of Cadmus.

Deceptively delicate, it was forged of orichalcum, the sacred metal of the gods. At its heart, an emerald glimmered like a serpent's scale, and within it lightning writhed—fragments of Zeus's bolt, alive and desperate to be unleashed.

A necklace of legend.

And of misfortune.

It elevated her power, but at the cost of control. At the cost of herself.

Why in the gods' name did she bring it here?

Zeph let out a low scoff, shaking his head. "I haven't seen that in centuries...last time you wore it..." He trailed off, jaw tightening.

He didn't need to finish. I remembered.

A battlefield drowned in blood.

Harmony gripping her throat—

A goddess of unity, never meant to wield that kind of wrath.

I forced my gaze away from the emerald and met her eyes.

"Promise me...restraint."

She didn't answer.

Instead, she slipped the chain back beneath her collar.

"Peace isn't only restraint, Cullen," she breathed. "Even mortals know—sometimes you burn the field to save the harvest. Sometimes you fight fire with fire. Be that fire, if it comes to it."

And there would be fires.

A sharp hiss of air escaped my lungs before I turned. With a single shove, I flung the heavy armory doors open, releasing us into the darkness of the night.

Astraios's Comet stretched wide before us, waiting.

Without another word, I spread my wings. One beat—and the ground slipped away beneath me.

Zeph summoned the wind, wrapping an arm around Harmony's waist. With a single gust, the three of us launched upward, swallowed by the sky.

"It's a trap," Zeph warned, his voice mixing with the howling wind.

I didn't look at him. My eyes were locked on the horizon, where the distance between Skye and me stretched.

"I know."

CHAPTER THIRTY-ONE

SKYE

Cullen. Zeph. Harmony.

The *Three of Wands* were gone.

Like the card itself—three figures standing together, ready to face whatever comes next—they stood united.

My reading.

They were moving forward.

The warmth of Cullen's touch still lingered on my skin, his kiss now a ghost on my lips—but that's all he was now. A ghost. A shadow swallowed by the night. My pulse thundered in my chest as I stared at the horizon, watching the last shimmer of his wings disappear into the darkness.

I exhaled slowly, opening my eyes.

Above me, the comet burned across the sky—a streak of fire carving its way through the stars.

Like a countdown had started.

And I wasn't going to sit here and do nothing.

Spinning on my heel, I marched down the corridor, my footsteps echoing Cullen's path to the armory. I didn't know exactly what I planned to do, but standing still wasn't an option. Cullen had gone to fight. I wasn't going to be left behind.

Unfortunately, I wasn't the only one with strong opinions about that.

Euryale was already waiting at the armory entrance, arms crossed, her expression a shield against whatever I intended to wield. "No."

I huffed. "Move."

She lifted an unimpressed brow. "You're storming in here like a woman possessed, and you think I don't know exactly what's going through that stubborn little head of yours? You want to go after him. Not happening."

Before I could fire back, Sara stepped forward, concern etched across her face. "Nyx will inform the Olympians. They'll find the others. We need to stay put."

I let out a sharp breath, frustration simmering. "And how long will that take? Days? Hours? I know one Olympian who can give us answers right now."

Euryale's glasses looked like they were on the verge of steaming, if that were even possible. "Absolutely not."

Sara glanced between us, confused. "Who?"

I met Euryale's gaze. "Aphrodite."

Euryale let out an almost snarl, her sharp teeth bared. "We're not going to the very goddess who ordered your execution. Your immunity to her Command won't stop her from killing you on sight, even with your bond to her son."

I flinched but didn't back down. "You said it yourself—in some deranged way, she cares for him. She could stop Phobos and Deimos with a single word. If there's even the slightest chance she'll help, I have to take it."

Euryale exhaled slowly, pinching the bridge of her nose like she was already regretting this conversation.

I hesitated, then played my last card. "Lydia wouldn't have stood back and done nothing. She would've fought for the people she cared about."

Euryale didn't move—but she went still in the most dangerous way. Silence thickened around her. She shifted slightly, and even with her glasses in place, I could feel her gaze pressing into me like the weight of the stone curse itself.

My pulse thundered in my throat, but I held my ground.

Her fingers flexed at her sides, as if torn between using them to stop me or help me.

"Damn you," she muttered.

That was as close to a yes as I was going to get.

"We're going to need—"

We both turned toward the armory doors—and froze. A group of nymphs stepped out of the shadows, silently blocking our path. Their faces were calm, unreadable, but their presence alone was a clear message: we weren't getting through.

My stomach dropped. I tensed, glancing at Sara, who remained still beside me.

"Sara," I said carefully. "What's going on?"

She stepped forward, brushing past Euryale and me, then turned to face us—her back now aligned with the others. "I promised I would do whatever is necessary," she began, her voice cracking. Her eyes refused to meet mine. "He wouldn't want you to leave. He just wants you safe."

I swallowed hard and looked at the nymphs. They weren't armed, but they didn't need to be. The palace's magic ran through them like blood through veins. If they didn't want me past that threshold, I wasn't getting through.

Euryale stepped toward Sara, her tone cold and measured. "And what if Cullen doesn't come back? Are you going to keep us locked in here forever?"

Then, slowly, she raised her hands to her glasses.

"Don't make me..." she whispered. "Please."

Sara's eyes widened, shock blooming across her face. Around us, the other nymphs stirred, their movements suddenly uncertain, tension rippling through the air like a warning before a storm.

"Wait!" I stepped in front of Euryale without thinking, planting myself between her and Sara. I didn't know exactly how immortal nymphs were —or how Euryale's curse would affect them—and I wasn't about to find out.

Euryale's grip on her glasses tightened.

"I know he wants me safe," I went on, pushing forward. "But if we don't do something—if we wait too long—then what? What if it's him who needs saving?"

Sara's gaze flicked between us, her lips pressed into a tight, uncertain line.

"I know you don't want to betray Cullen," I continued, softer now. "But this isn't betrayal. This is fighting for him. Just like he'd fight for us."

A heavy silence stretched between us. Then, slowly, Sara let out a breath and turned to the others.

"Stand down."

The nymphs exchanged glances. One by one, in perfect, graceful unison, they stepped aside, clearing our path.

Sara popped a hip, giving Euryale a pointed look. "I can't believe you actually threatened me."

"Well—" I started.

"Says the nymph who drugged me. Twice," Euryale cut in flatly, jabbing a finger at her.

Hmph. Sara turned on her heel and waved a hand at the others to open the armory doors.

I leaned closer to Euryale, whispering, "Were you seriously going to turn Sara to stone?"

"She wasn't going to turn to stone," Euryale replied as she calmly readjusted her glasses.

"How do you—wait. Has she already seen your eyes?"

Euryale didn't answer, just strode after Sara like the conversation was over.

I exhaled and shook my head. The two of them, walking side by side—they were light and power, sunshine tangled in a storm.

The three of us entered the armory.

Like the library, the armory was pristine and meticulously organized—but pointier. Rows upon rows of weapons stretched across multiple levels, each section curated for a different kind of war.

Euryale strode forward, selecting a sword with the ease of someone slipping back into an old life. She tested the weight in her hand, rolling her shoulders like she was reawakening muscle memory forged in battle.

Two nymphs approached me with protective gear, their hands quick and practiced as they secured straps around my wrists and shoulders. Black leather cinched tight against my skin. Their efficiency told me this wasn't the first time someone had stormed out of the palace on a warpath.

I buckled the belt at my waist, slid my harness into place, and reached for the daggers I'd been training with. The diamond pommels flared under the lanterns above as I sheathed them, the cold metal brushing the ring Cullen had given me.

My hand stilled. I started to take the ring off my finger but stopped. Taking it off felt like losing a piece of him, and I wasn't about to let go. I shoved it further on instead and flared out my hand. It was remarkable how similar the ring was to Cullen's bracelet.

When I moved to adjust it, the bracelet pulsed faintly, as if acknowledging me. It had cursed me before, but now...now it felt empowering, having it under my control.

My eyes caught on Euryale as she tossed a blade toward Sara, who caught it easily. But instead of taking it, Sara set it back on a rack and shook her head, tapping her small crossbody bag that looked as if it had been woven straight from the vines of trees.

"I've got everything I need."

Euryale raised an eyebrow. "And that is?"

Sara offered a sly smile. "Sleeping powder. And sustenance."

Euryale snorted. "Great. So if we get captured, at least we won't be hungry."

Their bickering—like an old married couple—blurred into background noise as I turned away, drawn to something else.

My eyes landed on a pedestal set apart from the rest. On top sat a box —a box I recognized.

My steps slowed as I approached, each one echoing through the armory. My fingers hovered over the lid, trembling with the weight of knowing exactly what was inside.

I lifted the lid.

There they were.

A pair of golden scissors lay nestled inside. The etched snake devouring its own tail—its eyes seemed to adjust, glowing faintly as if registering me.

The Fates' scissors.

I hesitated.

Take them, a voice whispered in my head. *You need them. You know this.*

My breath hitched.

I reached out slowly, my hand hovering. The moment my fingers closed around the handle, a jolt ran through me—

It's all connected. I know it.

Decision made, I tucked them into the bag at my belt.

The moment I did, a new weight settled in my body, as if I'd just added their very soul to my own. There was no turning back now.

CHAPTER THIRTY-TWO
CULLEN

Deep in the mountains, shattered columns clawed toward the sky like skeletal fingers. This was the domain of Phobos and Deimos.

Their temple—usually veiled in a choking haze of black clouds meant to unhinge any unwelcome minds—stood unsettlingly exposed.

Ahead, the tall black gates pulsed as if shedding skin, creaking open with a sound like a coffin lid. They were waiting for us.

I stood at the edge of the clearing, bow and arrow ready, my wings half-furled as I scanned the ruined landscape. Zeph and Harmony flanked me, her golden spear catching the faint light of the stars.

A shadow flickered across the rubble.

And then—they appeared.

Phobos and Deimos stepped into view, dressed in black suits like funeral undertakers. They wore no armor, carried no weapons—only their grins, which might as well have been twin blades. They looked like this was mere entertainment, as if they were hosts for tonight's main event.

Zeph leaned in—a whisper. "I don't sense the sisters here."

My grip tightened on my bow. "Where are they?"

Phobos spread his arms. "Ah, brother. So quick to violence."

Deimos tsked. "And here we were, just hoping to talk."

I flexed my fingers around the arrow. "I won't repeat myself."

Phobos tilted his head, exchanging a glance with Deimos. Mock surprise danced in his eyes. "So much concern for family all of a sudden."

Deimos clicked his tongue. "Funny, considering how easily you cut ties with us." He gave an exaggerated sigh. "You still don't grasp the severity here, do you? You think we're the enemy—but the real chains, the ones binding us, are up there." He pointed toward the sky. "Olympus."

His gaze slid to Harmony, and his smirk twisted into something cruel. "Tell me, sister, how does it feel to spend eternity preaching peace while being shackled to their will?"

Harmony raised her spear, its golden shaft gleaming. "Peace is not submission," she answered. "And unleashing hell on this world won't bring balance. It will destroy everything."

Phobos sighed, shaking his head like a disappointed teacher. "Such wasted potential."

Deimos cracked his knuckles, grin stretching wide. "Well then. Guess we'll have to show you what true freedom looks like."

He lowered his hands, palms pressed to the ground.

From the shadows at their feet, shapes slithered forth—twisted, writhing apparitions barely clinging to form. Their faces were locked in silent screams as they clawed their way into the mortal realm.

Harmony didn't hesitate.

She lunged forward, her golden spear flashing as it sliced through the dark. The weapon ignited on impact, cleaving clean through the nearest apparition. It shrieked—a hollow, earsplitting sound—before disintegrating into air.

Zeph lifted his hands, the wind stirring like a storm beneath his helmet. The mountain air crackled with power. Each strike he summoned rippled outward, tearing through the apparitions and scattering their smoke-formed bodies. But for each one that fell, more surged forward—shifting, multiplying, relentless.

I rolled my shoulders. "No new tricks?" I called out.

Then I raised my bow, drew back the string, and loosed an arrow straight into the heart of the dark. The shaft vanished into the mass, but the shadows only thickened. I clicked my tongue.

Phobos's voice slithered into my mind, warped and vibrating like a struck bell. "Still fighting?" he crooned. "Against what—a war already begun? Against the inevitable?"

The air congealed into a thick, suffocating fog. Shadows dragged themselves across the ground, secreting the scent of blood and decay like poisonous flowers releasing their pollen.

I tightened my grip on the arrow, muscles straining as I drew the bowstring back again—

The fog pressed into my lungs. The ground seemed to shift, tilting beneath my boots. A low hum vibrated in my skull, drowning all thought.

The world twisted.

The ground cracked open, black gas spilling upward like smoke from a cursed altar. It wrapped around me, hot and stinging, burning my eyes.

I blinked against the sting, my vision swimming—and then cleared.

And I saw them.

Bodies. Dozens. Maybe hundreds. Scattered across the broken earth, twisted in agony. Their faces frozen mid-scream. Eyes sunken, empty—turned toward me.

All of them stared.

And at the center of it all—

Skye.

But it couldn't be.

She stood, but her body sagged as if it barely remembered how to hold itself up. Her hair was tangled and soaked in something wet and dark, clinging to her pale skin. Her lips parted as if to speak, but no sound came.

Her eyes...

Gods, her eyes.

Those forget-me-not blue eyes—now glassy and blood-soaked. Wide. Bottomless. Staring straight into mine.

She reached for me, fingers trembling. Her mouth formed my name.

I stepped forward.

But the shadows moved faster.

They surged up her legs, wrapped around her waist, crawled into her throat—dragging her toward the abyss tearing open at her feet.

Help me.

The words didn't come from her lips.

They echoed around me—inside me—vibrating through my very core.

I reached for her, pulled her into my arms. Her body convulsed against me.

I cupped her face, desperate to soothe her, but her features twisted in agony, lips turning blue.

I looked down—

And froze.

My hands—my own hands—were wrapped around her throat.

I tried to wrench them open, to force them back, but my fingers only tightened. Bruises bloomed under my grip, darkening against her skin.

Skye clawed at my wrists, gasping, her wide, terror-stricken eyes locking onto mine.

No.

No.

I wasn't doing this. I would never—

"Yes, my son."

I turned.

Untouched by the surrounding carnage, a figure faded in and out like a ghost on the wind—a ghost with my mother's face.

"Did you really think you had a choice?" it whispered, its voice a perfect copy of hers. You exist because I allow it. You obey because I Command it."

I tried to move—tried to let go—but my body was no longer mine.

The ghost of Aphrodite raised its hand.

And my grip tightened.

Skye gasped. Her struggles weakened.

My pulse thundered in my ears, drowning out everything but that voice.

"This is what you were made for," it whispered. "Love. Desire. Destruction. You can't save her. You can't protect her."

Skye's lips parted, but no sound came—just a soft, choked breath as her body went limp beneath my hands.

I clenched my teeth.

No.

I wrenched my mind from the abyss, fighting past the suffocating weight of the vision. I reached for something real—something beyond the nightmare.

Her.

Skye.

The *real* Skye.

I pictured her smiling, fingers dancing across the piano, eyes glancing at me through her lashes.

The nightmare gripped me tighter, like a demon refusing to be exorcised, but I clung to her harder.

Her voice.

The way she challenged me.

The way she looked at me—like I was more than what Aphrodite had made me.

Shatter.

The battlefield snapped back into focus.

Phobos's growl of frustration ripped through the air as his illusion splintered like glass.

I holstered my bow, drew the Roman gladius, braced my stance, and launched forward.

The short sword flashed toward him—he twisted, the blade barely skimming past.

"Is that my father's?" he sneered. "You little thief...I'm sure he'll be pleased to know who carries it."

"You can give it back when it's through your chest!"

I swung in one fluid motion, but his shadows coiled around the gladius, twisting it off course. I released, pivoted, yanked my bow from my back, and in the same breath, nocked an arrow.

The string hummed with power—then screeched as I let it fly.

The arrow tore through the darkness, burning a path through the wraiths swarming around me, straight toward Phobos's chest.

His eyes widened.

At the last second, shadows coiled around him, warping his form—but not fast enough.

The arrow struck—not dead center, but enough to send him stumbling backward, his smirk finally faltering.

I loosed arrow after arrow, each one tearing through Phobos and Deimos's shadows. The apparitions they'd summoned flickered and warped, their hold on this realm weakening with every strike.

Where the fuck were the Olympians?

"You're all disappointments," Phobos clipped, voice flat with disdain. Then, as if signaling, he nodded once toward Deimos.

Deimos reached into the folds of his dark suit and drew out a curved horn. He raised it—and blew.

BRAAUGH!

The sound tore through the battlefield like a rift in the air itself.

Then—something shifted.

The shadows recoiled, curling inward like animals sensing a predator far greater than themselves.

I didn't lower my aim.

I listened.

Harmony exhaled sharply, her grip tightening around her spear. Beside me, Zeph went still—his posture rigid. Not with relief...but with dread.

Real dread.

Like he knew.

Like he could *feel* something.

And then it came—the wind.

It swept across the battlefield like a plague, cutting through smoke and ash, carrying heat and the sting of ice in the same breath.

Zeph cursed under his breath. "No—"

The shadows convulsed.

Then thickened.

Then warped.

And from that dark coil, two figures stepped forward.

Boreas. Eurus.

The Anemoi—the wind gods.

Boreas, god of the north wind, moved first. With every step, the temperature dropped. Frost cracked beneath his boots, spreading through the wounded earth in jagged veins. His hair, moon-white and wild, snapped in the sharpening wind. His skin had taken on a bluish hue, and his face was carved into a mask of frozen disdain.

Eurus, god of the east wind, followed—his brother's opposite in every way. Where Boreas chilled the world, Eurus shimmered with heat. The air rippled in his wake, thick with the dry, scorching scent of parched earth and sunburnt stone. The desert walked with him.

Boreas and Eurus moved to stand beside Phobos and Deimos. The four of them aligned—united.

Zeph didn't move.

Not a breath.

Not a word.

"Zeph!" Harmony's voice cracked through the tension, snapping him back.

He blinked, then raised his arms. Wind surged around us, forming a barrier just as we instinctively stepped into formation—the three of us, shoulder to shoulder.

Boreas fixed Zeph with a hard, unbreakable stare. "Little brother," he sneered, his voice like ice cracking across a frozen lake. "You should've stayed out of this."

Eurus exhaled, waves of heat distorting the air with the breath. "You always did choose the weak."

Zeph let out a short, hollow laugh. He looked around with mock curiosity. "Missing someone? No Notus? Don't tell me the south wind was too smart to join your little villain squad."

Boreas's expression didn't change, but Eurus's lips curled into a smirk. "Notus lacks vision. But you...you know better—"

Boreas struck before anyone could respond, his power sweeping across the battlefield in an icy gust sharp as knives. Eurus followed, moving like a specter, his strikes a blur. Zeph barely had time to react before Boreas's wind sent him crashing into a broken column.

Harmony's spear spun in a continuous arc, deflecting the force. Her feet slid against the shifting ground, the winds threatening to rip her off balance. With a sharp breath, she adjusted her grip and slammed the heel of her spear into the earth. A shockwave rippled outward, anchoring her as the storm howled around her.

My wings snapped tight, folding into a shield against the force.

Phobos and Deimos lifted into the air, their feet tracing the currents as if dancing a waltz—completely at ease amid the chaos.

"You didn't really think we came unprepared, did you?" Deimos's voice cut through the current.

I launched myself at them again, wings propelling me forward—but I didn't make it far. A blast of wind slammed into me midair, hurling me off course. I reached for the daggers at my side and flung them—only to watch the gusts twist and hurl them into the void before they ever came close.

Their laughter rippled through the storm as the air around us warped.

A massive, roaring vortex ripped open, spiraling upward and tearing at the sky. The ground shuddered beneath our feet as the tornado consumed everything in its path.

The wind screamed. The world blurred.

My vision darkened at the edges. The storm crushed my chest, determined to drive the breath from my lungs.

Harmony fell first.

Her knees hit the earth hard. She fumbled for the necklace of Cadmus —but before her fingers could reach the pendant, she collapsed. Her spear slid from her grip, dropping at her side.

Zeph staggered, choking. His own brothers were suffocating him with the very element that had once bent to his will.

I tried to stay upright, to push, to move, to fight. But darkness closed in.

And above it all—Phobos and Deimos hovered in the storm's eye, hands in their pockets, serene amid the destruction.

"Time to begin."

CHAPTER THIRTY-THREE

SKYE

Outside the armory, at the edge of the floating palace, a misty waterfall of clouds spilled into the abyss below, its droplets mingling with the endless void.

The comet still blazed across the sky—a fiery warning streak, as if to say time was running out.

I flipped it off, giving it a warning of my own.

Then I looked down at the swirling void beneath us and turned to Euryale and Sara.

"Well," I said, glancing between them, "how do we get down?"

Sara exhaled, brushing a hand across the small bag slung over her shoulder. "We nymphs usually use Zeph's winds to travel," she admitted. "But...he's not here. I'm sorry. I didn't even think about—"

Sara moved toward the edge. "There's still wind...maybe—"

"No." Euryale cut her off, throwing out an arm to stop her. "We're not risking jumping to our deaths. Not without Zeph."

"She's right," I agreed.

Fuck. I knew she was right, but something in me still knew there was something...

Sara moved closer. "We'll think of another plan—"

But I didn't hear the rest of her sentence.

My thoughts fractured.

No.

No.

No.

I threw my head back and screamed, "Zeph!"

The name tore from my throat—like sheer will alone could summon him from the wind.

My voice shattered against the sky, swallowed by the vast sea of clouds.

Please.

Please, you idiots have to come back—so I can yell at you for being stupid enough to leave in the first place.

But the sky gave nothing back.

No wind. No whisper. No sign.

I dropped to my knees, the weight of everything I'd been holding in since coming here crashing down all at once. My fingers curled into the cool grass, clutching it like it could anchor me to something—anything—as I choked on silence and sky.

"Zeph!"

Behind me, the cries of Euryale and Sara rose to meet mine. Their desperate voices echoed, carrying upward into the clouds—fragile, fleeting, unanswered.

I lifted my head, vision swimming with unshed tears. Gritting my teeth, I forced myself to stand. I refused to crumble. I refused to let silence be the end.

One last time—together—we screamed his name.

Lightning ripped through the clouds, as if even the storm joined our plea. Still, not a strand of my hair stirred.

I looked down into the endless dark, the sea of nothing waiting below. One card rose in my mind—*The Fool.* The cliff. The leap of faith.

Was this a test?

Was everything a test? Had I not risked enough, proven enough?

But no—I wouldn't risk Cullen.

Or Harmony.

Or Zeph.

Not one of them.

I leaned forward, toes skimming the edge—

And then—

The wind struck. A violent gust slammed into me, whipping my hair across my face, clawing at my gear, shoving me back from the brink with a force so fierce it stole the air from my lungs.

The three of us stumbled backward.

The wind roared alive—wild, relentless. But it wasn't Zeph's usual gentle breeze.

It was warmer. Heavier. The clouds parted, swirling as a figure stepped forward from the mist.

And what stepped forward was not Zeph.

He had Zeph's sharp cheekbones. The same golden eyes. But his hair was a deeper russet, tousled as if fire and wind had waged war and then made peace in his curls.

Sara stiffened. "Divine Notus," she breathed, her grip tightening around her bag.

"I came to warn Zephyrus," he said, his voice smooth, almost soothing, as if to prove he wasn't a threat. "But I fear I am too late."

A knot of dread twisted in my stomach. My fingers itched toward Cullen's bracelet. "Too late for what?"

The wind paused—stilled—as if it, too, was bracing for the answer.

Notus stood before us, his form shimmering like heat on the horizon—never fully there, never fully gone.

"North and east have taken west," he answered, his voice calm, distant. "Along with others. Down beneath the very ground."

"Down where?" I asked, my voice sharp.

"Tartarus," he replied.

The name hit like a shock, and a sharp breath hissed through my teeth. "And you just watched it happen?" I snapped, each word a dagger.

"I do not meddle in the feuds of my brothers," he said evenly. "The winds move as they must. We do not choose sides."

My stomach twisted. Rage burned beneath my skin, and my body shook with it. "Standing aside doesn't make you neutral," I retorted. "It makes you complicit."

Notus didn't strike back. The wind didn't rise in defense of him—it shifted, slow, circling us like it was listening. Considering.

"You came to warn Zeph, didn't you?" Euryale pressed, stepping forward. "That means you're already involved."

Sara had moved closer too, her hands lifting, palms open to the wind as if coaxing it, her voice soft but steady. "Your winds are a gift," she murmured. "But if things keep going the way they are…there might not be a world left for them to move through."

For a long moment, the air was still. I thought he might vanish entirely—slip back into the sky and leave us stranded.

"You speak as mortals do," Notus observed, his voice quieter now, almost curious. "Of guilt and blame. But the wind does not choose where it blows—it simply moves, as it always has."

I squared my shoulders and met his not-quite-there eyes. "Then move us," I demanded, my voice clear and steady. "Get us down there. Let *us* choose."

Notus was silent for a beat. Then, slowly, his image began to fade.

"No, wait!" I shouted, desperation cracking through my voice. I reached out, but Euryale and Sara caught me, pulling me back from the edge before I could fall.

He was gone.

Silence wrapped around us again.

Then, faint and nearly imperceptible, the air began to hum.

My hair whipped around my face as the gusts shifted and swirled, pressing against us with invisible hands. The three of us grabbed onto each other, our arms locked in a circle as our feet lifted from the ground.

We were falling.

No—not falling. Being carried. The wind surged beneath us, guiding us through the mist. The sky opened below like a curtain parting, and just as we pierced the last layer of clouds, Notus's voice floated up to us—

"I will do what I can," he said. "For as long as the wind allows."

"Thank you," I whispered back.

And I knew he heard me—because a cool breath of air brushed my cheek, soft as a kiss.

Yeah. He was Zeph's brother, without a doubt.

CHAPTER THIRTY-FOUR

SKYE

Out of everything I'd done, this...this was one that was going to get me killed.

The elevator doors slid open with a soft chime, and I stepped out alone.

A sleek, sterile hallway stretched ahead, polished floors reflecting the cold glow of artificial light. A voice crackled over the intercom.

"Welcome to Arrows Align."

I ignored it and kept walking, my boots squeaking against the floor, my heart pounding louder with every step. I wanted Euryale and Sara with me, but I couldn't risk Aphrodite's Olympian Command on them.

No—this had to be me. Alone.

At least for twenty minutes—the maximum Sara managed to bargain out of Euryale before they both stormed in to drag my ass back out.

I continued down the hall, my hands hovering near the daggers strapped to my thighs.

As I rounded the corner, a secretary's desk came into view—empty.

Beyond it, two massive doors stood wide open, as if Aphrodite didn't expect threats. Like she'd never had reason to.

I stepped through.

The room was a glass slipper—perfect but painful. The walls were smooth, uninterrupted gray, and the glass desk looked more like a statement piece than something functional. Behind it hung a piece of modern art—a chaos of jagged, abstract shapes. A slash of deep blood-red streaked down the center. The exact shade of human blood. Which was probably the look they were going for.

A woman—presumably the secretary from the abandoned desk—turned as I entered, irritation already twisting her expression.

"Excuse me, what are you doing here? It's after hours."

And then I saw *her*.

Aphrodite.

She moved like a swan gliding over water, so poised it was hard to believe she was actually touching the ground. Then she slipped off what I was fairly certain were fake prescription glasses. Her golden eyes flicked to me, a flash of surprise crossing them for just a fraction of a second—like she wasn't used to being surprised.

The subtle tilt of her head—I recognized it immediately.

The resemblance was uncanny.

Cullen's.

Strangely, it made me less afraid of her.

"Well, if it isn't my new daughter-in-law," she purred sweetly—but I knew an insult when I heard one.

"Thank you, Vanessa. You may leave for the night. Close the doors on your way out," she added with a careless wave toward the secretary.

Vanessa looked rattled but nodded, retreating without another word.

And just like that, it was only the two of us.

I had rehearsed what I was going to say—how I'd convince her, how I'd make her listen. But this wasn't about reason or pleading. Aphrodite didn't respond to desperation. She responded to power.

If I wanted her to hear me, I couldn't show weakness. I couldn't show fear.

I had to out-bitch my mother-in-law.

"You must be so proud," I began, keeping my voice steady, my chin high. "Your son's finally grown up enough to make his own choices."

Aphrodite's smile didn't waver, but something sharper twisted at the corners of her lips. "Bold," she said coolly. "But let's drop the pretense, mortal girl."

Uncrossing her legs, she pressed her perfectly manicured nails to the glass desk and rose—as if I dared to be taller than her.

As she walked toward me, her hips swayed in that tight pencil skirt with exaggerated rhythm—like she wanted to remind me just how impossibly, unfairly gorgeous she was.

"You think I don't see it?" Her voice was silk wrapped in steel. "Cunning little thing, aren't you? Tricking my son into bonding with you."

Her gaze dropped to the arrowhead resting against my chest.

"Tell me...did you spread your legs before or after he cursed you?"

I met her gaze without flinching, then slowly tilted my head back as a dramatic, exasperated laugh escaped me.

"Are you saying your son has no self-control? Sounds like a parenting issue—not a me problem."

Then—before I could talk myself out of it—I mirrored her.

Shifted my stance. Tilted my head just so. Let a slow smile pull at my lips.

"And for the record? After. He *worships* me between my legs."

I winked, sealing my death sentence with a smirk.

She moved in a blur—too fast to track.

One heartbeat, I was standing.

The next, I was slammed against the wall, her forearm pressing hard against my throat.

My breath caught. Panic clawed at my chest.

"You seem to think I'm no less deadly than I am beautiful," she murmured against my skin, her glow deepening as her rage flared beneath it. "You should see me with a swoooord."

She drew the word out like a blade itself.

I held her gaze, refusing to look away—refusing to let her see me struggle for breath. Then, in one sharp motion, I raised my arm and activated Cullen's bracelet.

A golden shimmer burst into the air with a crackle of power—Cullen's bow, quiver, and arrows materialized in my grasp.

Aphrodite's eyes widened. She staggered back. "How...?"

I exhaled hard, adjusting my grip on the bow. "Cullen gave it to me. He gave it to me because of Phobos and Deimos. They had taken him—"

Aphrodite's dark, humorless laugh cut me off. But I saw it—the flicker of tension in her shoulders, a crack in her perfect composure.

"Is your mind simple?" she sneered. "We are immortal."

I stepped forward, fire igniting in my chest.

"They've found the bloodline that can power the torch—the one that could restore the Titans. Cullen challenged Zeus. Said he'd take the throne if—"

"He challenged the throne?" Aphrodite's voice sharpened. "Over you?"

"Yes," I answered, the bowstring tightening in my grip with every word. "So unless you want your son—and the rest of this world—destroyed, maybe it's time you started taking this seriously."

Aphrodite didn't answer.

She tilted her head, studying me—not with fury now, but with something else. Something *curious.*

Then, slowly, her gaze drifted toward the window.

Rain tapped faintly against the glass—barely audible—until a flash of lightning lit the sky, casting the city in stark silver. A beat later, thunder cracked in the distance.

Aphrodite's eyes narrowed. She stepped closer to the window, as if confirming something only she could see beyond it—and flinched.

"You're going to have to prove yourself, girl," she said at last. "If you want the allied forces of the Olympians, if you want their help, you need to show them why you're worth it."

My eyes narrowed. "Even if Phobos and Deimos are trying to release the Titans?"

For a moment, I could've sworn her mask cracked. Just for a blink. A flicker of something—fear, maybe—passed through her golden eyes. Then she nodded.

"*Especially* if that's what they're planning."

I didn't lower my weapon.

My aim remained steady, my pulse pounding.

But Aphrodite didn't strike.

Instead, she turned away.

Her heels clicked across the pristine floor like punctuation marks. She stopped at the glass desk and pulled open a drawer, her shoulders squared as she reached slowly inside.

When she turned back, her hand was outstretched.

"Lower the bow," she said.

There was no heat in her voice. No challenge.

Slowly, cautiously, I lowered the weapon.

She stepped forward and seized my hand. I winced as her nails scraped across my skin, but my focus locked on what she pressed into my palm—a ring forged of black metal.

It was heavy, radiating a warmth that sank into my skin, burrowing deep—like heat settling into muscle.

"This," Aphrodite explained quietly, "was forged by Hephaestus. It's a portal to the Underworld, where he resides."

Hephaestus.

Cullen's father.

She didn't say *my husband*. Didn't claim him—not even with a hint of possessiveness. She said his name like a technicality.

Cullen told me Aphrodite had chosen Ares—that Hephaestus was the one she turned away.

And yet...he was the one who forged this. A ring. A key. A portal.

He gave her a way back to him.

But what about Cullen?

Had he done the same for his son? Was there a ring waiting for him, too, hidden somewhere in a forgotten drawer of the palace?

I didn't know.

And not knowing—not being able to ask him right now—hurt.

Before I could think further, the office doors slammed open—shattering the silence and ripping me out of my thoughts.

Dark hair.

A black suit, worn like well-tailored death.

Ares.

Something dragged behind him, scraping against the tile, grating like a sword on stone.

My throat closed.

He hauled them forward.

Euryale.

Sara.

My stomach hollowed out.

Ares's grip was unyielding, as though he were presenting prisoners to a throne.

He stopped in the center of the room, radiating smug satisfaction. His smile was pure arrogance—like a gambler who'd just gone all in and hit the jackpot. Twice.

Euryale twisted violently in his grasp. He readjusted with mechanical ease, not even sparing her a glance.

My heart jolted. "Let them go!"

Aphrodite didn't even turn. She just sighed, long and exasperated. "Must you *always* make an entrance? You're going to make all my—"

"—meetings more entertaining?" Ares finished for her, his eyes glinting with amusement, like a mouse toying with a cat.

He leaned down—first toward Euryale, then Sara. His breath ghosted over them like a predator savoring the scent of fear.

"I found them outside," he drawled. "No doubt scheming. Thought you might want a taste of their pain before I had my fun."

Sara flinched, every muscle taut, like a cornered animal. She yanked her head back again and again, refusing to meet his gaze—his teeth—as he drew closer. Inch by inch. Like he was deciding whether to bite.

Euryale bared her teeth back at him, her nails raking across his skin, but Ares didn't flinch. Didn't even blink. Nothing marked him. Her fury only seemed to entertain him more.

Aphrodite brushed her long hair back, as if this were merely an irritating delay in her schedule. "Ares, drop them."

He hesitated—clearly expecting permission to play further—but after a beat, he obeyed.

Sara stumbled but caught herself, throwing him a look of pure, focused loathing.

Euryale yanked herself free and straightened, still burning. "You arrogant—"

"Silence."

His voice cracked through the room like a whip.

Euryale's mouth moved, but no sound followed. Sara's hands flew to her throat, her eyes wide with panic.

My pulse spiked.

He used the Olympian Command.

Ares turned back to Aphrodite, a flicker of smugness playing at his lips. "I see you've caught something, too."

His eyes dragged over me—slow, appraising, cold. Like I was an object to be cataloged and discarded in the same breath. Then, just like that, the interest vanished.

He pivoted to Aphrodite, and his expression shifted. The teasing dissolved into something darker. Possessive.

He stepped in close, fingers grazing her waist as he dipped his head.

The kiss he pressed to her neck wasn't a greeting.

It was a brand.

A message: *Mine.*

Aphrodite's smile curved—subtle, indulgent, perfectly controlled. She allowed him the moment, tilting her head just enough to grant access, like a queen bestowing favor.

When he pulled back, her fingers drifted across his wrist—a light, deliberate touch. As if to say: *You may stay.*

Satisfied, Ares smirked and turned away, dropping into a nearby lounge chair with lazy elegance, limbs sprawled like a predator full on blood.

But to me, he still resembled a dog—waiting for a reward from his master.

My fists clenched. "Release them."

Ares didn't even look at me. "Cute."

Aphrodite, already growing bored, flicked her hand. "Let them speak, Ares."

Ares exhaled with theatrical weariness, rolling his head back like allowing them to speak was an unbearable chore. "Speak."

The invisible pressure lifted.

Sara scowled, still catching her breath. "You...I've never been fond of—"

"He's an ass," Euryale cut in, cracking her neck. She nudged her glasses up at the side, a gesture that was both a warning and a reminder of who she was and what she could do.

Ares grinned, clearly amused. "Second-best ass in the room," he quipped with a wink toward Aphrodite.

Aphrodite waved a hand, already dismissing them. "Childish nonsense. All of you."

Before I could react, Aphrodite grabbed my hand—the one with the ring—and pressed it flat against the towering glass pane overlooking the city.

The instant the metal touched the surface, ripples bloomed outward, distorting the skyline like heatwaves off asphalt.

A portal.

The room shifted.

Ares went still.

Utterly, dangerously still.

His gaze snapped to the ring. And in the space of a single breath, recognition lit his eyes.

Then it twisted.

Curdled into something darker.

"You had *that* in your possession?"

His voice dropped to a chilling hush—the kind that exists only in the breath before a storm breaks.

And then the storm broke.

Pressure spiked. The air thickened. The walls groaned, bearing the weight of his fury. Overhead, the lights flickered. Loose papers ripped from the desk and scattered like panicked birds, drawn toward the gravitational pull of his rage.

My lungs seized. I coughed, choking on what felt like smoke—though there was none.

But Aphrodite didn't flinch.

Her power flared in answer. She didn't shout or lift a hand—she simply *became.*

A beacon. A light. The eye of the storm.

Radiant beams poured from her skin like sunlight breaking through thunderclouds—piercing and utterly blinding—pure beauty made lethal.

She stepped forward.

"Do not presume you own me. For I belong to no one."

Ares's nostrils flared. His jaw clenched, fists curling so tightly I thought his knuckles might split. Power thrummed beneath his skin, muscles coiling like the earth itself was about to snap.

For one suspended heartbeat, I thought he'd lose it. That he'd rip the world apart just to prove he could.

But then—he looked away.

The tension snapped.

The room exhaled.

Heat vanished—like a flame swallowed by shadow.

The lights steadied.

Silence fell.

Maybe even war had a line it wouldn't cross.

Or maybe Aphrodite was the one line it couldn't.

I blinked hard, rubbing my eyes as the glow on her skin faded—her radiance dimming back to something merely *goddess-level* instead of blinding.

My gaze slid to Euryale. Then to Sara.

Their eyes found mine, and I saw it reflected—

That same silent question: *Were we really going to do this?*

Trust Aphrodite.

Step through a portal.

Follow a path forged by her rejected husband to the deepest place in existence.

To the Underworld.

To whatever waited.

Maybe—to our deaths.

And yet...

I curled my fingers tighter around the ring.

Some things were worth the risk.

I turned back to her. "Where does this lead?"

Aphrodite didn't answer.

Right. *Prove myself.*

Euryale drew a sharp breath and stepped forward. "I'll go first."

"No," I snapped, grabbing her hand before she could move. My other hand shot out for Sara's, gripping tight.

"We go together."

The window rippled faster and faster, bubbling and popping, distorting the air until it felt like it was creating its own atmosphere—dragging us closer with every breath. I could feel their pulses racing through our joined hands, and my own fear thrumming back at them.

Our fingers locked tighter.

Our feet moved as one toward the portal.

Gods help anyone who tried to tear us apart.

And together, we stepped into whatever hell waited on the other side.

CHAPTER THIRTY-FIVE

CULLEN

Bzzzzzzz.

A low, grating buzz filled my ears—static, distant, pressing in from all sides.

My head rocked forward—*thud*—then slammed back. *Crack.*

Everything blurred, teetering on the edge of a dream.

My eyes were shut tight. Muscles tense. I squinted, struggling to drag myself back—to piece together where I was, *when* I was.

I couldn't move.

Why couldn't I move?

Then—*whuff.*

Warmth. Soft. Familiar. My fingers curled in something smooth and cool beneath my touch.

Sheets.

My sheets. Twisted in knots around my waist.

That didn't make sense.

I forced my eyes open. Everything swam. Shapes blurred. Light bled across the edges. The room tilted, refusing to focus.

My room.

I was in my room at the palace.

In my bed, to be precise.

But none of it felt real.

Like a dream trying too hard to be one.

Click.

"Look who's finally awake."

A voice slithered through the silence.

Skye?

She moved toward me, hips swaying with every step. Her hands reached out—

Her touch barely grazed my skin, but I leaned into it. Into her fingers tracing lazy, looping patterns across my chest. Fingertips skimmed my collarbone, then climbed to the line of my jaw. Her breath, warm and steady, ghosted over me.

Like she belonged here.

Like I'd never been without her.

She wore lace.

Sheer. Delicate. Useless.

The candlelight burned through it, casting her in molten gold, outlining every curve—every promise I ached to claim. The fabric shifted as she leaned in, brushing against me.

I breathed out—slow, shaky.

Surrender.

I dipped my head toward her.

Her lips grazed my temple. Drifted to my cheek. Lower.

Teasing.

I turned to her. Caught her mouth with mine.

Tasting her.

But—

This wasn't her taste.

Copper.

Salt.

I tore away, gasping.

And froze.

Her lips weren't just bleeding.

They were *pouring.*

A torrent—thick and red—spilled down her chin, soaking the lace, the sheets, my skin. More blood than a body could hold.

Drip.

Drip.

Drip.

I jolted awake.

My chest heaved. Sweat clung to my skin. Each breath came sharp, ragged.

Snap.

A hand gripped my chin—fingers like sandpaper, clamping down and jerking my head upward.

Deimos.

He crouched in front of me, his face a breath away, wearing a grin like a demon savoring its next possession.

"Brother," he murmured, tilting my head like a child inspecting a broken toy. "Having a nightmare?"

I tried to pull back, but my body jolted and stopped. I twisted as much as I could, but my wrists—heavy, bound by thick iron chains—bit into my skin, anchoring me to the jagged ground. My limbs were stretched taut, forcing me into a bowed, submissive position as my knees dug into the gritty, uneven stone.

Deimos released my chin, his nails dragging along my jaw like a barber's blade.

I forced my gaze upward.

We weren't in the Underworld.

We were deeper.

Sulfur scorched my lungs and stung my eyes. The cavern walls fractured and surged molten red, pulsing blood through the very stone. Above me, shadows writhed—not cast by flame, but born of hell itself. They moaned, echoing the tortured screams that trembled through the ground beneath my knees.

Tartarus.

To my left—Zeph.

To my right—Harmony.

Both bound like me, chains stretched taut. Their heads hung low, black clouds coiling around them, faces twisted in torment.

Nightmares.

"Enjoy your rest, Cupid?" Deimos's chuckle yanked me back to his attention.

I bared my teeth, and the chains groaned against my pull. "Wake them," I snarled, the words reverberating off the shackles that bound me.

He sighed—long and exaggerated, dripping with mock boredom. Then, in a blink, he vanished—his form unraveling into smoke that slithered through the shadows. The scent of sulfur curled through the air, acrid and clinging. His voice lingered from behind me.

"Can you really trust what you see? Are they even there?"

My head throbbed; his words settled like rot in my mind, burrowing deeper.

Phobos stood motionless, his suit swallowed by a shadowed cloak that clung to his shoulders and pooled at his feet. His face was a mask of perfect indifference, utterly unreadable.

"Enough," he said coolly, nodding toward the edge of the abyss. "Attend to our guests."

Deimos's shadow form hissed low, displeased, but obeyed. His wraithlike figure dissolved into darkness, flying off until even the shape of him was gone.

I turned back to Phobos.

And then—with a flick of his fingers—

Tartarus fell away.

The chains vanished.

The ground softened.

The stench of damp stone and ancient blood evaporated.

In its place, a golden glow. The air grew crisp and sweet. Olympus stretched before me, pristine and eternal. We stood at the edge of paradise, overlooking the world below.

It burned.

Fields consumed by flame. Forests reduced to ash. Smoke curled into the sky like a black crown. But in Olympus, above it all, everything remained untouched—quiet, beautiful, immune.

"You see?" Phobos's voice came from beside me, a sudden warmth that felt strained, unnatural. He stood there with a smile that never reached his eyes.

"While the Titans walk the earth, destroying what's left apart, we—our family, our allies—could remain here on Olympus. Free from their Command. Free from their tyranny. Just...peace."

I turned to him, jaw tight. "Peace?" I gestured toward the devastation below. "That's your peace?"

His exhale was long, quiet, edged with disappointment. A shadow crossed his face—and with a flick of his fingers, the illusion shattered.

And we were back.

The heat.

The chains.

Tartarus.

The silence that followed was loud enough to swallow hope.

Phobos cracked his neck. "Well, can't say I didn't try." He stepped back, giving me a once-over. "Looks like the three musketeers get a front-row seat to history in the making. Who knows? Maybe we'll reevaluate your stance in a century."

A scream pierced the air.

High-pitched.

Female.

Skye's sisters.

The sound echoed from the direction Deimos had vanished.

Phobos hummed, glancing over his shoulder. "Don't they make beautiful music?" He turned back to me with a lazy smirk. "But let's focus on something more important—Skye."

With a casual wave, Phobos summoned a book from the shadows of his cloak. He opened it and began flipping through the pages, scanning as though searching for a particular passage.

"It's funny we're not closer," he said, almost conversational. "Given our shared distaste for our mother. She made our fathers look like fools."

I recognized the book instantly—an exact copy existed in my library.

Hephaestus's journal.

Phobos tapped the page and smirked. "Your father forged a torch to steal power from the Titans—not just to stop them, but as some pitiful declaration of love for our mother. Pathetic."

"Why don't you bring it up with him?" I replied, letting the faintest hope edge my voice—however unlikely—that my father might use his Olympian Command to end this.

Phobos rolled his eyes, amused that I'd even suggest it.

"Nice try. But we don't need him," he chided, flicking the thought away with a casual wave. "We already know where the torch is."

He motioned downward toward the massive crater carved into the earth. Deep within it, the torch pulsed—its flame burning brighter, as if it *knew* we were speaking of it.

"And," Phobos added, "we have the Praxis bloodline."

I flinched.

"Yes, we've known about the bloodline for a while," he went on, voice smooth. "But it was difficult to trace. We had to be sure. You know how it works—gods can only bond once. When Skye broke the Olympian Command, we knew she was different. It didn't take long to confirm her ancestry."

"If you already knew," I gritted out, "why haven't you bonded with her sisters?"

"As I said—we had to be certain. We even consulted the Fates. They want the bond broken as much as we do. Their vision confirmed it." He snapped the book shut with a sharp flick, the sound cracking through the still air like a whip.

Then Phobos moved.

He crouched in front of me, eyes gleaming through the shards of his hair. As he leaned in, his breath brushed my cheek.

"Without the nectar, she'll die one day, you know," he whispered, tilting his head as if savoring the idea. He tapped his chin, eyes flicking upward in feigned thought. "Maybe I'll send you the funeral arrangements. Or..." His mouth stretched into a monstrous grin, sharp as shattered glass. "Maybe I'll force the nectar down her throat and let her live an eternity—alone, untouched, unloved."

His eyes glimmered. "Decisions, decisions."

I lunged against the chains, every muscle straining, fire tearing through my limbs as the metal bit into my wrists—but I welcomed the pain. It meant I was still alive. It meant I could still fight.

Phobos stood and turned his back, as if disgusted with himself for wasting breath on me.

"Phobos!" I roared. He didn't respond—just slipped into the darkness, where screams rose to greet him like a doorbell chime.

I would end them.

Rip them apart and scatter their remains across every cursed corner of Tartarus.

Skye...

I tilted my head up, straining—reaching—for even the faintest trace of our bond.

I'll tear through every realm, every curse, every layer of stone between us.

You are not alone.

Not while I still breathe.

I will carve my way out of Tartarus to get back to you.

And with the gods as my witness—

They will not keep me from you.

CHAPTER THIRTY-SIX

SKYE

Hiss.

"Fuck!" Pain shot through my finger.

I looked down to see the ring Aphrodite had given me flicker—then violently snap free, launching off my hand like it had been burned by me.

We stumbled out of the portal, and I barely managed to catch my balance before the ring vanished with a sharp, final *hiss*. The portal sealed shut behind it, leaving us in suffocating darkness.

Apparently, the ring didn't appreciate being worn by someone who wasn't its true owner.

Well. No turning back now.

I turned—Euryale and Sara were already on the move, their heads tilting in sync as they scanned above.

I followed their gaze.

Jagged black rock stretched, cracked, and scarred in every direction. The air reeked of sulfur, which I recognized instantly from helping Lydia patch a gas leak back at the apartment. I forced my breathing to steady, each inhale a conscious act to keep from coughing.

Sara crouched, pressing her palm to the ground. Her voice was low and unsteady. "I...I can't feel the earth's life force here."

"It's like another world," I murmured, my eyes snagging on a warped iron gate ahead. Massive and crooked, its bars twisted like clawed fingers reaching for the jagged ceiling.

Euryale dusted off her shoulders as if we hadn't just crash-landed at the gates of hell and commanded, "Forward."

A narrow path of damp stone wound ahead, with a rusted railing and line of torches clinging to the wall beside it. Murky fog swirled at the entrance, as if gravity dragged it inward.

I stepped forward—one foot, then the next. Euryale led; Sara fell into place behind me.

As we walked, Euryale's voice stayed low and cautious, as if something in the dark might overhear. "The Underworld has many levels. At its center is the palace of Hades and Persephone. Every soul must pass through their domain before moving on."

"Okay," I said. "So Tartarus is on one of these levels? What are the others?"

She nodded. "Beyond the palace is Elysium, for particular souls who have passed judgment and found peace. Then there are the Asphodel Meadows—a place that isn't necessarily good or bad, just...neutral, for souls still clinging to the thought that they have something to offer the world."

The Gorgon shoved a boulder aside like it weighed nothing. "The Fates dwell here, too," she added, her hand brushing her weapon—as if the name alone might summon them.

A chill ran down my spine. "And Tartarus?"

"Tartarus," Euryale repeated. "A pit at the very bottom of the Underworld. So deep, even the gods fear it. It's where the Titans were cast after the war."

"Great," I muttered. "Exactly where we're headed..."

Sara touched my shoulder and offered a soft smile, but I saw the tension behind her eyes.

She was scared, too.

The fog thinned, pulling back to reveal something shifting ahead. The torches' light flickered against the dark and rippled.

A current.

A river.

It stretched endlessly, vanishing into the horizon. The water lapped at the shore in a steady, pulsing rhythm—like it was waiting for us.

I swallowed hard. "I don't suppose this is one of those peaceful, scenic rivers?"

Euryale exhaled, grim. "Welcome to the Styx."

But it wasn't water. Not really.

The river was black and thick, viscous as oil. It moved sluggishly, with tendrils of mist coiling off the surface, twisting into shapes before dissolving into the air.

Then the water stirred.

Something rose from its depths with a slow, sloshing sound—a boat. Small, almost like a fisherman's skiff, but with sharp edges that curved upward. It glided silently across the river, leaving no ripple in its wake, as if it wasn't bound by the rules of physics.

Someone stood inside—tall, unnaturally so—draped in tattered robes that pooled at his feet, swallowing the floor of the boat. A deep hood obscured his face, but in the darkness beneath, I caught a glint—bone. His form shimmered and wavered slightly, like he wasn't fully anchored to this world.

He looked like he'd stepped straight out of the *Death* card in my tarot deck—the skeletal ferryman standing at the threshold of the unknown.

Euryale and Sara edged closer, their movements syncing with mine. I felt our heartbeats align, a silent, shared rhythm of dread.

The ferryman lifted his head just enough to acknowledge us. When he spoke, his voice came in fragmented whispers, like dry leaves scraping together. "Passage...three."

I took a breath and stepped forward, forcing calm into my voice. "We need passage."

He tilted his head slightly, as if not understanding why he was having to repeat himself. Then he rasped again, "Three."

Euryale exhaled sharply beside me, arms folded tight. "He wants payment," she said. "You don't cross the Styx without paying the ferryman."

Instinctively, I reached into my pockets—nothing. My stomach twisted.

"Do we have any money?" I asked.

Euryale and Sara exchanged glances.

No.

The ferryman didn't move, his hooded figure still as a shadow. But the boat began to retreat, slipping backward, sinking slowly into the black water. The ferryman descended with it.

Without hesitation, Euryale lunged forward. She slammed her foot onto the edge of the boat, gripping it with both hands to keep it from vanishing.

The ferryman tilted his head back and shrieked—a sound that wasn't one voice, but many. A chorus of agony, layered and fractured, as if every scream he'd ever carried was echoing at once.

I clamped my hands over my ears, but it was useless. The sound drilled through my skin, rattled my bones, and ricocheted inside my skull like it was trying to split me open from the inside.

Then, through the folds of his robes, the ferryman raised a staff.

The barbed tip swung forward, stopping when it leveled directly at Euryale's chest.

She didn't flinch. Didn't move.

Slowly, she reached for her wrist. Her fingers unclasped something small—a delicate chain. She held it out, letting it dangle between them.

Lydia's bracelet.

My breath caught.

Euryale's jaw was clenched tight as she forced the words through her teeth. "Enough?"

The ferryman tilted his head slowly, the motion jarring and unnatural—like rusted machinery grinding back to life. A long, excruciating pause passed.

Then, at last, he lowered his staff.

With a single nod, he accepted the offering.

His voice cut through the air like dry leaves scraping against stone. "Two."

Two more offerings.

A lump rose in my throat. If Euryale could give jewelry...then I knew what I had to do.

My hand trembled as it moved to the ring on my finger—my wedding ring. The metal felt heavier now, like it understood what was coming and resisted, clinging to my skin.

I hesitated. My fingers curled tightly around it.

Swallowing hard, I pushed Cullen's face from my mind—his voice, his touch, the way he slipped the ring onto my finger. I couldn't think about that now. I couldn't afford to.

Stepping forward, I slowly extended my hand, palm open.

The ferryman's hood tilted slightly—as if acknowledging the gesture. Then he nodded.

My breath hitched as I held the ring for one final second...then let it go.

It fell into his palm without a sound.

"One," he rasped.

Sara didn't hesitate. She reached into her bag and pulled out a small loaf of bread. Cradling it in both hands, she lowered herself onto one knee, bowing her head slightly—as though her offering were a sacred gift.

"For you, honorable ferryman," she intoned, her voice laced with sincerity. "A humble offering, given in gratitude for safe passage."

The purity of it radiated off her—like a child proudly presenting a crayon drawing for the fridge.

The ferryman didn't move.

Euryale crossed her arms. "Yeah, I don't think he's interested."

Sara's smile faltered. She glanced between us, then exhaled softly through her nose. "Guess you'll have to go without me."

"No." The word ripped out of me, sharp with panic. "We're not leaving you behind."

Euryale stepped forward, seized Sara's wrist, and yanked her closer. Sara didn't resist, her gaze meeting Euryale's as if they shared a silent understanding.

"We don't have anything else to give," she said in a calm, steady voice.

At that, the ferryman stirred.

His skeletal hand rose and pointed.

At me.

At my chest.

I froze.

My necklace. The arrowhead shimmered faintly, reacting like it sensed the danger ahead.

"No," Euryale snapped, moving Sara behind her and planting herself between me and him. "Choose something else."

The ferryman didn't respond. His skeletal finger lifted again, this time pointing unwaveringly at the necklace around my neck.

The cursed arrowhead.

My hand rose to it, fingers brushing the metal. I hesitated.

It was the only thing keeping the visions away—the only barrier between me and madness.

But if I didn't give it up...Sara wouldn't be allowed to cross.

And I wasn't leaving her behind.

Forcing a smile, I unfastened the chain and held it up. "Well...I guess no one should touch me from here on out."

"Skye..." Sara protested, but I shook my head. My mind was made up.

The ferryman extended a hand. The moment the necklace touched his skin, it vanished—absorbed instantly, like ink seeping into parchment.

Without a word, the ferryman turned and stepped back into the boat, waiting.

I drew a sharp breath and climbed in, moving to the far end where a plain wooden plank jutted out like a makeshift bench. Euryale and Sara followed, neither speaking.

The instant we were all inside, the vessel lurched and glided forward, smooth and silent, as if the abyss carried us.

My hand drifted to my now-bare chest. Beneath my skin, I couldn't help but sense something beginning to stir deep within my heart...my soul.

Not even the river lapping against the boat made a sound.

The only noise was the ferryman's rowing—slow, agonizingly slow. Each oar stroke let out a low, rhythmic *creak* that echoed through the silence, making it feel heavier. Denser. Like sound itself was suffocating.

I wasn't sure what I'd expected from the ride. Something dark, sure—but it felt like we were trapped in a nightmare version of *It's a Small World*, if you swapped the animatronics for death and despair.

I shifted in my seat, restless.

Sara leaned over the side of the boat, curious—like she half-expected to spot a fish...or worse, the face of some drowned, lost soul staring back.

Across from her, Euryale sat with a straight spine, one hand hovering over her sword, her entire body carved from tension.

The silence stretched on. So long, I thought I might scream just to hear something—anything—again.

Then, finally, the boat slowed.

We were approaching land.

Or at least, what I *thought* was land.

The boat skimmed to a stop without even a splash. The ferryman gestured silently, his skeletal hand extending toward the shore.

We stepped out.

The moment our feet touched the ground, the boat—and its ghostly pilot—melted back into the water without a ripple, vanishing as if they'd never existed.

I turned around once, just to make sure.

Gone.

Sara clasped her hands together, the sound startling in the silence. Her eyes were wide, voice barely a whisper. "Amazing...the home of Divine Hades and Persephone."

Before us, a palace rose from the dark earth, seemingly *grown* rather than built. Its towering obsidian pillars stretched into the shadowed sky, their fractured stone veined with molten gold. Every crack had been mended as if by kintsugi—but here, the art wasn't about honoring imperfection. It was a warning: the palace had been reforged stronger.

There was no path around it. No alternate route.

If we wanted to move forward—

We had to go through.

Sara and Euryale moved first, their steps steady as they headed toward the palace. I hurried to catch up, the soles of my shoes crunching softly against the black stone beneath us.

"Skye, do you remember when I first spoke of the Olympian gods?" Sara asked, her voice hushed but clear.

She meant her lessons back at Cullen's palace. "Yes. Why?"

"Hades is Zeus's brother, but he's not one of the Twelve. He rules the Underworld, not the heavens or the mortal realm—so he doesn't wield the Olympian Command."

That was a relief. Not having to deal with that was a small mercy.

"But don't get comfortable," Euryale warned, her voice sharp as a blade. "Hades may not have the Command, but that doesn't mean we're safe. He won't have any goodwill toward us."

I frowned. "Why?"

Euryale scoffed, the sound low and bitter. "Aphrodite," she spat. "Her envy is the reason Hades is even bonded with Persephone in the first place."

Sara nodded solemnly. "The story goes, Aphrodite wanted to punish Persephone—because she was..." She waved a hand, searching for words. "So, she sent Divine Cullen to shoot Hades with an arrow. He did, and Hades took Persephone as his queen...and well, the rest is history."

Fucking Aphrodite and her petty jealousy.

I let out a breath as we continued up the path to the palace doors.

Euryale stopped, her grip tightening on her sword. "We move carefully. If we can slip through unnoticed, all the better. I'd rather not test how long Hades holds a grudge."

Sara hummed thoughtfully, tapping a finger to her chin. "Hmm... wasn't there something else in the palace with them?"

Euryale froze.

She drew her sword in one fluid motion, glasses flashing toward the shadows just beyond the entrance.

And then I heard it.

Low. Deep. A growl that vibrated through the stone beneath our feet —like the earth itself was warning us to run.

The shadows ahead stirred.

Then, with slow, thunderous steps, it emerged.

Sara turned back to us, her lips forming three distinct syllables: *Cer. Ber. Us.*

The beast was enormous—easily the size of Mystic Soulstice. Its three massive heads moved in different directions, each set of burning golden eyes fixed on us. Its fur was black—blacker than the river we'd just crossed—and its snarling jaws dripped saliva that hissed when it hit the stone, scorching it on contact.

None of us moved.

Maybe if we were just still enough—

A blistering wave of heat rolled over us as the creature exhaled. One head turned—

The other two snapped.

And it lunged.

Euryale reacted instantly.

She shoved Sara and me behind a cluster of jagged rocks and, in the same breath, unsheathed a dagger and hurled it at the beast. It struck the middle head square across the muzzle.

The beast didn't even flinch.

Instead, it reared back and roared, three jaws snapping in fury. Teeth longer than my arm gnashed inches from where Euryale rolled beneath it.

I pushed off the rock, my heart slamming against my ribs.

I wasn't fucking standing aside.

With a sharp inhale, I grasped my bracelet, cool metal biting against my skin. Power surged through me—a golden pulse that rippled outward. In the next breath, Cullen's bow and arrows materialized in my grip.

I notched an arrow, heart hammering.

Don't hesitate.

But they were fast.

Euryale gritted her teeth, rolling to dodge another swipe and slashing at the nearest head. The blade bit deep—but Cerberus adapted, its second head snapping down to disarm her. The sword went flying, clattering across the stone.

She barely had time to react before it lunged again.

Cursing, she whipped out her baton and jammed it between its gaping jaws. Cerberus clamped down, one massive paw crushing her torso, pinning her to the ground. The force rattled her whole body—but she held firm, the only thing keeping those fangs from tearing into her.

I steadied my aim on the beast.

Will it, Cullen's voice echoed through my mind.

I exhaled. Let the arrow fly.

It hit—dead center, a clean shot—

Then shimmered...

And vanished.

Dissolved into the beast like mist.

What the—

Cerberus halted.

One paw hung midair. The growling faded into a low, questioning rumble. Then silence.

All three massive heads turned—slowly.

Not toward Euryale.

Not toward me.

Toward Sara.

Its golden eyes locked onto her, unblinking.

A tail twitched.

Once.

Twice.

Then—wagged.

I blinked. "What..."

The second head tilted. The third let out a soft, curious huff. The tail wagged faster, scattering dust.

Euryale, still pinned but stubbornly unbowed, braced herself. "What did you *do*?"

Sara blinked, wide-eyed. "Why...why is it looking at me like that?"

Then I felt it.

The hum of power still pulsing through the bow.

Not the sting of a curse—

But the warm, steady pull of something else.

An arrow of love.

I'd been thinking of Sara.

Of how much I wanted to protect her.

My eyes widened.

"Oh..." I breathed.

Euryale looked between us, utterly deadpan. "Did you just make the dog fall in love with Sara?"

"I...think so?" I said, staring down at the bow in disbelief.

Sara, bless her innocent soul, reached into her bag and pulled out a loaf of bread.

"No sudden moves," Euryale hissed.

But Sara, completely unfazed, stepped forward like she was approaching a lost golden retriever.

"Here, boy," she cooed sweetly, voice light and melodic. "Who's a good guardian of the Underworld?"

She tore the bread into small pieces, tossing the first chunk just shy of the creature's front paw.

The massive hound sniffed. One of its heads lowered, nose twitching. Another gave a curious whuff. The third stared, unblinking, right at Sara.

Then—

A soft, high-pitched sound broke—a whine.

Cerberus whimpered.

And then—slowly, impossibly—it lowered itself to the ground with a heavy, echoing *thud.* Stone trembled beneath its weight.

I just...stood there.

Blinking.

Mouth slightly open.

Euryale, still flattened beneath one of Cerberus's enormous paws, turned her head just enough to gape at the scene.

"You have got to be kidding me," she grumbled, her voice caught somewhere between exasperation and disbelief.

Cerberus, unbothered, licked up the bread with three happy tongues, its once-snarling jaws now busy gnawing on crust like it was a feast from Olympus.

Sara beamed, hands on her hips like she'd just solved world peace.

"Seeeee?" she said brightly. "Good thing I brought sustenance."

A startled laugh bubbled up my throat. I bit it back and hurried over to help Euryale.

She groaned, grabbing my extended hand as the giant paw finally lifted from her.

Cerberus was far too preoccupied with Sara and her bread to care.

"I don't want to hear it," Euryale muttered, brushing herself off with whatever dignity she could gather as we slipped past the world's most terrifying—and now oddly obedient—guard dog.

We were just steps from the massive palace doors when Euryale's sword shot out, blocking Sara and me. "Not a sound until we're on the other side. Understood?"

I nodded, still clutching the bow—an arrow already notched, my fingers resting lightly on the feathers. Not aimed, but ready.

The doors loomed open, held apart by thick, ancient chains. They looked like they hadn't closed in centuries, as if Hades himself had been forced to witness every soul that passed through.

I had expected the throne room of the Underworld to be cold, empty, lifeless—but as I stepped further, it smelled like a greenhouse.

Sara's eyes lit up as she took in the green vines draping along the walls, curling from the ceiling like leafy waterfalls. I could've sworn her skin even looked a shade less pale, as if she were soaking in some long-lost sunlight.

Our footsteps softened against the moss-covered floor as we moved deeper inside. It was quiet—only the faint rustle of leaves brushing one another, like the whole place was breathing.

Crimson blossoms dotted the greenery, but they were unlike any I'd seen before. They seemed to twitch—just slightly—as if reacting to our presence.

Poppies.

Curious, I crouched down, my hand hovering above one. The scent was thicker here, cloying. I leaned closer—

The vines snapped forward.

I didn't even have time to scream before they wrapped around my arms and legs, yanking me backward. The bow and arrow slipped from my hands, vanishing in a shimmer of light as they returned to the bracelet.

A strangled cry rang out—Sara. She twisted, whispering to the ivy, but the vines refused to obey, coiling around her torso and binding her arms. Euryale slashed at the creeping tendrils, but more surged upward, snaring her wrists.

The vines pulsed—tightening. My heart thundered in my chest.

One bud turned toward me. Slowly, its petals unfurled, brushing my chin. A sharp puff of fragrance burst out, spraying my face.

My muscles went slack. My vision swam.

Just before the world went dark, I saw the flower tilt toward another—as if whispering.

Then everything faded to black.

CHAPTER THIRTY-SEVEN

SKYE

A low, resonant hum filled my ears as consciousness clawed its way back to me. My limbs felt heavy, like I'd been submerged in warm water for too long. My nose scrunched—something thick hung in the air, clinging, like I'd inhaled too much pollen.

Slowly, I pried my eyes open.

We were no longer in the moss-covered, poppy-lined entryway.

No...my head was resting against something hard. I pushed my hands against it, feeling the cool surface beneath me as I lifted my head, disoriented.

We were somewhere else now—a place that looked like a gothic cathedral, but with no pews. Just darkness and towering pillars. They were entwined with ivy, their blooms the color of dried blood, throbbing faintly like beating hearts.

And then I saw them.

A staircase climbed toward two thrones. One was carved from dark stone, its edges jagged and spiked like onyx spears. The other was draped in wisteria, pale blossoms woven through its frame, blooming softly in the dim light—as if they had learned to thrive in darkness.

The figures seated upon them were as striking as the thrones themselves.

The man wore a gladiator-style breastplate that looked forged from volcanic rock, a dark cape pooling at his feet. His hair was slicked back, a neatly trimmed beard framing his mouth.

Handsome—but it was the woman beside him who stole the breath from my lungs.

Her skin was deep and radiant, glowing as if kissed by sunlight itself. Dark curls cascaded over her shoulders, threaded with garlands of flowers, and her full lips were painted the color of ripe pomegranates. She was breathtaking—so much so, she could rival Aphrodite herself.

No wonder Aphrodite resented her. No wonder she cursed her, though she wasn't the one struck by the arrow. She wanted to ruin a purity and innocence she could never possess.

I cautiously pushed myself upright, my legs unsteady. Beside me, Euryale and Sara groaned, shaking off the lingering effects of whatever magic had knocked us out.

I winced, rubbing my arms and wrists, still sore from where the vines had clamped down too tightly.

Then a jolt of panic sliced through the haze.

Cullen's bracelet—gone.

My gaze dropped to my wrists. My hands trembled as the realization settled. It wasn't just the bracelet—my daggers were gone, too. *The scissors.* Only my protective leathers remained.

Before I could speak, a voice cut cleanly through the stillness.

"You are not of the dead, and you enter my home uninvited."

Hades.

He paused, his gaze sweeping over us before landing on Sara. His brow twitched. "And you entranced my dog."

Well, this is awkward.

Sara perked up beside me, clasping her hands together.

"Oh! He's such a good boy! We had some bread, and he liked it—"

Euryale yanked her back so hard Sara let out a small yelp. Hades raised an eyebrow at the exchange but said nothing. Instead, he exhaled through his nose, tilting his head slightly before continuing as if the interruption hadn't occurred.

"I would choose my next words carefully—and your motives for such an intrusion."

I swallowed hard, recalling Aphrodite's words: *Prove yourself.*

"We didn't mean any disrespect," I said, keeping my tone steady. "If there had been another way to reach Tartarus, we would've taken it. We wouldn't have"—my eyes swept the chamber, and even the poppies and blooms curled toward me, straining as if to listen—"disturbed your peace."

Hades didn't blink. Didn't speak.

But his fingers tapped once against the armrest of his throne—a silent cue to continue.

I drew in a breath and kept going, even as it felt like laying my throat bare to a blade.

"Phobos and Deimos are planning to restore the Titans," I explained. "They want to break the Olympian Command, even if it means destroying everything."

I hesitated for half a second, then gestured to the Underworld around us.

"Even here."

A beat passed. The silence stretched taut.

"And I..." My throat tightened, but I forced the words out. "I'm bonded to Cullen—Cupid."

A muscle in Hades's jaw ticked. Yeah—he already knew who I was.

I clenched my fists and pressed on. "If anyone understands the power of love, it's you. That's why we're here. If—"

Hades raised a hand, cutting me off.

"You assume I take sides."

I took a step forward, earning a flicker of surprise from him.

"I just thought—"

"You thought wrong." His gaze sharpened, tone flat with irritation. "Phobos and Deimos are not my concern. Nor is your bond with *Cupid*." He said the name like venom. "The affairs of gods and mortals beyond my realm hold no interest for me."

I opened my mouth to protest—

"You should be grateful I allow you to leave at all," Hades went on, his voice dipping lower, colder, as if trying to sever me from Cullen. "Your presence is insult enough, but to expect aid?" He huffed, and I swear smoke left his nostrils like a dragon. "You are fortunate I do not punish you for Cupid's transgressions."

Beside him, Persephone tensed, her gaze shifting away at the mention of Cupid's name. A shadow crossed her face—like the mere thought of him held pain.

Euryale stepped forward, fury radiating off her. "What did they offer you?"

Hades's eyes flicked to her, but she didn't falter. If anything, she leaned in, coiling like a snake ready to strike.

"What could Phobos and Deimos possibly give you in exchange for turning a blind eye?" she pressed. "Power? Freedom?" Her lips curled in a bitter, almost mocking smile. "Or is it revenge?"

The air thickened, heavy with tension.

Euryale tilted her head, the challenge in her gaze unmistakable. "After all, your brothers tricked you into this throne, didn't they? Zeus claimed the skies, Poseidon the seas—and left you with the dead. You've never been an Olympian, never held their Command. Wouldn't you want Phobos and Deimos to break their rule?"

A low rumble shuddered through the palace, rattling the stone beneath our feet.

Hades rose.

And the room darkened—no, it was swallowed. Spirits surged from the shadows like they'd always been there waiting, the despair of a thousand lost souls woven into their forms. They stretched unnaturally, rising in defense of their king.

The floor cracked beneath us, fissures spiderwebbing outward as the ground split open.

The air turned colder, pressing against my chest, dense as packed soil, each breath harder to pull in than the last. Like I was already being buried alive.

Power. Unfathomable power.

Euryale tensed but didn't move.

"Mind your tongue, Gorgon," Hades barked, his voice alone enough to make the spirits tremble.

Sara suddenly stepped forward, hands raised in an open gesture. "Forgive her, my Divine," she said, her tone soothing, careful. "The universe cannot fathom the strength of the love you possess."

Hades's gaze snapped to her, his expression still as carved stone.

Sara held firm. "You're no tyrant, Divine Hades. You are the merciful keeper of the dead—the one who ensures they find peace. Even the souls forgotten by the living—you remember them." Her voice softened, reverent. "You love them."

For a moment, nothing moved.

Then Hades clenched his fists—as if angry with himself for losing control. The spirits withdrew, dissolving back into the shadows once they sensed the threat had passed. He sank into his throne again, slower this time.

Hades narrowed his eyes. "You claim to know my love?"

Sara hesitated, but before she could respond, Hades shifted, his body angled subtly toward Persephone.

Persephone...his love.

It was there—in his eyes.

The same look Cullen gave me.

Before I could talk myself out of it, I stepped forward. "Persephone."

The moment her name left my lips, Hades's gaze snapped to me—deadly. The mere thought of me addressing his queen was a death sentence. His fingers twitched against the arm of his throne, but Persephone lifted a calm, deliberate hand—halting whatever storm had begun to rise in him.

Her eyes met mine—unblinking, unwavering.

I inhaled slowly, each word tipping a scale I couldn't afford to break.

"We need to get to Tartarus," I began. "And in exchange, I can offer something. A truth."

I paused, waiting to see if divine wrath would strike me down.

"I can show you Hades's feelings for you."

Persephone's eyes widened.

Beside her, Hades surged halfway from his throne, voice a low growl. "No—"

But Persephone didn't flinch. Didn't even look at him.

Her gaze stayed locked on mine as she slowly stood, wisteria rustling around her like a living veil.

"Yes."

Hades turned to her, jaw clenched. "Persephone—"

She stepped forward, and that single movement silenced him.

"And how do I know this isn't a trick?" she asked, calm but curious.

I lifted my chin, meeting her gaze. "Because I'll tell you something only you and Hades would know."

Persephone studied me like someone who'd spent lifetimes guarding herself against deception.

She let out a low, thoughtful hum.

Her gaze flicked to Hades, whose expression remained carefully neutral. Then, after a long pause, she turned back to me.

"Very well," she agreed at last, though her tone carried caution. "But if this is a trick, my husband will be the least of your concerns."

I could see the fire in her eyes—she may have looked angelic, but she seemed more than capable of handling a few demons of her own.

I nodded and started forward.

Euryale stepped in front of me. "Absolutely not," she snapped.

Sara stepped closer beside her, voice lower but no less urgent. "Skye, this is dangerous. You don't know how this place might twist your visions."

"You're no good to anyone if you're dead," Euryale added, not holding back.

I straightened. "We're all dead if I don't."

They looked like they wanted to argue more, but I lifted my chin. "It's my choice. So let me make it."

Euryale and Sara relented, letting me pass. I moved back toward Hades and Persephone.

"Cullen also cursed me with his arrow," I said. "I can see visions of someone's thoughts through touch. I can't promise how long I'll be able to hold it—but I'll hold on as long as I can."

"You are cursed and bound to him," Hades murmured, his gaze sweeping over me—measuring, dissecting—as if only now registering the full weight of what tied us together.

Both marked by Cullen.

He, by love.

Me, by madness.

Two sides of the same curse.

Persephone tilted her head slightly. "You would do this—show us this vision of truth—even if it could wound you?"

I nodded. "Yes. As long as you keep your word and help us reach Tartarus."

A slow smile curved her lips. She turned to Hades, her expression shifting into something fierce and resolute. "Then this is it," she declared, stepping toward him. "The proof you've always wanted."

Hades's gaze darkened. "Persephone—"

"No." She cut him off, her voice commanding. "You've doubted yourself for too long. You refuse to trust your love for me because of his arrow." She gestured toward me without breaking her gaze. "But now we have a way to know. A way to see what's real."

Hades's jaw clenched, but he said nothing.

Persephone stepped closer, undeterred. "If you truly believe your feelings aren't your own, then let her prove you wrong."

A tense silence filled the room, thick as the shadows curling at the edges of the great hall.

Hades didn't move, his expression carved from stone—but a flicker passed behind his dark golden eyes.

Persephone closed the space between them. He parted his legs so she could step between them. She reached for him, cradling his face in her hands—her touch tender yet resolute.

His jaw tensed beneath her fingers. For a moment, he didn't move, his gaze fixed somewhere past her shoulder, refusing to meet hers. But she didn't let go. She held him as if grounding him—as if reminding him of everything they'd built together.

Slowly, Hades turned his gaze back to her.

They stared into each other's eyes, as if her soul were caressing his.

Then, finally, he exhaled. "Very well," he grumbled. "I will grant passage for your vision."

I took a slow, steadying breath. Even I wasn't sure what I was about to pull from the depths of his past.

The visions before—glimpses of truths I wasn't meant to see—had torn through me like a goddamn hurricane. I couldn't control them, and each time, they took a piece of me...of my sanity.

I had no clue how many more visions I could endure before my mind unraveled completely. Headaches. Nosebleeds. What would be next?

I shook the fear away.

Cullen was in Tartarus, and I didn't know what the hell had happened to him. If there was even the slightest chance this vision could bring me closer to him, then I had to take it—even if it wrecked me. Even if it meant leaving a piece of myself behind.

I climbed the last step, heart pounding. What if I saw something Hades and Persephone didn't want to face? What if, despite everything, their love really was just a lie?

Doubt crept in, tightening around my ribs, but I shoved it down.

A pair of golden eyes held mine. *Move forward.*

I raised my hand slowly. The way Hades shifted—as if I were holding a branding iron to his face—told me he wasn't used to being touched. Not like this. Not by someone trying to uncover the truth of his heart.

"Think of her," I instructed, motioning toward Persephone.

Hades nodded.

My palm hovered just above his. A breath. A heartbeat. Then, with the smallest movement, I closed the space between us, pressing my hand to his.

The moment I felt his cool skin, the world around me shattered.

A vision exploded through me.

I saw Persephone as she was then—young, untouched by the Underworld, the warmth of the sun still clinging to her skin. And I saw Hades watching her from the shadows...longing for her, aching to be near but never daring to step into her light.

My head snapped up.

Aphrodite stood at a distance, whispering something beneath her breath—then pointed.

At Cullen.

And then—

The arrow.

The moment it struck Hades, everything changed. His thoughts spiraled, consumed by her—Persephone's laughter, her voice, the way she moved through a field of golden wheat like she belonged to the earth itself. The arrow didn't just pierce him—it embedded itself in the deepest part of him, warping every rational thought into obsession.

The curse of the arrow didn't discriminate against immortality. He was a god, but now he was completely powerless against his own heart.

And still—

Even under the thrall of the curse, he fought it.

I felt it. His magic surged, pushing back against the curse—desperate to keep his thoughts his own.

Yes, he brought Persephone to the Underworld—

But he never took her.

Not against her will.

He waited.

He watched.

He gave her space, even as the curse in his chest screamed to act.

Then came the seeds—six glowing crimson pomegranate seeds.

A shield.

He'd crafted them himself, pouring his magic into their very core—so that if she stayed, it would be by her choice, not his obsession.

And Persephone had chosen.

The time they shared.

The patience in his touch.

The respect.

All of it shaped something stronger than the curse.

Something real.

Something true.

The vision tore away, ripping me out like I was being yanked through a vortex.

Pain slammed into me. My head throbbed, the room spinning like a car rolling end over end after a crash.

Warmth trickled down my upper lip.

Blood.

I swayed, my legs buckling beneath me—

But strong arms caught me.

Euryale on one side.

Sara on the other.

Their grips were firm but careful, never touching bare skin, like holding shattered glass.

"Skye."

Sara's voice cut through the haze, laced with worry I could feel in my bones.

"I'm—" My voice came out hoarse, brittle. I wasn't sure what I was, but I was still here—still standing. "I'm okay."

I drew in a shaky breath and forced myself to look up.

At Hades.

At Persephone.

Both frozen in place, staring at each other.

Hope in their eyes.

I wiped my nose with the back of my hand, smearing blood across my cheek, and straightened as best I could.

"It wasn't the curse," I rasped, meeting Hades's gaze head-on. "Not entirely. Yes, you acted on pure impulse. You desired her above all else. But love...that wasn't the arrow."

I turned to Persephone. Her lips parted, a quiet breath catching in her throat.

I staggered forward. "You did that yourselves."

Hades's eyes flickered—something raw surfacing, something long buried beneath the weight of centuries and silence.

"You fought it," I continued, my voice steadier now. "You resisted. And when you couldn't push her away, you didn't cage her. You protected her."

I swallowed hard. "The pomegranate seeds you gave her...they weren't to keep her against her will, were they?"

Persephone's breath hitched.

"They were a shield," I said, louder now. "Your magic. Your love. You crafted something that could only bind her if she chose it. You gave her that power. You gave her a choice."

A tremor rippled through Persephone. She turned to Hades, eyes wide, searching his face as if seeing him for the first time. Slowly, gently, she placed her hands against his chest.

He didn't move at first.

Then, after what felt like an eternity, he raised one hand and brushed his fingers over hers. Barely a touch—but it carried the weight of everything unspoken between them.

I exhaled, body sagging between Sara and Euryale, the only things keeping me upright.

I'd given them the truth.

A truth that had always been theirs.

Blood still trickled from my nose as I pressed a hand to it.

Persephone glided toward me, closing the distance like a swift breeze. "Thank you."

She drew something from her pocket and motioned to my hand. I lifted it—careful not to let her skin touch mine—and she placed it in my palm.

A handkerchief. Blush silk, embroidered with gold. Her hands lingered just above it, and the fabric shimmered. Then she gestured for me to unfold it.

I raised an eyebrow but slowly unfolded the cloth. Tucked inside was a small sprig of yarrow. My fingers brushed the delicate white flowers.

I glanced up, startled. "Yarrow?"

She offered a small, knowing smile. "It helps with blood flow. And perhaps the visions, when they take too much."

A breathy laugh escaped me as I pressed the handkerchief to my nose. "You know your plants."

Her smile widened just a touch as she gestured to the surrounding greenery. "Of course. I'm the goddess of spring."

"Thank you," I breathed—meaning more than just the herb.

Hades stepped beside her.

"You have proven your truth," he said. "I will keep my word as well."

He raised a hand, and the air around us shifted—

Thick with magic.

Shadows peeled open beside his throne, unraveling like smoke to reveal a swirling black void. From its depths, our belongings spilled out—bags, weapons, everything we'd been stripped of when we entered.

Euryale moved first. She strode toward the pile, snatched up her sword and baton like she was reclaiming a limb, and with a sharp huff, tossed Sara's bag to her without missing a beat.

I descended the stairs, my fingers trembling as I reached down and slid Cullen's bracelet from the pile, fastening it back around my wrist.

It wasn't much—but it was a piece of him.

And right now, that meant everything.

I tightened the straps of the dagger sheaths against my thighs, then reached for my belt, where I'd hidden the scissors in one of the bags tied to it. Carefully, I adjusted it as though it were nothing, unsure what Hades and Persephone would do if they discovered them.

My fingers brushed the hidden metal, tracing its hard edges, following the length until I felt a faint pulse of power thrumming beneath my touch—a silent whisper telling me, *Yes, we're here.*

And then—footsteps.

Persephone approached, something gleaming in her hands.

Not a weapon.

A mirror.

Its frame was a dark gold, curling like tendrils around the edges, studded with tiny gemstones that glimmered faintly. The glass didn't reflect like normal—it moved, liquid and alive, like the surface of a disturbed pond.

"This will guide you," she offered, placing it gently in my hands.

I narrowed my eyes, studying the shifting glass. The surface rippled—within it, winding paths, rivers, and twisting caverns bloomed like flowers.

A map.

A map of the Underworld.

Persephone leaned in slightly, her voice dropping to a near whisper. "But be cautious, Skye. This mirror is more than a guide. Those with powerful desires—freedom, connection—they will be drawn to it. If it falls into the wrong hands, it could be used to escape the labyrinth that binds them here."

So...don't lose it. Got it.

I curled my fingers tighter around the mirror and nodded.

"The scissors of the Fates are with you," Persephone murmured, as if speaking only for me.

My heart clenched.

"While others cannot wield them, they still hold powerful magic. Be strong, Skye. And may the Fates guide you all."

She knew. She knew I had them.

Before I could speak, Hades raised a hand.

The massive doors of the palace groaned, ancient hinges straining as they opened to reveal the darkened path ahead.

I glanced at Persephone one last time.

She met my eyes—a token of respect. Recognition.

As if risking my life had proven I'd earned even a sliver of their help.

I offered a faint smile in return, then turned away.

Euryale and Sara fell in beside me without hesitation.

The doors slammed shut with a thunderous *thud* that echoed down the stone corridor.

We were back in the depths of hell.

But hey—at least this time, we had a map.

CHAPTER THIRTY-EIGHT

CULLEN

Pain was the only constant.

The apparitions Phobos and Deimos commanded coiled around me—black, shifting forms that seeped into my skin and burrowed into my mind. Nightmares bled into one another. Some old. Some new. All crafted to break me.

But I didn't break.

I adapted.

The moment I felt a nightmare tighten its grip, I lashed out—sharp, violent, headfirst.

A sickening *crack*.

Bone met shadow.

The thing shrieked, a high, piercing sound, before unraveling into nothing but vapor.

My chest heaved as I stumbled back against the chains, vision swimming.

It wasn't over. Another would come.

I blinked hard, forcing my focus back to where it needed to be.

Harmony and Zeph.

Still trapped in nightmares.

Dark clouds still coiled around their heads, feeding them horrors I couldn't see.

I had to get to them.

I strained forward.

Chains pulled tight.

Agony tore up my arms as the metal bit into my skin. I twisted my wrists, testing for any give.

Nothing.

But maybe I didn't need to break them.

Maybe I needed something else...

I forced myself to look—*really* look.

Darkness.

No weapons. Nothing I could use—

Gods, even the burning rocks beneath me were useless.

...*Rocks.*

A slow grin pulled at my mouth.

Rocks, I could work with.

I shifted my weight. Slowly. Every inch screamed through my shoulders, chains groaning in protest. My arms stretched forward, wrists grinding against metal. Tendons pulled taut. My fingers splayed against the heat.

Dust.

Ash.

Then—roughness.

I angled my palm.

Brushed.

Found the jagged edge of something sharp.

Small—crumbling at the corners.

A shard.

I coaxed it toward me with two fingers, careful not to lose it to the cracks below. I held it in my palm, feeling its heat bite into my skin.

Steady.

I moved, measuring the distance, the angle, and the height of the shadow hovering over Zeph's still form.

Breathe.

Then I flicked.

A clean, practiced motion—like pulling back a bowstring.

The shard flew.

The wail echoed, high and shrill, as the shadow above Zeph ruptured into smoke. He jolted upright, gasping like a drowning man dragged from the depths.

One down.

My fingers were already searching the ground again, sifting heat and dust, ignoring the sting. A second shard—longer than the first, more brittle. I gripped it between my knuckles.

My gaze found Harmony.

Her body lay limp, half-curled on her side. The dark clung to her, rippling like it was feeding on her.

I lined the shard against my palm.

My muscles screamed, but I pulled back, holding the shot like it was my last arrow.

It had to be enough.

I loosed it.

The rock arced through the air, spinning once—twice—before striking the darkness with a sharp *crack*.

The shadow recoiled violently, bloating with a hiss—then exploded in a spray of mist and ash.

Harmony's back bowed. She gasped sharply, hands clawing at the ground, eyes flying open, blinking against the darkness.

"What—" she rasped. She shook her head, as if trying to clear the fog —as if the nightmare still clung to the edges of her vision.

"No time," I croaked, my voice hoarse. "We have a problem."

Zeph gave a humorless laugh, still catching his breath. "Yeah, no shit."

Harmony inhaled deeply, steadying herself. "Where are they?"

"Gone—for now," I answered tightly. "We find Skye's sisters. We get out."

Her breath caught as she looked down—throat bare.

The necklace was gone.

Her expression darkened. "They took it."

No weapons. Not ideal.

Zeph rolled his shoulders, testing the chains binding him. "I can cause a distraction. Might give us an opening."

The moment Zeph used his winds, his brothers would feel it.

He knew it, too—and he was still willing to sacrifice himself.

Fuck that.

I leaned in, voice low, the chains clinking softly behind me.

Gave him a half smile.

"Nice speech. But I'm not letting you play the martyr."

Zeph returned it, dry and steady.

I held his gaze. "We walk out together—or not at all."

Before he could respond, the air split with a deep, thunderous *boom*.

The ground trembled.

We froze.

Then—footsteps.

Each one echoed through the cavern, followed by the bite of icy, blazing wind curling around us.

From the shadows, two figures emerged.

Boreas. Eurus.

With a sudden gust, they lifted off the ground, gliding across the cavern. Robes whipped behind them, flowing up as tall as my wings. They descended on Zeph without hesitation, barely glancing at me or Harmony.

Boreas landed first. His boots struck stone with a heavy *thud*. His face, all hard angles and frostbitten disdain, looked carved from ice.

"The deal was him," he said flatly. "He's ours. Along with his winds."

Before Zeph could react, Boreas seized him by the collar and hauled him upright. The chains snapped tight, locking him in place.

Zeph let out a hoarse laugh. "Fighting over me? Didn't know I was such a prized stag."

Eurus rolled his eyes, thoroughly unimpressed.

Phobos and Deimos watched from the sidelines with idle amusement, eyes gleaming.

Deimos stepped forward. "Do I need to remind you who you serve?" he asked, his voice like silk over steel.

Phobos released his shadows, which rose upward like fingers. "No one leaves. Not until it's done."

Boreas's grip tightened. His jaw flexed, but he stayed silent.

Eurus, however, cast a glacial glare at the twin gods. "You think we've forgotten?"

Phobos chuckled, low and pleased. "Good."

Then a dark, gleeful look stole across his face, his gaze flicking toward the cavern entrance.

"Our new guest should be here soon," he said, voice low with anticipation. "It's almost time."

Someone else was coming?

Phobos moved closer, pointing a sharp, accusing finger at us. "Interfere, and we'll rip the air from your lungs again."

Deimos chuckled beside him, low and cruel. "Aww, I hope you interfere. Just to watch you choke again."

Beside me, Harmony tensed; Zeph remained silent.

We were forced to do nothing but watch.

"Begin," Phobos ordered.

Boreas and Eurus moved in unison, their hands slicing through the air like warriors performing a practiced, deadly dance. The winds stirred instantly, obeying without hesitation.

A roar built around us. Wind howled to life, a keen edge carving through the cavern.

A sudden gust slammed into the walls, carving deep fissures into the stone. The ground lurched. The earth groaned as cracks splintered outward.

Boreas pivoted, sweeping his arm wide. Air surged with him, hurling loose stones like shrapnel.

Above us, the ceiling trembled. Stone groaned and cracked, forced apart by invisible winds. Then—light.

A single beam broke through the rupture. A white light—

Astraios's Comet.

Its glow poured down, humming, illuminating the darkness like a tear from the heavens.

Phobos and Deimos turned toward the light, eyes gleaming—like it had arrived right on time.

I braced myself.

A voice echoed from the light.

"Good...good. Everything is right on schedule."

I turned, certain I would be numb to surprises.

I'd never been more wrong.

A figure emerged, stepping into the fractured beam of light.

And in that instant—I knew.

Betrayal had a face.

"Don't look so disappointed," he chided with a shrug, casual, familiar. "It's just business."

Then the mask slipped, and something colder sharpened in his gaze.

"But honestly? This one's a little personal."

Hymenaeus.

The god of marriage. God of...bonds.

Now standing here. Among *them*.

His golden wreath caught the comet's firelight, gleaming like a crown. His robes were unmarked—pristine, as if untouched by the rot and ruin around us. As if he still believed he was holy.

Hymenaeus stepped forward, hands folded, as if presiding over some sacred ritual. "You, along with so many others, insulted me," he said smoothly. "You let *her* conduct the bonding ceremony in my place."

His gaze flicked toward the twin gods. "Hera," he added, his voice dripping with contempt.

Harmony's chains rattled as she lunged forward, fury crackling in her voice. "You know he didn't have a choice!"

Hymenaeus tilted his head, mock sympathy curving his mouth. "Oh, I know. And that's the problem, isn't it? The Olympians take what they want. They treat the rest of us like obedient little servants."

He paused—for effect. "Their reign ends today, for I am no lesser god."

I let out a dry laugh, shaking my head. "Did you rehearse that monologue in front of a mirror? Practice your dramatic pause?"

Zeph snorted beside me.

Hymenaeus didn't react. His smile never faltered. He stepped closer, eyes flicking to the chains binding my wrists—close enough to provoke, just far enough to be safe.

Coward.

He scanned Harmony, then me. "You both look so much like your mother," he murmured. Then his tongue dragged across his lips—slow. Revolting. "I can't wait to pay her a visit once the Olympians fall. Feel those golden waves of hair through my fingers...just like your sister."

His gaze slid to Harmony, dragging over her in a way that made my stomach twist.

Harmony didn't flinch. Her stare burned molten, the wrath of Ares alive in her eyes.

Hymenaeus only chuckled, sick with satisfaction, and turned his attention back to me. "And then, of course," he drawled, savoring every syllable, "there's your newly bonded wife."

Not a smile. A curl of the lip—darker, twisted, eager. "I wonder what it'll be like...to finally lay my blessed hands on her."

My vision went red.

The chains groaned as I lunged, fury erupting like a tidal wave through my chest. I was an inch from his face—so close I could feel the smug heat of his breath.

He smiled, savoring the fact that I couldn't reach him.

So—like the rocks—I used what I had. My spit struck his cheek, sliding down. I imagined it as my fingers clawing across his skin, leaving burning trails that would burrow to his core.

Hymenaeus didn't even blink. He dragged a finger through it, slowly, and licked it clean. His eyes gleamed, sick with pleasure.

I was ready to tear him apart—

But movement at the cavern entrance stopped me cold.

They were dragged forward, two frightened figures barely staying on their feet. Even in their fear, the resemblance was unmistakable—the eyes. Skye's sisters.

They were shaking. Traumatized. Who knew what Phobos and Deimos had already done to them.

Phobos chuckled as he approached, voice thick with mockery. "Ah, look at them—Skye's dear, sweet sisters. So fragile. So breakable." He tilted his head with a sneer. "Don't be rude, girls. Say hello to your new brother-in-law."

Deimos laughed darkly, circling them like a chimera scenting blood. "That's right. This is Cullen Eros—Skye's newly bonded husband. She never mentioned him? Shame. And here we thought family was supposed to be close."

The sisters clung to each other, fingers locked tight, arms pressed together, as if that alone could keep them safe.

Phobos sighed theatrically. "Shy, are we?"

Without warning, he seized one sister and yanked her forward, forcing her arm through his like some grotesque parody of a courtship. She whimpered but refused to release her sister, their grip straining even as he pulled her away.

I lunged against my restraints, rage surging through me.

If I could just—

Deimos leaned in, flashing teeth. "Careful now. Wouldn't want to upset your in-laws."

Hymenaeus exhaled like a bored priest, stepping forward with a coaxing smile toward the sisters. "It will all be over soon," he said softly—comfort offered before an execution.

Then he moved toward a jagged column of stone that rose from the ground like a towering, makeshift pulpit.

Phobos and Deimos flanked him—true gods of chaos.

Hymenaeus raised his hands.

The air shifted.

And when he spoke, his voice carried—echoing through Tartarus.

The Titans wailed in response.

The bonding ceremony had begun.

I knew the words—had heard them the same day Skye and I were bound.

But this was different.

There was no choice. No consent.

One sister for Phobos.

The other for Deimos.

They didn't want this.

Their eyes were wide with terror, limbs rigid as they moved through the ceremony—wrung from them by fear alone.

I yanked against the chains until my muscles screamed, fury humming through every nerve.

"Cullen." Harmony's breath tore out sharp and ragged, her eyes—

I followed her gaze.

The comet's glow flared brighter, pulsing in rhythm with the unnatural stillness. Boreas and Eurus moved in unison, shaping the stone above—carving channels that funneled the celestial light into a basin, like a baptismal font.

"This isn't possible," she whispered, disbelief scraping her throat. "The comet...it shouldn't be able to produce nectar."

But it was.

At the center of it all, Hymenaeus placed two golden vials into the cradle of carved rock.

They shimmered in the basin's core, catching every drop of divine light.

Inside—liquid fire.

The nectar of the gods.

"Like I said—we've done our research." Phobos's drawl was almost academic, as if this were a carefully calculated experiment. His smile sharpened. "If a bond is sealed beneath the flare of Astraios's Comet, nectar will flow. The heavens' own gift—turned into their undoing."

Hymenaeus lifted his arms, voice echoing against the stone.

"It is done."

Phobos and Deimos didn't hesitate. They forced the vials to the sisters' lips. The girls writhed, twisting away, but the golden liquid slid between their teeth—thick and searing.

Their cries drowned.

Bodies convulsed. Backs arched. Gasping turned to choking, then—

Collapse.

One. Then the other.

I threw myself forward, chains screeching. I would've torn my own arms off if it meant getting to them—

Too late.

They lay still.

So...still.

Then—a twitch. A breath.

Their bodies calmed, the seizing turning into small shivers. Something was settling in their veins.

Power.

One stirred first. Her head lifted just enough to find me.

Her eyes locked on mine—pleading, desperate.

The other followed, mirroring her perfectly. Two sets of matching gazes—silent cries screaming through the stillness.

The blue of their irises had vanished, replaced by a shimmering gold.

Faint at first—but spreading.

A divine light.

My breath caught.

They had made them gods.

CHAPTER THIRTY-NINE

SKYE

I tilted the reflective surface, squinting at the shifting, liquid-like lines that formed our supposed path. No matter how I angled it, the map warped—its markings flickering and changing—making it near impossible to read.

"This thing is bullshit," I muttered.

But Cullen was close—I could feel it. I *had* to find him.

I adjusted my grip on the cool glass, my fingers tightening as the tunnel ahead split. I glanced down at the mirror, which pulsed faintly, its warped reflections bending toward the right.

The only sounds were the soft *crunch* of Sara and Euryale's footsteps and the occasional drip of moisture echoing overhead.

"This way," I said, stepping forward.

"Skye, how are you feeling?" Sara asked, her voice soft but laced with concern.

Euryale glanced at me, too—not outright asking, but watching closely.

I rolled my shoulders, forcing my posture straight. I wasn't about to admit how drained I felt, as if all my energy had been siphoned away. My head felt light—almost like I had an iron deficiency, but infinitely worse.

"I'm fine," I clipped. "Let's keep moving."

Neither of them looked convinced, but they didn't argue. We didn't have the luxury of slowing down.

Euryale exhaled sharply. "At this rate, we'll be wandering in circles all night. Let me see it—there might be a cut-through path."

She paused, scanning the tunnel, then strode to the wall and yanked a torch free in one smooth motion.

The moment the firelight hit the mirror, the reflections fractured. Jagged beams whipped through the cavern like the frantic sweep of a searchlight—a beacon that sent a signal into the dark.

A signal that said: *prey*.

Euryale jerked the torch away from the mirror.

Too late.

The air shifted.

Something moved.

Then—

SKREEEEEE!

From above, dark, two-winged figures uncurled from their perches in the shadows. Their bodies were long and skeletal, their leathery wings expanding and cracking as they stretched. Clawed hands—gnarled and elongated—gripped the jagged ceiling before they dropped, landing effortlessly above us.

The larger of the two cocked its head, lips curling into something between a snarl and smirk.

"Furies," Sara said softly behind us.

"The females can drag fully armored soldiers off. I've seen them do it," Euryale added, her feet shifting on the dirt as if bracing to lunge.

"Look what we have here," the smaller one rasped, her voice a dry scrape against the silence. "Trespassers in the land of the dead."

The larger one scuttled forward, a claw scraping the ground. "Sinners," she corrected.

I clutched the mirror tighter to my chest.

Sara and Euryale pressed in, the three of us forming a tight circle, backs together.

"We pass judgment on those who evade justice," the larger one declared, her gaze flicking between us. "You"—her glowing red eyes settled on me—"are a liar. A fraud who deceives others under the guise of power."

My stomach twisted.

Euryale shifted closer, her head bent low to our ears. "We need to—"

The smaller Fury snapped her gaze toward Euryale, lips peeling back to reveal rows of rotting, jagged teeth. "And you—how many innocents were scorched by your rage?" Her voice dripped with accusation. "Murderer."

Euryale didn't flinch, but her jaw locked tight.

"That's not true!" Sara shouted, stepping forward.

The Fury turned to her in a flash. "Disobedience," she hissed, venom thick in her voice. "Defiance against the god who gave you purpose."

Sara's expression hardened, darkening.

It was as if these creatures could see into our deepest guilt and twist the knife.

The larger Fury lifted a clawed hand, pointing directly at the mirror in my arms. "But perhaps there is penance," she mused. "A price for mercy."

The second one shrieked, "Give us the mirror!"

The sound split the air—sharp, piercing. My ears rang.

I glanced at Euryale and Sara. "Fight?"

Euryale didn't hesitate. "No."

The Furies' wings flared wide, eyes burning like coals.

"Run."

My lungs burned, but I didn't stop. Couldn't stop. The cavern walls blurred past, the path twisting and splitting, but we had no choice except to keep moving.

I clutched the mirror tightly, my grip slippery with sweat. Every time I glanced back, all I saw were those glowing red eyes locked onto us.

"Glasses!" I shouted at Euryale. If there was ever a time to turn things to stone, it was now.

Euryale and Sara answered in unison, breathless but exasperated—"They're blind!"

Oh, just fucking perfect.

More piercing shrieks tore through the air—more of them. I didn't look back. Instead, I tossed the mirror toward Euryale like a quarterback throwing a Hail Mary. She caught it with a grunt, barely keeping pace, before passing it to Sara.

The Furies were getting faster. Closer.

One swooped low—I could feel the gust of wind as it passed, sending a cold shock through me. Another lunged at Euryale, but she ducked just in time.

Then—Sara screamed.

I turned just as a Fury's talons sank deep into her arms, ripping her off the ground as if she weighed nothing.

Her face twisted in pain, fingers spasming around the mirror. Blood—greenish, slick—splattered onto the stone below.

"Sara!" I shouted, sprinting after her.

The Fury reeled her close, its rotting face hovering inches from hers, hissing like dry ice on metal.

Sara thrashed in its grasp, kicking, twisting—but it was no use. She was trapped.

My pulse hammered in my ears. I whipped toward Euryale, but she was surrounded—her sword flashing, wings of shadow mixing with steel, too far to reach us.

No hesitating.

I ran—then skidded to a stop.

I summoned Cullen's bow and arrows, nocked an arrow, and pulled the string back.

The Fury snapped its soulless gaze toward me just as I let the arrow fly.

I thought of how it had hurt Sara.

Will it. Will it—pain.

The arrow struck deep, piercing flesh and bone. A blood-curdling shriek tore from its throat as its grip instinctively loosened.

But not enough.

Sara twisted midair, fumbling for the pouch strapped to her side. With a desperate flick of her wrist, she hurled a vile of sleep powder into the Fury's face.

The creature recoiled, screeching as the fine dust clouded its vision. Its talons spasmed—

Sara fell.

With a choked gasp, she crashed to the ground, her limbs twisting into a protective knot around the mirror, binding herself to it like a vine.

"Euryale!" I screamed, moving toward Sara.

With one swift slash of her blade, Euryale struck the Fury blocking her path. It collapsed, black sludge pouring from its side, wings contorting as if trying to stop the flow. She closed the distance between us. With her free hand, she grabbed my arm, and together we formed a tight huddle around Sara.

I looked up, past Euryale's shoulders.

Above us, the Furies circled, their numbers swelling until they blotted out the cavern ceiling.

A layered chorus began—voices pressing in, echoing, and burrowing into my skull.

Liars.

Murderers.

Sinners.

Each word dragged every ounce of guilt I'd buried straight to the surface.

Liar.

Liar.

Liar.

The chant tunneled through me, as if they weren't speaking to the air but to me alone.

The lies I told to keep Lydia's shop alive.

The lies I used to convince my heart to suppress what it felt for Cullen.

And the gnawing truth that if my lies ever cost someone I loved their life, I would never forgive myself.

I tightened my grip on Euryale, fighting the guilt as it threatened to consume me.

Then—

A new sound tore through the cavern.

Low at first.

A single note, rising.

Then another...like music. *How?*

SKREEEEE!

The Furies shrieked, their cries distorting as they flew, crashing into one another. But the melody only swelled, weaving through them and growing stronger.

My knees nearly buckled.

It felt like...Cullen.

My eyes slipped shut, helpless to resist.

It was as if beauty itself had been given sound.

The music caught in my chest like a memory—the same ache, the same depth—just like Cullen when he played his violin.

Every note, every line of melody, felt spun from the very threads that wove souls together.

The Furies faltered. Then—

They broke, scattering into the shadows, wings thrashing in panic, as if unable to withstand its purity.

And then the final note dissipated.

Silence swallowed the cavern whole.

Then—

Heavy footsteps approached. They were more than sound; they were a force, like the ground itself had no choice but to acknowledge him.

A figure emerged from the shadows above us. Tall and broad-shouldered, he moved with restrained power, as if he knew exactly how much force to unleash. A silver flute, barely larger than a pen, gleamed faintly in his hand.

The cavern's dim light skimmed over the hard planes of his face, the sharp cut of his jaw. Crisscrossed leather straps bound his chest over a dark tunic, sleeves rolled to reveal burn scars twisting up his arms—scars that looked like blurred tattoos etched into his flesh.

There was no question.

Cullen's father.

Hephaestus.

"If you value her life," he said, his voice rolling down to us as he gestured once with a massive arm—then waited. No words. No Command.

Euryale didn't hesitate. She crouched low, slipping Sara carefully onto her back. Sara's head lolled against her shoulder, arms still clutching the mirror, but Euryale's grip was iron as she carried her forward.

I fell in behind them, my eyes fixed on Hephaestus with every step. He didn't move—just stood there, waiting.

When we finally closed the distance, Hephaestus pressed his palm to the cavern wall.

The stone shuddered beneath his touch, like some great beast answering its master's command. Then—with a thunderous *crack*—it split open, fissures spiderwebbing outward until they framed an arch. Light bled through the fractures, as though another realm awaited on the other side.

A door.

WARMTH.

That was the first thing I noticed.

Thick wool blankets cocooned me, their weight oddly grounding after the chaos of our escape. The steady crackle of a fire filled the room, flames licking at cedar logs and perfuming the air with smoke laced faintly with iron—like a blacksmith's forge hidden inside a mountain cabin.

Across from me, Sara lay stretched on her back, sunk into the deep green cushions of a couch in the middle of the room.

And at her side, Hephaestus worked in silence.

His large hands moved with a precision that didn't match the roughness of his calloused skin. Thick, scarred fingers handled Sara's wounds with...gentleness. Each cut cleaned, each bandage wrapped with the expertise of someone who'd done this before—of tending to the wounded, of fixing what had been broken.

I swallowed hard, my gaze catching on how his fingers moved—how they were so different from Cullen's, yet carried the same quiet strength.

Cullen.

I needed to find him. I didn't know how much time I had left.

Sara winced as Hephaestus tightened the final bandage.

Euryale stood beside her, arms crossed, watching every movement like a hawk. Not that she'd ever admit it, but I could tell—she was relieved Sara was being cared for properly.

After a beat, Euryale scoffed. "Honestly...letting some oversized bat carry you off like a damn damsel."

Sara let out a tired breath. "Oh, *sorry* for the inconvenience."

Euryale rolled her neck with a grunt, grabbed a folded blanket from the loveseat I was sitting on, and shoved it behind Sara's head—hitting her in the face in the process.

"Hey!" Sara glared. "I just survived a Fury. Do I really need to add Gorgon assault to the list?"

Euryale didn't bother with a response. She let go of the pillow and sat on the loveseat beside me.

I raised a brow at her. "You're more attentive than I expected."

She scoffed again—louder this time, like she was trying to drown out the accusation.

Hephaestus didn't say a word. He just kept working. Calm. Steady. Focused.

I glanced at Euryale.

Would he use his Olympian Command?

Order us out?

But he didn't.

He simply continued tending to Sara, his movements unhurried and methodical—like a man who'd known pain all his life and chose, despite everything, to heal what he could.

Hephaestus exhaled, the sound low and heavy.

He rolled the sleeves of his tunic back down, the firelight catching on the burn scars twisting up his forearms.

His eyes met mine briefly, silently, before he turned away. He gathered the remaining medical supplies and, with a long stride, moved toward the dark mouth of an adjoining room.

I hesitated. My muscles ached, every bone protesting, but I pushed myself to stand and follow.

He moved like someone used to silence, someone who'd been alone long enough to make peace with it. Maybe even preferred it.

But unfortunately for him...I had plenty to say.

"He's here."

That made him stop.

Encouraged, I stepped forward again, the words rushing out before I could overthink them. "Cullen is here. Phobos and Deimos took him to Tartarus. Will...will you help us?"

He turned slowly. Set the supplies down carefully. And then, finally, he looked at me.

Really looked at me.

His eyes tightened—not quite with resistance, just with weight.

Then he said, flatly, "It's not my place."

My jaw clenched.

Not his place?

"You do know how we got here, right?" I snapped. "Aphrodite gave me a ring. A ring that you made—to help find your son."

That surprised him.

It was subtle, but I saw it—the slight widening of his eyes, the way his fingers curled slowly into fists. But then he shook his head, like he didn't want to believe it. Like believing it would cost too much.

I stepped forward. "Can you help us?" I dared to ask again.

Hephaestus stared at me, silent and unmoving, disbelief etched in his gaze. But underneath it, something else lingered.

He *did* care.

He just didn't want to admit it.

And that pissed me off.

Anger flared in my chest, hot and fast. "So that's it?" I demanded. "You're just going to let Cullen suffer? Abandon him—again?"

He tensed.

Still said nothing.

I pushed harder. "You're no better than Aphrodite."

That hit.

I saw it in the way his shoulders locked up. The twitch in his jaw. But instead of snapping back, instead of defending himself—

He turned away.

"You can rest here," he said. His voice was low, controlled.

Like a door quietly shutting.

Rest?

Was he serious?

"We can't rest," I snapped. "The comet—"

"The comet is not at apex," he cut in. "There is time."

And with that, he turned—vanishing into the shadows of the corridor, his footsteps swallowed by the dark, leaving me standing alone in the flickering firelight.

My fists clenched.

My heart pounded.

I wanted to argue.

To shout.

To make him *do* something.

But the words caught in my throat—hot and useless.

I stood there, breathing hard, anger buzzing beneath my skin like static.

Then slowly—I turned back.

I just...I hoped there was more to him than what Cullen had seen.

Because how could *that* man be Cullen's father? How could someone so empty have made someone like him?

I crossed the threshold in silence, the warmth of the fire brushing my skin. Euryale had already dozed off, arms crossed, chin dipped. Sara stirred slightly but didn't wake.

The moment my head hit the cushion—

Sleep dragged me under before I even had the chance to close my eyes.

CHAPTER FORTY

CULLEN

Immortal.

Skye's sisters were still trembling—but they were immortal now, and…they could touch that damn torch.

I yanked on the chains instinctively.

Useless.

My strength alone wasn't enough, not against these.

But Harmony…

Even without the necklace to amplify it, she still had power. She'd always had it.

I turned to her, voice low. "Harmony."

She caught my look instantly and gave the faintest shake of her head. "I can't."

I drew a steady breath. "You were always stronger than that necklace. It didn't make you powerful—*you* made it powerful."

"You're more than enough, princess," Zeph added, his eyes shining like he wanted her to see herself reflected there, to believe the truth staring back at her.

Her gaze moved between us, then settled on Phobos and Deimos. They were distracted, circling their new brides like twisted collectors admiring prized possessions. Overhead, Zeph's brothers stirred the winds, lifting Hymenaeus out of Tartarus like the coward he was.

Slowly, Harmony straightened, spine rigid against the chains that bound her. "This is your plan?" she asked, her voice vibrating with power, every word echoing back at them in small reverberations. "You might restore the Titans' power—but do you truly think you can control them? Control *Cronus*?"

Phobos let out a low chuckle, amused. "Oh, our little sister thinks we're afraid."

But Deimos didn't laugh.

His eyes narrowed, something darker moving behind them. He stepped away from his bride, and in a blur of smoke, he was on her.

His hand clamped around her throat, lifting her high enough that the chains snapped taut, forcing her onto her toes. Harmony's eyes widened, gasps choking out of her as she clawed for air.

Zeph surged—but before his winds could rise, Boreas and Eurus were on him, locking him down with their own.

Deimos leaned in, voice dripping with scorn. "You are nothing," he hissed, sensing what she'd tried to do. "Our nightmares weakened you. You can't even conjure a flicker of your power. You're useless."

And something inside me snapped—not just fury, but guilt. His words mirrored my own.

I met Deimos's eyes, my voice low and hard as my arrows. "You're wrong."

He didn't release her—but I saw it.

That doubt.

I pressed on, my voice cutting through the space between us. "You're afraid of her, aren't you?" I glanced at Harmony, then back to him. "Even without that necklace. Even in chains. She's still stronger than you'll ever be."

Then I looked up at her. "You're strong, Harmony. The nightmares might've shaken you, but choosing to rise—choosing to keep using your voice—that's what makes you powerful."

Her fingers twitched.

And then, faintly, a light pulsed beneath her skin—soft at first, like a heartbeat. It glowed steady, quiet, but unrelenting.

Her gaze locked on Deimos.

"Let. Me. Go," she rasped.

Deimos's grip faltered.

I saw the flicker of confusion in his eyes, the slight slack in his hand, like he'd forgotten why he was even holding her.

The light within Harmony grew bolder. Her breathing leveled out, even with his hand still clamped around her throat. Her power seeped into the air like heat rising before a storm, threading through the cracks of his control.

"Fuck you," Harmony spat, her voice clearer.

Deimos blinked, hard. Like he was trying to shake off a fog. But Harmony didn't stop. Her glow pulsed again—stronger this time. Warmer. Radiant.

His breath hitched. His fingers trembled.

He was going to release her.

Then—the cavern shook.

From the pit below, a roar erupted—countless voices rising together in a volcanic scream.

The Titans.

With that, Deimos released her.

Harmony dropped, hitting the ground hard as the chains went slack. Coughs wracked her body, and her glow dimmed, her natural complexion returning.

Above us, the comet flared brighter.

Blinding.

Burning like a second sun bleeding into Tartarus.

And from the pit—

A single word rang out. Echoing off the walls. Then again. And again. Gaining strength, gaining speed—until it swelled into a fevered chant:

Apex. Apex.

Skye's sisters clung to each other, trembling. Their wide, fearful eyes darted between Phobos and Deimos.

Phobos stepped behind one of them, placing a hand on her shoulder with mock tenderness.

"Don't be afraid, my little bride," he murmured, his breath brushing her ear. "Do this for us. Release the bind, and you'll have your freedom."

She stiffened. Her golden eyes were vacant, unfocused. Her lips parted slowly, as if the word had to claw its way through fog.

"Freedom," she repeated, voice flat and mechanical.

Phobos's grip tightened slightly.

"Yes. Freedom," he said again—softer this time, like it was a promise instead of a trap.

The other sister turned, mirroring the first. Her mouth formed the same word.

"Freedom," she whispered.

Deimos grinned, tilting his head as though admiring a well-trained pet.

"That's right. Go on, then."

They hesitated—but began to move.

Phobos coaxed them faster.

"Yes. You'll have your freedom. Everything will go back to how it was."

I lunged against the chains, fury burning through every nerve.

"Don't listen to them!"

The sisters froze. Their fingers tightened around each other's.

For one suspended moment, I thought they might actually hear me.

Phobos let out a long, exaggerated sigh and shook his head. "See how he shouts? How desperate he sounds?" His voice coiled around them like a noose, tightening with each word. "Of course he would say that—he's *her* husband. Do you really think he wants you to be free?"

Deimos stepped closer. "Skye was never a true sister," he murmured, his tone soft, poisonous. "Wasn't she always the most beautiful one? The one who never had to try while you struggled just to be noticed?"

Phobos leaned in, his long nails tracing from one sister's eye to her cheek. "You deserve this freedom. A life of your own—not one spent in her shadow. Do this, and you'll be remembered. She'll be forgotten."

A shudder passed through them as the words took root. Phobos and Deimos's influence slithered deeper, wrapping around their minds like a drug that promised peace but was nothing more than a noose.

Damn it—their eyes were already clouding, slipping away.

"Submit...for it is fate," Boreas intoned, the air pressure around me suddenly dropping. Eurus drifted closer to Zeph and Harmony. They felt it, too.

Fate.

The word vibrated in my ears, a siren's call to let go and let the strings tethered to my soul decide my path. No. I would not bow. I would not surrender. I would seize the strings and defy even fate itself.

Obediently, the sisters turned toward the pit. Their steps were slow but steady, as if the words had wound them up like clockwork dolls.

The pit gaped before them—a vast abyss of churning darkness whose depths writhed with movement. A jagged stone pathway jutted out from the edge, winding downward into the chaos as if its very hosts had carved it.

And the instant the sisters stepped closer—

The pit roared to life.

Shrieks and growls thundered up from the depths, shaking the cavern walls. Shadowed figures strained against their chains—hulking forms barely visible, hands like boulders clawing at the rock. Even their words hit like acid rain.

Free us.

Take it.

"Go," Phobos commanded, his voice fraying with impatience.

One sister took a trembling step forward.

But the other buckled.

A strangled sound escaped her throat as her knees gave out, her body collapsing. She clung to her sister's leg, fingers digging in like a frightened child. Her golden eyes were wide, locked on the writhing pit below—the Titans, monstrous and endless, their furious bellows shaking the cavern walls.

She couldn't move.

Deimos chuckled and leaned down. "Or do you need us to help you?"

Phobos sighed, as though this were nothing more than an inconvenience. He reached down and gripped the fallen sister's arm, easily pulling her to her feet.

"You will go," he murmured, brushing a lock of hair from her face with unsettling gentleness. His tone turned coaxing, sweet. "And you will do what we ask."

The sister trembled but nodded, reaching for her sister's hand again.

Phobos smiled. "Good girl."

Together, they stepped forward, movements stiff and uncertain. Each footfall scraped along the narrow stone path, pebbles skittering into the abyss below with every hesitant step.

I yanked against my chains, desperate to see over the edge.

Far beneath us, lit by the crimson flicker of the pit, the torch burned—suspended in the dark like the pulsing heart of Tartarus.

The sisters quickened their pace as the Titans' howls grew louder, more frenzied, as if they could already taste freedom. When they reached the center, they stopped, their gazes locking on the torch—a false promise of salvation only a wave of their hair away.

Then, in perfect unison, they reached out.

The moment their fingers wrapped around the torch's golden handle, the flames detonated outward, devouring the dark.

Light pulsed from the torch, casting jagged streaks across the cavern walls. The air itself seemed to shudder, humming with thick, electric power. Below, the Titans roared, sensing their moment—freedom so close they could taste it.

The ground quaked. The pit trembled. The torch flared—

And then came the screaming.

Skye's sisters' bodies convulsed violently, backs arching as if caught by invisible chains. Their hands, still locked around the torch, spasmed but couldn't release it. Golden cracks split across their skin, glowing like molten veins, pouring light from within.

Their mouths stretched in silent agony, their voices lost beneath the roar of divine power surging through them.

Gods...no.

Their skin peeled away first—shredding from their limbs in curling ribbons. And beneath it, their bones glowed. Not white.

Gold.

The nectar of the gods, glowing like a liquid fungus, webbed around them.

Their golden skeletons cracked—then shattered—disintegrating into dust. Not even ash remained. Their very essence, everything they had been, was erased.

Gone. Not even immortality had spared them.

The torch hovered once more in the air, its flame steady, untouched.

Bind unbroken.

I swallowed hard, my throat tight. Skye's sisters were gone.

I turned my gaze toward the murderers.

Phobos and Deimos stood frozen, their eyes fixed on the empty space where the sisters had been, save for the flickering light of the still-bounded torch.

Phobos crouched low, biting his thumb as he stared at the empty air. "Well. That's unfortunate," he muttered.

Deimos stepped up beside him, arms crossed. "It was worth a shot. We even made them immortal—figured that might give them a chance at surviving."

What...?

From the depths of the pit, the Titans howled.

One shadow rose above the rest—larger, louder. His mouth stretched wide, like it could swallow the pit whole.

Wrong blood.

Cronus.

A chant surged from the pit, echoing the Titan king's fury, shaking the very stone beneath us.

Wrong blood.

Wrong blood.

"Yes, yes, we heard you," Phobos snapped, standing with an irritated roll of his shoulders. He glanced at Deimos, his tone sharpening. "Plan B?"

Deimos's eyes flicked to the flame—and a slow, gleeful smile spread across his face. "Plan B," he echoed. "The comet will stay at apex a little longer. And hey...the vision never showed them touching the torch."

Then—they turned to me.

My stomach dropped.

Phobos straightened, his gaze flicking toward Zeph's brothers—guard dogs waiting for their command.

His shadows flared, and Deimos joined him. Apparitions swarmed over Zeph and Harmony, smothering them instantly. Their heads snapped back, eyes rolling white, as they were dragged screaming into nightmares once again.

I thrashed against the chains, muscles burning, adrenaline tearing through every fiber of me.

Phobos blurred forward, pressing two fingers to my temples as Deimos's palm clamped down on the crown of my head. The pressure was immediate, stealing my breath and locking me in place.

Phobos chuckled, low and smug. "Stronger than the others," he mused. "You're so high maintenance, Cupid. I'll actually have to put in some effort."

His fingers dug deeper, and a searing heat bloomed beneath my skull.

"Let's see how you handle...*this*."

The shadows rippled, congealing into a sphere larger than any nightmare I'd ever faced.

From its surface unfurled ashen tentacles, each one dripping with weightless fog. One slithered toward my cheek, trailing a cold that bit deep into my skin before crawling to the corner of my eye.

Then—it pierced.

Darkness surged, plunging straight into my mind.

My body convulsed, chains clanging as I thrashed against the pull, but Phobos's grip burrowed deeper—fingers hooked as if they'd threaded into my skull.

My vision blurred, black spots spreading at the edges. I was slipping—spiraling into the abyss—

"Boreas. Eurus. Fetch the girl," Deimos ordered.

Phobos's grin split wide as he glanced at his twin. "I fear...not. She won't be far."

CHAPTER FORTY-ONE

SKYE

Sleep didn't feel like sleep here.

I looked down. My protective leathers were gone, replaced by a yellow sundress that resembled one from my childhood. It flowed softly around my legs, light as air.

I stood in a vast, endless field of wheat, bathed in muted gray light. The air was thick with the scent of earth and something faintly sweet, like dried flowers. Above me, the sky stretched wide in a hazy shroud—no sun, no stars—just an eternal twilight pressing against the horizon.

The Asphodel Meadows.

Euryale had said what it would be—just...existence.

But how did I get here?

I began to walk, not knowing where I was going, my fingers brushing the tops of tall wheat stalks as I passed.

Then I saw a figure in the distance.

Euryale? Sara?

I kept moving.

Closer now, a woman knelt a few feet ahead, slowly plucking flowers from the ashen soil as if time were meaningless. She wore a white dress that stopped at her ankles, its fabric light against her frame. Her hair was tied back in a long braid that trailed down her back.

When she looked up and smiled at me, my heart stopped.

That smile—it was hers.

Lydia.

There she was, as if she'd been waiting for me, expecting me to be here.

My breath caught. I took a shaky step forward. "How...how is this possible?"

She dusted off her hands, expression calm, as if seeing me here in the land of the dead was the most natural thing in the world. "The Underworld works differently, sweetheart. Even in dreams."

My body moved before my mind could catch up. I ran to her, throwing my arms around her like I was seven again—bursting into her shop after school. She smelled the same...that familiar trace of sage clinging to her as her arms wrapped around me. One hand stroked my hair with the same gentleness she always had, like a mother comforting her child.

Her touch was light as the wave of a feather across my skin, but I could still feel it—feel her touch.

My mind struggled to process it. Lydia was holding me, but no visions came. I didn't have the arrowhead to protect me, so how was this possible?

I didn't know, and at that moment, I didn't care.

Relief surged through me, stealing the breath from my lungs. I squeezed my eyes shut.

"I've missed you so much."

"I know," she whispered into my hair. "I've been watching over you."

I pulled back just enough to see her face, searching her expression for something—anything—to help make sense of this.

She gave me a small, mischievous smile. "You always did like cats."

I froze. My breath caught in my throat.

No...

She nodded, her eyes full. "I've been with you this whole time. Watching over you. Over Euryale, too."

My hands gripped her arms. *Lydia...was...is...Marnie?*

My mind scrambled to understand it all—and then I remembered the book about the kingdom of Praxis.

Marnie had found it. She'd brought it to us. Led us to it.

She'd known.

"I-I don't understand. How? Why?" My voice cracked beneath the swarm of thoughts.

Lydia cupped my face, her thumbs gently brushing away tears I hadn't realized were falling. "Because you needed me. And because you still do."

I swallowed hard, trying to put it all together. My aunt...my cat...my guardian? My guide?

"You've been so strong...done so much," she said softly. "But there's still more to do. You'll need to speak with the Fates."

I stiffened. "The Fates?"

Lydia's expression darkened, her voice growing heavier. "They won't give answers easily. They speak in riddles. You'll have to listen carefully. Think carefully."

She wanted me to go. To leave her again. It wasn't fair. I'd already lost her once—and now, after everything, I had to say goodbye again?

"Why do I have to go?" I whispered. "I...I don't want to leave you."

She smiled sadly, tucking a stray strand of hair behind my ear. "I know. I wish we had more time, too. But you must go to the Fates."

The air shifted around us. The gray light flickered, dimming like a candle on its final breath.

Lydia sighed, pressing her forehead gently to mine, her touch lingering—an unspoken goodbye. "The comet is ready," she murmured. "It's time for you to wake up."

I clung to her, desperate to stay a little longer. Just one more moment. Just one more word.

But the dream was already unraveling, as if the candle had finally gone out.

I WOKE WITH A SHARP GASP, the dream's weight clinging to me like damp fog I couldn't shake. For a moment, I didn't know where I was.

The scent of smoke and metal grounded me—the forge, the hut. Not the meadows. Not Lydia.

My arms curled tight around myself, as if I could conjure the dream of her embrace, hold it long enough to stop the hollow ache in my chest.

Slowly, I turned my head.

Euryale sat upright, hands clasped, her forehead resting on them. She was so still, her breaths shallow and uneven. A single tear slipped down her cheek, catching the rim of her glasses before she brushed it away and turned her face toward me.

She didn't speak.

She didn't have to.

She'd seen Lydia, too.

The silence was as heavy as the blankets wrapped around us—until Sara stirred across from us. "What's going on?"

My throat tightened. "Lydia...the comet," I choked out, the words sticking. I didn't even know where to begin.

Euryale pushed herself upright. "We need to move," she said, already on her feet.

I pushed up and crossed to the couch to help Sara. Slowly but steadily, she rose, testing her balance and running her fingers along the edge of her bandages.

"Good to go?" I asked.

She rolled her shoulder with a slight wince, then nodded. "Good enough."

Euryale crouched, tightening the laces of her boots with sharp, practiced pulls. "Then let's go."

I reached for Persephone's mirror and tucked it under my arm—but something tugged at me. A weight that wasn't there.

My wrist.

I froze, fingers brushing my skin.

Bare.

I rubbed it again—harder this time—like maybe I'd missed it. Like maybe I'd feel it if I just pressed harder.

Cullen's bracelet was gone.

I needed to fucking weld that thing to my wrist to keep it from coming off.

Panic punched through my chest. I spun in a tight circle, eyes raking over the floor, the couch, the table—anywhere it could've landed.

"What?" Sara asked, her voice cautious.

I didn't answer. Couldn't. My pulse thundered in my ears as I stormed out of the room, my heart pounding, anger radiating from me.

Hephaestus stood motionless at the mouth of the adjoining room, as if he'd been waiting for us to wake. Soot coated him, clinging to his skin and streaking his beard and wild snarl of curls, as though he'd spent the night sleeping in the ashes of his own forge.

His eyes met mine, steady and unblinking. "It is with me," he said, like he'd plucked the question straight from my mind.

Before I could speak—before I could even demand answers—he turned on his heel and strode into a narrow corridor.

I followed, with Euryale and Sara close behind, shadows at my back.

The hallway opened into a smaller chamber, the walls flickering with low forge light. And there, resting on a stone worktable, were two objects glinting beneath the glow.

Cullen's bracelet.

"It was worn," Hephaestus explained without turning. "Frayed—from time, from magic. I reforged it. Strengthened it."

I stepped closer, breath catching—not from panic this time.

Beside it lay a second bracelet—a perfect twin.

Except...

This one was different. Flames and feathers twined across the band, etched as if a phoenix itself had been caught mid-flight.

My fingers brushed the metal before I realized I'd moved.

Hephaestus picked up both bracelets, turning them in his massive hands. "If you're both fighting, you might as well have equal protection."

"Thank you," I whispered. He held them out in offering, and I slid one onto each wrist. One for Cullen. One for me.

He grunted—his version of acknowledgment.

But I saw more—the exhaustion etched into his face, the soot clinging to him like black coffee, its bitterness the only fuel keeping him going.

He hadn't just reforged the bracelets. He'd poured everything he had into them. Into *us*.

And apparently not just the bracelets.

Euryale picked up her sword and gave it a test swing, checking its balance. The blade appeared reinforced, deadlier, and she gave a small, approving nod.

Sara rolled up her sleeve as Hephaestus handed her a pouch of medicine and bandages. He pointed and grunted once, and Sara nodded as if she understood him fluently.

Then Hephaestus turned to me and slowly reached down, pressing something small into my palm.

A ring.

It looked almost identical to the one Aphrodite had given me—the one that could draw her from the Underworld.

"A way out," Hephaestus said simply.

He was giving us the same chance.

I swallowed hard, words caught behind the lump in my throat.

Instead of speaking, I slid the ring into the pouch at my belt beside the scissors. My hand lingered there. Did Hephaestus notice them? Slowly, I lifted my gaze to him.

"There is another matter," Hephaestus added, his tone deliberate—almost as if he'd chosen not to acknowledge what he might've seen. Then he turned toward the door.

Outside, the Underworld's eerie glow stretched endlessly across the cracked horizon. Shadows danced in the distance, but my gaze locked on the massive machine parked just beyond the forge.

It looked like an ATV—if an ATV had been forged by a god and built to survive literal hell.

Thick metal plating wrapped around its frame, reinforced with layers of dark iron that shimmered faintly in the gloom. The wheels were enormous, spiked and armored, meant to crush anything in their path. Pipes snaked along the back, hissing steam, and the engine pulsed with a dull, molten glow—like it had a heartbeat of its own.

It wasn't a vehicle.

It was a beast.

Sara gave a low whistle. "I'm driving."

"Absolutely not," Euryale snapped.

"Why not?"

"Because I actually value my life."

The two of them launched into a full-blown argument as they marched toward the machine, voices rising, hands gesturing wildly.

I stayed where I was, standing beside Hephaestus.

I let out a breath, shaking my head slightly as I took it all in—everything he'd done. For *us*.

"I'm not apologizing for what I said about Cullen," I said finally.

He didn't respond.

Then—he smirked. Just the faintest twitch of his lips, but I caught it.

Cullen's smirk.

"Wouldn't expect anything less from my daughter-in-law," he replied.

I blinked. "What—?"

But he was already walking away, leaving me frozen, mouth parted in surprise, thoughts spiraling.

Hephaestus paused, rubbing a hand across the back of his neck like he was bracing himself for something uncomfortable.

Then he turned back to me.

"I don't know if anyone's explained," he said slowly, "but the bond... isn't only a ceremony."

My face must've shown my confusion—because I was.

"It's a connection," he continued, his voice rough, as if the words themselves resisted leaving him. "There will be times you'll be able to sense him. Feel him. Even when he isn't there."

A chill crept down my spine, burrowing deep. My soul was already reaching for it—this connection.

The unease twisting in me wasn't just worry.

Cullen was in danger.

And I could *feel* it.

"Can I talk to him?" I asked quietly. "Like—with my mind?"

Maybe we could communicate through this place and get out of here.

Hephaestus shook his head. "It's not that simple," he answered. "You'll understand and know when the time is right."

Of course, nothing ever was simple anymore.

I shifted on my heels, trying to process everything. Hephaestus watched me, his gaze heavy—like there was more he wanted to say, but the words refused to form.

Cullen told me his father was barely a shadow in his memory—distant, cold, irrelevant.

But...now.

I opened my mouth. The words hovered there.

Come with us.

It was so close to slipping out.

But Aphrodite's voice slithered through my memory: *Prove yourself.*

So instead, I asked the question that had been on my mind since seeing the panels in Cullen's library.

"The torch you created..."

My voice faltered. I shifted again, uneasy now.

"If we're too late and the bond is broken, can the torch be destroyed?"

Silence fell like a dropped blade.

Hephaestus froze. Even Euryale and Sara went quiet, their argument cut short as their heads turned toward us.

"The torch," he said slowly, like each word was weighed before release, "is one of the most powerful weapons I've ever made."

That wasn't a *no*.

His jaw flexed. "Blood was used to make it." A tense pause followed as he weighed the words. "Blood can be used to destroy it."

He didn't say it; he didn't have to—my blood.

The realization hit before his final word, whispered, almost reluctantly: "All."

Just one word, as if anything more would dilute the truth.

Not just a drop. Not a cut on the palm.

All. Enough to kill me.

I stared at him, willing him to say he was wrong. To say there was another way. But he didn't.

I tried to laugh, but it came out thin. Brittle. "Well...let's hope it doesn't come to that."

He didn't answer. Just looked at me. And that silence said enough.

I climbed into the ATV, gripping the edge as Euryale revved the engine and the machine rumbled to life beneath me.

I looked back one last time.

Hephaestus stood there, arms crossed, soot still smudged across his skin. His head tilted slightly, eyes locked on me.

A slow smirk tugged at the corner of my mouth. "You and Cullen do that same thing, you know," I observed, mimicking the tilt. "The way you look at people—like you can see right through them."

Hephaestus blinked. And for just a second, he looked genuinely caught off guard.

I leaned further out, my voice low but certain he could hear me. "Cullen is just as much your son as he is Aphrodite's."

His shoulders tensed, the words landing like a hammer strike somewhere deep inside. Cullen was his son. I wondered if anyone had ever dared to say that to him—and if he'd ever, even for a moment, believed it.

Euryale jolted the ATV forward, a sudden lurch that kicked up a wave of soot and ash behind us. The forge disappeared into the Underworld haze, but in the rearview mirror—Hephaestus still stood there.

Unmoving.

Watching.

I didn't look away until he vanished from sight.

Then I turned my gaze downward and gripped Persephone's mirror tightly, the cool surface grounding me.

I closed my eyes, Lydia's message echoing in my mind: *Go to the Fates.*

When I opened them, the mirror began to shimmer, like light bending through water. Slowly, it shifted, and ripples swirled as shapes formed beneath the glass.

A path was revealing itself.

CHAPTER FORTY-TWO

SKYE

When the map led us here—this place…

"Lydia told you to come here?" Sara asked, frowning, her gaze narrowing on the path ahead.

It ended at the gaping mouth of a cave—the kind you'd expect in the opening scene of a horror story. Jagged rocks glistened as water dripped steadily from their edges, like saliva from the fangs of some ancient beast waiting for us to step inside and feed its hunger.

We climbed out of the ATV, boots crunching against slick, uneven stone. Just as Sara moved forward, Euryale's hand shot out, catching her arm—not rough, but firm.

"Skye goes in alone."

Sara jerked back. "What? No."

Euryale's grip didn't loosen. "Lydia said it had to be her. Alone."

I glanced at her, a chill running through me. *What else did Lydia tell her?*

Her head dipped, hand still locked on Sara's arm—not so much holding Sara back as holding herself together.

I stepped between them. Only then did she let go.

"I trust Lydia," I said softly. And I meant it. I trusted her with my life.

My breath shook as I exhaled. At least they'd be safe out here if I didn't come back—*if*—at least they'd still be alive. That was all that mattered.

I turned back toward the cave.

It didn't just look dark—it *felt* dark. Like it had pupils. Like it was watching me.

My fingers brushed the pouch with the Fates' scissors inside.

Maybe this was why I had them. Why Lydia told me to come here.

Maybe I was meant to return them.

Only one way to find out.

I adjusted the bracelets on my wrists and checked the daggers at my sides. I wasn't about to walk into the unknown without weapons.

With one last look at Euryale and Sara, I drew in a breath. "If I'm in there too long, don't wait. Just go."

Sara's brows pulled together. "Skye—"

"I mean it."

I wouldn't let them get trapped down here if things went wrong.

Sara didn't move.

Euryale gave me a single, solemn nod.

I gave a sharp nod back, then focused solely on my feet, pushing off the ground as the rock path disappeared beneath my boots.

Faster. Faster.

The words were a silent plea to my trembling legs.

The cave's maw grew larger until it swallowed me whole.

THE DEEPER I WENT, the heavier the air became.

Each step was like walking through a fog made of ash and breath. My lungs strained. I kept moving, trying to ignore the way my breath caught at every shift of shadow, every faint *plink* of dripping water—at least...I hoped it was water.

Hsssss.

Whissssk.

Whispers—circling, drifting in and out of my ears.

Then louder.

She's here.

We knew she'd come.

We told ourselves so.

The voices tangled over one another—layered and circling, arguing with no one and everyone all at once.

I forced myself forward into the darkness, my heartbeat pounding in my ears—louder than the whispers.

The space ahead widened, and I stopped, scanning. The darkness shifted—less black, more blue-white, like a beam of moonlight shining down from a passing cloud. But when I looked up, there was no source—no sky, no light—just the illusion of it.

Then—like they stepped out of the air itself—a figure emerged.

Hunched. Cloaked in layers of heavy fabric. But even the folds couldn't hide the way it shifted—twisted.

My body locked up, nerves flaring as if my mind were reaching for something beyond comprehension.

One body, but three faces. Each one vying for space beneath the hood.

My eyes focused on the first. Its skin was a tapestry of overlapping wrinkles, eyes milky and far-off, as if remembering something lost to time.

The second looked mummified—skin stretched tight over sharp bones, eyes wide and unblinking, forced to see what was happening right in front of it.

And the third...frozen mid-scream, only half-formed. Its features were warped in terror, mouth twisted, and eyes bulging, as if it were seeing something that hadn't happened yet.

The Fates.

I forced myself closer, my knuckles white as I gripped the pouch at my side.

"I have something of yours," I said, my voice barely pushing through the heavy fog separating us.

I opened the pouch and slowly drew out the scissors, holding them just far enough to show I wasn't hiding them. "I'm here to return them."

A rasping chuckle rippled through the shadows.

"Returned, but never taken. Given, but never lost. A gift, a curse, a thread that must be undone," their voices intoned in perfect unison.

The screaming face twitched, like it was trying to smile.

I swallowed hard. *Never lost.*

They knew I'd bring them back.

The Fates shifted beneath their hood, their single head jerking, restless. Gnarled fingers spasmed at their sides, clenching and unclenching as if grasping at something only they could see—as if every second of existence was an unbearable torment.

But they didn't take the scissors.

Instead, they turned—retreating deeper into the shadows.

"Wait!" I called, stepping after them, the word sharp in the silence.

Lydia had told me to come here.

There had to be a reason.

"How do we stop Phobos and Deimos? How do we stop the Titans? How do I save Cullen—"

A sharp hiss sliced through the space like a pressure valve releasing, freezing everything.

The Fates went still, their body pulled taut like a puppet yanked by invisible strings.

"No. No questions."

Their hooded head twitched, jerking once—twice—before their body convulsed in short, snapping bursts. Then it slumped, sagging like the effort had drained them.

"You are here for answers. *Answers,*" they rasped.

I bit the inside of my cheek, frustration sparking. "Okay, well, how else am I supposed to—"

The air thickened around me, as if the cave itself pressed closer.

Answers...Answers...

The word echoed through the damp air, like it had replaced the humidity.

They speak in riddles.

Lydia's voice rang in my mind, floating on a wind that pushed against the cave's echoes.

Answers. Not questions.

I took a slow breath, shifting the scissors in my grip. If they wouldn't answer me directly...then maybe I had to show them what I already knew.

"My bloodline is the key to releasing the Titans," I said—low, but certain.

Their hands spasmed.

All three faces flinched at once—one wincing, one stretching wide, one cringing as if struck. Then...they nodded.

The sound was awful.

Crack. Click.

Each vertebra, each joint grinding into place with unnatural force.

Were they in pain?

I tightened my grip on the scissors, the cool metal biting into my palm. "You showed Phobos and Deimos the future," I continued, my voice steadier now. "You showed them my sisters would break the bond."

The Fates' head snapped toward me—three faces in perfect, unnatural unison.

"*Wrong*!"

The word struck the air like a gunshot, and the cavern trembled. Shards of rock broke loose from the ceiling and clattered to the ground around me. I flinched, instinctively bracing for more to fall.

"We never showed them your sisters would break the bond," they hissed.

I echoed their words back, the full weight of them crushing me. "My sisters won't break the bond."

"The descendants of Praxis's living blood—yes. But untouched by the hands of death," they chanted. "To sever what was bound, both must weave together—life untouched...and life returned."

The words twisted in my mind.

Untouched. That had to mean immortal—or, in my case, someone bonded to an immortal.

But *returned...*

My breath caught. My pulse thundered in my ears.

You were...stillborn.

Cullen's voice echoed through my memory.

I died when I was born. I was returned.

I carried both.

"I will break the bond," I whispered. The words were barely audible—but they surged through me, rushing outward like water from a broken dam.

The Fates jerked as if my words had unlatched something inside them. Their body seized, limbs trembling before halting altogether. Slowly, they raised their hands.

The cave shuddered.

Stone groaned and twisted above me, jagged shadows peeling away from the walls. The darkness shifted—gathering, bending—then bloomed into thin rays of light that split the air like cracks in glass.

Images flickered overhead, burning and warping like flame.

A vision.

The shadows unraveled into chaos: fire curling through fractured stone, golden chains snapping, the earth bracing the weight of something—something coming.

Cullen's hands braced against the ground, his wings limp at his back, and his eyes held me in their reflection.

Harmony and Zeph—fighting back-to-back, surrounded by beasts spilling from the torn seams of a crumbling world.

Monsters. Demons. Beings shaped like men, but giants.

The Titans.

And towering above them all, one stood like a king.

Then—me. At the center of it all.

A torch clutched in my hands.

Its flame wasn't just fire—it was part of me. Burning through *me.*

The Fates chanted:

"Truth revealed, balance restored.

Inner power tames the wild.

Endings pave the way for new beginnings."

I knew...I *knew* those words.

I'd seen them on my tarot cards:

Love.

Strength.

Death.

The vision snapped apart. The images vanished into shadow, leaving only the echo of their words behind.

The ground trembled beneath me, and my knees gave way. I dropped to the stone floor, cold rock against my palms the only anchor I had left. I gasped, chest heaving, heart hammering like it was trying to break free.

"What—" The word caught in my throat. I swallowed, tried again. "What happens to me?"

The Fates' faces turned toward me together, slow and solemn.

"To know one's future," they rasped, voices cracking like dry earth, "is to know one's misfortune."

Misfortune.

I looked at them—at the way they clutched at themselves.

Twisting. Trembling.

I knew what it was to live with visions clawing at the edges of your mind.

I knew what it meant to lose yourself inside them.

They were suffering.

They were cursed.

Just like me.

And somehow—impossibly—what rose inside me wasn't fear.

I *saw* them. Their desperation—for all of it to stop. To just *stop*.

I swallowed hard, then forced myself to stand. My legs trembled beneath me, but I pushed through it. "Can you stop the pain?" I asked, the words spilling out before I could second-guess them.

The Fates stilled.

Then—slowly—their head turned. Their eyes fell to my hands.

The scissors still hung there, cold and heavy in my grip.

"You carry our end," they murmured. "It is our time at last."

Their hands reached toward me—open, unarmed.

Not a threat.

A plea.

They had known.

From the beginning, they had known who would carry the scissors. When it would happen. How it would end.

Me.

They wanted me to end it.

To free them.

But to touch them...

Without the arrowhead to shield me, the visions would come flooding through again.

How much of me was even left?

The pressure was already building behind my eyes, my sanity curling inward like burned paper.

But the vision—it had shown me holding the torch. Which meant maybe, just maybe...I had one more touch left in me.

Just one more.

I stepped forward. The Fates shifted, cloak sliding from their shoulders as if they'd been waiting.

My hand trembled as I lifted it, pressing my palm against the Fates' chest—right above where a heart should've been.

Their skin wasn't like flesh. It was neither cold nor warm, but somehow both—like pressing my hand to the edge of a dream.

The Fates trembled under my touch, a sound like a dying breath escaping their throat.

And then—

The vision hit—a tidal wave of color and agony crashing through me.

I saw myself gripping the scissors in both hands, plunging them into a precise point in the Fates' chest. Not just anywhere. *There.* The one place that would end it. That would free them.

I felt the shudder in their body, the stillness that followed, the way their faces twisted into something that looked, impossibly, like relief.

And then—

As if the vision had spilled over the edge of time—

It wasn't the future anymore.

It was now.

My hands moved without hesitation, the cold handle of the scissors anchoring me as I stepped forward. The blades slid between their ribs—like snipping the last thread of a tapestry.

A low tremor rippled through the cave.

The walls seemed to exhale.

And the endless whispers—the voices that haunted every corner—fell silent.

I caught the Fates as they collapsed, guiding them gently to the cave floor. Their hood fell back just enough for me to see their face—no longer twisting in agony, no longer pulled across the weight of time.

Just stillness. Peace.

Their lips lifted—barely. A ghost of a smile. Soft. Almost grateful.

As if, for the first time in their existence, they were free.

I knelt beside them, the scissors still in my hand, slick with something I didn't look at too closely.

And then, as their final breath slipped from their body, a whisper rose around me—coiling through the shadows like thread finding its needle. The voice didn't come from their mouth. It came from everywhere.

A thousand echoes spun into one:
"What is severed is never truly lost.
What is held may yet unbind.
Keep the blade, child of sight—
for the weave is not yet undone."

The sulfur-thick air of the Underworld hit me like a wall as I stumbled out of the cave, my legs barely holding me as my breaths came in ragged gasps. The weight of what I'd done clung to my hands, the cold metal of the scissors biting into my palm. With a swift motion, I threw them down, needing them *away* from me.

And then—

I dropped to my knees and vomited. First bile. Then blood—dark, too much of it, pooling on the ground.

Killing the Fates had been nothing like fighting for my life. Nothing like defending myself against monsters or gods who wanted me dead. This...this had been a choice. One I made.

Footsteps crunched against the rocky ground. A hand—Euryale's—gripped my shoulder straps, steadying me.

Sara crouched beside me, her voice tight with worry. "Skye—what happened? Are you—"

I wiped my mouth and forced myself upright, grabbing the scissors without really looking at them. "I know what needs to be done." My voice was hoarse, but steady. It had to be.

Sara shook her head, eyes flicking between me and the cave as if trying to piece together what I wasn't saying. "What does that mean? What did they show you?"

Euryale's glasses caught the glint of my reflection. "Skye."

I didn't answer. I couldn't. If I said it aloud—if I spoke the vision—it would make it real. *Too* real.

So I turned toward the ATV and climbed in, gripping the bars like they were the only thing keeping me grounded. "We need to go."

Euryale and Sara exchanged a look—one I didn't acknowledge. Then, without a word, they climbed in.

The engine roared to life.

And we tore across the wasteland, the mirror shifting once more.

To Tartarus.

CHAPTER FORTY-THREE
SKYE

The ATV jolted across uneven terrain, tires kicking up dust as Euryale pushed the engine harder. The dry wind lashed my face, stinging my skin—but that wasn't what made me suck in a sharp breath.

Pain.

It hit me like a drop in altitude, like the air had been ripped from my lungs. A raw, searing ache that didn't belong to me.

Cullen.

I gritted my teeth, gripping my side as if that could somehow ease it. After what Hephaestus had said about our bond, I knew this wasn't just in my head. Our bond...it must be stronger now. Maybe because we were getting closer. Maybe because it was evolving.

Sara's worried eyes caught mine. "Skye—what's wrong?"

I barely heard her. "Go faster," I told Euryale.

Euryale didn't hesitate. She nodded and slammed her foot down, the ATV surging forward, devouring the distance to Tartarus.

But it wasn't enough.

I needed more. I needed to reach Cullen *now*.

The bond tugged at me again, and this time I didn't resist. I focused on it, homing in, trying to make sense of the invisible thread that tethered us.

My instincts took over. I reached for the connection—not with my hands, but with my mind, trying to grab onto anything.

Cullen, I whispered in my thoughts, squeezing my eyes shut to sharpen the bond between us.

My fingers curled tightly around the mirror in my lap, knuckles white. The metal frame was cool against my skin—until it wasn't.

I opened my eyes.

A faint glow shimmered along the mirror's edge—soft at first, then pulsing brighter until my reflection wavered, blurring...then shifting.

The mirror—*I could see him.*

How?

He was slumped against cold stone, wrists bound in shackles that pulsed with a sickly red light. Tendrils of inky blackness coiled around his head—their faces swallowed by a swirling void.

I reached for him.

And the moment my fingers touched the mirror's surface—the world tilted.

The wind vanished. The roar of the ATV disappeared.

Suddenly, I wasn't in the vehicle anymore.

I was falling—plunging through the mirror like it had turned to liquid, not glass.

I braced for impact, but it never came.

Instead, I stumbled forward, breath catching in my throat.

Where am I? What just happened?

I turned slowly.

It looked familiar.

Felt familiar.

I blinked hard as the blur sharpened into focus.

A room.

A bed.

My heart stuttered.

It was Cullen's palace—our bedroom—but twisted, distorted, as if the whole place were reversed.

I walked toward the bed, fingertips grazing the edge of the sheets—black silk, smooth and cool to the touch.

I stepped around it, hesitant. Another step. My gaze drifted toward the corner—

Was that...my piano?

I took one more step—

And froze.

Cullen.

He was on his knees, shoulders hunched, golden curls wild and matted like he'd torn at them in desperation. His wings sagged behind him, trailing along the ground like broken limbs.

He didn't see me.

Didn't sense me.

He was curled over a body.

My blood turned to ice.

I crept forward, barely breathing. The body was crumpled at his feet, splayed like a broken doll.

And then I saw the face.

My face.

No.

No, no, no, no.

It was me—pale and lifeless. Lips tinged gray, eyes half-lidded, reflecting nothing back.

Cullen clutched that version's hand like a lifeline. His entire body curled in on itself, as if he were trying to hold it—*me*—together, even though it was gone.

"I couldn't save you," he whispered. "I couldn't get the nectar in time."

I froze.

I'd never seen Cullen like this. Never seen him *broken*.

"Cullen," I breathed, stepping forward. "I'm still here."

Cullen said nothing.

I dropped to my knees beside him, shaking him gently by the shoulders. "Cullen, look at me. I'm here!"

He didn't flinch. Didn't blink. His gaze slid past me, as if refusing to meet my eyes.

And then—

The lifeless version of me vanished. Gone in an instant, as if it had never existed. Cullen remained, fingers curled around empty air, still trembling like the loss had just happened.

"It doesn't stop," he choked out.

Before I could respond, the door creaked open behind me.

I turned.

Another version of me stepped into the room.

My heart slammed against my ribs as I stumbled backward. This version walked right past me, not even glancing my way—as if I didn't exist.

She knelt beside Cullen, cupping his face in her hands with excruciating gentleness.

"It's okay," she whispered. "I love you."

I felt sick.

Cullen sucked in a sharp breath, his whole body tensing as he clung to her words, reaching for her like—like she was me.

Then suddenly, her body went stiff.

Her face paled.

She choked on nothing.

And collapsed.

Lifeless.

Cullen let out a strangled sound—raw, broken grief tearing through him as he crumpled beside her.

The version of me vanished into nothing.

And I realized—this was a nightmare. The cycle was repeating.

He was losing me over and over.

I clenched my fists, nails biting into my palms.

No. No more.

I turned back to Cullen and slapped him.

Hard.

His head snapped to the side, and for the first time, his eyes flickered with something besides agony.

"Cullen," I said, my voice softer now—urgent, but gentle. "It's me. I'm here. I swear to you, I'm here."

I cradled his face in my hands, brushing my thumbs over his skin, grounding him in my touch.

Then I pressed soft kisses to his forehead, his cheekbones, his jaw—anywhere I could reach.

Cullen exhaled shakily, his hands coming up, hesitant, as if afraid to believe it.

I caught them in mine, squeezing tight.

"I'm real," I murmured against his temple. "And I need you to wake up."

The door creaked open again.

I didn't turn this time. I already knew what I'd see.

My nightmare self stepped into the room, gliding toward Cullen like clockwork—like a damn evil doppelgänger.

But I was done playing this game.

"Enough of this," I snarled, stepping into her path.

She barely seemed to notice me—until I shoved her hard, sending her stumbling back.

And then something changed.

Her vacant expression twisted into something sharp. Something aware.

And then she lunged.

I barely dodged in time, her hands swiping where my throat had been seconds ago.

She...she can fight back.

"What the hell?!" I barely had time to get the words out before she was on me again—faster, stronger than me.

We crashed, my back slamming into the floor as she landed on top of me. Her fingers curled like claws, reaching for my face, and I barely got my hands up in time—locking around her wrists, straining to keep her nails away from my skin.

Her eyes were mine...yet warped, like a reflection in a circus mirror. Blue burned where the pupils should've been, and the irises were black—like dark holes, swallowing everything around them.

And then—

A sharp inhale behind her.

Cullen.

His body jolted, like something had finally snapped. He staggered forward, blinking, dazed—but his eyes found me.

Real me.

His expression shifted in an instant—from confusion to horror to fury.

"No," he breathed—and then he moved.

In one swift motion, he closed the space between us. His hand shot out, fingers locking around the back of nightmare-me's neck, and with a snarl, he ripped her off me like a parasite from flesh.

She twisted unnaturally, kicking out, her strength nearly matching his.

She squirmed free.

I scrambled to my feet just as Cullen's wings snapped open, striking her with a powerful beat.

The blow sent nightmare-me staggering backward. Her form glitched, a static flicker between her solid self and shadow.

Then Cullen moved—fast, a blur of motion. His wings snapped again, propelling him forward as he caught her mid-lunge, one arm hooking tightly around her throat.

She thrashed, snarling, trying to claw free—but he held her steady in the air, just long enough.

I moved, daggers flashing into my hands.

Surging forward beneath them, I ducked low and drove upward—blade first. The dagger sank into her chest, the impact jolting through my arm.

It screamed—raw, piercing, not human. The sound echoed through the room, vibrating in my bones.

Her body buckled, folding inward. The illusion collapsed into itself, twisting, churning into thick black smoke—the same tendrils I'd seen coiled around Cullen's mind.

The smoke shrieked, writhing—and then—

Gone.

Silence.

Cullen turned to me.

He reached for me like he couldn't stop himself—like he needed to feel me, needed to make sure I was real.

I met him halfway, crashing into him, my arms locking around his neck, his hands gripping my waist, pulling me flush against him.

His mouth found mine in a bruising kiss—desperate, consuming.

Then suddenly, I was weightless.

Cullen lifted me effortlessly, pressing me against the wall, his hands gripping my thighs as my legs wrapped around his waist. His body was fire against mine, his tongue devouring every inch of my mouth like he could never get enough—like not even the end of time would be enough to stop this.

I gasped against him, my fingers twisting in his hair, clinging to him like letting go would drag me back into the nightmare.

But he broke the kiss, just enough to press his forehead to mine, his breath coming fast and uneven.

A moan escaped me—frustration at the loss of contact, the ache of missing him, the sheer need to have him closer. It didn't matter where we were. I just needed *all* of him.

His fingers traced along my cheek, his touch sacred, as if he feared he might never get a chance to touch me like this again. His eyes were wild—like he was battling the same hunger, the same restraint.

"It's you," he breathed—more growl than whisper, as if he didn't trust his senses, as if seeing me might vanish if he blinked too hard.

His gaze searched mine, desperate, every emotion flickering at once.

A crooked smirk tugged at his lips, a reflex he couldn't control. "Only you would slap me like that."

A sound broke from me—half laugh, half sob—as I buried my face in his shoulder, arms tightening like I could hold him here, keep him from slipping away again. "You weren't listening."

He slipped a finger under my chin, tilting my face up—then, softly, achingly, his lips brushed mine again, like he was finally allowing himself to believe.

"I'm listening now," he whispered.

He pulled me closer, like he could fuse us together, as if any distance left between us still hurt.

"If you're coming here..." he murmured, lips brushing my ear, "looks like I'll have to chain you to our bed after all."

A breathless laugh escaped me as I dragged my fingers down the back of his neck, feeling the heat of his skin. "I don't hate that idea right now."

His grip tightened, golden eyes bright with desperation. "I miss you," he whispered. "I need you."

I cupped his face, thumbs tracing the sharp lines of his jaw—grounding him, grounding *myself*.

Then I leaned in and kissed him—slow, lingering.

"I'm coming," I promised.

The room began to tremble, cracks spiderwebbing through the nightmare like shattering glass.

Cullen's breathing faltered. "Skye—"

I held his face. "We have a plan," I explained. "No matter what I say or do—trust me."

His jaw tightened. He hated that. Hated not knowing. But after a beat, he let out a sharp breath.

"I trust you," he said. "But trust that I can't live without you."

I brushed a curl from his forehead, my throat tightening.

"I—"

The nightmare collapsed.

And everything went white.

THE UNDERWORLD SNAPPED back into focus.

I gasped, my body lurching upright as the hot wind from the ATV slammed into my lungs.

"Skye! Oh, thank the gods." Sara's hands flew to her chest. In the driver's seat, Euryale sat rigid, her grip vice-tight on the wheel, watching me carefully.

"What happened?" Sara asked, scanning my face. "You just—froze."

"I—" My voice came out raw. "I saw him. Cullen. I spoke to him."

The mirror lay in my lap, its surface rippling once more, as though it hadn't just dragged me into its universe moments ago. Sara snatched it up and shoved it into her bag, as if burying it could somehow stop it from pulling me in again.

Just as Persephone warned...it wasn't only a mirror.

It was a connection.

Our bond.

Euryale exhaled sharply. "You tell him we're coming to save their—"

The tires screamed.

Euryale slammed the brakes.

I threw my hands out, bracing against the dash, as Sara let out a startled yelp.

"What the—?" she gasped, gripping the edge of her seat.

Euryale didn't answer. Her gaze was locked ahead, knuckles bone-white on the wheel.

I followed her stare—and my stomach turned to lead.

Figures blocked the path.

Two of them.

Tall and still, their forms shimmered, flickering like heat mirages—half wind, half flesh.

Just. Like. Zeph.

Notus had told us. His brothers took them.

Now they were here.

Hovering. Waiting.

For us.

For *me*.

The air thickened, the wind pressing inward—coiling for a fight.

Euryale's hand drifted toward her sword.

Sara's fingers slid into her bag.

But I—

I unbuckled my seatbelt.

"Skye—!" Sara's voice cracked, but I was already stepping out into the open.

I knew what they wanted.

And I wasn't going to run.

Sara appeared beside me, silent. Her eyes said it all: *I hope you know what you're doing.*

Gods, I hoped so, too.

I wasn't the smartest. I wasn't a warrior.

But none of that mattered.

I would keep moving. Keep fighting—until my heart gave out or my body refused to stand.

I stared down Zeph's brothers, shoulders squared, voice sharp as the daggers at my sides.

"Well?" I snapped. "What are you assholes waiting for?"

I lifted my chin, eyes blazing.

"Come get me."

CHAPTER FORTY-FOUR

SKYE

I fought to steady my breathing against the winds of Zeph's brothers swirling around us.

Every instinct screamed at me to fight, to run, to do something—but I forced my mind to still. This had to work. It *had* to.

The vision hadn't shown me what came after I broke the bond, and I sure as hell didn't have a plan beyond that.

The Fates' last riddle had told me to keep the scissors—that had to mean they were part of this. Heat flared at my side, as if the blades themselves were bracing for battle.

The air cut.

Euryale, Sara, and I slammed against the rocky ground.

I caught myself with my hands, the terrain scraping my palms. The air here felt even heavier than before—if that was even possible.

I looked up.

Phobos crouched low in front of me, his gaze locking onto mine. "Welcome to the show."

I sucked in a breath, eyes darting past him—

Harmony. Zeph. Cullen.

All of them bound in shackles.

Like animals.

Cullen's chest heaved in ragged breaths, his shirt torn, golden curls matted to his forehead. And his eyes—those same eyes that once looked at me like I was the center of the world—now shimmered with something else.

Fear.

For me.

But my sisters—

They weren't here.

Am I too late?

"I can feel your fear," Phobos said, standing tall, eyes glinting. "No, you're not too late. You're *right* on time."

His gaze flicked toward Deimos, who lingered near Cullen, Harmony, and Zeph like an executioner awaiting his signal.

Harmony's eyes locked onto mine. "What are you doing? Get out of here!"

Zeph tensed beside her, his eyes darting to his brothers. One of them—the taller one—tilted his head slightly in silent warning: *Don't even try it.*

We were outmatched.

Outnumbered.

Outpowered.

"Divine..." Sara breathed, her voice breaking as she stared at the chains around them.

Phobos chuckled, strolling over to Deimos.

He reached down and gripped Cullen's chin, forcing his face upward—forcing him to look away from me.

"Let him go!" I yelled, my voice trembling as I pushed myself to my feet. Euryale and Sara stepped up beside me.

Cullen's lips parted, his voice hoarse. "Skye."

Phobos's smirk deepened as he crouched beside him. "Someone helped him break out of his nightmare," he said, almost admiringly. "I'm guessing that was you." He released Cullen's chin, but not before Cullen jerked his head away in disgust.

Phobos only grinned wider, utterly unbothered. "You really are something special, Skye. You're the one we've been waiting for," he proclaimed, like it was some great honor.

I didn't flinch. "I'll break the bond. But we"—I swept my arm toward the others—"we all walk away."

Deimos took a slow step forward, studying me with a predator's patience.

"Interesting," he murmured. "You offer to release the torch's bind so freely...while everyone else here fights to stop it."

There was accusation in his tone.

They weren't fools. They'd need more than just empty words.

So I would give them something else—truth. Some parts of it.

"You think I want the Olympians in power?" I asked, stepping forward until I met Deimos's gaze. "You think I want Cullen bound to them, forced to be the one with blood on his hands?"

My voice dropped, quieter but firmer—as the next words settled in, more real than I realized.

"I'd rather watch the world burn than see the people I love suffer. And now, all of them are here...suffering."

Phobos and Deimos exchanged a glance, and I felt the shift. The tension didn't vanish, but it changed—

Slowly, those twin expressions twisted into matching, gaping, tooth-filled grins.

In perfect unison:

"Deal."

I moved past them without hesitation, ignoring the hand one of Zeph's brothers extended toward me. I'd seen the vision, and I knew where I needed to go.

"Stay with the others," I said over my shoulder to Sara and Euryale.

They didn't argue.

I approached the edge, my boots brushing the lip of the pit.

A breath caught in my throat as I forced myself to meet Cullen's eyes.

Trust me, I mouthed silently.

His face twisted, torn between fury and anguish—but he didn't speak.

"Watch your step," Deimos sing-songed, gesturing grandly toward the jagged descent of stairs.

The stairs, carved into the pit, yawned open—a maw of stone so dark I couldn't distinguish one step from the next. It looked ready to devour me whole, as if the pit itself knew who was entering.

A low, constant rumble echoed around me—*whsss-sss-sss*—as though voices were being carried from the deep.

Shadows twisted at the corners of my vision. Half-formed figures flickered at the periphery, darting just out of reach. But I didn't look. I kept my gaze locked on my feet, refusing to give the darkness more than it already wanted. I couldn't trust what I might hear—and I sure as hell wasn't about to trust what I might see.

At the bottom, I saw it.

The torch.

It floated in the center of the pit, suspended in the thick air. Its flames were alive—flickering wildly. The glow pulsed, as if the fire itself were reacting to me. Calling to me.

I couldn't explain it. But I could *feel* it.

The heat from the flames rolled in waves, pulling at me—like gravity itself. It was as if it recognized me, as if I were part of it.

I stepped forward, breath shallow, eyes locked on the torch.

"Little blood of Praxis."

The voice wasn't loud, but it rumbled through the cavern like a seismic wave.

My blood turned to ice.

I froze.

Then, slowly—heart pounding—I turned.

Just like in the vision, he was larger than anything else in the pit. His form was a fusion of flesh and stone, as though he'd become one with the walls themselves. His skin resembled cracked clay, veins of red and blue pulsing beneath the surface, as if I could see his heartbeat. His eyes—two vast voids—watched me with something far worse than rage.

Hunger.

Inky chains, forged from what looked like the Styx, coiled around his massive limbs. They wrapped him tight, anchoring him to the pit's walls —but not enough to conceal who he was.

Cronus.

The Titan king.

He moved—slowly, massively—as if the very act of shifting forced the pit to adjust around him. Stone groaned. Dust fell in sheets from the walls.

"Cronus watched where your blood fell," he rumbled, his voice grinding through the cavern like boulders tearing across the earth. The floor trembled beneath me.

My stomach twisted.

My blood...my sisters.

"Cronus remembers their screams. Their fear. They thought their actions would be enough."

A low, guttural laugh rolled from his chest. "They were nothing. They died for nothing."

The words hit like a knife twist.

I staggered back a half step, as if I could somehow dodge the truth of it—but it lodged deep inside me anyway.

My sisters...gone. Dead. And it was my fault.

My throat closed. Tears burned, but I clenched my jaw until it ached.

I wouldn't cry.

Not here.

Not in front of him.

No—I would avenge them.

I stepped forward, forcing each breath past the tight knot in my chest. The ground was cracked, unsteady—shards of stone shifting beneath my boots—but I didn't stop until I stood at the very edge, the torch just beyond reach.

Before hesitation could set in, I reached out—and seized it.

The burning handle met my skin with a *hiss.*

Flames exploded to life, roaring outward in a spiral of heat and light. One flame lashed around my wrist just above where my bracelet rested, searing into my skin with a sharp, electric burn. I gasped, smelling my scorched flesh, but didn't let go.

The fire slid across my arm, as if tasting the blood it had drawn. Testing me.

I gritted my teeth, swallowed the pain, and held firm.

The torch pulsed.

Then—like the fire had made its decision—it unleashed.

A crack split the air. Flames shot upward, clawing into the dark, stretching higher and higher—reaching for the comet above as if they could grasp it.

And in their wake—light.

A constellation of glowing orbs emerged, suspended on threads of fire. They hung there, trembling like stars yanked from the heavens.

One by one, the orbs shot downward, slamming into the chained bodies of the Titans below.

The moment each one struck, the chains shattered—bursting apart in flashes of searing heat and sound, fragments spiraling into the dark.

The pit shuddered. Stone moaned and split as if it were screaming, fissures racing across the walls like the world itself was coming undone.

I staggered back, choking on ash and heat.

And then—

Cronus roared.

A sound no mortal could've made—like the end of the world had a voice.

All around him, his Titans answered.

Their freedom had come.

And the world would break.

I looked down at the torch, now nothing more than dead weight in my hands. Its flame had gone out.

Then a blur—too fast for something so massive—rushed past.

I dropped just in time, the force of its passing nearly throwing me off balance. My knees slammed into the broken stone, the breath ripped from my lungs. My heart thundered, but I pushed myself up, every muscle burning, the extinguished torch still clutched tight in my grip.

Then came the laughter.

At the edge of the pit, Phobos and Deimos stood like proud spectators to a symphony of destruction.

"*Finally*," Phobos breathed, eyes alight with victory. "They will kneel. Olympus will burn."

Deimos stepped forward, a dangerous, confident smile stretching across his lips. "We have freed you. Titans—go. Olympus awaits. Prepare our thrones."

He turned toward Cronus, towering and unmoving, his mountainous form still half-wrapped in shadow. Each breath from the Titan king shifted the stone around him, as if the world itself were bracing.

Phobos grinned, adding, "Our reward, Cronus. As promised."

Dark energy swarmed around the twins, radiating outward like coiled tornadoes. It pulsed and whistled through the air—a threat, a demand, a promise of power ready to be unleashed.

For a moment—silence.

Then Cronus smiled.

A slow, creeping thing.

"Yes," he rumbled, voice deep enough to crack mountains. "Your reward."

He moved forward, unbothered by the swirling shadows the twins had conjured. He passed through it like fog—untouched, unshaken—as if their fear-born power held no sway over him.

Before they could react, his mouth opened.

Too wide. Far too wide.

It wasn't just a mouth anymore. It was a void—a churning black hole where no light returned.

The sound that followed was wet.

A sickening *squelch* as Cronus's jaw unhinged—bone and sinew tearing, stretching beyond reason.

Phobos and Deimos barely had time to register their arrogance.

And then he devoured them. Whole.

Silence crashed down.

No bodies.

Just...gone.

The pit still trembled. Titans and monsters clawed their way out of the darkness behind him—but I couldn't focus on them.

Because Cronus was looking at *me* now.

He smiled.

"Cronus wants little blood."

CHAPTER FORTY-FIVE

SKYE

The ground lurched with his first step. The walls shook so violently they cracked apart, sending fractures spiraling around me.

I bolted—scrambling toward what was left of the stairs, if they could even be called that.

Chunks of ledge had already crumbled to ruin. I veered toward the wall, my free hand tearing at the rock as I climbed—skin splitting, fingers slipping on blood-slick stone.

"Skye!"

Voices above.

Euryale and Sara—arms outstretched, reaching.

I lunged.

Fingers grasped blindly. Boots scraped uselessly against breaking stone.

I hurled the torch upward. Euryale caught it with one hand, her other shooting down to seize my collar. Her grip locked like a live wire. Sara grabbed me, too, and together they pulled. My feet barely touched the rock before I was yanked upward and out of the pit.

I collapsed, breath ragged, heart hammering—the torch still clenched in my shaking hand.

No time to breathe.

The cavern ceiling groaned, stone raining down as it split apart. The night sky tore open, and a comet's beam flooded Tartarus in blinding light.

Was it the Titans forcing their way out? The monsters clawing from the pit?

No.

This was something else entirely.

A pulse of energy rippled through the air.

And then—

The cavern above split wide, light shattering into shadow.

Wings unfurled, spanning so wide that their silver tips seemed to dip and kiss the space between stars.

Nyx.

A sound followed—like thunder tearing itself apart.

She wasn't alone.

The Olympians had arrived.

A golden chariot sliced through the cavern ceiling, lightning lashing wildly from its wheels.

Zeus.

Beaming like a star come to earth.

Two figures flanked him: Hera, and beside her, gripping a massive trident—Poseidon.

Winds howled behind them, a blur streaking in their wake.

Notus.

He cast me a small, knowing smile—*he came.*

Carried on his winds, the Olympians descended one by one, like the Titanomachy panels come to life—my memory of the carvings with their names etched alongside them.

The first landed with a force that cracked the stone. Her spear gleamed like morning sun on steel, her stance rigid, sharp, eyes locked on the pit. Nyx hovered at her side.

Athena.

Two more followed in perfect tandem, bows raised and arrows already notched.

The twins—Apollo and Artemis.

Hermes appeared in a flash of light, a gust of Notus's wind marking the beat of his winged shoes.

Beside him stood a figure rooted in the very earth itself.

Demeter.

Dionysus descended next, a wooden staff bracing his fall. Without hesitation, he arched his back and flared his chest, revealing a tiger tattoo. The ink rippled—and the beast leapt free, the same tiger from IVY.

Ares followed, grinning, ready—as if a worthy fight had finally arrived.

Light flared behind him, so bright it burned through the chaos. Vengeance carved into every line of her glowing form.

Aphrodite.

I turned slowly, taking them all in.

They came.

They actually came.

The ground shook.

Hephaestus?

No.

Something deeper.

A fracture split the Underworld's foundation as darkness poured into the chasm like blood from an open wound.

Hades.

And beside him—Persephone.

They stood together, shadows and spring entwined.

For all his talk of neutrality—his silence, his absence—

Hades had made his choice.

He'd come.

He raised a single hand.

The ground split.

From the depths they rose—shambling, hollow-eyed warriors clawing free from forgotten graves. Bones cracked and popped in protest, armor and tattered cloth slipping from them, nothing left to hold it. Still, they reached for rusted weapons, fingers curling as though memory itself dragged them into place.

The army of the Underworld had answered their king.

Hades unleashed them against the creatures and Titans spilling from the depths of Tartarus.

He turned to Zeus and Poseidon.

The three brothers exchanged a single, heavy look.

No words. No hesitation.

They moved as one—sky, sea, and death surging forward. A trinity of force crashing into Cronus with the power of the cosmos behind them.

And I—

I ran.

Torch clutched tight, feet pounding over fractured stone, I tore through the chaos with Euryale and Sara at my side.

Because I wasn't stopping.

Cullen, Harmony, and Zeph were still chained.

No matter what was happening behind me—I was getting to them.

Beings and creatures swarmed around us, their focus not on us but on the sky above, as if it promised their freedom. Dionysus's tiger leapt overhead, the god astride its back, a creature thrashing as its limbs were clamped in the beast's jaws.

Every muscle in our bodies went still.

Blocking our path was something my mind struggled to comprehend. Its sheer size rivaled Cronus himself—a colossal mass of scales and bone. The head was human, but from the waist down stretched the coiling body of a serpent, thick as pillars of stone.

It tilted its head back, jaw unhinging, and a hiss reverberated through the cavern—sharp enough to rattle in my chest.

Euryale stepped in front of me, steady and braced, her hands lifting toward her glasses.

A voice thundered behind us, delighted and savage.

"Typhon—ohhh, I've missed you."

Ares.

His grin stretched ear to ear, his spear catching the comet's light as if it drank from the chaos. His helmet flashed as he surged forward—not running but launching like a cannon shot, hurling himself straight into Typhon's torso.

The monster shrieked, the sound splitting the air like a collapsing star.

"Go! Get to him!"

Aphrodite streaked past me, golden belt gleaming at her waist. In one smooth motion, she drew her sword—then pulled it apart, twin blades flashing as she leapt to join Ares. Her movements blurred, grace and fury entwined, as together they clashed with the serpent—gods against monster.

I turned to Euryale and Sara. No words—just one sharp nod between us.

I ran, the name ripping from my chest.

"Cullen!"

I could see him now—just a breath away.

Closer.

Closer.

I dropped to my knees, skidding hard, pain shooting up my legs—but I didn't stop.

The torch clattered beside me as my hands flew to the chains around Cullen's wrists.

"Come on," I gasped, breath ragged. "Come on—"

But the chains didn't budge. It was like they were fused to his skin.

Behind me, Euryale and Sara fought just as fiercely to free Harmony and Zeph, but the metal held—its magic stronger than our will.

Cullen jerked against the restraints, frustration rippling through his muscles. "Skye, get out of here!" His voice cracked—half command, half plea.

I refused to answer.

"Skye—" He twisted toward me, golden eyes locking on mine, fierce and desperate.

"I'm not leaving," I said, bracing in front of him as I yanked at the chains from another angle.

He let out a breath that sounded like both a curse and prayer. "So fucking stubborn."

Leaning in, he pressed his forehead against mine, grounding me like a tether at the edge of the world.

The battle vanished—

The Titans, the monsters, the roar of gods—

All of it blurred.

All I could feel...was *him.*

Even if this was it—our last moment—at least I had him.

And he was enough.

A metallic *clang* shattered the stillness.

Something massive landed beside us, the earth cracking under the impact.

The figure stood tall—broad-shouldered, heavy as a mountain. His coat groaned under the weight of weapons—blades, hammers, gears, contraptions I didn't even recognize—strapped to every inch of him, as if he carried an entire forge on his back.

I didn't have time to breathe before he moved.

He swung.

Hephaestus's hammer struck Cullen's chains with a force that sent a shockwave through to the ground.

The chains shattered.

Cullen was free.

He sucked in a sharp breath, his arms falling slack, as if he hadn't realized how much pain he'd been in until it vanished.

"...Father?"

The word barely made a sound.

Hephaestus grunted and kept moving—brutal efficiency in every step. Two more swings, and Zeph's chains broke. Harmony's followed, bursting apart in a shower of sparks.

Zeph exhaled like he'd been holding his breath for hours, the wind rising around him as if a missing limb had reattached. "Finally."

Hephaestus turned. From somewhere within the endless arsenal strapped to his frame, he pulled a blade and tossed it to Harmony.

She caught it on instinct.

"I didn't forge these to collect dust," he said gruffly, already reaching for another weapon. He tossed a second blade to Zeph.

"You—" Cullen's voice caught.

He stared at Hephaestus, shaking his head slightly, like he couldn't believe it. "You're here?"

Hephaestus didn't flinch. Instead, he turned to me, bent down, and picked up the torch from where I'd dropped it. He placed it deliberately in my hand, his gaze lingering on mine like he already knew—

Like the torch was always meant to stay with me.

Then, slowly, he looked back at Cullen.

"You are my son."

Four words.

But somehow, they seemed to rival the weight of the torch in my hand.

Cullen inhaled sharply—then went still.

"Here," I cut in, pressing his bracelet into his palm.

He looked down.

His gaze snapped to my wrist, where its twin gleamed under the firelight—the one Hephaestus had forged for me.

"I got my own," I assured him, raising it proudly.

RRAAAUUGHHH!

The sound ripped through the cavern as Titans and monsters surged forward, every eye locked on me.

They knew what the torch could do.

And they wanted it gone.

Beside me, Cullen exhaled, fingers tightening around the bracelet. Power shimmered, releasing like a pulse through the air.

In a blink, the bow was in his hands, arrow notched, his eyes scanning—locked in.

He released.

Arrows flew, each shot a flash of silver slicing through the chaos.

I moved with him, torch close to my chest.

He didn't take his eyes off the mix of Titans and monsters flooding from every side. "Skye, you and the others—find a way out."

I ducked as another arrow sang past my ear. "Not without you."

His jaw tightened. "Skye—"

"We." I slipped beneath his arm as he aimed and fired again. "*We* need to get out."

He cursed under his breath, but the next arrow he fired was sharper, angrier. His stance shifted closer now. Protective.

Nearby, Hephaestus fought, swinging his hammer and sending creatures flying, bones crunching like brittle twigs. He didn't just fight—he demolished.

"The torch still has power," he called, his voice somehow calm over the carnage. "But it needs to be rekindled."

Cullen shot again, the arrow driving straight through a monster's skull. It crumpled backward, lifeless.

"What spark can—"

A sudden gust tore through the battlefield toward us.

Not Zeph's.

I turned. Zeph launched himself into the fray—directly toward Boreas and Eurus. Notus wasn't far behind, his winds slicing the air as he joined his brother.

"Brothers!" Zeph's voice cracked through the noise like a cyclone. "Phobos and Deimos are gone! There's no point to this anymore—stop!"

But Boreas and Eurus didn't stop.

They looked deranged—maybe they'd followed Phobos and Deimos out of fear, or duty. Maybe they no longer knew how to stop.

Zeph and Notus met them head-on—wind against wind, a cyclone crashing into itself, chaos swirling in every direction.

And they weren't alone.

Harmony's power swelled behind them.

She lifted a hand.

"Enough."

A pulse erupted from her—soundless, seismic.

It rippled outward, folding into the winds of Zeph and Notus, fusing into a tidal surge of raw elemental force.

It slammed into Boreas and Eurus.

They staggered. The wind around them stuttered. For one breathless moment, I thought they might retaliate.

But their winds turned—redirected not toward Zeph, Notus, or Harmony, but toward the Titans and monsters instead.

Enough. Enough. Enough.

The word echoed, chanting, reverberating—as if Harmony's voice had imprinted itself in the air. Boreas and Eurus's eyes went wide, hypnotized, their fury numbed by her command.

And just like that, they opened a new front in the battle.

Zeph blinked, hair whipping in the gale as he stared at Harmony's power crackling around her like lightning. "You sure you're okay, princess? Because—"

"I've got this handled," Harmony snapped.

And judging by the way half the battlefield was now airborne, yeah—she absolutely did.

Hephaestus crushed another enemy with a single hammer swing, then turned to us. "Get the torch to Zeus," he said. "The spark—" His gaze met mine. "Your blood."

Cullen bristled beside me. "Absolutely not."

Hephaestus didn't falter. "It needs to awaken."

My fingers curled tighter around the torch.

Blood. The torch had already tested me.

I carried the blood of Praxis—the living and the dead.

"We'll find another way," Cullen growled, his voice low and furious.

"There isn't," Hephaestus said simply, as if it were a law of nature.

I turned, taking in the battlefield around us. For a heartbeat, everything slowed—Tartarus burning, monsters and Titans tearing through the chaos. Hera and Demeter fought a giant with what had to be a hundred eyes, each one blinking in madness as they struck. Hermes flashed in and out of sight, his winged staff cutting through snarling creatures, dropping them into sudden, dreamless sleep.

And beyond it all—Zeus.

Sara and Euryale exchanged a look, something silent passing between them before Sara stepped forward. "We'll clear a path," she declared. "Get to Zeus."

Euryale didn't speak.

She simply stepped away from the group—calm as a storm waiting on the horizon.

Slowly, her fingers lifted.

To her glasses.

A few turned away—warriors, gods, monsters alike. But not me. I watched.

The glasses slid from her face.

In the same breath, her fingernails lengthened, sharp as obsidian shards. Her hair transformed, unraveling into serpents that lifted, coiled, and came alive. Their red eyes gleamed in the dark, fangs glistening like polished bone.

They hissed.

Low. Lethal.

Like death taking a breath.

Euryale didn't move.

She simply stood there—for one beat, maybe two—her Gorgon self reawakening, calibrating to the violence around her.

The screaming started.

Monsters froze mid-charge, their faces locking in horror as they solidified to stone. One after another, they shattered, then crumbled into dust. Even the Titans staggered, their movements slowing as if encased in ice, struggling to break free.

Through the mayhem, Sara moved like a shadow dancing in moonlight.

She slid through gaps, ducked under claws, flung vials of sleep powder that burst like glittering clouds. Every miss aimed at her hit something else—one monster tearing into another.

“Go!” she shouted.

Cullen was already moving. His bow vanished as his arms wrapped around me. His wings snapped open—one powerful beat launching us into the air.

I held tight to the torch. Wind tore past. The battlefield shrank beneath us, a vortex of war and fury.

Cullen flew fast—one arm locked tight around my waist, the other slicing through the wind as he steered us through the hell below.

Below, everything burned.

Titans and gods clashed, streaks of light blurring with flame and shadow.

And above—

Astraios’s Comet.

Blazing through the sky like some ancient eye had opened to watch us. To judge us.

Cullen’s voice was a ragged edge against the wind. “Hold on.”

I tightened my grip around his neck, pressing my face—and the torch—against his shoulder as we climbed higher.

His wings beat furiously, each stroke carrying us closer to the heart of the battle, closer to Zeus.

Lightning split the sky like wildfire, each bolt a cannon blast of fury and power. The trinity still fought against Cronus.

Cronus roared.

His breath became a hurricane—ripping monsters from the battlefield and hurling them skyward. Their screeches pitched higher as they spun helplessly, wings snapping, claws flailing.

The wind slammed into us next. My grip slipped against Cullen’s shoulders, and I clung harder, desperate not to be torn away. I would’ve focused on my breathing—if not for the monsters now hurtling out of the gale, straight at us.

Cullen dodged.

Nyx blurred past, tackling a winged creature before it could reach us.

Athena hurled her spear. Apollo and Artemis loosed arrows, cutting a path through the air.

Zeus's eyes met mine. Just a little farther.

My arm stretched, the torch reaching toward him—

The sky tilted.

Cullen lurched—

A strangled cry tore from his throat as a massive hand clamped down on his wing.

"No!" I screamed, slipping from his arms.

The world inverted—sky above, earth below—rushing up too fast.

A shadow lunged from the battlefield.

Three heads. Three snarling maws.

Cerberus.

Vines snapped tight around my waist, yanking me midair onto Cerberus's back with a jolt. My hands fisted in his thick, matted fur.

Persephone sat ahead of me—steady, commanding. She urged Cerberus forward toward the Titan, his roar thundering beneath us, the sound vibrating straight through my ribs.

I snapped my head up—

Just in time to see Cullen scream.

The Titan holding him gave one final, brutal twist—

And tore his wing off.

No.

Cullen's cry split the air as feathers exploded outward, drifting like ash. The Titan didn't stop. Its hands still gripped him tight, raising him higher—ready to rip the other wing.

Cerberus roared, rearing back before slamming forward, massive paws crashing against the ground as he charged the Titan.

Panic gripped me—fierce, blinding. My pulse thundered. There wasn't time. Zeus was too far. Cullen was going to—

Then.

Heat.

A pulse at my side—faint at first, then growing stronger.

The Fates. The scissors.

This...this was what they meant.

No hesitation. I slipped from Cerberus's back, sliding down his flank before hitting the ground hard. The impact knocked the air from my lungs.

I rolled, clutching the torch, as I heard Persephone yell my name. My free hand reached for the scissors, and in one quick, sharp motion, I sliced my palm open.

Blood welled hot and fast.

I pressed it to the unlit torch.

Flames erupted.

Not a spark—an inferno. The torch devoured my blood like it had waited lifetimes to taste it. Fire wrapped around my hand like living serpents, hissing, writhing, consuming.

I didn't stop to think.

I ran.

The torch felt forged from the marrow of my soul—mine in every way that made up my flesh and bones.

I no longer feared death.

The only fear left in me was a world where Cullen didn't exist.

So I burned that fear out.

With fire raging in my grip, I turned the torch on the Titan.

It screeched—an unholy, bone-deep sound—as the flames struck, latching on like claws. Light ignited beneath its skin, pulsing, struggling, as the torch tore into it.

The Titan convulsed, its colossal form collapsing inward, unraveling from the core.

A glowing orb burst from its chest—a shard of divine essence wrenched free with a sound like reality itself screaming. The torch pulled harder, dragging it in, wrapping it in flame. The essence twisted, fought—and then surrendered, sucked back into the torch like it had always belonged there.

The Titan's grip on Cullen shattered.

He dropped.

His wing flared—uneven—sending him into a spiral.

"Cullen!" I yelled, voice raw.

But I didn't move. I couldn't—not yet.

The torch flared in my hand, the heat pulsing like a second heartbeat.

There were more.

Across the battlefield, the remaining Titans staggered. Their limbs jerked. Their eyes glowed.

Light ripped from all of them. They collapsed one by one, gutted of power, crumpling to the ground—powerless.

I barely held on.

The torch screamed for more.

The Olympians surged forward, weapons flashing, voices rising as the weakened Titans and monsters were driven back—forced into the pit of Tartarus.

The pit consumed them one by one, their screams echoing into the void. Chains snapped shut, divine seals slamming into place with a sound like the sky cracking.

But the Titan king raged. Even stripped of the torch's power, Cronus fought.

He shattered every chain that bound him.

Swallowed every weapon hurled his way.

"Cronus!"

Zeus raised his arms, lightning coiling around them. He released a bolt toward Cronus as Poseidon hurled his trident, the two attacks fusing in a blinding snarl of power. Hades cloaked the weapon in shadow, veiling it as it tore through the air—

—and struck.

The trident pierced Cronus's chest, forcing him back. His massive form splintered, his essence howling as the pit rose to claim him. From its depths, the army of the dead surged upward—hundreds of skeletal arms seizing him, dragging him deeper, deeper, until only his roar remained.

Silence followed.

Then—

A chorus of triumph.

The Olympians raised their weapons, voices lifting in fierce, exhausted joy as the battlefield trembled under the weight of victory. The monsters... the Titans...Cronus—gone. Tartarus sealed.

I looked up. Zeph and Harmony carried Cullen, his one wing still hanging limp, his head lolling to the side.

He was in pain. And...he would suffer again.

I could feel it humming beneath my skin, the same deep ache that had haunted me since Persephone's mirror. The cycle was turning once more.

Though cracked, the torch was already stitching itself back together, its power pulsing faintly as it reformed.

What I had taken from the Titans wouldn't stay with me.

The Olympians would take it.

Reassert their Command.

Reinstate their thrones.

Restore everything to their perfect, gilded order.

And Cullen would be at their mercy again.

I couldn't let that happen.

My vision swam as I staggered forward, reaching for the scissors. Blood still stained the blades. They shimmered under the flickering remnants of the battlefield, humming softly—as if they knew what was coming. As if they understood this was final.

I didn't hesitate.

I drove the scissors into the heart of the torch.

The flames recoiled with a sharp, breathless gasp. Then they surged—wrapping around my wrist, spiraling up my arm in burning coils, as if trying to stop me. As if the fire itself was desperate not to be undone.

I gritted my teeth, muscles locking against the pain.

Then I met Hephaestus's gaze.

"Now," I rasped.

Recognition flared in his gaze. With a roar, he raised his hammer high and brought it crashing down on the scissors' rings.

The sound was a thunderclap, splitting the sky.

The torch cracked—

A frequency so sharp, so pure, it felt like the world had been flattened into a single, shattering note, stripping away sensation, thought, breath—everything.

And then—

The torch's power surged, shooting upward in a column of blinding flame that tore through the dark and reached for the heavens, drawn to the comet that still hovered overhead. The moment it touched—

The comet vanished.

Gone.

The battlefield fell silent.

The last remnants of Titan power were gone, pulled into the void. The sky hung still, empty where the comet had once burned. Around me, the wreckage of war—shattered stone, scorched earth, stone monsters—lay quiet.

I...was quiet.

The cracked torch slipped from my fingers. My knees folded as if gravity had forgotten me. I didn't feel the ground when my head met the stone.

Faint voices floated in and out, muffled and distant. Darkness crept at the edges of my vision. My body stopped answering.

Somewhere far away, a voice called my name.

"Skye—"

Cullen.

His voice tore through me, ripping my heart open.

I forced my eyes toward him.

He was on his knees, clutching his side, face pale with pain. One wing hung at a jagged angle as Harmony and Zeph steadied him. Even like that, his golden eyes searched for mine—reaching for me as if he could pull me back.

Sara and Euryale were shouting—urgent, commanding—but their words couldn't reach me.

My body wasn't listening anymore.

The pain was gone now, replaced by a strange, weightless sensation. I was drifting, the edges of the world smearing into a blur of color and sound.

No. I couldn't leave. Not yet. Not when—

Somewhere in the haze, Hades and Persephone's eyes found mine. And in that moment, I knew I was no longer just a visitor in the Underworld. I was becoming part of it.

Barely conscious, I saw Zeus step forward.

Without a word, he unsheathed a narrow blade and drew it across his palm.

Golden ichor spilled from the cut, shimmering as it fell, catching the last embers of battle's light.

The drops landed—my lips, my skin.

And then—

Fire.

Not the kind that burns, but the kind that births stars.

It exploded through me, igniting every nerve, flooding my veins, filling the cracks in my soul with liquid light. The darkness in my vision shifted—black dissolving into radiant gold.

"Zeus is king!" a voice rang out—just before a flash of white light swallowed me whole.

CHAPTER FORTY-SIX

SKYE

I pinched my wrist.

I could still feel pain—but it didn't linger. The spot that used to twinge from an old car accident felt...fine. No ache. No stiffness. I flexed my fingers and slowly rotated my wrist. It was gone—not in the slow, ordinary way injuries fade.

This was something else.

Like my body had been rewritten. Repaired from the inside out. Constantly working, endlessly renewing itself.

Strong.

Immortal.

But I couldn't dwell on that—not when I was already...somewhere else entirely.

The ceiling stretched impossibly high, upheld by marble columns that looked capable of supporting the sky itself. Golden light poured through open archways, filling the chamber with a divine glow as clouds drifted far below.

Mount Olympus.

No one spoke the name, yet I knew. The place itself declared it, radiating a presence that refused to be mistaken for anything else.

Before me, twelve thrones stood in a sweeping half circle. All were occupied, each one unique—as if crafted to embody the god who sat upon it.

The Olympians.

And then there was us.

Cullen and me.

His wings had vanished into his back. Both of us were clothed in white, as though the flash that carried us here had washed away every trace of battle, every scar of Tartarus. Cullen wore a pressed shirt and pants—reminding me of the *Abbey Road* album cover Lydia kept framed in her room.

I, on the other hand...

I wore a floor-length gown, pure as new snow. Lace butterflies clung delicately along the sides, their wings stitched in place, yet they looked as if they might take flight at any second—like they'd only just transformed. Like me.

I shifted slightly under the weight of their stares. Some curious. Some furious. All powerful. The bond was broken—and I was the reason.

"She purposely destroyed our power!" someone snapped. Though not shouted, the voice still reverberated through the columns.

"Hymenaeus has gone into hiding. Who's to say they haven't been working together?" another chimed in.

"They had no right," Poseidon growled, rising partway from his throne. "To sever the bond. To strip us of our Command. It was a betrayal of our authority."

"A betrayal?" I stepped forward before Cullen could stop me. "No. Binding gods like slaves was the betrayal. Phobos and Deimos were right about one thing—the bond needed to be broken."

A ripple of outrage surged through the chamber. Ares scoffed. Athena's eyes narrowed. Hera looked one blink away from smiting me where I stood. But Aphrodite—she said nothing. She only watched. Not agreeing. Not objecting. Just...watching.

"It's done," Cullen said, his tone matter-of-fact.

"Silence." Apollo's voice cracked through the chamber like a whip.

A Command issued by a god long accustomed to instant obedience.

But Cullen didn't move.

He met Apollo's glare and, with a voice forged in steel, said, "No."

It was undeniable now. The bond was severed—not a thread of it remained. Cullen had defied an Olympian Command, without even my touch.

He'd done it on his own.

The silence that followed was deadly.

Then Apollo stood, taking a single step forward, his eyes blazing.

Hephaestus rose next. He didn't speak—he didn't need to. The way he shifted, the tension in his frame, the subtle spike in heat that rippled through the air—it was a threat in itself.

But before anyone could act, the atmosphere shifted. A pulse of power reverberated through the chamber, heavy enough to rattle the marble beneath my feet.

Zeus.

"Am I still not the king of the gods?" His voice rolled—deeper than thunder—the weight of it settling across the chamber. It pressed into every one of us, a reminder of who he was. What he was. *King.*

His gaze swept across the room, a sovereign surveying his unruly court. "Order will be maintained," he declared, voice absolute. "If any of you wish to challenge that, then by all means—continue. But I will personally deliver you to Tartarus, where you can keep the Titans entertained for the rest of eternity."

Silence.

Apollo and Hephaestus sat back down

Then, one by one, the gods followed.

Not with the grace of divine beings, but with the heavy reluctance of those reminded of a power greater than their own—Zeus's power.

"Leave us," he ordered, his tone leaving no room for argument. He raised a hand that came down like a gavel, his gaze locked on mine.

I wasn't the one he was telling to leave.

They hesitated.

Even gods could hesitate.

And then, slowly, they filed out. Their footsteps echoed across the golden floor. No one challenged his words. No one looked back.

I caught Hephaestus's eye as he passed. He gave a small nod—reassuring—a silent promise: *I won't be far.*

The chamber doors closed behind them with a deep, echoing finality, sealing me inside with the king of the gods.

Except Cullen just stood there—like leaving me wasn't even an option he'd entertained for half a second. *Stubborn.*

Zeus turned to him, expectant—but the old Command no longer held. Cullen could not be ordered away.

Cullen squared his shoulders, gaze unwavering. "I'm not leaving."

Zeus exhaled through his nose—not in anger, but in something almost like amusement.

I reached out and squeezed Cullen's hand. "It's okay," I murmured. "Go."

He hesitated—his eyes locking with mine. I knew he could see the golden flecks in my irises now. What I'd become.

He stared a moment longer, then gave a slight nod. His fingers brushed mine before pulling away.

I watched him walk to the doors—each step reluctant. At the threshold, he looked back once, just once, before the doors shut behind him.

And then it was just...

Me—and the king of the gods.

The silence stretched.

Then Zeus moved.

He descended his throne with measured steps, circling me like a creature thought extinct—curious, assessing, dangerous.

"You think you are the first to defy the gods?" His voice was low, curling through the air. "That you are the first the Fates have whispered of?"

I went still.

Zeus's eyes gleamed. "I have seen the Fates, girl."

Even as an immortal, a chill ran down my spine.

"I have known of the prophecy longer than you've drawn breath," he continued. "You think I stood idly by when Phobos and Deimos rose to power? No. Because their rebellion was never the true threat."

My heart pounded. "The Titans weren't the threat?"

Zeus smiled, but there was no humor in it.

"The time of the gods has waned," he replied, turning toward the grand window overlooking Olympus. "The power we hoarded, the chains we forged—were destined to break. The bond shattering was only the beginning."

He sounded...tired.

Not weak—just tired.

He looked less like the almighty ruler of Olympus and more like someone who'd carried the weight of eternity for far too long.

Then his lips quirked in a faint, almost teasing smile. "Perhaps I'll take that boy up on his offer to be my successor."

I blinked. "Cullen wasn't serious when he challenged you for your throne."

He laughed—a short, dry sound. "Was he not?"

I wasn't sure if he was joking.

He turned back to me, his expression sobering once more. "Immortality has its advantages, but you should be cautious. You've made many enemies today."

I swallowed, the truth of it sinking in. Some Olympians—and other gods—would not take the breaking of the bond lightly.

"But," Zeus went on, "you've also made allies. Choose wisely, goddess of soul."

Goddess.

So it was true, then.

"I thought I had to wait until the solstice to drink the nectar."

Zeus lifted his hand—the same one he'd cut with the blade—as though inspecting it, or perhaps honoring it. His gaze drifted, distant, caught in a memory from long ago.

"As the one who struck the final blow against Cronus during the Titanomachy, the heavens granted me...privileges. Privileges bestowed only upon those who prove themselves worthy."

Aphrodite. She told me to prove myself.

Did she know? Did she give me a chance?

"What does 'goddess of soul' even mean?" I asked.

Zeus clasped his hands behind his back. "That truth is yours alone to bear. The strength of your will shall shape the goddess you are to become. Death was only your beginning."

I nodded slowly, as if the motion alone might help his words make sense.

He studied me for a long moment, then exhaled, as if dismissing me. "Your god is waiting for you."

And for the first time in history, Zeus gave a mortal-turned-goddess permission to leave Olympus on her own terms.

I walked toward the doors, each step carrying me farther from the weight of everything that had happened. The battle, the broken bond, my own immortality—it all settled within me like a story still being written, the ink not yet dry.

I thought about my life before all this. Before gods and Titans and bloodlines. I'd been human. A girl with a cat, a job, and a life that—strange as it had been—was mine. Would it ever feel like that again? Or was I something else now, something even I couldn't recognize?

The doors towered ahead—gilded, massive—and with one final breath, I pushed them open.

Cullen was waiting.

He stood with his back to me, staring out over the expanse of Olympus. At the sound of the doors, he turned—and when he saw me, he smiled.

Not a smirk. Not a teasing grin.

No...it was the kind of smile that felt like sunlight after a storm. The kind that belonged to someone who'd lived under another's control for too long—and had finally, finally—been set free.

Cullen would be free to make his own choices. His own mistakes.

And we would make them together.

We had to infinity's end.

EPILOGUE
SKYE

The world had changed. We'd changed. But here, in the quiet hum of my apartment, time finally seemed to slow.

Cullen and I lay tangled together on my too-small bed, his warmth pressed against me, his breath steady and even. His fingers traced slow, absent patterns along my arm—unhurried, like we had all the time in the world now.

Because we did.

My hand drifted to my collarbone. The arrowhead necklace wasn't there.

Gone.

After Zeus, the curse no longer wrapped around my mind. I could touch another's skin without any visions at all.

That part of me—mortal, cursed—was done.

But when I looked down, nestled back where it belonged, was my ring.

I twisted it between my thumb and forefinger, feeling the cool metal. I'd thought it lost forever—swallowed by the Underworld itself.

"You never told me how you got it back," I murmured, tilting my head to meet Cullen's gaze.

His lips curled, amused. "I expected a fight—or at least a favor I'd regret." His fingers slid down my wrist, brushing over the ring before lacing with mine. "Turns out, the ferryman has interesting tastes. He only wanted one thing in return...Sara's bread."

I blinked, then laughed. "Sara's bread?"

Cullen huffed, shaking his head. "Don't ask me why."

The thought of the ferryman—the dark guide of souls—trading a ring for a loaf of bread was...something. But after everything, it was hardly the strangest thing in my life now.

Cullen shifted, pressing his forehead against mine. He held himself there, as if the mere thought of distance would shatter him. "You don't know how much I hated seeing your hand without it."

His words sent something warm through me, a slow-burning heat curling to my toes.

I curled into him, closing the small space between us, my fingers sliding into his hair as I pulled him into a kiss—deep, all-consuming. His lips moved against mine, his hands sliding down my back, drawing me closer until no space remained between us.

My bed was far too small for this.

But with Cullen—his wings, now healed, wrapping around me, his fingers leaving trails of heat across my skin—

I didn't care.

Cullen let out a dramatic groan as he shifted, his arm slipping off the side of the bed. "I swear, Skye, this bed is trying to kill me."

I laughed as he barely caught himself before toppling off. "You're immortal. You'll survive."

"That's not the point." He propped himself up on one elbow, eyes narrowing at our ridiculously small bed before sweeping his gaze over the rest of my apartment with exaggerated judgment. "I'm just saying, if only there were somewhere else we could go. A place with, I don't know, a massive bed, maybe some silk sheets, a palace even—"

I rolled my eyes, cutting him off. "Hint, hint."

He smirked, but I only stretched out, making myself comfortable again. "I like it here. Mystic Soulstice is right below."

"Fine." Cullen sighed, dramatically defeated. "We'll keep your shoebox for now."

Before I could respond, he dipped his head, shifting my shirt aside to press a slow, open-mouthed kiss just below my navel, stealing the breath from my lungs.

His hand splayed across my stomach, thumb stroking idly—as though trying to speak to something that wasn't even there yet. But we both knew. Knew of *her*.

He exhaled against my skin, his voice softer now. "We'll need a room for her."

My heart squeezed.

I wasn't showing, not yet. But deep inside, I could feel it—an ember, a spark of something new taking form. Not just life, but a soul. A goddess's soul, cradled within my own.

Because I was no longer just Skye.

I was the goddess of soul.

I was still adjusting to my new title, as though a forgotten sense had awakened within me. It was more than seeing new colors—it was feeling them, breathing them, becoming them. Souls revealed themselves as fragile butterflies, their wings brushing softly against my own essence. And when one was caged, I could reach for it, coax it open, guide it gently toward the light until it found the strength to fly on its own.

The tarot was no longer just cards, but an extension of what I was now. I could glimpse butterflies behind every draw. I could heal. I could give people what Lydia had always longed for—what she dreamed Mystic Soulstice would become: a sanctuary. Her true legacy.

I swallowed hard, threading my fingers through Cullen's hair as he pressed another reverent kiss to my stomach.

Our daughter.

Our future.

I had no idea what kind of mother I would be, what kind of goddess she and I would become. But I knew one thing—

We would never be alone.

"*Faith* will be just fine here," I said, smoothing my fingers over Cullen's hand still resting on my stomach. "But...maybe a little more house wouldn't hurt. Not in the clouds, though. I can't imagine baby-proofing that."

He grinned, tilting his head slightly as he watched me. "And we're sure on the name Faith?" His tone was teasing, but I caught the curiosity beneath it.

I traced small circles over the back of his hand, warmth spreading through my chest. "It was Lydia's middle name," I murmured. "And I think we owe her a lot."

As if summoned, Marnie sauntered into the room and leapt onto the bed with a delighted meow. She kneaded her paws into the blanket, then flopped against my side, purring loudly in agreement.

Cullen raised an eyebrow. "Why do I feel like we've just acquired a full-time spy from the Underworld?"

I laughed, scratching behind Marnie's ears as she pushed eagerly into my touch. The idea that Lydia might still be watching over me—over us—filled me with a quiet, comforting peace.

"Good," I whispered, pressing a kiss to Marnie's soft fur. "I love you."

Knock, knock.

Cullen and I both turned toward the apartment door. Voices echoed from the other side.

"Princess...you can't just—"

Zeph's voice drifted up the stairwell, cut off by the sound of more footsteps—heavier, faster.

"Knock, knock!" Harmony's voice rang out—just before she pushed the door open and stepped inside without waiting.

Zeph, right behind her, smirked. "You do know how doors work, right? Generally, people wait to be let in."

Harmony rolled her eyes, flipping her hair over her shoulder. "And waste time? Please."

Cullen groaned, sitting up as his wings slowly dissolved into his back. He shot an exasperated glance at the intruders. "Oh yeah, just invite yourselves in. It's not like this is a private space or anything."

Euryale and Sara came in next, arms full of bags bursting with stuffed animals, baby bottles, and enough soft blankets to swaddle a small army.

Seeing them like that—together, actually smiling—hit me right in the chest. It was a quiet warmth that felt like...family.

"Where should I set up the bassinet?" Sara asked brightly as Euryale adjusted her grip and maneuvered around Zeph and Harmony with practiced ease.

Cullen sighed, loud and dramatic, crossing his arms as he surveyed the now-crowded room. "You see what I mean? This place is too small." He pinched the bridge of his nose, as if the very idea of limited square footage caused him physical pain.

I laughed softly, one hand resting over my stomach.

I could already picture it: Faith, surrounded by this mismatched, chaotic, fiercely loyal family.

She wouldn't grow up in silence or in judgment.

She wouldn't have to earn love just to feel it.

She would know—every single day—that she was enough.

Cullen moved beside me, his hand covering mine, our fingers threading together over the swell of our future.

When I looked up at him, I saw everything—the god, the man, the myth—and how none of those titles mattered.

He was mine. My love. My strength. My future.

Cullen drew me closer, his smile flicking toward the others as they moved about the apartment. "I must be a fool to think I could steal you away from them for more than a few hours."

I rose onto my toes, cupping his jaw, and kissed him with every breath and soul I had to give.

When I pulled back, I whispered against his lips, "*The Fool* represents new beginnings. And when faced with the unknown"—I smiled softly, our hands resting where our daughter grew—"it means a leap of *Faith*."

ACKNOWLEDGMENTS

As a mother, I've often heard the phrase "It takes a village." And it's true—not just in raising children, but in writing, too. I couldn't have made it this far without those closest to me.

Firstly, thank you to my friends Megan and Haleigh, queens of the romance genre, who always answered my midnight messages without hesitation. You never missed a beat—even when I needed clarification on, let's just say, certain...anatomical details.

To my parents, who wanted to read this right away—and I made them wait until I'd polished it and made it beautiful for them—thank you for your patience, support, and unwavering confidence in me.

To my editor, Sam—my fairy godmother who sprinkled the magic of track changes over everything. You are a kindred spirit, and you've made me want to send Christmas cards to stay in touch (and I don't even send Christmas cards!). You're amazing, and I can't wait to work with you again.

Thank you to the cover designers, artists, and interior designers who pulled this from my head and into the real world. Your talent gave my story a home in reality, and I am honored to have worked with you.

Lastly, to my husband. When I thought I couldn't do this, you told me to sit my ass down and finish, because you knew I loved this. Thank you, *quack quack.*

Now, to my little readers...you being here is everything.

And we're just getting started.

ABOUT THE AUTHOR

Kimberly Rison lives in Maryland with her amazing—and most handsome—husband, who definitely isn't standing behind her as she writes this. Together, they share a chaotic toddler and an even more chaotic tabby cat.

When she isn't writing about gods and goddesses, she's watching K-dramas and eating popcorn with hot sauce, which you're now imagining—and yes, it is delicious.

www.ingramcontent.com/pod-product-compliance
Lightning Source LLC
Chambersburg PA
CBHW020931310726
48980CB00007B/729/J

* 9 7 9 8 9 9 3 1 4 4 3 1 3 *